EMOTIONLESS

CAMILA FERNANDEZ GOMEZ

authorHOUSE®

AuthorHouse™ UK
1663 Liberty Drive
Bloomington, IN 47403 USA
www.authorhouse.co.uk
Phone: 0800.197.4150

Published by AuthorHouse 11/09/2018

ISBN: 978-1-5246-6276-9 (sc)
ISBN: 978-1-5246-6274-5 (hc)
ISBN: 978-1-5246-6275-2 (e)

Contents

# Chapter 1

Date: 3 February 102 AW
Location: The Government
Narrator: Aliana

"WE'RE SCREWED." ROMA sighed as he crossed his arms over his chest, his white uniform was tidy for once. "I'm sorry but we're screwed."

"Maybe you're screwed, I'm confident I'll pass... even if we fail group strategy." Iris replied, standing next to Roma. She was putting her red hair up in a bun, her honey eyes avoided mine as she spoke.

I tried my best not to seem annoyed by her comment, it had been a while since graduation and I still couldn't look at Iris without anger rising in me.

"We have to trust each other," Mathias stood beside me, I looked up at him. He looked very handsome in his white uniform. His chestnut hair was messy from the helmet he had just taken off, his light blue eyes found mine, he smiled at me before he carried on, "Most importantly, we have to trust Aliana, we picked her for a reason, right?"

I wanted to thank him for his trust and his words but I knew it was pointless to do so and I knew better than to open my mouth, I would've been a stuttering mess.

I took a deep breath in and tried to keep my hands from shaking. We were so close to the end of our last preparation module and I was not doing as well as I would've liked.

1

There was a lot of pressure on me, not only from my parents but from pretty much everybody. I couldn't fail this module, I *had* to get the highest score no matter what.

The pressure of all of it made my chest feel heavy, my hands ached with the need to reach for my pocket where I always kept my pills. I had been trying to not be so dependent on them but it was getting harder and harder each day and thinking about it only made me wish I had stopped taking them ages ago but after graduation, I couldn't even go a day without them.

When I graduated, I had the second highest score in the female category and for someone like me, someone who came from one of the most important families in the Government, that was unacceptable.

I still remember my father's eyes when the results were put up on display for everyone to see. The way he looked at me... I knew he was disappointed and even though I barely had a relationship with him, it still hurt. He didn't allow me to explain, he didn't want to hear what I had to say; for once I wanted him to hear me out but he was so disappointed that he didn't even want to look at me.

Ever since my grandfather, the members of the Keenan family have been nothing but the best. The most sophisticated, smartest, the bravest... Oh, the glory of being a Keenan. My family was perfect in the eyes of strangers, with the exception of me. I was the odd one out.

I couldn't fail. I simply couldn't but strategy was never my forte and everybody knew it.

"Roc knows all your moves; in strategy, we can't win," Eden spoke then, reminding me of the reason why I wasn't so confident about today's test.

My best friend, Roc Meylor was great with mind games and strategy, that was his *thing*.

"Will you fail if we don't pass group strategy, Roma?" Mia asked with a confused frown. If I didn't know better, I'd say she was concerned, worried that Roma could end up jobless and without a purpose in life.

2

"Not that it is any of your business, but yes, of course I'll pass, can you say the same?" Roma glared. I rolled my eyes at him, he was always so rude without a reason.

"We need to come up with ideas, not argue." Liz groaned, taking a step back from the group. Her blonde hair was up in a ponytail, her brown eyes found mine and she raised her eyebrows as if questioning me.

I swallowed hard, my mouth was dry and the palm of my hands sweaty.

"Roc's probably going to hide to make us go out there and look for them," I began, clearing my throat and trying to steady my hands as I fixed my uniform's jacket. "He'll want to play with our minds, tire us, make us angry, frustrate us so we lash out."

"What are we supposed to do then?" Chris asked. He was sitting next to James, both watching us all from their seats.

"Their beacon light's on," Eden informed us, looking over at the far end of the room. Roc's team was ready and their blue light was on to show that. Seeing the flashes of the blue light only made my anxiety grow. "They're ready."

"We could... I don't know, wait until they attack first?" Iris asked, making eye contact with all of us.

"Or we could just shoot each other and save ourselves the embarrassment." Roma shrugged sarcastically.

"*Enough*," I snapped, glaring at Roma as I did so. "I didn't ask you to pick my team, Roma. I didn't ask any of you to do so."

"I'm just saying—"

"I don't care about what you're saying." I interrupted him, the rest of my team must have understood the change in my voice because Chris and James quickly stood up and got inside our circle again, the rest stood up with their back straight and facing me.

"Liz, James, I want you guys to find the highest place in this room. Liz, you go east, James you go west but stay within the central perimeter. You're our eyes, so let us know what you see and if one of us is in danger, help out but only if you believe the other person cannot come out of a situation. Do not take an opportunity from one of your teammates just because you want to add another body to the count, alright? And that goes for all of you."

They all nodded, Liz and James walked over to where we stored the long-range rifles.

"Eden and Chris, I want you guys to blow things up, not people, *things,*" I carefully pointed at them, Eden smirked and nodded. "I want you two to draw them to the centre of the room. I don't know how and I don't care either, make noise, cut the path, whatever it is you do, I want them all running to the centre of the room, yes?"

"Yes, ma'am," Chris saluted me and followed Eden to where the explosives were.

"Mia, Iris, Mathias, and Roma... you guys are with me." I sighed, walking over to where the rest of our equipment was.

The guns and explosives weren't real, they did inflict pain but in electric shocks. It was mostly just paint, though.

I grabbed two grenades and an assault rifle. When we were all ready, we grabbed our helmets and I turned the beacon light on, letting the captain and the other team know we were ready.

Soon enough, the room went dark and after I put my helmet on, the training hall turned into an old city ruined by war.

In silence, we entered the room. As planned, Liz and James communicated when they were in position and Eden and Chris didn't need to report their location because not long after, I began to hear explosives going off.

"Disperse but don't wander too far off," I ordered, Mathias nodded and slowly began to walk away.

"Copy that." Roma, Iris, and Mia replied at the same time as they too began to walk away in different directions.

We were safe as long as we were within a walking distance from each other. That way if Roc's team tried to attack, we had a better chance at counterattack.

"Hayes here," Mathias spoke, he was breathing hard. "Problem on the east side, too many, can't retaliate."

"Echo 4 here, help's coming your way, Hotel 2." Eden's voice broke through my earpiece, I could tell by the way he spoke that he was smirking.

"Leigh, I *told* you not to call me that," Mathias groaned, I rolled my eyes. "Over."

"Aliana, four o'clock," James spoke, before I could move, I was being shot at. I ran to cover behind an old car. "Mia's out, can't see Iris."

I counted to three, giving myself the confidence to attack back. I couldn't shoot back, not if they kept shooting my way.

"Roc shot Mia." Iris spoke between breaths, "I almost got Ben but Roc saw me and— I don't know where they went. Roc shot me, I'm out." I took a deep breath in, trying to calm myself. I needed this, I needed to win and I was not going to get anything by hiding.

"Aliana straight ahead, shoot straight ahead in three, two..." And right when he said three, I popped up from behind the car and fired three times, hitting my target.

"Eden, straight ahead, 15 metres away," Liz informed, "Nine, seven, five— *now.*"

Not a minute later, a loud explosion was heard throughout the whole room, making me wonder just how much explosives they used. I heard Eden's chuckle through the earpiece.

"Charlie Nine here, you're good to go, Hayes," Chris informed us.

"Ben's out, Roc's on the run." James said, "He's heading north."

"I got him, I got him," Roma said loudly, hurting my ear. "Roc's in the city centre, he's entering a ruined building, I think he's wounded. Say the word and I'll light him up."

"Permission denied," I ordered with all the authority I could muster. "Keep your eyes on him. If he moves, you follow. Everyone else, to the centre."

Roma was waiting for us to arrive, when everybody got there, he pointed at the building where he saw Roc going in. I took a minute to think about what to do, we only had two loses, Mia and Iris.

It was by far the best I had ever done in group strategy and we all knew it. It wasn't like I had done much either, I just... went with it and we weren't done yet. Roc was still in and knowing him as well as I did, he wasn't going to give up just because he was outnumbered.

My thoughts were rudely interrupted when Chris shook me, trying to get my attention.

"Mate, she's thinking, she stays still when she thinks." Roma pushed Chris away from me, I could've laughed at the comment in any other situation because who would've thought Roma knew something like that about me, but I needed to come up with a plan. "Let her think. I wanna win; mostly I wanna see Roc's arrogant face when we win."

"Okay, surround the building but do not be open, if he sees you he will fire, do not underestimate him just because he's on his own," I told them, I took a deep breath in and slowly let it out. This was going to be my time, I was not going to let Roc win.

When what was left of my team got into position, I swallowed hard and tried to sort out my ideas properly. A couple of days ago, I read in a book that sometimes, if you know your enemy well enough, you can use their flaws against them; if you know how, it can be fatal to them. I knew Roc well enough to know that his biggest flaw was his arrogance, so I silently hoped the book wasn't wrong.

"Aim at the building," I ordered, supporting my gun on the old rusty car I was using to cover myself, I aimed at the house, "Open fire on five... four, three, two... fire."

The noise from our guns wasn't loud enough to disturb my ears, after all, they weren't real guns. When our guns ran out of ammo, my team reloaded but I waited, I waited because I was expecting him to do something, he wouldn't stay in there for long, he had to come out at some point.

"Hold your fire," I ordered, squinting my eyes as I tried to see through the smoke.

"He's coming out, Roc's coming out," Mathias informed, I felt my whole body relax.

"He's holding his gun," James stood up, aiming his gun at Roc and also letting Roc know where he was. Before James could fire,

Roc shot him and began to shoot from left to right without an actual target.

When Roc was shooting in my direction, Mathias used that to shoot him in the back, making Roc fall to his knees.

"Roc's out," Mathias said and at that, I had to clench my jaw to not shout at him. Winning didn't mean anything; winning gave me points but not as much as eliminating Roc would've given me.

I needed the extra points to be on the lead. If I wasn't on the lead everything I've been trying to do since graduation meant nothing, I was still nothing but a second.

"Wait, that's not—" Eden was saying, but he was interrupted by a grenade that exploded a metre away from them, filling them with paint and electroshocks.

"I thought only Roc was left." Mathias groaned, taking cover behind a wall.

"Recount," Liz said, "Eden and Chris took out four people, I took out one, James didn't take out anybody, Aliana took out one, Roma took out two, Mathias?"

"One," He said, "I know Mia and Iris didn't take out anybody."

"We're still in the simulation, that means there's someone in there still," I spoke up, hoping Roc was still there. If Roc was there, I still had a chance and I wasn't going to let anyone take it from me, not even Roc.

"Come out, Roc," I shouted, loud enough that my voice echoed. "I know you're in there, so you might as well just come out."

"How do you know Roc's the one up there?" Liz asked.

"I just do," I whispered, hoping I was right.

A long minute went by, the tension was making my body rigid and there was still no sign of Roc. Groaning, I took one of the grenades I still had and threw them at the building, making sure I aimed and it went where I wanted it to.

Not long after, Roc walked out of the building; we were all aiming at him and he was aiming at me. I couldn't help but smile at the sight. If he was still here, I still had chances of getting the points I needed to be on the lead.

7

Roc was tall and muscular, his shoulders always firm and strong. You could tell by the way he walked that he thought highly of himself. I stood up and walked slowly to get closer to him, counting every step as I went. Roc was as still as a statue, aiming his gun at me, not caring that the rest of my team was still aiming at him.

"What are you doing? Just shoot him already." Roma muttered, I ignored his questions and reminded myself to tell him not to question me.

When I was close enough to Roc, my smile grew, if we fought, Roc's chances of winning weren't as high as mine. If I won, which I knew I could, it meant I had finally beaten Roc at his own game.

"I've won, Roc,"

"You're not going to shoot, are you?" Roc asked as he took a few steps forward until he was right in front of me, "You don't want them to shoot, but you don't want to do it either, do you? Don't tell me you're really going to choose the easy way out?"

"Do you even have to ask?"

"Let's get to it then," He replied.

I didn't reply or give him time to prepare himself. I quickly kicked the hand in which he held his gun. Roc was *way* taller than I was but I was very flexible, and my legs were the strongest part of my body.

He wasn't ready for my kick. He let out a groan of pain, but he was still holding the gun. I'd have to work harder this time to beat him.

Roc quickly recovered from the kick and with an open hand, he hit me in my chest, pushing me back a few steps. He might not have been a great fighter, but he was very strong.

Roc used the distance he had created to aim his gun at me. He shot three times, not at my torso but at the floor, near my feet. It was easy to dodge the bullets as I ran up to him. It was nice to know he wasn't going to shoot me – not just yet, anyway. He *wanted* to fight me as much as I wanted to fight him. I had won strategy, something that was his strong field, he wanted to show me that he could fight me, that he could win in something I was good at.

8

Often my siblings spoke out about how my friendship with Roc was sort of unhealthy but they didn't understand. Yes, we fought each other, we were competitive but we did it because we had to. The world wasn't going to go easy on us, we didn't need pity, we needed strength so we made each other strong.

When I reached him, I took the gun by its barrel and pushed it back, hitting his stomach with all the strength I had. He fell to his knees as I used the gun to hit him on his chin this time. Roc didn't give me enough time to hit again, he grabbed the gun by its butt and pulled it, taking it away from me and throwing it away.

For a moment, I couldn't help but to feel a bit afraid, seeing big Roc standing in front of me, his chest moving at the rhythm of his rapid breathing, he looked like a rabid animal. If it was anyone but Roc, then I would have been in trouble, but it was Roc, Roc wouldn't *really* hurt me.

I went into my defence pose, expecting Roc to attack me, which he did. As always, he threw his punches at my body. I had told him over the years to mix his punches but he never listened. His punches were too easy to dodge, way too easy. I didn't realise what Roc was doing until I felt the impact of his huge fist on the left side of my helmet.

Good one, Roc.

"Just shoot him already," Mathias spoke, his voice sounded distant. I had to shake my head a few times, trying to get rid of the long beep in my ear. I could even hear heartbeat pounding in my ear.

For a moment I couldn't focus, I felt pressure on the side of my face and all I wanted was to calm my heart rate, I needed to focus.

Roc was waiting, standing still a couple of steps away from me and lowering his fists. He was waiting for my reaction, for me to make a move. He didn't mean to hurt me as much as he did.

Roc started to run towards the gun he had thrown away. I quickly took a rock from the ground and threw it at the back of his legs, making him fall flat on his face. I ran as fast as I could towards his gun. My gun was too far away. Besides, where was the fun in going for mine when I could go for his? It was more interesting that way.

When I passed by Roc, he grabbed me by the ankle, making me fall. *What a bastard!* But we both knew the rules: *there are no rules.* Everything was permitted, everything in order to win.

However, unlike him, I placed my hands in front of my body, trying to roll off instead of falling flat. I could still feel Roc's hands trying to grab my ankles, so I kicked him until I made sure he wasn't trying to grab me again. Damning me under his breath, he let me go. Smiling at nothing, I used my legs and hands to crawl as fast as I could until I reached the gun.

Raising it to aim, I shot Roc in his back, once, twice. And then the game was over.

When I stood up, Roc was still lying on the floor, trying to calm his breathing. I took my helmet off and I was back in our training hall, the simulation was over and I had won.

Roc turned around and looked up. Taking his helmet off, his blue eyes found mine. His lip was bloody and he had a serious look on his face. But with one look at his eyes, I knew he was pretending.

"Congratulations," he said while he sat on the floor, his hands resting on his knees. "Been reading a bit, have you?"

"No, I told you I didn't need that book." I lied as I held out my hand to him, helping him up. Roc was the one who gave me the book, he said it could help with strategy.

Roc and I made our way back to where our teams were. Waiting for our captain to dismiss us.

"Did I hurt you?" He asked, pointing at my face, a little frown in between his eyebrows. I shook my head and looked up at the huge window at the far-right end of the room, where the captain was watching us from the second floor, supervising the training. "Don't worry, you did great."

"She shouldn't be worried, she owned you back there." Roma mocked, walking away to the weapon cabinet.

Roc was going to reply to Roma's comment but before he could, the captain's deep voice came out of the speakers, filling the whole room with his voice.

"Interesting method, White Team," the captain began. "She caught you by surprise, Meylor. She left you alone with little backup. A bit overdone at the end – too much violence, which you two could have spared us – but good job, Soldier Keenan. And congratulations, Keenan, you're back on top."

I had to force myself to stay still and not to seem too hyped. I felt like I could finally breathe with ease, this meant so much. I couldn't wait until I got home, my mother was going to be so proud.

"Session finished, you can head to the changing rooms now."

Roc and I walked at a slow pace, staying behind so we could talk without worrying too much about who could hear. I liked to think I was close with all my teammates but I couldn't talk to them like I could talk to Roc. Even with Mathias, whom I've known practically since we were babies.

"I'm going to shower," Roc told me, walking backward as we headed to the changing rooms, "See you in a bit."

I headed over to my locker, smiling as some of my teammates stopped to congratulate me. The changing rooms were mixed. Obviously, no one was going to do anything that went against the law, so there was no point in separating males from females, you had privacy in the bathrooms and showers, though.

I took off my clothes until I was in a sports bra and my trousers before I took my toiletries from my locker, I grabbed my communicator, I looked up for my mother's contact and I typed a quick message letting her know I had good news and I went straight to the showers.

Showering was my favourite part after training, it relaxed my muscles and washed away all the dirt and sweat. I felt new and for once I felt content with myself.

Heading back to my locker, I tried to change as quickly as I could, I really wanted to meet my mother for lunch like we always did after my training. I grabbed my dirty clothes and went over to the basket when my pills fell from my trousers' pocket. And just my luck... Roma picked them up.

"Are you sick?" He asked, looking at me and then turning his attention to the pills. I don't know if I imagined it or not but I could've sworn his face expression faltered for a second before he turned to look back at me.

"That's none of your business." I snapped, snatching the little bottle of pills from his hands as I walked away from him.

"You need to chill, Ali," Roc whispered loud enough that I could hear. "You get upset really quickly sometimes, somebody can notice."

I rolled my eyes, sitting down by the bench in front of his locket. He was putting on his tank shirt, facing me as he did so.

"Chill? I'm very chill, when am I not chill?" Roc chuckled at my comment, shaking his head as he sat down next to me.

"When you don't take those, for example." He pointed at my pocket where my pills where. I sighed getting a little annoyed, I knew what was coming.

It was easy to be myself with Roc, I didn't have to hide. He had seen me in my darkest moments and he kept quiet even though he was supposed to report me. I was an emotional person, despite how much I hated to admit it, I was. The pills helped me control it, it kept me in line and out of danger. We both knew perfectly well that any sign of emotion would mean a great deal of trouble because, in the Government, emotions were a weakness, mistakes that the Government tried to erase.

I was a mistake. I was... not supposed to be. I felt everything too deeply and it was never good. I felt rage, I felt a burning anger within me that I couldn't control and the pills helped with that, the pills purpose was to block all my emotions and help me maintain a normal life. Roc, on the other hand, didn't need the pills as much as I did. It was easy for him to hide everything, even when he was hurt or angry, he could smile through it and I admired him for that.

"You need to learn to control yourself," He whispered, leaning down to tie his shoelaces, "The pills aren't always the solution."

"Easy for you to say, you don't live with Johan."

"You can't hate him forever," He carried on, turning to look at me. His hair was dripping wet. "Also, at some point, you're going to have to accept that these emotions aren't a bad thing, Ali."

"I really don't want to argue." I sighed, looking away from him.

"Are you meeting your mum for lunch?" Roc asked, changing the subject, I nodded.

"Well, I have to do rounds with Mathias," He groaned, tiding his other shoelace, "Shoot me now and save me the boredom."

"Mathias is nice, give him a chance and you'll like him." I rolled my eyes, Roc didn't like Mathias, he never did.

"No, I'm okay, thank you." He sighed, standing up as he reached for his uniform's jacket.

I was going to carry on our conversation when the captain's voice filled the room through the speakers.

"Soldier Keenan, your presence is requested at the CB. Please head there right away."

"What've you done?" Roc smirked, playfully shaking his head at me.

"It's probably my mum, maybe she has too much work and can't come out for lunch." I groaned as I put on a white T-shirt, my white jumper, and my collar shirt. I tied my hair up in a ponytail as I headed out to the Central.

The Central Building, or the CB, was literally at the centre of the Government. From the training centre it was about an hour walk. I could've called for my family vehicle but I felt like walking. Vehicles were mostly used to travel to the farms and the harbour that were both too far away from the city for people to walk.

I was entering the upper-class sectors, my sector. All the houses were white and larger than the houses in the other sectors. People in elegant black suits and black or grey jackets were walking and talking peacefully. There were tall light posts with white and light blue strings at the bottom on every side of the road. Every four metres, there were trees. The trees didn't have any leaves yet. Maybe soon. I knew summer was coming. At least I hoped it would come soon, I never really liked winter.

When I finally arrived at the Central, I couldn't help but stop and admire the building. There was a walking path surrounded by grass, and in the middle of that, there was the building, white with light blue windows. It was a ten-storey building and it had underground facilities.

As soon as I stepped into the building, warm air from the AC hit my face, it wasn't too warm and it smelled new and fresh.

The ground floor was very bright thanks to the glass walls allowing all the light in. There was also a little waiting area decored with fancy white furniture and a glass table that had an information projector, a hologram. At the time, there was no news to be projected, but the blue hologram light that came out of the projector showed the time, date, and temperature. I thought it was wrong because it said the temperature was 11°C. To me, it definitely felt hotter than that. The date was 3/2/102 AW.

AW stood for After War, once we came here, it was supposed to be a new beginning to humankind, so we started from zero.

At the reception was an elegant lady with black hair, brown eyes, a little nose, and thin red lips. I greeted her and went straight to the lift. Normally, there was no need to talk to the receptionist since I was always expected by my mother and the receptionist already knew that, which is why I was surprised when she stopped me.

"Miss Keenan," She spoke politely, standing up with her hands held together before her lap. "I'm afraid you're going to have to go to the tenth floor."

"I thought my mother was expecting me?" My mother worked on the eight floor and was often there or at the underground facilities.

"The Board has called for you, Miss Keenan, they're expecting you." She said, pressing some buttons behind her counter and then she pointed to the lift at the far right.

The gesture made my heartbeat quicken as my brain tried to think of all the possibilities why they would want to talk to me. I didn't realise I was holding my breath until the receptionist called out my name, making my legs move forward to the lift.

My palms were sweaty and no matter how many times I tried to dry them on my trousers, they felt too sweaty. I took deep breaths in intents to calm myself down and I went over what I had to say. Good afternoon, a firm salute, I shouldn't look at them in the eye for too long, stand firm and strong, show nothing. I had it all under control.

As soon as I stepped out of the lift, I was met with emptiness. There was no one there, not even the assistants. My feet felt heavy as I walked by their offices. The door by the first office read A. Jones, Aurora Jones, there was another office nearby but without a name yet, there were no successors for the Jones family. The next office belonged to Frank Hayes, Mathias's father. Then there was Robert Frayn's office. And last but not least, my father's, Johan Keenan.

I had to prepare myself, I was nervous and I needed to be calm no matter what. I had no idea what they wanted, I needed to remain calm no matter what but it was hard because even the idea of being inside the building gave me the chills.

The building held all the Government secrets, all that we were and how we came to be could be found within the walls of the CB. The underground facilities were locked under extreme security. I've never been further than the first underground level, it was as far as I could go. Apparently the last levels were underwater and so far down that the silence could drive you insane, he said you could even hear your own heartbeat. Roc said that it was a great idea to have prison cells down there because it could drive the prisoners crazy; what better punishment than that?

Roc was the only one of the students who had been any further than I have. He was chosen to help Frank Hayes with whatever business he had down there, Roc never told me what it was and I never asked. In the Government, the less you knew, the better off you were.

With a sigh, I walked to the meeting room and after knocking twice, I opened the double doors.

The first thing I saw was a very large wood table with eight black chairs around it. On the white walls were photographs of the founders, their successors, and their successors' successors. Nathaniel's picture was one of the last. There were also pictures of Mathias and William Frayn.

At the end of the room, by the glass wall, looking out the window with his back turned was my father. I couldn't see his face, but I knew it was him by the way he stood, relaxed and tall, his hands inside the pockets of his black trousers.

My brother was there too, he sat at the far end of the table, staring up at me. His eyes, a mixture of bright green and blue, were watching me carefully with a seriousness that sent chills down my spine. His lips were in a straight line; his face lacked emotion.

Just like our father, Nathaniel was wearing a plain black suit, a grey collar shirt, and a nice navy blue tie. I guess that was why Nate looked so much like Father, perhaps it was because he dressed like him, he talked like him, he *wanted* to be like Johan. The idea both warmed my heart and left a bittersweet feeling in the pit of my stomach.

Behind Nate, our mother was sitting with her hands crossed over her lap. Seeing her there made me frown, she wasn't part of the board, she shouldn't be there and the fact that she was there meant something had happened or was about to happen.

My mother had her blond hair tied up in an elegant bun. Her blue eyes were looking at everything except at me. She had white flawless skin, a pointy little nose, and high cheekbones. She was practically the definition of beautiful.

I looked around the room and found the other member of the board. Aurora within them. Aurora Keenan, née Jones, Johan's mother.

"She's finally here." I didn't have to look at Aurora to know she was the one who spoke. Her voice was enough to send chills down my spine. It was like fingernails scratching a chalkboard.

"Mrs. Jones." I saluted, swallowing my disgust. I knew she didn't like to be called Mrs. Jones, but she wasn't a Keenan. She married one, but that didn't make her one. "May I know why I am needed?"

I despised Aurora. I *hated* her. And the feeling was mutual. She never liked me. Sometimes I was convinced Aurora went out of her way to make me feel so insignificant as if I was nothing but dirt on her clean, white shoes. What bothered me the most was my family's reaction to this. No one ever said a word when Aurora laid her hands on me and when she humiliated me and belittled me. Johan knew all this and he still said nothing, he did *nothing.*

After a while, I just stopped caring. I stopped trying to make Aurora like me. I didn't waste any more time wondering why my grandmother was like that with only me. That's how I learnt in the worst way that no one would ever rescue me or stand up for me. No matter how small or dangerous my demons were, I'd have to face them alone.

"Oh no," Aurora replied with a frown. "I didn't ask for you. As a matter of fact, I don't think you should be here at all. I don't think you ought to know."

"Enough," Johan spoke with a warning in his voice. This was serious.

"Ought to know what, Johan?" I asked. My father turned around. His eyes were watery and red, making his green irises stand out. His nose was red too because of the cold he had caught weeks ago. His lower lip was fuller than his top lip. He looked pale. He normally had tan skin, but at that precise moment, he looked so pale that my heart stopped for a moment. I had never seen Johan like that, as if he was in pain.

"That's no way to speak to your father," Aurora snapped at me before Johan could reply. "Or your *superior.*" I knew what Aurora meant by *superior*: not just that Johan was older, but also the fact that he was better than me. *They* were all better than me. I tried really hard to bite my tongue, but Aurora deserved a response. Just when I was about to say something back, Johan spoke.

"It's about Samirah," he said, ignoring Aurora's comment.

My heart picked up its pace. I tried to control my facial expression, keeping it as straight as I could. I would never allow myself to make a mistake in front of Aurora, or anyone who was part of the board for that matter. It was like trying to run through a minefield. If you made a mistake, a wrong move, you died. That's how I felt. If I showed an emotion, I'd die.

"The board has gathered here to give us information about what happened. Mr. Hayes will fill you in," Johan continued, pointing at Frank Hayes.

Frank Hayes was standing up behind the table, his dark blond hair combed to the side, the usual hairstyle every man had in the Government. His eyes were a light blue, and he had a small smile on his face.

I maintained eye contact with him and his smile grew, making me look away. He was wearing a plain black suit with a black collar shirt and a plain black tie. Mr. Hayes had stunning blue eyes. He had a grin on his face as he moved closer to me.

Perhaps it was the fact that I did not like Mr. Hayes at all that helped me see past his charming smile. He was very full of himself. He thought he was better than everyone, and he took any chance he got to say it out loud. Mathias was nothing like the man standing in front of me. Father and son but they were *nothing* alike.

Frank was a violent man behind closed doors. I knew because if you were observant enough, you saw the little details, like Mr. Hayes's knuckles or Mathias's face when he was training and in pain, and you noticed the fact that he never took his T-shirt off. Or if you pay enough attention, sometimes you'd see Mrs. Hayes wince in pain.

Frank Hayes was a snake and I hated him more than ever when he opened his mouth and let out those four words.

"Your sister is dead."

 **Chapter 2**

Location: The Government
Narrator: Aliana

A WAVE OF pain went through my whole body as I tried my hardest to keep my facial expression straight and not let it betray me.

Sam couldn't be dead. This was a mistake.

"Or at least that's what we think," another man at the end of the table, Robert Frayn, stepped in. His voice was full of empathy.

"It really is just a matter of time," Frank Hayes added.

I was going to throw up. *Samirah is not dead.*

I wanted to say something, I wanted to speak but I couldn't. To show any sort of emotion would mean that I was able to feel, which would put Johan at risk and I knew that if I did try to speak, I was not going to be able to control whatever left my mouth.

"It seems that Samirah was around the bridge doing some natural research. Fact is that she's probably dead by now. Either she got lost in the woods or they took her." *They.* Frank Hayes didn't have to say who he meant by "they".

They were the rebels, the unspeakable rebels. The scum of the earth, the savages, whatever people want to call them.

Sometimes people would disappear and the board would make sure everyone knew that the rebels had taken them. Some people speculated, saying that it was probably for rituals and "savagery stuff". Everyone believed what the board said because they had no other choice but to trust blindly. That's how the Government worked, people followed whatever the Board said. The Board controlled everything, they were the ones that said what was dangerous and evil, what was pride and what was shame, what was wrong and good. The Government dictated the lives of everybody.

The Government wasn't always right, though. There were a lot of secrets, their lies didn't always make sense, a lot of wrongs that were never set right. But who was I to go against the Government? The board was the law and to go against the law was treason, and I was many things but a traitor was not one of them.

My world shattered at my feet as Frank's words replayed in my mind. My throat was getting tighter. My body felt heavy, I wanted to move, to do something but I was glued to the floor.

I felt sick. My mind was spinning. My hands were shaking, so I hid them behind my back. My breathing became heavy and unsteady. I was about to lose control but then I found that Johan's green eyes were focused on me. A slight shake of his head stopped me and whatever it was that I was thinking of doing. I stayed still and tried to calm myself.

I swallowed all my pain, putting my emotions aside where they had been building up, in that place I had created at the back of my mind where I locked all my anger and hate.

Taking a deep breath, I tried really hard to make my voice as steady as I could as I looked back at Mr. Hayes. "If that's all I was being informed of, I ask permission to be dismissed," I said.

"You are dismissed, soldier," Hayes said with half a smile.

"Her life shall be an example of bravery, and she shall be remembered as a loyal servant to the Government," I said once I was ready to leave. It was what you were supposed to say when someone was gone, the last thing you said before you never again raised the subject.

"And together we shall endure the emptiness," Johan replied. Nathaniel and our mother stayed quiet. Aurora gave me a glare of superiority.

Once I left the Central, everything was a blur. I walked and walked without any direction. I was numb. When I snapped out of it, I was at the beach. Sitting on the sand, I didn't even know when I had gotten here or how long I'd been here. The sun was already down. My eyes were burning, and tears were making my face wet. It didn't feel real. Samirah wasn't gone. She couldn't be.

I felt a need to shout or punch or kick someone. I wanted to get this feeling out of me, but I couldn't because it was so unknown, the tears and the pain, I had never experienced pain like that. It hurt, my body hurt, even breathing hurt. Everything in me felt like it was breaking and I did not know how to make it better.

I was trying to find my pills, as I didn't know where they were. My hands were shaking, so I put them on my knees to steady them, forgetting about the pills. I tried to control my breathing, but every breath I took was just another stab in my chest. My anxiety attacks normally came when something scared me really bad or when I was stressed. It was Sam who helped me through them. Who was going to help me now?

My father and my brother thought for some unknown reason that Sam needed me way more than I needed her, but that wasn't true. I knew it and Sam knew it. *I* needed her. The thought of her being gone knocked the air out of my lungs.

Tears kept coming out of my eyes. My chest was hurting as if I had pressure on it. I kept trying to move, but my body wouldn't respond. All I could feel was a horrible feeling of suffocation and pain everywhere in my body.

A hand shook me to my feet. Someone would see me cry, someone would see me suffering, and it would be all over. Everyone would know I had emotions, and God knows what the board would do to me then. But no matter how hurt I was, I was not going to go down without a fight. At least a fight would help me get some anger out of my system.

I slapped the hand away, looking up at the person. I found a pair of blue eyes looking down at me, blue as the crystalline water beyond the beach. For a moment I thought it was Frank Hayes, but as I took in the rest of the face, I saw Mathias's kind smile fading as he regarded me.

"I just got the message," I could tell by the way Mathias spoke, he was trying to be careful. "I'm sorry."

A part of me was convinced that if I lied to Mathias, if I told him I was okay, he'd believe me. He didn't have a reason not to. Roc and I had tried it before, tell people very obvious lies and they'd believe us. All we did was follow orders, people were basically robots with basic common sense and knowledge of certain emotions that would allow them to react a certain way like being surprised, or anxious, knowing when to be cautious when to be worried, basic things such as knowing when they were in danger. I was no threat to Mathias and he had no reason not to trust me.

"No. I don't – I don't know. ... I was—" I was trying to calm myself down, trying to say something coherent, but the words wouldn't leave my mouth. I relaxed my shoulders. Maybe it would be better if they all knew, Sam was gone, what was the point?

I was about to break down, cry my eyes out, and finally let out all that I had been building up inside me. I had lost my sister, and I felt no hope.

"Calm down and take a deep breath," Mathias said, his voice suddenly changed. "No one can see you like this."

This was the beginning of my end.

Or it would have been if Mathias hadn't helped me. It was impossible for him not to know, not to see I was hurting, because I was emotional., I was a mess of emotions and he didn't care, actually, he acted like he knew.

"Look at me," Mathias cupped my face with his hands and dried the tears off my face with his thumbs, "There are other soldiers around, try to stand straight and don't look anywhere but at me."

"Mathias, what are—"

"It doesn't matter what I'm doing. What matters is that no one can see you like this. I'm sorry about Sam but you have to get yourself together, Aliana." His tone was strong, serious and demanding. "I'm calling my driver, he'll take you home."

"But, Mathias—"

"We will talk another time." Mathias interrupted me again. I wasn't used to obeying orders from my soldiers. I was the captain of the team. I gave the orders. But I didn't question him again.

I stayed still just like he had asked. He didn't say much, didn't even look at me. And when his driver finally came, he leaned down and kissed my forehead.

"We've always been family, you and I, you take care of me and I take care of you, that's how it is, no questions asked." He said, opening the back door of the car and making me sit down. "Take your time and when you want to talk, I'll be here but for now go home and talk to Johan. Just remember not everything they say is true."

Before I could ask him what he meant, he closed the car's door and I was being taken home. Mathias knew and he was just like me. I could see it in his eyes, the worry, and fear. Mathias had emotions just like me.

Mathias's words kept replaying in my head. It was like he knew something I didn't. Everybody knew something different and nobody could be trusted, that much I knew. I couldn't ask anybody else but I could ask Johan and if he lied to me, I'd know.

I locked all the pain I felt behind that door in my mind. I didn't want pain; I didn't want anything.

Thinking of Samirah made my heart ache. It was unbearable to even think that I'd go to my room and not find Samirah there. She wouldn't be in the living room reading a book with two different-coloured socks on. She wouldn't be there to fight me every single day or to hold my hand at night when the nightmares made my skin feel like it was being ripped open. Sam was gone and the thought killed me. My whole body trembled. A huge ball was forming in my throat. I felt out of breath. I shook the image of Samirah out of my head. I just had to get home, to Johan. Johan had the answers I needed.

I got out of the car as soon as the driver stopped, making my way inside my house.

Home was a white house with two floors, three bedrooms, Johan's office, a huge living room, three bathrooms, and a kitchen. It smelled of lemon and mint mixed with a hint of sweetness. Home was where

I stayed up late on Saturday nights and slept in on Sundays, waking up to Samirah's complaints about me sleeping too much. Nate and Sam bickering over something stupid, Johan reading a book, Mum engrossed in her paperwork that she wasn't supposed to bring home but she did anyway. Sam picking a fight with me over the silliest thing and Nate mocking her over it. That was home.

I headed to the dining room, ignoring Sam's pictures as I went in. It was dinner time, so I figured my family would be there. Cynthia, my mother, was sitting where she normally sat, next to Johan, but he wasn't there.

Her dark blond hair was still in a high, tight bun, her rounded blue eyes looked heavy and her lips were in a straight line. There was no polite smile, just a cold stare. Next to her was Nathaniel, sitting in Samirah's place. His face was serious too. Nathaniel was two years older than I was. My mother had him when she was very young, only 16 years old.

Aurora had wanted to marry her son to the best candidate she could find, and she wanted to do it fast. Cynthia was the only one who met Aurora's criteria. She did not care that Cynthia had just turned 15 or that Cynthia didn't want to marry Johan. My mother had ambitions, she wanted to *be* somebody, to make something out of her name, she didn't want to be recognised because of her husband's name.

Once my parents were married, Nathaniel soon arrived. Couples were supposed to be 16, 17, or older before they got married, but Aurora didn't care. Every time she came home to visit, she would give the talk to Nathaniel about how it was better for him to marry while he was young, but Nathaniel never cared for what Aurora had to say. With his charming smile, he would tell her that he had better things to do than to marry and raise babies. And because he was a future member of the board, he could do as he pleased. Surprisingly enough, Aurora listened to him. Her favourite grandchild spoke so she listened.

"Where's Johan?" I asked. Cynthia and Nathaniel both looked up at me.

"Not now, Lynn," Cynthia sighed tiredly. She liked calling me Lynn, she didn't like the name Aliana. It was Johan who wanted to call me that. I didn't have the heart to tell her that I didn't want to be called Lynn. "Please, just come and sit with us," my mother pointed at the seat next to her, where I normally sat.

I always did as she asked, *always*, no matter what she asked, I agreed but this time I couldn't.

"In his office," Nathaniel blurt out before I could answer my mother, who sighed and put her hand to her temple. I said nothing. I left them and walked to Johan's office.

His office was next to the living room. The double doors were closed. Without knocking, I walked in.

As soon as I walked in, the smell of mint and lemon hit me – mint and lemon mixed with old books and liquor. The mint and lemon scent came from Johan. He had a cream made of lemon and mint for his nose and his hands. When he rubbed the cream on his hands and applied it to his nose, it helped him breathe better. There were a lot of books, too many and I was sure Johan had read them all at least twice. But the books were out of place. He had a bunch on the floor and others on his sofa at the end of the room. There was another bunch of books laying around near the door.

In the middle of the room was a long desk with a family portrait and three transparent computer screens in front of Johan, he was sitting in his black chair. He was wearing his white-collar shirt with the sleeves rolled up, and his tie was loosened around his neck. The first button of his shirt was undone, and his hair was messy. I had never seen him like that, not even when I found out his secret.

The door of his liquor cabinet was wide open and he had a glass in his hand. The bottle on his desk was almost full. Johan didn't drink much, but from time to time he'd have one or two glasses.

Johan seemed to be hurt. And I found joy in that. I've always felt a certain pleasure when I knew he was hurt. I remember the first time I caused him pain and he told me how sorry he was for everything he had done, for what I knew about him. I remember how proud I was of myself for hurting him. I remember seeing the worry and the sadness in his eyes and I remember the joy I felt when I knew I wasn't the only one in pain.

I tried to hate him, I tried so hard to hate him but, in the process, apart from failing, I began to hate myself.

"Aliana?" Johan's voice brought me back from my thoughts. I wanted to be angry at him, but all the anger I had felt when I walked inside had dissolved, all I felt was pure pain.

Johan to me was a hypocrite, a liar, a traitor, a man I once loved blindly, someone I had once thought of a hero, I had his image up high on a pedestal above the clouds, but one day, when I discovered who Johan Keenan really was, that image I had of him fell and it shattered. He asked for forgiveness many times, and forgiving was easy. I could forgive, I loved him enough to forgive him, it was the forgetting part that I was struggling with and there was no forgiving without forgetting. Every time I tried to forget, there was a fire in me reminding me that there was one thing I could never forget. A horrendous scar I had from my rib cage to my hip.

"Is it true?" I muttered, pushing the thoughts away. I wished he would tell me that it wasn't true, that it was just a dumb occurrence to test me, but deep down I knew it wasn't a test. Seeing Johan like this ... Samirah was gone, and he was in pain.

If you're not ready to hear certain answers, sweetheart, don't ask certain questions, my grandfather used to tell me. Sometimes I wished I would listen to people's advice. Seeing Johan's face, I didn't want to know the answer to my question.

"No." He sighed, not looking at me.

My soul went back into my body. I could breathe again. Samirah wasn't dead. I would've felt it somehow. She was okay. Sam couldn't die; she wouldn't leave me.

"Where is she? What happened?" I demanded, angry at the lie.

"Aliana, please not now."

"Tell me where she is!" I snapped, banging my hand on his desk.

"Have you taken your medicine yet?" he asked, exanimating me from head to toe, it wasn't like me to lose control. He didn't wait for me to answer, he opened a drawer of his desk. I had forgotten to take the pills once I finished training today. When the captain had called me in, I was too worried to think about it and then they said Samirah was gone...

"Where is she?" I asked again, trying to keep my tone steady this time. "You have to tell me."

"Take this," he said, extending his hand to me with one blue pill in the middle of his palm. Even if I did take it, one pill wouldn't be enough but that's something Johan didn't know.

"Not until you tell me."

He looked at me with his green eyes. His jaw was tight, and he looked tired, very tired. With no time to argue, I took the pill and put it in my mouth, biting into it as the bitter, disgusting chemicals dissolved in my saliva.

A moment of silence passed. I felt myself calm down a little. My shoulders relaxed and my body felt a little heavier. *This* I liked. It was a challenge to train like this, but at the same time, it was helpful as it helped me focus on something other than the fears of revealing my emotions. Taking my time to find the courage to ask the question that had been spinning in my mind, I took a long breath.

"So, was it really *them*?" I asked. "She came; she took Sam?"

"And who exactly do you mean by 'she'?" Johan asked tiredly, looking away from me.

"Don't pretend you don't know who I'm talking about," I snapped, trying to keep my voice low, I didn't want anyone hearing this conversation. "You know who. That *woman*."

"Why would she—?" Johan stopped talking to scratch his eyebrows, he looked genuinely confused, as if it wasn't possible, as if I was crazy for even thinking it. He had dark circles under his eyes and his skin still looked pale, he looked older than he was.

"Then why did they take her? I don't see any other reason."

"No one took Samirah away. Sam left."

"What do you mean, she left? How did she leave? She wouldn't do that." *She wouldn't do that* to me, I wanted to say.

"Do you really think she would even try to come back *here* after everything that has happened? Samirah leaving was not her doing."

Johan chuckled as he shook his head at me. "Do you really want to know why Samirah left?" he asked. I nodded. "Two reasons. The first one is that she was being prepared to take her role on the board committee as Aurora's successor and what she learnt could have frightened her."

That didn't surprise me. Aurora did prefer Sam and Nate out of all her grandchildren, even out of Johan's sisters. But why would Sam run away because of that? It would have been great for Sam to have *that* position. She had always wanted that, as it was essentially a free pass to do whatever she wanted – not to mention the salary that came with the job.

"The second one, I'm guessing, is this." Johan took a bunch of papers from his second drawer and held them up for me. I looked at him and then at the papers, waiting for him to explain. Rolling my eyes, I took the papers and leafed through them.

"What's this?"

"Documents," Johan answered. I looked at him, lifting an eyebrow as if I were going to read about fifty pages when he could just tell me. Realising the same, he sighed and carried on. "Rocco Meylor asked someone, Frank Hayes to be exact, for you to be his bride. When Frank brought this up, it was, of course, denied. They put forward someone else's name."

"Who?" I asked, swallowing hard, avoiding Johan's eyes as my cheeks warmed up. I had come to terms with the fact that Roc and I were never going to happen. Roc never accepted it; I moved on, he didn't.

"Samirah," Johan answered me with a forced smile. Every single muscle in my body tensed up. "It's no secret to any of us that you have a – a friendship with Roc. Perhaps she felt that if she were to accept this, this *thing* with Roc, then she would be betraying you. Perhaps she thought it would hurt you."

"That's a lie. Besides, I don't care about *this*," I tossed the papers on the end of the desk. I didn't care and she should've known that. "What did you do to her that made her leave?"

"She will be okay," he told me after a long pause. He didn't want to tell me what Sam was learning because it was secret.

I was so done with secrets.

"How do you know? She can't just be alone out there. Make someone go and find her!"

"I can't do that," Johan muttered, lowering his gaze. "You more than anyone should know that. We can't cross the bridge."

I looked back at Johan, trying to find his gaze, but he kept looking away from me. He wasn't tired as I had thought; he was sad. Of course he was sad. Samirah spent literally every day with him. Sam and Nate followed him around like little ducks following their mother. Johan looked miserable and I had to accept the truth. Even if I wanted to go after Samirah, even if there were hundreds of soldiers available, we couldn't cross the bridge. No one could cross the bridge that separated us from the rebels. If someone was gone, they remained gone. And we, the ones who were left, were not supposed to speak of the lost ones again. And that I couldn't bear.

"This is all your fault," the words left my mouth leaving a bitter aftertaste. It was his fault Samirah was gone.

I felt an emptiness in my chest. The void in me was getting deeper and bigger, consuming me a little more. Without Sam, it was unbearable and there really was no solution, no fixing whatever that was wrong with me.

"You are going to blame me for this too, sweetheart?" Johan finally looked back at me. His eyes were glassy and his thick eyebrows were curved, causing a sad expression to appear on his face. I regretted ever wanting him to look at me in the first place. He had this wounded expression that made my heart shrink. And the way he talked, his tone, broke my heart. I couldn't bear it, so I did what I always do: I walked away.

"You can't run away from everything, Aliana," Johan's voice followed me as I walked out of the room.

Of course I can, Dad. I can run away from anything as long as I run fast enough.

I passed through the hallway and went into the dining room, where my brother and mother were still eating. I passed my hand over my mother's shoulder and pressed my lips against her temple. I wasn't supposed to do that, but I didn't care. I wasn't the type of person who liked physical affection, but with my mother I was different. With her, I didn't hide anything.

"You should eat something," she said without looking at me. She hadn't looked at me since the meeting. She did look in my direction, but not *at* me.

"Not hungry, Mum. I'll eat later."

"Where are you going?" Nate asked, standing up to follow me.

"I don't know. I just need to get out,"

"You shouldn't be out so late. Remember curfew. The last thing we need is you getting caught out at night when you know it isn't allowed," I turned back to look at him, curfew was at 10.00pm. There was no need for people to be out later than that time, as the shops closed at 9.00pm. "Do you need credits? I can transfer some."

I didn't need credits to buy anything. I had my own credits. I shook my head and turned around to walk away from him.

Once outside, I walked around my neighbourhood, all the houses looked the same as mine. I was trying to figure out what I was supposed to do, but I came up with nothing. Before the clock hit 9.00, I went into a shop and bought a bottle of water.

My payment had just come through that morning. My family was rich, being an important family and all, but I didn't like using Johan's money. As soon as I began to work, I used my own money. We didn't really use actual money, as it was seen as something vulgar. Papers and coins were a waste, so we used credit points. A microchip was implanted in our hands, so when you paid, the shop employee took the credit points instantly.

In the Government, you could easily tell the difference between poor and rich, we were divided into sectors. Imagine a circle and within that circle, imagine nine more circles. Three circles for each class: lower, middle, and high class. I lived in the first ring, the closest one to the CB, the richest sector.

I didn't know what to do or where to go, but then a crazy idea popped up in my mind. And I knew just the person who was going to help me. My sister was alone in the woods. She had crossed the bridge and was alone at night – Samirah, who couldn't even find her own socks and always took mine. Samirah couldn't even find her way through the Government's streets on her own. She still got lost from time to time, saying that all the streets looked the same. But the truth was that she was *always* distracted.

All I knew was that I needed to do something. I needed to find Samirah to be whole again, to be complete, to have a chance at being fixed.

There was only one person who was always willing to help me: Roc. Roc was my best friend. He always had my back, so I made my way to Roc's.

His house, just like every other house from the middle-class sector, was smaller, houses were closer together, they were like smaller versions of my house. I knocked on his door and waited for a few seconds until he was in front of me. He had a serious expression on his face, as always. His dark blue eyes looked down at me, expecting something, just like always.

Roc was the same age as me, 17 years old, although we both looked kind of older than that. We weren't kids. We weren't teenagers. We had to be adults because in the Government you stopped being a kid at the age of 10. There was no time to play and people already expected much from you.

"Ali, I tried to call you but—" he sighed, his eyebrows joined together, making his facial expression appear sad. I knew what he was going to say. "May her life—"

"*Don't*," I interrupted, walking inside his house. I couldn't hear that again. "I came to ask you a favour."

Roc followed me until we were in his living room. I saw the little hologram on the table showing Samirah's picture next to the news story of her being gone. I looked away from the projector and back at Roc's face. I needed to concentrate.

31

And I told him what my father told me and showed me, that Samirah probably left because of the petition. I told him that my sister wasn't dead as the Government said, that she had left. Roc didn't move a muscle of his face while he listened to me. He looked like a perfect statue.

"It's my fault, Roc," I said once I finished explaining, scratching my thumb with my nails. "And it's my responsibility to go after her."

"It isn't your responsibility," Roc said while he folded his arms across his chest. "Hypothetically speaking, if Samirah did really leave – which she didn't, because the news is on every informative hologram – she stopped being your responsibility the moment she decided to leave you. This isn't your fault."

"It's *our* fault. If you had listened to me when I told you I was not going to be your trophy wife, then Samirah would have never had a reason to leave. But you just couldn't let it go, could you?"

"I— I'm sorry but she's dead, Aliana. Let the gone stay gone."

"You don't understand. *She's out there,*" I pointed at the door, growing anxious as each second went by. "And I'm going to find her."

"Are you listening to what you're saying, Aliana? Look!" He took me by the arm and dragged me to the table with the hologram on it. There was a black-and-white picture of Samirah.

I didn't need it to be in colour. In my mind, I could put the light shade of bronze in her skin, the light green in her eyes, and the light brown in her hair, which was not wavy like mine but straight. That was my sister, my beautiful and elegant sister. Her full name was on the photograph, along with her birthday, her work position, and the date of her death. At the bottom, it read, "May her family find peace." But there would be no peace knowing that she was out there, that she could die at any time, and that I wouldn't know it. I would have no peace without my sister. Even if it was my sister's body lying in the woods without a heartbeat, I needed to see it. I needed to find her, alive or dead.

"That's a lie, Roc!" I snapped, shaking his hand off me. "I – I thought that maybe you would understand, but you don't. She's there and I will find her, with your help or without it." My voice shook a little at the end. I had nothing else to say, so I turned around to walk away.

I would find her on my own.

"If you leave this house with the intention of crossing that bridge, know that I will call the commander and inform him of your plans," Roc threatened me, his voice cold and sharp. I stopped right where I stood. I turned around, staring at him, taking in every little detail in case I missed something in the last twelve years I'd known him. Had Roc really just threatened me?

"She needs me, and *I* need her. You can call the commander if you like. Call Johan, or call the board, member by member if you like, but she's my sister."

I turned around again, having decided to go and find Samirah, but then Roc took me by my elbow, this time more gently.

"I'm not going to let you leave. Think of your family. If you leave my house thinking of crossing, I will find whoever I can to stop you before you make a mistake we can't come back from. Think of the pain you'll put your family through – your mum, your brother, even Johan. They already lost Samirah."

I felt Roc's words like a kick in my stomach. He was right. It could cause them a lot of pain to lose Samirah and then lose me too. But the only one of them who could actually feel pain was Johan. And I wouldn't be causing much pain. He would probably be better off if I left.

"She was my only chance, Roc." My voice broke when I spoke, I allowed myself to sit down, my vision was blurry because of my tears and my eyes began to sting. "Don't you understand that I hate this? She knew about me, she knew there was something wrong with me all along and she was trying to fix me."

"There's nothing wrong with you." He snapped, getting on his knees to look at me, "These feelings do not mean you need to be fixed."

"That's not what I mean and you know it!" I snapped back at him, standing up so fast that he fell on his back, "You're so blinded by what you want to see, you're just like everybody else. You created

33

an image of me choosing and picking what you liked the most about me. That's not me Roc."

"Oh, come on..." He interrupted me, shaking his head at me in disbelief.

"I need help and Sam was going to help me," I carried on, "You should've seen what she wrote about me, the things she thought of me... and she isn't wrong, Roc. You and I both know it."

"Just because you made a mistake—"

"You don't mistakenly empty your gun on someone," I muttered through my teeth, looking at him in the eyes as I spoke, my tears were running down my face and I did nothing to stop them. "I— I can't live like this, Roc. I need help."

"You did what you *had* to do," He stood up and cupped my face with his hands, "You didn't tell Samirah about that, did you? Aliana, you didn't tell anybody—"

"I need her, Roc," I cried, there was a huge amount of pain going through my body but I couldn't quite pinpoint where it was coming from, it was everywhere. Pain flowing through my veins making my body shake and crumble. "Can't you understand that? I need her."

"If you leave, they will say you're gone and I won't be able to say your name ever again. I won't be able to cope if *you* leave me too," Roc's blue eyes met mine, pleading me desperately to understand him. "If you stay, we can be together."

I shook my head, Roc didn't understand, he didn't *want* to understand because he didn't care. If Roc didn't care what could happen to Samirah, who was a part of me, then how could he say he cared for me? I was literally breaking inside just thinking that I may never see my sister again. How could he not see that I needed her? How could he not see that it took all the strength I had to keep my voice from breaking, to stand straight and not fall to my knees and weep until I was void of any emotion. How could he not see?

How could I believe his claims of love when he refused to help me find the one person that was willing to find an end to my mental suffering? Was that what love meant? To manipulate and ignore the other's suffering because it meant you got to be with them?

I couldn't love Roc romantically, but I had to a certain point, I did help build up his so-called love for me. And I hated the fact that I did so, however that didn't give him the right to manipulate me.

"I don't know how to live without her," I whispered after a long silence, allowing myself to feel the pain I was trying so hard to contain. Roc hugged me then, placing his chin on my forehead and running his hand up and down my back. "I don't think I can handle this for much longer, Roc."

"You will learn, it hurts but you can endure it, together we can endure everything." I wanted to push him away. How could he?

I hated lying, I thought it would have been very wrong of me to lie to others when I had been lied to for so many years. I hated lies and I promised myself I wouldn't lie, there were some things I had to keep hidden but I always tried my best to be honest. Lying to Roc was hard but if it was what I had to do to get my sister, I would do it.

Just this once. This will be the only time I ever lie to him. Just this time, for Sam.

I stepped back, pushing myself away from me. I looked up at his blue eyes and I thought about it, about lying to him, about how I'll be giving him hope of something that I know will never happen.

"Together," I said, swallowing hard as I held his hand.

And he believed me. He had this radiant smile as if I had just made his night with one simple word.

I had convinced him. Now I just needed to figure out how the hell I was going to leave.

 **Chapter 3**

Location: The woods
Narrator: Aliana

IT HAD BEEN five weeks since Samirah left. When the fourth week of her disappearance rolled around, I left home.

For a week I had been walking around the woods, looking into every little clue that might lead me to my sister. On the third day of my search, I found some kind of villages. People walked around and spoke in a language I did not understand but they didn't look much of a threat. I did not dare to go in, though. There was no way Sam would be there, so I turned back and walked half a day to where the bridge began, where I found an empty bottle of water, surely Samirah's.

The villages were an inconvenience, I didn't want to be seen so I had to wait until the sun went down to properly search. It was harder but I could walk around without worrying too much.

It was very hard to find any evidence in the woods. Although Samirah did leave some stuff behind, it still led me nowhere.

My days began very early in the morning. The sun rose at 5 a.m. and went down at 7 p.m., if not earlier. Winter was gone and with it so was the snow. It was hot all day long, but at night it was kind of chilly. I was trying to wake up earlier than 7 a.m. to make good use of the sunlight because in the dark I couldn't see anything.

I felt useless, I was walking around in circles. I had been gone for days and I found nothing. There was no way to make the days longer, the woods smaller, or my eyes faster in taking in details; there was no way to make the search less agonising.

The last bit of hope I had of finding Sam was slowly fading. I was coming to the realisation that sooner or later, I had to accept I wasn't going to find Sam. If anything, I'd find her body, but at least that would give me some peace. I knew I wouldn't be able to go back to the Government, as the board wouldn't allow me back in. But without Sam, what was the point? I'd miss my family and my friends every day, but I knew the consequences of my actions and I accepted them willingly. I knew what I was leaving behind. I knew what I was coming to, and I accepted it. If I had to live on my own for the rest of my life or if I didn't live at all, then so be it.

I waited for days until I left home. It was impossible to do it sooner because Roc kept watching me, he didn't completely believe me. When he began to believe me, he started to talk about our future and all the things he wanted for us. I listened to him, thinking how naive he was to actually think that we could ever be happy.

That day, when I got home I grabbed the biggest bag I could find and filled it with things I might need: water purifier, food, a compass, small-size weapons of all kinds, ropes, clothes for Samirah once I found her, a bunch of little bottles with my pills, and a family portrait where we all looked happy and like a proper family. It was a bit sentimental, but whatever; Sam would like to have it. And once Roc gave me space, I took my bag and left.

I had to sneak out on everyone. It wasn't hard to sneak out, I had been ignoring and avoiding everybody.

I did see William Frayn. He was friends with Sam and Nate, he was also part of the Board. Once William saw me, he came up to me and told me that if I needed anything in particular or if there was anything he could help me with, he'd be pleased to do so. I politely thanked him and kept making my way.

Over the week I had been in the woods, I realised that the white uniform wasn't the best thing to wear. The radiant colour must have been an easy target for miles – another reason I had to move slowly and carefully. Also, I noticed that the last two days when I'd been getting close to the village, there were traps all over the place – easy to spot, really.

Stupidly enough, I got trapped in one. It was in plain sight, very obvious, so I missed it. I stepped on it and I went flying into the air. A rope wrapped around my ankle, hanging me upside down from a tree. *Great.* Luckily for me, I always had my knives strapped to my ankle and in several other places. Once I reached the knife at my ankle and cut the rope, I had to pretend that this was another exercise, a high drop, as I had practised several times before. With a backflip, I landed perfectly on the ground.

Once I was on the ground, I inspected the area to look for more traps. In total, I had found ten, all of them the same type. The traps were new. I'd walked around and hadn't seen them before, which meant that their intent was to trap me.

Looking at the traps, I was thinking about Sam falling into one of them. Maybe she was alive. Maybe I still had a small chance of finding her. An idea popped into my mind: I would never find Sam in the woods, most of all because I had never been in the woods. For all I knew, I was walking around in circles. *Rebels* knew the woods – they lived there.

Quickly I undid all the traps I could find, putting them in another place around a well-hidden circle. I waited until it got dark, and then I hid my bag. I couldn't find Sam on my own, so they were going to help me find her.

*   *   *

It wasn't the sunlight that woke me; it was the raindrops. It was drizzling and it was kind of chilly; I put on my hoodie and my white field jacket, rolling the sleeves up to my elbows. I tied my long hair into a bun and wrapped a white bandana around my face, putting the hood over my head as well. I didn't like the bun or the bandana, but I didn't want the rebels to see my face. Nor did I want to interact with them but I had no other choice. I would do anything for my family and right now I needed to find Sam.

The day was cloudy; the ground was wet, making my boots sink in a little; there was no sunlight at all, so my uniform wouldn't be much of a problem. And after a boring morning, just as I had planned it, two rebels showed up. I couldn't see their faces, I was hiding behind a tree.

One of them was easy to spot, big and muscular, about 5'10". His skin was tanned, and his long hair was light brown maybe. The other one was about the same height, maybe taller. Although he looked muscular, he didn't look as big as the other one. His hair was brown and short, and his skin was light brown, which reminded me of Roma's caramel skin colour. The rebels were playing around, punching and pushing each other.

They were so distracted; they didn't seem to notice me. How were they supposed to come running after me if they didn't even seem to care that I was making noises or waving my *white* uniform around? I got tired of waiting for them to notice me, so I dramatically sighed and walked out of my "hiding" spot.

They didn't notice me then either.

I saw the big rebel push the taller one into some bushes. I couldn't help but roll my eyes. What the hell were they doing? They were supposed to be big and scary savages. They were supposed to behave violently, not play around like little boys.

Sighing, I stepped on a branch, making enough noise to be heard. The big one looked at me as he helped the other rebel get up. I looked back at them silently, daring them to come after me. The taller, skinnier one had a smirk on his face.

As soon as I knew I had their attention, I sprinted away, knowing they'd follow. I had thought it wasn't going to be easy to fool the rebels. After all, it was the savages who had made the Government burn all those years ago, it was the rebels that killed almost half of our population when they rebelled against the Government. Fooling them wasn't supposed to be easy, but right at that moment, seeing them play with each other like little kids, it didn't seem too hard.

All I had to do was to get to where the traps were. And once I did that, I'd have to make them help me, tell them they had to or else I'd kill them. Not that I was going to do it, but they didn't have to know that.

The two young men were running after me. The big one with the light brown hair was far behind the other. One of them – I guessed that it was the hench one – was really loud. I was surprised to see how fast they were. I couldn't help the smile that was forming on my mouth. I loved this, the running and the adrenaline. I felt free.

I pushed myself to run even faster. I felt the clean air in my lungs. Each breath made my lungs burn, but I loved the feeling. I loved the feeling of the raindrops hitting my face and my heartbeat racing. I felt amazing at that exact moment, nothing mattered but running through the woods.

It was unexplainable how something so simple could fill the void in my chest, could make me forget about all the wrong I've done. It was when I did the things I loved most that I felt a hint of happiness and freedom. That was something no one understood.

There were tree branches on the ground, so I had to jump to dodge them and not fall on my face. I looked back and saw the boy with dark brown hair jumping over a big branch. However, the bigger one didn't see it in time, so he tripped over it and fell to the ground, rolling on his back. For a moment there, I thought I was going to have to slow down because I thought his rebel companion would stop and help, but he didn't. He kept running even faster. Of course he wouldn't stop, these people weren't like that.

I carried on running until I heard the rebel scream, or more like a groan when he was about to catch me – he was literally centimetres away – but before he could, I jumped over one of the traps, rolling to the middle of a meadow surrounded by trees, which camouflaged the traps perfectly. The rebel stepped right into my trap, which made him fly sky-high. He yelled out of surprise with a hint of humour in his voice. He was spinning around, his hands moving about while he tried to stay still to look at me.

"Impressive. What we do now, huh?" he yelled with a hint of mockery in his voice.

"Now we wait," I answered, my voice serious and sharp. I didn't want to talk to a rebel, or work with one, or look at one. But desperate times call for desperate measures.

"Hold *on*," he asked, laughing, His accent was a horrible thing. I didn't answer. "Oh, dude, you a girl?"

I let out a long sigh. I didn't want him to know if I was a girl or boy. I didn't want him to talk to me at all. I stayed quiet, and so did he for a time, but then he carried on.

"Alrighty, so, my friend gonna come and he'll get me down. You're gonna have a lot of explaining to do, so if I were you, I'd drop the attitude, *amiga*." I didn't say anything. I was grateful for the bandana covering my face. After what felt like hours, another scream broke the silence.

"That friend, you mean?" I said with an air of superiority, pointing to where the big guy was hanging from both his ankles.

"Well, this is cool. This is great, awesome," the guy with brown hair said, letting his arms hang. "We all hanging upside down. Now what, smartass?"

I could hear the mockery in the rebel's voice, but I wasn't fooled by it, it was accompanied by a hint of frustration. I didn't answer. Instead, I reached for the knife strapped to my left ankle.

"I am going to bring you down. Do not run," I told him while I walked to the tree where the robes were tied. "There are more traps, and only I know where they are. I will tie your feet, your hands, and your neck with a rope. You run; I pull."

"Two shits in a stick! You can—"

"*Shush.*"

"Bossy much." The one with light brown hair snorted.

"Oh, little girl, when I get a hold of you—" I cut the rope before he could finish, making him fall onto his back. From the sounds of it, it was rather painful.

He groaned in pain. I smiled.

"Oops, it slipped," I said.

"Isaac, you okay?" the big guy with light brown hair shouted as he kept spinning around.

The brown-haired rebel called Isaac growled as I put my knife on his neck. That kept him still while I put a rope around his neck and hands. If I pulled the rope that was tied to his neck, he would choke.

The rebel named Isaac stared directly at me the whole time, his jaw clenched, he was angry and I did not feel intimidated. When I finished tying him up, I held his stare. He had a scar on his left eyebrow, right at the beginning of it. His eyes were the same colour as his skin, light brown, with a black line surrounding the iris. His nose was a little wide. His lower lip was bigger than the top one. He had a three-day beard.

I was actually surprised when I began to take him in. He didn't look like some evil savage or some violent person. He looked kind of boyish – if it weren't for his ugly beard and his big muscular body. The beard made him look rather dirty, but probably because I was used to boys being cleanshaven. He smiled, showing his white teeth. I stood up, not wanting to look at his dirty face.

"Walk." I pulled the ropes. The rebel Isaac growled again but he did as I ordered.

When we reached the tree from which the hench guy was hanging, I told him the same thing I had said to rebel Isaac. However, when he fell to the ground, he ran. I caught hold of his rope and pulled it, which was harder to do than I had expected, I mean, he *was* huge after all.

"What part of what I said did you not understand, savage?" I shouted, a wave of frustration and anger shaking me. "Do not make me repeat myself, do *not* run," I added.

"Sebas," the rebel Isaac said, he could barely talk, "Stop."

I turned to look at the one called Isaac. I hadn't realised I was pulling the rope around his neck, my anger had taken control of me for a split second. I hadn't taken my pill that morning, and I could feel the burning desire to reach for them but I had to focus.

Relaxing my muscles, I loosened the rope around the rebel Isaac's neck. Tying up the hands and the neck of the other rebel, Sebas, he didn't even bother to look at me.

Once I got hold of my bag with my belongings, the three of us started to walk. I was poking them with a stick so they would keep moving forward. I didn't know how to approach them or how to ask – how to order – them to help me. While we walked far away from where the traps and the little village were, almost reaching the bridge, I thought about ways to tell them that they had to do as I said. I was trying to find a way to say it without sounding nice or doubtful or needy.

After a while, I stopped wondering about the ways I could torture them if they refused. I started to look at the two young men. They were different. They both had wide backs, but rebel Sebas was bigger. He was taller too, but not by much. Rebel Isaac had brown skin and mixed facial features, which led me to believe that he was of mixed race, like Roma was.

The two rebels were different but similar – maybe even siblings. Different mothers, perhaps? Loving didn't come as a taboo for rebels. They were savages after all so maybe they had different partners.

I couldn't help but wonder if this was how people saw me and Sam. We were twins but we had our differences. We both had Johan's nose shape. Samirah had his light green eyes, whereas my eyes were a darker shade. Sam's hair colour was lighter than mine. It was also short and straight, whereas mine was long and wavy. I was a few inches taller than Sam. And while Samirah had a delicate, perfectly golden body, I had strong muscles and my skin was darker than hers. Sam was delicate, smart, and overall just perfect. I wasn't.

Walking back to the bridge took at least two hours, but I needed to be far away from where the rebels might look for their friends. I was tired and wanted to stop halfway, but I knew I couldn't. The fact that rebel Sebas was talking non-stop the whole way didn't help either. He asked me questions the whole time, "Who are you?"; "Where we goin'?"; "What you want?" He also said things like, "Am thirsty"; "You making a mistake"; "I need to stop"; "Am hungry"; "I need a bathroom break"; and "Am tired." It was very irritating, even more so because of his harsh accent, the way he rolled his *r*'s… I had never heard anything like it before. It got to the point where I just needed him to shut the hell up.

"Good God, don't you *ever* shut up?" I snapped at him. "Bloody hell, I'm not surprised you're tired and thirsty; you keep talking and talking. You're a very annoying little thing. I wonder how people can be around you."

"I ain't little," Sebas spat. It seemed like it really annoyed him to be called little – such a big guy with such a dumb insecurity. But hey, we all had our insecurities, I wasn't one to judge when I had so many myself.

"Oh, for God's sake," I groaned loudly. I was so tired of rebel Sebas that I took the bandana off my face and wrapped it around his mouth.

He kept trying to talk, though. I knew I would never again wear that bandana. Rebel Isaac let out a little cough – disguised laughter. I didn't want him laughing either. This wasn't a laughing matter; it was a serious matter.

We could finally walk in peace now that rebel Sebastián wasn't talking or complaining thanks to the bandana. By the time we reached the bridge, I was so tired that all I needed was to sit down. We sat in the first little camp I had made after I ran away.

Right after we sat down, I got up to start a fire. I tried to use the trees to cover the fire from the few raindrops that were still falling. The sun went down an hour late. Not one of us said a thing. I just stared at the fire. I needed to find a way to make them help me. Perhaps I could tell them I was going to give them to my government if they didn't help me. We were just a bridge away …

After an hour of silence, rebel Sebastián tried to say something that sounded like "I'm hungry." I couldn't deny it, I was hungry too, but I wasn't about to leave them and go get food for them. After another hour, the two rebels were asleep. I could tell because their breathing was very relaxed and one of them was snoring.

I tied their ropes to a tree and moved away to set a trap for an animal. The fact that I didn't like the two rebels didn't mean I was going to let them starve. I needed them to be well and strong enough to help me. If only I could be brave enough to form the words in my mouth: "I need your help." But those words – those words were too much to say to someone I knew, so I couldn't fathom saying those words to *these* people.

After a while, a little brown bunny fell into the trap. Its rear paws were tied up together. I grabbed the rabbit, keeping my knife in my other hand. The rabbit was defenceless, small, and hairy. Its heart was beating so fast; I could feel it in the palm of my hand.

Who was I trying to fool? I could never kill an animal. I didn't even eat meat, for God's sake.

I petted the rabbit's head and ears. I petted the creature for a while as I sat and watched the two rebels. Then I let it go. If the rebels asked me for food, I could always say that I didn't want to give them any. I still had biscuits, cereal, and bread with jam.

Empty-handed, I stared at the rebels. I took the ropes back into my hand and was ready to pull if anything went wrong. I didn't get to sleep, as I had to keep an eye on them. I didn't know rebels, didn't know what they were like, so I couldn't possibly know what to expect from them. But my eyes grew heavy. I was very tired. I kept rubbing my eyes with the palm of my hand, but all it did was make them feel heavier. Once I closed my eyes, it was a fight to open them again.

I was looking for Sam. I was desperate to find her. Something had happened to her. I didn't know what had happened, but I knew that something had. I could feel it. I was still in the woods, still looking for Sam. One moment I was running in the woods, and in a blink of an eye I was at end of the bridge. In front of me, I could see the main street to the Government. I was going to walk across the bridge when a raindrop fell on the top of my head. Only it wasn't a raindrop. I stepped back as I took in the picture: Johan, Cynthia, Nathaniel, and Samirah were hanging from one of the bridge's posts.

Their clothes were filthy with blood, and they were looking at me with anger in their eyes. I could feel the bile rising in my throat. I dropped to my knees, my eyes were burning, but tears wouldn't come out. I looked back at the Government, expecting someone to show up and help my family, but all I saw was a man in an elegant black suit, his hands in his pockets, an evil smile on his face. His eyes bluer than any blue I'd ever seen. When I blinked, Frank Hayes was no longer at the end of the bridge but was right in front of me. Holding me by my arms, he pulled me up to my feet. His eyes were beautifully blue.

I blinked and tried to look past him to my family, but they were far, far away. I wanted to look away from Frank's eyes, but I couldn't; it was as if they took all my attention.

Frank had a wicked smile on his face, he then opened his mouth and he was saying something but I couldn't hear him. I couldn't hear his voice but I could hear everything that was surrounding us. I was frozen, my legs wouldn't respond, fear was taking over my body. I wanted to run away, far away because I had never felt such fear as I did right at that moment.

And then, everything got quiet, it was like the world was mute and all I heard then was Frank's voice.

"It doesn't hurt," he whispered, making me shiver. "Once you hit the ground, it'll be quick. The hard part is the falling. That's when all the regrets come, when you think of what could have happened if you had taken a different turn in your life. Would it still have led you to this? But there's no turning back, you were at the top and now you're falling and once you're falling, there will be no one to catch you."

I frowned as I followed his eyes to where he was looking. Frank had me hanging over the edge of the bridge. When I looked down, my stomach dropped to my feet. Where there was supposed to be water was now nothing but blackness. All that was holding me from falling were Frank's hands. Instantly the hair at the back of my neck stood up. I couldn't breathe. And then Frank Hayes let go of me. I was falling. I was falling, and it was all my fault.

Gasping, I woke up. I pressed my hands to my face and rubbed my eyes hard. It was just a nightmare. My family was okay. They were members of the board, so no one could hurt them. The heartache kept me awake. When I felt like I was about to fall asleep again, I poured water over my face after taking three pills.

My nightmares were always bloody. Someone always died, and someone else always blamed me. Mostly, my nightmares were about a woman who tried to kill me. In my dreams, I was always trying to run away from her but she always caught me and then made me watch as she killed, one by one, every single person I ever cared about and when she was about to kill me, I woke up.

46

My mother once told me, "Control your mind or else it will control you." I always allowed my fears to control me and that made it very hard for me to remain calm. She was right, she was always right.

Looking back at the two boys, I couldn't help but feel a bit guilty. Was I keeping them from their families too?

"What am I doing?" I sighed while looking up the sky full of stars.

What a lovely night full of regrets.

Chapter 4

Location: The woods
Narrator: Isaac

I WAS TRYING TO get a good look at the girl. At first, I couldn't see her face because of the bandana. But even when she took it off to shut Sebastián up, she wouldn't look at us for longer than a second.

She first had her hair tied up in a bun, but as we walked, she put her hair up in a ponytail instead. Her clothes were very bright and baggy; it was no surprise I had confused her with a boy. She was wearing a white shirt buttoned up all the way to the top, white cargo jeans, and grey combat boots. I knew better than to think she wasn't strong. After all, she had us both on a rope. Although I didn't want to admit it, she looked pretty badass with her belt full of knives and her gun.

When we finally stopped to rest, I was a little scared because we were near the bridge. All the hope I had for the girl to let us go, thanks to Sebas's big mouth, was long gone when she put the bandana around his mouth. He actually looked kind of funny. It took time and patience to get used to Sebastián's big mouth. After a while, it was actually kind of comforting.

When the sun went down and night came, Sebas fell asleep quickly as always. His snores were so even, there was no doubt he was asleep. I was pretending to be. I had to keep my eyes open to figure out a direction to go when we ran away. There was no way I was going to let myself or Sebas be a lab rat for the Government.

I looked at the girl while she just stared at the fire. I am not gonna lie; she was beautiful, but she looked pissed off. There was a moment when she got up and for a second, I thought she was going to kill us in our sleep but she got up to hunt. She trapped a rabbit. My stomach rumbled with hunger. But, she didn't kill it. She sat down and petted it. At that point, I knew she wasn't going to do it. If you play with an animal you're going to have to kill, you'll end up not killing it. She wasn't capable of killing it.

Softy little girl.

I hit Sebas with my elbow to get him to wake up, which he did. I pointed to a sharp rock, hinting at him to use it to untie his ropes, which he did while pretending to be asleep. But his snores became uneven and louder. Once Sebas had untied his hands, all I needed was for the girl to be distracted so Sebas could run away and get our people to help me.

Then the girl shook herself awake. Her breathing was uneven and she looked scared. She reached for her bag, took out a bottle of water, and splashed some of it on her face and took some blue pills.

"If you let us go, we won't go after you," I said, breaking the silence. The girl jumped and looked at me.

"Why would I believe you?" she answered. She spat the word *you* as if I was the worst species in the world. "You're a rebel."

She was waiting for an answer, I was trying to figure out why she called me a rebel and if I should feel insulted. She had a little frown that made her eyebrows curve. It also gave her face a sad kind of look, sad and pissed off. She looked like a doll, like a Government doll. She reminded me of someone but I couldn't quite know for sure.

"It's very simple, actually. See, I can't go home and tell everyone that I've been captured by a smartass from the Government, now can I, doll?"

"What, and a girl can't do that?"

"That's not what I meant, a girl can do this and more, but not a girl from the Government."

"As if you knew anything about girls from the Government."

"Well, I know some, smartass."

"Stop calling me that."

"So, entertain me, *smartass*," I smirked. Seeing how it annoyed her, I thought I may as well do something to keep myself entertained. Besides, it annoyed me the way she kept calling me a rebel or a savage. "What are you doing here?"

"I said, I'm not a smartass; I am a soldier," she said, shooting me a look. God, that look; it was like she wanted to pull my eyes out. It seemed to be very easy to annoy her. I wanted to burst out laughing.

"A soldier!?" I gasped, opening my mouth to pretend to be surprised. I laughed in her face and boy, did she look pissed. "So, what are you doing here? What's the plan, lil' soldier?"

"For now, you sleep," she ordered me with a sigh.

"I'm not sleepy."

"Then make yourself be sleepy."

"Can't do." I shook my head. I needed to distract her so Sebastián could go. He was almost free of all the ropes. The one around his neck was the last.

"Then shut up," she said with more authority in her tone of voice while she pulled the rope tighter around my neck.

A wave of anger shook my body. She was choking me and didn't even realise she was doing so, or she simply didn't care. She couldn't kill a bunny, yet she was about to choke me to death with surprising ease.

"They gonna know we ain't back yet, my people. And they will come looking for us. When they find us, you won't know where they coming from. These are our woods, our home. You're nothing here." I looked at her in the eye, "Your first mistake wasn't crossing the bridge. Your first mistake was thinking you could survive here. And when my people come, they will free me from these ropes and they'll beat you up so bad no one will recognise you. You will be so miserable that you will crawl at my feet begging me to let you go because I'm nothing compared to the others. You will be my slave, and I will– I will make you feel things that your cold heart has never even imagined. I will humiliate you and make your life a living hell until the thought of your precious Government is nothing but a sad memory in your pathetic little life. Your life will belong to me. You and your emotionless ass will belong to me."

I never threatened anyone before. It wasn't my strong suit. I had often seen Miguel do it, though. He made real good threats, but I was not Miguel. There was a first time for everything and perhaps my first time with threats didn't go as I had expected.

After I said it and went through every word I said, I realised just how pathetic it sounded. We never kept slaves, and I wasn't about to torture anyone for no reason at all. It took too much cruelty to torture someone daily, never mind that I certainly didn't have the time to do it. Maybe I could if I hated her or something, but I actually found her kind of funny – someone I'd like to annoy from time to time when I was bored. However, the girl didn't know this. For all I knew, I was the most dangerous person she's ever seen. But not a muscle of her face moved an inch as I let the words out as if I had not just said I was going to make her life a living hell.

Maybe threats weren't my thing.

"And you call yourself a rebel, a savage?" she asked, frowning. Technically speaking, I ain't never been called that. Maybe a savage, but a rebel? Nope. "What kind of threat is that, anyway? *They* will beat me and you'll do what, exactly? Watch while they do it? I don't understand how that makes you sound evil or cruel. It just makes me fear you less. I think you talk too much."

Now she was the one making fun of me. I growled as I tried to get up and run away, but she was fast.

She pulled the rope tied to my feet, and I fell on my face. She got me up on my knees and pulled the rope around my neck. With the rope getting tighter around my neck, it was getting hard for me to breathe. She pushed me against a tree, pressing her forearm against my throat, which made it even harder to breathe. We were face-to-face and she was staring a little too much.

"Watch it, love. I know I'm attractive, yeah, but keep the distance," I smirked, she frowned confused. "Handsome, huh?"

"*Please*, don't flatter yourself," she snapped, raising one of her perfectly curved eyebrows. "You're a savage with bad manners and a big mouth. You dress like a vagrant. With messy hair and horrible haircut, ever heard the word *comb*? You smell like a horse. You're ugly, idiotic and annoying. And on top of all this, you're a narcissist. Not my type." She kneed me in the stomach, making me fall to the ground.

Ugly!? I felt very insulted. Maybe I was a bit of a narcissist, just a little, but I *was* handsome.

"Oh, but you people have types?" I coughed, looking up at her, and prepared myself because she was probably going to hit me once I said this. "In that case, I doubt *you* are anyone's type. All angry and bitter. No one likes sour lemons, *love*."

The girl laughed, amused by my comment. I knew it wasn't going to take too long until she realised that Sebas was gone.

And as if she heard my thoughts, she turned around and Sebas was gone. I allowed myself to laugh out loud, I distracted her and Sebas was gone.

"Yeah, I take it back. I guess you really not so smart after all." I laughed again, looking at her while she turned around to face me.

The look in her eyes ... it was rage. I felt a hint of pleasure at seeing her so angry. At least I had done that.

"Oh, don't be so angry, soldier. That's an emotion, and you aren't allowed to feel those. I do wonder though, how do you manage to hide it from everybody?"

I was laughing hysterically and I couldn't stop. I was very nervous. I've never been this close to the bridge.

She pulled the rope and I felt as if my breath had been knocked out of me. I put my hands on the rope around my neck, trying to loosen it but it was too tight. My sight was blurry while she knelt and pulled my hair back, making me face her.

"My only mistake was getting distracted. Yours? Thinking you know anything about us." Her tone was full of anger; she was *really* pissed.

She put a hand on my neck and loosened the rope a little bit. I coughed, taking big breaths. For a moment I thought I was going to pass out.

"Anger? You think you know something about anger, rebel?" she continued. There was so much coldness in her voice, and even though I could tell she was infuriated, she still managed to talk very slowly. I think the slow way of her talking was what made her words sound worse than they were, it made her sound scarier. "Anger is the only feeling I've ever known. Now walk and show me where your friend went, or so help me God I will lose the last bit of self-control I have left. And trust me, you do not want that to happen."

She was so close to me; I could literally see the burning anger in her eyes. She wasn't lying. She was able to feel; that much was obvious. But could she be cruel?

The girl punched me in the face with a great amount of strength. When I felt her fist meet my jaw, I lost my balance. The next thing I felt was a huge pain at the back of my head. After that, everything went black.

Chapter 5

Location: The woods
Narrator: Aliana

FOR A MOMENT there, I thought I killed him.

I punched him and he fell back, hitting his head on a rock. If he was dead, it wasn't really my fault.

I looked at him for a moment with my hands covering my mouth, waiting for a movement or something, but he was so still that I really did think he was dead. Regretting my little loss of control, I got close to him to check for a pulse. I let out a breath of relief when I felt his pulse.

I wanted to wait for him to wake up, but I didn't have time to waste. Who knew where the other one was? I threw water on his face and slapped him around a couple of times until he woke up. The rebel Sebas ran away. He was probably on his way to his village. I had already lost a lot of time and if Isaac was telling the truth and his people would come after me, then I had to find Samirah fast. And then everything would have been for nothing.

I had to make him help me. This was when I needed Roc the most. He wouldn't let anyone escape, he would come up with an idea to make the rebel help me. Roc would have never been so easily distracted.

As soon as the rebel was on his feet, we began to walk. God knows where we would go, but we had to go somewhere. I was thinking about this absurd thing I was doing. I needed to ask him to help me. I needed to find my sister and then get out of this place.

I was in the middle of nowhere, surrounded by huge trees and with a hostage. *I* had a hostage. I felt guilty and a horrible sorrow that made my body heavy to move. My eyes started to burn. Tears were threatening to come out, and I was afraid wasn't going to be able to stop them.

The tears were rolling down my face and the anger was overwhelming me when the rebel's voice brought me back from my thoughts.

"I didn't know you people cried," he said with a stupid chuckle. I had knocked him out about an hour ago and now he wanted to make jokes? Where was his common sense?

"You think you know all about us, and yet you have no idea," I sighed as we walked around a little pond. I was so tired, all I wanted was to rest.

"Why didn't you kill the bunny?"

I tensed without meaning to. I didn't think they'd see that. He probably thought I was weak. But then again, I had many ways to prove the opposite.

"Because I don't kill animals,"

"Kill people instead?" he joked, chuckling as he lifted an eyebrow. I looked away from his curious eyes.

"Wouldn't be the first time,"

Silence. I smiled to myself.

"What are you looking for, anyway?" He carried on after a minute.

"How do you know I'm looking for something?" I tried to keep my paranoia and anxiety off my facial expression.

"If you wanted to take us to the Government, you would've done it right away, but you didn't. So, I'm guessing something brought you to this side."

I said nothing. I didn't know what to say.

"I can help you, you know? You ain't done nothing bad yet, I don't completely dislike you. Besides, I'm kinda curious about what you do. So, you're a soldier. I didn't know you guys had soldiers. Who you fight? It sounds like a joke—"

"You'd really help me?" I asked, interrupting him. This changed everything. I knew I couldn't completely trust one of them, but for a moment I felt a hint of hope again. I had to put my pride aside, without help I would never find Samirah.

"What, don't I look like the helpful type?" He smirked.

"Looks can be deceiving," I looked up at him. He did not look like a guy who would help *me*. Besides, the ropes around his neck, the ones *I* put there, were a big sign screaming *no*.

"Appearances can be deceiving," he said, looking at me. Maybe he was referring to the both of us. I didn't expect a rebel to be like *him* and he probably didn't expect someone from the Government to be like me. "I can very well be a demon in the skin of an angel. And let's be honest, I *do* look like one. I mean, look at me."

I rolled my eyes at his comment.

"It can just be a trick so I untie you. And then you'll show me your real face and try to kill me *or* run away. I'd say the latter." That was meant to be an insult, but he didn't seem to take offence.

"Yeah, that's the beauty of it, ain't it? Not knowing what the other's intentions are and still putting your trust in them. It's almost like giving me a knife and expecting me not to kill you simply because I say I won't. That's kinda deep, if you think about it, for you to trust someone like me."

"I don't trust you," I told him. If he was trying to get himself out of the ropes, he was doing a bad job. But I needed his help. This was strictly a necessity. I needed him, but that didn't mean I trusted him.

"But you need my help."

"I do."

"So," he said after a long pause.

"So, you're going to help me?"

"What you looking for?"

"You'd really help me?" I asked again.

I could hear Roc's voice at the back of my mind telling me not to trust one of them, but before I could regret my decision, I pushed Roc's voice away and put my pride aside. I didn't care about showing my weakness; I cared about finding my sister.

"I already said I would, and my father told me a man should always keep his word," he said with a smile on his face.

"Which means that your … let's call it a threat … is something you're also intent on keeping?"

"Look, I—"

"I accept your help," I interrupted him before he got the chance to talk, "I don't know if you're saying this so I let you go or if you actually do keep your word, but I've ran out of options. I have one condition: once we find the person I'm looking for, help me take them across the bridge to safety." This was crazy but it was the only solution I could see. "You can make me your slave or whatever, but I need this person to go back to where they belong, safe and sound."

I met Isaac's eyes, hoping my emotions weren't written all over my face.

The boy looked at me for a long minute. I didn't like this deal, but what other option did I have? The woods were too big for me. And by the time I got used to them, Samirah would probably be gone – *really* gone this time.

"Whoever it is, this person seems to be very important to you," he said with empathy. Something crossed his face but I ignored it, I didn't need his empathy or his overly emotional self.

"So, you're going to help me, with my condition and all?"

"Yes, you have my word,"

I looked at him trying to find something that would give him away, something to show me it was a lie and that I was being an idiot for believing in him, but there was nothing. Sighing as I got closer to him, I knelt to cut the ropes around his feet. Then I cut the ones around his hands and, last, the one around his neck.

I stretched out a hand to him, looking at everything but his eyes. I knew he was looking at me – I could feel his eyes boring into me – but I still couldn't bring myself to look at him. He was one of them and I was about to shake his hand.

I had a real chance of finding Samirah.

But then Isaac grabbed my hand and, with his free hand, took a big branch. I was going to attack him, but he already had his hand up, ready to strike a blow. The last thing I saw was his face until everything went black.

*   *   *

I woke up with a horrible pain on the right side of my head. I was dizzy and bouncing; the world was upside down. I blinked a couple of times, confused with my surroundings.

The world was upside down because the disgusting, horse-smelling rebel was carrying me on his shoulders. I tried to move my hands, but they were tied and so were my feet. When I tried to remember what had happened, an image of Isaac hitting me with a branch popped into my head.

"You said you were going to help me!" I shouted, trying to kick him, I groaned trying to get a good blow at him. "Put me down, you *savage!*"

By now we were probably halfway back to his village. The sun was already coming up. I brought my tied hands to my head, I had an open wound. I was stupid enough to trust a *rebel*.

That was the only chance I had to find Sam, and he took it from me.

"I will *kill* you!" I screamed, allowing my anger to take over me.

"You bluffing, you can't kill an animal, you gonna kill me?" He snorted. "You softy little soldier." I groaned louder, trying to hit him harder.

"Stay still!" he snapped at me, tightening his hold on my thighs. It was a rather uncomfortable position. He had my mid-body bent over his shoulders.

He put me down on the ground, taking my face in one of his hands. I tried to move away, trying to get away from him but before I could get too far from him, he took my whole face in his hand and pushed it up so I would look at him. It wasn't an aggressive hold, and maybe that's why it felt so uncomfortable because he did it softly and with care.

"I *will* help you." His eyes were wide open as he spoke. His voice was calm, but his accent was still annoying. "I will help you, but I'm doing it my way, okay? My friend must have already made it to the city. He probably already spoke with our leader. My people will come looking for me. Trust me when I say you don't want 'em seeing me with a rope around my neck and you holding it. They won't care if you're a defenceless girl, even though you sure as hell ain't. I'm going to help you, but you have to do things my way now, so relax and don't be stupid, *love*."

He winked at me – he really did wink at me again – and then he put me back over his shoulder. I gasped my mouth at the cheeky gesture and tensed my muscles.

"Can you please stop calling me that!" I snapped at him, pinching his back. He put me down with a frown. Irritation was written all over his face.

"Listen here, *love*," he spat, "I am the one in charge now. If I wanna call you love, I'll call you love. If I wanna call you smartass, I call you that. If I wanna call you a sour lollipop, I call you that too. You need to shut up and get back on my back so we can make it in time before they come."

My mouth dropped open. Sour lollipop? God, this boy is worse than an 8-year-old. Actually, an 8-year-old behaves better than this guy.

"You call me any of those things and I will cut your tongue out, *rebel*," I muttered. He sighed and, without notice, picked me up and carried me over his shoulder.

I said nothing after that, as I did not want to argue with this boy who looked like a grown man. After about three hours of him walking and me bouncing, I told Isaac to let me walk, so he put me down.

"We ten minutes away," Isaac informed, "When we get there, say nothing about you being a soldier or that you looking for someone.

You don't fight or have guns. I'll hide your bag so they don't see the armoury you have. They will probably take you to interrogate you, so drop the attitude, 'cos they ain't like me. I didn't lie when I told you that I would help you."

I nodded. I didn't have a choice anymore.

"You got any more weapons? Knives? Daggers? More guns, maybe? Deadly weapons like a Lego?" he asked, laughing at his own joke. He rolled his eyes at my lack of amusement. "You got more weapons? Yes or no?"

I did have two more daggers under my shirt, two knives strapped to my left ankle, and one more gun strapped to my right ankle – well, a little higher than the ankle. Yeah, I had more weapons, but I shook my head in reply.

"I don't believe you."

I shrugged.

"Either you tell me or I'll search you myself. Up to you, Smartass."

"My God." I rolled my eyes. "In the sheath strap around my leg muscle, a little higher than my ankle, there are two knives. There is a 6-mm strapped to my right leg, same height as the other." He looked at me with raised eyebrows, knelt, and took out the razor-sharp knives. The 6 mm was special to me. Nathaniel had given it to me as a birthday present. It was a beautiful matte colour. It even had my initials engraved in it: A. L. K.

It was pretty and very expensive. Of course, the price was nothing to Nate. His income was almost as big as Johan's.

"And two daggers under my top in my back. If you don't mind, I'll take them out myself," I said, taking the daggers out of their holders. They were each six centimetres long. I sharpened them every week. My favourite daggers, they each had a little hole I could fit my finger into. They were small but deadly.

"Jesus, who you gonna hurt with all this?" He took the daggers and his index fingers through the holes, spinning the weapons around. "How you use it?"

"Don't play with those or you're gonna get hurt, you moron! They're sharp," I snapped at him. I didn't care if he got hurt or not. I didn't like people touching my things.

He threw his hands up in the air and then put the daggers inside the bag. We kept walking. At one point, Isaac hid my bag well enough that you could barely see it.

It was morning when we finally got to the large village I had seen before.

"Please don't make me regret trusting you,"

"That must have been hard for you." He laughed, making me want to take it back. "I don't know how they will react, just be chill, okay? Keep the smart comments to yourself. Oh, by the way, I also have a condition."

"What do you want?"

"You have to tell me stuff about the Government and people over there and stuff. You have to answer all my questions." I relaxed and nodded. If I found Samirah thanks to him, nothing would be enough to repay him. Answering questions about the Government would be nothing compared to what he was giving me.

He kept walking forward, my heartbeat was beating faster with each step I took. By the end of the day, I was going to be surrounded by those who I was supposed to hate the most: rebels.

Chapter 6

Location: La Cruz
Narrator: Isaac

WHEN WE GOT to the city, I was still holding the girl over my shoulder. She had been so quiet the whole way that I thought she was angry again. Such a small body, but full of so much anger.

The first person I saw was Miguel, Cairo and José were at each side of him. Miguel always had his head shaved. His hands were folded across his chest as he stopped to take me in. Cairo's arms were full of ink. If you didn't know him, you'd be afraid of him, but Cairo was a family guy. He was calm and all jokes, but he was a beast when he needed to be, like everybody else, I guess. And last but not least was José. His hair was always in cornrows. He was the one with an attitude. Out of the three of them, Cairo was the biggest, followed by José and then Miguel. But appearances were deceiving. Out of the three of them, Miguel, with his silent personality and his innocent smile and serious eyes, was the most fearsome.

Sebastián was with them. He had been talking when he caught sight of me. He burst out running to me, shouting my name.

I heard the girl breathe in as if trying to prepare herself for what was coming. She was very calm and very still, like a warrior preparing for battle.

I was curious about the girl. She was totally different from what I had thought people who lived the Government were like. I had met some people from the Government but none like her. This girl, there was something about her, the way she carried herself, the way she spoke, the way she moved, the way she did *everything*. She looked very confident and very deadly at the same time. I was very intrigued by her, people from the Government weren't supposed to be like that, not even the ones who were normal.

"I had to tell Miguel. We were just on our way to find you." Sebas was out of breath, I could tell he was sorry but he did the right thing, even if it got me in trouble.

"When you ran away, she got distracted and, well, I attacked her and then made my way here," I told them. Miguel, Cairo, and José were already there listening. The girl pinched me when I spoke my lie. I tried not to laugh. It was obviously a lie, but I couldn't say the truth. Miguel, Cairo, and José would call me naive and stupid for trusting one of them like that.

"She crossed the bridge, Miguel."

"I think she wanted to take us as lab rats," Sebas opened his big mouth, I swear sometimes he had such a big mouth. Saying that she wanted to take us as lab rats … it was not good, not in our city, especially not in front of Miguel and Cairo.

I put the girl on her feet. She wasn't heavy, but my shoulder had gotten numb from carrying her and her heavy ass bag since last night.

"José, take her and interrogate her. I wanna know why she's here," Miguel ordered. José smirked and took the girl into a tight grip. She flinched and looked at me but quickly looked away.

"You all right, kid?" Miguel grabbed my face with his hands and began to look me up and down.

"Yeah, I'm good, I'm good," I answered, watching as Jose practically dragged the girl through the woods, "Shouldn't we go with them?"

"Not you." Miguel stopped me, slapping me a couple of times, it wasn't hard but it still hurt, "You go talk to your aunt. She's worried, I promised her as soon as I got you back you'd go straight to her. She's at your mother's."

I wanted to roll my eyes, my aunt was very overprotective and very paranoid, and she would do anything to make sure Miguel gave me simple tasks, sometimes I didn't even get to leave the city at all.

And of course, Miguel listened to my aunt because if Miguel listened to anyone aside from his sister Luna, it was his wife, Andrea, my aunt.

"She's my prisoner. I don't want her to be interrogated yet." I was looking right into Miguel's eyes.

"So why did you bring her then?" Miguel held my gaze. I stayed quiet, not knowing what to say. "José will interrogate her," Miguel concluded, turning around.

"Why José, though?" I insisted, walking next to Miguel. José wasn't the greatest guy ever, and the girl wasn't very nice either. That mouth she had … "Let someone else interrogate her. Let Cairo do it."

Miguel turned to look down at me, he gave me a cold, harsh look. "Don't question me, Isaac. And don't act like a child, you ain't one. Do as I said and go see your aunt." Miguel put his hand on my head and mussed my hair, "Or stay and we talk about how a girl from the Government captured you."

"In my defence, the girl's actually quite smart. And I wasn't expecting it." I chuckled. Miguel wasn't angry; he had a mocking smile on his face. Cairo laughed as he walked past us, shaking his head.

"Tomorrow, if you like, you can come see your 'prisoner'."

"But Miguel—"

"Tomorrow, Isaac," Miguel repeated and I knew that was the last of it. Miguel walked away from me heading back to our city and probably to the Church, where the girl would be interrogated by José.

I really hope she listened when I told her to keep her attitude to herself.

Narrator: Aliana

I was scared and I was trying my best not to show it.

As soon as the man called José grabbed me, I knew he wasn't the type to play games, just like Isaac had said.

While the man dragged me around the city, I had a chance to get a good look. It seemed like a simple village, easy to escape if I wanted to.

Although it must have been really early, there were already a few people walking about, there was an old lady with some sort of wooden cart and there were lots of fruits inside. She stared at me while I walked by with a confused frown and a mango halfway to her mouth.

Everything had so much colour. It looked so alive. The houses looked old, some in need of paint, some others were painted in bright colours, some green, and some orange. I had never seen so much colour in my life.

The man took me to some kind of old building, the white paint was fading and it had a lot of windows, our steps echoed as we walked. The inside was pretty, it smelled nice. The windows had strange drawings on them, some of the drawings near the window looked like angels.

I thought that was where I was going to be interrogated, but the man walked past and dragged me into a hallway by the end of the room. Along the hallway were a few doors, he opened the second one to the right. The room was grey. It had two chairs, some dirty mattresses on top of the other, and a big mirror on the front wall. Next to the mirror was a door. It was an interrogation room. We had one similar at the Government, but ours was clean.

José sat me on one chair, tied my hands behind me, and then tied them to the chair. He sat down in front of me.

For the first time, I could look at the José guy. He was big and muscular. His arms were about the same size as my head. His hair was in braids, his eyes were brown, his skin was darker than mine, his lips were fleshy, and his facial expression looked angry – very angry.

"Name," he ordered, his voice strong and deep, just as I expected.

I didn't answer so he repeated the same question harshly.

I should have probably been smart and just said my name, Aliana Lynn Keenan. It was not hard to do…

What happened next, happened so fast that didn't even see it. But I felt it. José slapped me across the face. He was fast. The side of my face he had slapped felt like it was on fire.

"Tell me your name."

"Didn't your mother teach you manners?" God, I was so stupid.

José slapped me again, this time harder. I laughed a little. He held back, but it still hurt.

"Why you here?" José asked.

"I think I'm being interrogated," I shrugged. "However, I highly doubt the lack of words could get us far. Perhaps if you—"

He slapped me again, this time so hard I tasted blood in my mouth.

"What a bitch," I let out a gasp, followed by a forced chuckle.

"Why are you here?" he asked again, marking every word. His accent wasn't as harsh as the others', but there was a hint of anger in his voice that, surprisingly enough, hadn't been there before. He seemed to be running out of patience very fast.

I knew it was a bad idea to play around. Isaac had told me to leave the attitude. I should have listened to him, but it was too late to go back now. I wasn't going to show this man any sign of pain or fear. And if I began answering his questions, he'd know if he slapped me for a bit, I'd end up doing as he said.

"Go on, scum," I muttered with a daring smirk on my face, "I'm sure you're capable of more than that."

José hit me again, harder than before. All I could hear with my right ear was a loud beep. José's hand was so big that he could literally slap my whole face with it. I hated myself for being so stupid and not answering right the first time, but now I couldn't give up my act. I knew my lip was broken as I tasted blood and my right cheek was probably going to be bruised. My face felt hot and itchy.

"For somebody as big as you, you sure do hit a little soft." I was interrupted by another slap, I took a deep breath and it let it out slowly, I was so angry my body was literally shaking.

"Soft, son of a bitch, scum..." José repeated while he slapped me, chuckling as he spoke. Well, at least I knew the name calling bothered him.

"You are all the things that are wrong with your kind. Actually, you're just proving my point."

"And what's your point?" He asked me and I should've stayed quiet, everything in me told me to be quiet, but the stupid side of me took over my mind and my mouth...

"That your kind should be erased from this earth," I smirked through my bloody lips and as I looked up at him all of my anger, all the years I had been holding everything in, all the hate I felt towards what his people meant to me and all of my resentment decided to take over my mouth and I couldn't stop myself. "That you and your people are a waste of space and sooner or later you all will be nothing but dust and bones that we'll step on."

I was talking more than I should have, I didn't really mean any of the words that I said. I've never met anyone like José... But to José, this could all be true, and when he slapped me, he slapped me so hard that for a moment I forgot my own name.

José kept asking questions, and I kept saying things I didn't mean or think. He was getting angry, and so was I. I had never in my life felt so much rage. I wanted to hurt him, but since I couldn't do it physically, I tried the best I could to hurt him verbally, which seemed to annoy him but not hurt him.

"Your name," he demanded again, rage in his tone. I was the one wounded and in bad shape, but José had run out of patience and he still didn't even have my name. That was something.

I looked up at him. It was hard for me to breathe. I was coughing, and blood was coming out of my mouth. Not wanting to show any emotion, I gathered all my strength, sat straight up in the chair, and looked directly at him, serious and firm, as any good soldier would do. I wasn't going to give him the pleasure of knowing how I really was feeling, that I was actually scared and weak, that I couldn't breathe, and that I was sure I was going to faint at any moment now.

"Losing your temper, aren't you, José?" I mocked, my voice as hard and as cold as I could manage.

José punched me with his tight first. I wished he would start hitting me on the other side of my face. My right side was probably filled with bruises and swollen. My left side hurt, but not as much.

I felt numbness in my jaw. That was it; I couldn't hold it anymore. I was going to give up. But then José lifted his fist again and punched me harder. He was asking me something, but I understood nothing. My sight was out of focus, everything was going dark, and my muscles hurt like hell, so I just let go, letting the darkness take over.

Freezing cold water woke me up. My muscles tightened. I coughed a few times and tried to stop shaking. When I could focus again, I saw José standing in front of me with a stupid little smirk on his face and a bucket in his hands. I didn't know how long I passed out for, but José looked calm again.

I wasn't calm, I was far from it. I could literally feel my whole body shaking with anger, I wanted to break the ropes around my wrist and kill the bastard, choke him with my bare hands, kick him, punch him, rip off his fingers one by one, cut his tongue out, break every bone of his body, and make him suffer for this humiliation.

They will beat you up until no one will be able to recognise you. You will be so miserable that you will crawl to my feet begging me to let you go. Those were Isaac's exact words, and that was what was happening now. *I will humiliate you and make your life a living hell.*

Isaac lied to me and I believed him, what was he expecting of me now – to beg him for mercy as soon as he walked through the door? Well, I wouldn't do that. Never would I lower myself to that level again. If I was going to die today and never see Sam again, then so be it, but I was not going to let them see me break.

I had nothing to lose, so I didn't care what José was asking me. I just kept quiet and sat up straight. He kept hitting me until I broke my silence and insulted him again. And then he kept hitting me until I fainted again and again. They didn't wake me up until the next day – with another bucket of freezing water.

There were three men in the room now. José was sitting in front of me. One of the men was next to José, standing up looking down at me. He had his head shaved. The other man was at the back of the room. His arms, full of drawings, were crossed over his chest. He was looking at me, too.

The three of them had serious expressions on their faces. They all looked quite scary to be quite honest. There was no need for more words than those to describe them: big and scary.

"Rise and shine, little girl," the man next to José said, the one with the shaved head. "Feel like talking today?"

 **Chapter 7**

Narrator: Aliana

QUESTION AFTER QUESTION I remained in silence.

The other two men didn't help much either, the one with shaved hair, I've come to know his name is Miguel, asked the double of questions José did and José slapped me around when I didn't answer, which was every time I was asked a question.

I was so tired and every inch of my body was sore; my head was hanging like it didn't belong to my body. I was in and out of consciousness, I wanted to stay awake, I wanted to hear what they were saying but the voices came and went.

"She won't say anything, Miguel," I heard José's voice, he sounded annoyed.

I don't remember how much time I was out, but I do remember that I woke up when someone burst into the room and began shouting.

"What the hell did you do to her?" It was a familiar voice; I knew I had heard it somewhere but I couldn't keep my thoughts in place long enough to remember. "She looks dead!"

Funnily enough, I *felt* dead.

"No, not dead. She fainted. I think." That, I did recognise, it was José. A hint of mockery in his voice, I heard his steps getting closer to me, I heard the metal of the bucket as he raised it from the floor and pour the water over my head. "And why do you care what happens to her? She did that to you. Remember that."

Oh, Isaac. That was the voice. I felt a burning sensation flowing through me, I believed him, I was ready to trust him and he betrayed

70

his word. I was naive, stupid for believing him. His kind, his people probably didn't know what honour was.

"Yes, but still—"

"But nothing, Isaac," I've come to recognise Miguel's voice, he always kept calm but his voice had a force in it, it made everybody in the room stay quiet. "You know well what happens when they take you to the Government."

I wanted to look up but I didn't have the strength to do so, I wanted to laugh and say: "He's the liar, he's the one that can't be trusted!"

"She won't say anything," The other man said. I didn't know his name since he barely got involved and when he did, his name wasn't called out. "José has been beating the girl since yesterday, non-stop, and she keeps making fun of him. He didn't even get her name. She's a tough one, this one. I say, leave her in the woods and let her get to the bridge on her own, or to Alex's city or to Príncipe, whichever she finds first."

"Why does it have to be like that?" Isaac asked. "She can't go to Príncipe city because Kiko will reject her if they know she came from here. Miguel, you've let others stay. Why not her? She ain't different from the rest."

"But she is," a faraway voice was heard, it was a girl's voice, I think. I wanted to snap at whoever that was, why do rebels think they know so much about us? "Different, I mean. Look at her, her clothing … she's a soldier, and soldiers are different. They are trained to do things without even questioning, even if it means giving their own life for no reason. They're supposed to know how to adapt to any situation. I knew a guy who could manipulate anyone to make them do as he pleased. I don't know how to explain it, but perhaps it would be better if you let her go back."

"Isn't that better for us, then? We can use her to—" A loud bang on the table, interrupting Isaac.

"Why," Miguel snapped, making me jump. I forced myself to look up, and I found a lot of people in the room but I couldn't see properly, my vision was a little blurry and I couldn't really open my right eye. "Explain to me why she should stay in *my* city. Explain to me why you never cared about how we treated our guests but that now you care what we do with this one."

"I'm sorry, but *this* is how you treat your guest?" I chuckled, trying to find Miguel in the little crowd. "Anyway, this little moron here gave me his word. He also threatened me." I swallowed, tasting my blood. "He said that you savages keep your—"

And everything stopped. I could see, I could see every single person in this room and I could see *her*.

She was wearing colourful clothes; her hair wasn't combed or in its usual bun. Her eyes found mine and all colour drained from her face. My vision was getting blurry once again but this time it was because of the tears.

"Sam?" My voice was barely above a whisper. It was her, it *had* to be her, I was not seeing things. "Samirah," I said again, this time I tried to speak louder but my voice broke.

She didn't say anything, she just looked at me. A muscular guy, which I recognised as Sebas moved closer to her. He whispered something to her, but she didn't seem to be listening.

"No way. No," Her voice was breaking and a few tears fell down from her eyes. I knew it was her. "What did you do? Why would you come here?"

I frowned at her questions, trying to find the words to answer her. She tried to get close to me, taking each step carefully, José tried to stop her, but Sebastián grabbed him and pulled him away from her.

José and Sebastián started to argue, but I was too focused on Samirah, she was coming closer to me and I still wasn't sure if I was hallucinating, if it was real or if I was dying. Samirah knelt right in front of me and put her hands down my wet top. Her cold hands made my body shiver, I knew what she was looking for, and although I had never allowed anyone to touch my scar, I figured she needed to make sure it was me.

"What are you doing here, Lynn?" Samirah cried, moving the wet hair off my face. "Why did you come? Lynn, you shouldn't be here. Look at what they've done to you…"

I wanted to answer her, I really wanted to but my eyes were closing, my body felt so heavy.

"How?" I demanded once I found the strength to do so. "With them?"

Sam sighed, stopping herself before she could answer me, she looked up at me once again, her eyes cold and distant as she spoke, "You shouldn't have come. You should have stayed there, where you belong."

I had never felt so angry as I did right then, I wanted to hold Samirah still, make her face me again, but she stood up and walked away from me.

"What are you talking about?" I snapped, I tried to get rid of the ropes around my hands, tried to move the chair in any way possible but I couldn't. "Look at me. *Look at me,* Samirah. Are you saying you belong *here*? You'd rather be surrounded by filth than with your own family!? You'd rather be with *these* people!? Look at you; you even look like one *them*!"

I was so focused on Samirah, so concentrated in finally getting what I had wanted for weeks that I had completely forgotten about the people surrounding us, José was no longer in the room and it seemed that it was now the other big guy's turn to hit me. Before I had time to react, the guy with no name yet was ready to backhand me. I closed my eyes, expecting the sting from his slap but it never came.

"That's enough, Cairo," Miguel's voice interrupted, finally breaking his silence. "Y'all are giving me a headache. Especially you." Miguel pointed at me, I wanted to laugh.

The big guy, Cairo, took a knife from his belt and bent down to face me.

"I'm going to ask you once, and you best not answer me with your dumb, stupid jokes, I'm not José. What are you doing here?" His voice was rather scary and threatening. He spoke in a low, raspy voice but in all honesty, I've seen worse.

"She's m—"

"My, my," I interrupted Samirah before she came to my defence, "you lot need to mind your own business. That information is none of your business, you filthy animal."

73

"You think you brave, don't you?" He asked me, playing with his knife. He pressed it softly against my face, moving it from my temple to my chin. I could feel the soft touch of the metal, it made me tense and my breathing quickened against my will. I tried to move my face from his knife but there was nowhere to move. "All night you've been someone's punching bag and you've said nothing. Maybe that's because a beat-up doesn't scare you. But how about scars? No one likes scars, especially your people. Y'all wanna be so perfect. Let's see how much you say while I deform that pretty little face of yours."

"You dare mark me, you savage, and I swear I *will* kill you," I muttered through my teeth, looking at him directly in the eye, my tone of voice as sharp as his knife.

"You may have fooled these two," He pointed at Sebas and Isaac. Smirking as he spoke, probably happy that he was getting the reaction he wanted from me, "And made them think you bad, but you ain't never hurt a fly. I see it in your eyes. Your posture and your attitude tell me one thing, but your eyes tell me another – and eyes don't lie."

"Oh, try me," I dared him with a wicked smile, "You wouldn't be the first."

The man was pressing the knife harder against my face. He was going to cut me, he was going to do it but right before he pressed deeper, Samirah spoke.

"She's my sister!" Samirah shouted. "Please, stop."

"Your sister?" Sebas asked with a frown.

"Yes, she's my twin, Lynn– *Aliana*."

"Hold on," Isaac spoke, "You don't look alike—"

"We *do* look alike," she glared, "We're fraternal twins, different placentas."

"You two sisters?" Miguel looked at me, taking two steps towards Cairo and moving him away from me.

"Yes. She's my sister." Samirah spoke again with desperation.

"Untie her and get her cleaned up." Miguel spoke, looking at me with a frown. It was my turn to be confused, I stared back at him. "No one touches her; until I'm back."

Without uttering another word, Miguel turned around and left.

Chapter 8

Location: La Cruz
Narrator: Aliana

IF I WAS asked to explain what my life had turned into, I'm very sure I couldn't find the words to do so.

Things didn't turn out the way I had expected them to. A few days ago I had two prisoners and no idea if Samirah was alive or dead. Today I'm the prisoner, but on the good side, Sam's alive and well.

I was relieved to see her alive, even though we weren't precisely on speaking terms. It was as if what I had lost the day I was told she gone, returned to me. I was once again complete. However, my moment of relief was cut short; I wasn't allowed to be with Sam, I was allowed to stay for the time being, just not with her.

The days that followed my arrival to this horrible place, I had been locked in some sort of prison cell. The man called Miguel came a couple of times the first day, he didn't talk to me, he just stood there and looked at me like he knew me, like he knew who I was and for a split of a second, I thought that maybe he did know me. Maybe he knew who I *really* was. But before my anxiety could get to me, I pushed the thoughts out of my mind. There was no way Miguel could know me, *really* know about me.

The third day, he came with a healer and an apprentice. The healer didn't do much, she allowed her apprentice to do all the work and even though I didn't want to be touched by them, the girl was patient with me. Also, I was in so much pain that I couldn't reject anything that could help me feel better.

I was in a lot of pain so I didn't hesitate to take whatever they said would help. I don't know what they gave me but I think I slept entire days. When I woke up in the morning, it felt like I had slept for weeks. The prison cell's door was opened, folded clothes were by the door, a little note on top. I sat up, closed my eyes and took a deep breath in. *I can do this.*

Every step I took hurt. Getting up was hard but trying to reach up for the clothes hurt even more. The note had a simple message, a messy handwriting that read: "Someone will show you to the bathroom, be ready when I get there. Today you earn your stay." At the end of the note was his name, Miguel.

It wasn't like I had much of a choice, at least for now.

Once I walked out of what had been my prison cell, I found a girl about my age sitting on the floor, reading a book. She was so concentrated that I didn't want to interrupt her. I stood there, half asleep and half dead. Standing still, surprisingly hurt as much as walking did. I cleared my throat, making the girl close the book right away, she turned to look at me with her eyes wide open, they were the same colour as honey.

"Holy cow, you scared me." She gasped, bringing her book up to her chest, her narrowed eyes taking me in. "You look like shit."

I feel like it too.

"Thank you, I do try." I couldn't help but smile, looking down at the clothes and the note I had in my hands.

"Miguel said I should take you to the showers, and to be honest, you need it, no offence but you smell." She chuckled. I looked away from her, a little embarrassed by her comment. "No worries, though, the smell is mostly because of the medicine we put on your bruises and wounds, José fucked you up pretty badly."

"Ah, I've had worse." I looked down at her, she was still sitting, taking her long curly hair up in a ponytail. Her hair, a big mess of beautiful chestnut curls, it was … amazing, to say the least. She had narrow honey-coloured eyes and a nose that fit perfectly well with her face, big and wide. Her lips were fleshy and turned upwards in a polite smile.

"I bet you have." She replied sarcastically, "Anyway, I'm Natalí. I don't know if you remember me, I don't think you do, it has been weeks and you were in a bad condition when Miguel allowed us to come patch you up. I'm the one who cleaned your wounds."

"That was you?" I narrowed my eyes at her, to be honest, I was in so much pain and so tired that I didn't remember much. "Well, thank you. If you don't mind me asking, how long have I been out?"

"Don't worry about it." She sighed and stood up, she was a little shorter than me. "We practically put you to sleep for almost a month, sorry about that, Miguel's orders." She shrugged and looked at me with an apologetic expression, I didn't have time to process what she was saying because she carried on talking. "In another life, I'd let you sulk about the fact we put you to sleep for almost a month but there's honestly no time for that, Miguel will be here soon and he doesn't like waiting."

I followed behind her, trying hard not to limp as I walked.

"So, listen," She began, walking backwards so she could look at me, waving around the book in her hand. "I'm supposed to go in with you while you're in the bathroom but that would be a little awkward. So I'm just gonna wait outside while you're in there."

I nodded, feeling relieved, I wanted to thank her but before I could, she carried on talking.

"However, I can imagine that you're feeling perhaps a little trapped, so if the idea of hitting me and running away crosses your mind at some point, it won't work. But if you still wanna try, don't hit the face, okay?" Natalí joked as she pointed at her face, a hint of a smile on her lips. She turned around and carried on walking normally, turning her head around to look at me from time to time.

"I know you have some kidnapping tendencies, so if you're going to use me as a hostage to escape, don't waste your time, I'd make a really shitty hostage. Also, José's outside, waiting for Miguel … and you."

I wanted to tell her that it wasn't necessary to tell me all that, I understood my position, for now, I was a prisoner. I had to do as they asked and behaved the way I was expected to. Sooner or later they'd let down their guard and I'll be able to escape. Besides, I needed a plan. I still hadn't been able to talk to Samirah and to be honest, it wasn't a conversation I was looking forward to. I had missed her a lot but I felt betrayed.

"Please hurry up, if you're late, Miguel will get in a bad mood, if Miguel gets in a bad mood, he complains, if he complains I get in trouble with the healer and it might not be important to you but this is important to me and—"

"I won't take long." I interrupted her mumbling. She sighed and nodded, laying against the wall.

I went inside the bathroom. I don't know what I was expecting but it was a pretty normal bathroom. I stood in front of the mirror, taking myself in. I did look like crap. I took off my shirt and was left in my white sports bra that was stained with blood as well. My torso was filled with purple to yellow bruises, but my eyes weren't focused on them. My eyes went straight away to the huge scar. It was a nasty looking scar, the length of my whole hand and the width of four of my fingers.

With a sigh, I caressed the scar with two fingers, sliding my fingers up and down the skin that wasn't mine but somehow belonged to me.

When I was a baby, a woman stabbed me with a pair of scissors, she cut through my skin, leaving a massive hole where there was once skin. The doctors tried to sew it up, but the hole the woman had made was so large that it couldn't be done. I lost a lot of blood. The skin that was used to 'repair' me was my mother's, Cynthia, she made the doctors cut skin off from her back and sew it on me. She said there was no time for synthetic skin, so she said to use hers. It was like I had a little bit of her in me. The funny part is that you can tell the skin isn't even mine, you can see how it goes from my bronze skin colour, to my mother's pale skin colour.

A knock interrupted my thoughts, I jumped and quickly tried to cover my scar, even if Natalí hadn't come in, it was reflexes.

"Dude, you have like 5 minutes and I'm not hearing the shower." Natalí's voice seemed desperate, I chuckled to myself, finishing undressing and getting in the shower.

The cold water did wonders. It was refreshing to have a shower after so long, the water was a little bit cold but after a minute, my body got used to it. I quickly washed my hair with what looked like soap, it smelled nice. I washed as quickly as I could manage and when I was ready to get dressed, I found myself staring at the clothes for far too long.

The clothes were of different colours, bright colours that I had never seen in clothes. The t-shirt was oversized which I was grateful for, it was bright blue which made me feel a little anxious because bright colours attracted attention and that was the last thing I wanted. The jeans were of a dark blue colour and baggy, I had to keep pulling them up. Luckily for me, I still had my boots.

I felt out of place dressed like that. I never was the centre of attention, people rarely even noticed me, but I stepped outside these doors dressed this way, I'd just be putting myself on a spotlight. I had to remind myself that I wasn't in the Government anymore. These people probably wouldn't even look twice and if they did, it would be because I was a prisoner.

I had to remind myself of that.

Once I got out of the bathroom, Natalí was still reading. When she looked up at me, she smiled and stood up, motion for me to follow her.

"Guess what?" Natalí wiggled her eyebrows at me, I looked at her with what I imagine was a disinterested facial expression. "Woah, calm down, don't get too excited. Anyway, I think you'll be working with my dad. He doesn't like people and I heard they wanna keep you away from people. Can't think of a better place than my dad's shop."

"And what does your dad do?"

"Miguel will explain it to you." She sighed and stopped walking, I stopped next to her. "He'll be here any minute now, so just wait here. If you're in pain just take this," Natalí handed me a plastic bag with a bunch of little green ball-like things inside it. I looked at it, inspecting whatever that the thing she just gave me was. "Don't look at it funny, I know it doesn't look nice but trust me, it'll be enough to help you with the pain. I made those myself."

I wasn't too sure if I wanted to take whatever it was that she gave me, however I *was* in pain and who knew how long it would be until I could take my actual pills, so I just nodded and placed the plastic bag inside my pocket. Without saying goodbye, Natalí turned around and walked away. I was left in a huge hall, waiting for Miguel to show up.

Miguel showed up about ten minutes later. For someone who didn't like to wait, he sure did make people wait for him. In the Government that would've been so disrespectful, no matter if you're a member of the board, if you're a shopkeeper or a farmer, you show up on time.

Miguel was a big man, he was tall and not as muscular as his trusted men, but big enough to make you think twice about how to approach him. However, muscles didn't always mean much, you could be strong and have muscles to show off but if you didn't know how to fight, how to defend yourself; you were useless, brute force, which was useful but not so much when fighting a person who had been practicing different martial arts their whole life.

Miguel stood two steps away from me, his eyebrows furrowed as he looked down at me, he waited a minute until he spoke. "Do you know who I am?"

"You're ... the leader?" Judging by his reaction, that was not the answer he was expecting but he nodded anyway.

"Let me be straight up, so... for now, you're a guest, you're going to have to earn your stay." He turned around and walked away, I figured I had to follow him, so I did. "It took me a while to figure out where you could be of help, I think you'll do well with Junior. You've taken 10 precious minutes of my day already, so José will take you."

I frowned, taking a deep breath in as we approached José. José stood up once he saw Miguel, he didn't look at me once. However, I couldn't keep my eyes off his hands. He had a rusty chain with handcuffs at each end. My heart dropped to my stomach at the sight of those.

"Your hands." Miguel's voice made me look up at him, I knew what he meant but I still couldn't bring myself to do as he asked. I looked at the rusty chain. "This is just for precaution, at the end of the day José will take them off," Miguel added, tension clear in his voice. I swallowed hard, biting my tongue, I slowly extended my hands out to him.

I ignored José's smirk or the way he smugly looked at me as he chained my hands. Miguel said something to José, something I couldn't understand. The pair of men were having a heated conversation, Miguel stood tall and even though José was bigger, Miguel's presence was threatening. Suddenly, Miguel pointed at José and with his index finger, a fire in his eyes that could've scared me. He said one simple word, something that even I understood, "No." There was no room for discussion.

Seconds later, Miguel walked away, leaving José awkwardly standing halfway through a sentence. I should have stayed quiet but I couldn't help myself. I chuckled.

"Just... how irrelevant are you?"

José glared at me but didn't say anything at all. I smirked to myself, ready to make another remark but before I could, José pulled the chains, hurting my wrist as he dragged me out of the building into the streets.

* * *

In my mind, I had the idea that I was going to be treated like a slave. Isaac had said so himself. However, the work I was given was not what I had expected.

I was in some sort of repair shop.

José dropped me at a rustic house, the outside layout wasn't different to the others. The inside was unlike anything I had seen before. As soon as I entered, there was a small living room, the furniture was made out of a material that seemed to be leather, brown and worn out leather. The only thing that really caught my attention was a black and white photography of a woman and a man.

The woman was smiling at the camera, she was holding a bouquet of flowers, wearing a beautiful dress. It was simple but sometimes simple things worked better. The man was not looking at the camera, instead, he was smiling tenderly, looking at the woman with his arm around her waist. He was wearing a button up shirt, pants and barefoot. They were both barefoot.

"My wedding day." A man's voice startled me. I quickly turned around. A tall man stood beside me. He was chewing on a slice of mango as he stared at the picture with longing in his eyes. "Happiest day of my life, I tell you that."

I remained in silence, what could I say? It was just a picture and yet I couldn't tear my gaze from it. Pictures captured moments, they weren't supposed to capture emotions. It seemed impossible to feel anything from a picture yet I could tell they were happy, I swear I could almost feel it radiating from the picture. The way he looked at her, the way she smiled like there was not a single bad thing in the world... For a moment I felt as if I was intruding something intimate, something that belonged to the man and the woman in the picture and only they could understand it.

Was love supposed to look like that?

"I'm Junior," The man continued, I looked away from the picture but he kept staring as he chewed on his mango, he seemed nostalgic. "And this is my repair shop."

"I thought this was a house." I muttered.

"Yes, this is my home," He nodded quickly, turning around and walking away. He limped as he walked. "But also my place of work."

I followed him into a large room, some sort of garage. In the middle of the room was a large table with a few chairs around it, there was a pile of different tools and objects. There were other tables that were packed with different items.

"This is the workshop, and all we do is repair, sometimes even create." Junior said tiredly as he walked towards the table in the middle, "The important stuff, the things people come to collect are either on this table or on that one," Junior pointed at the first table to the right. I nodded. "It isn't complicated, if you don't know what's wrong with something, find the notebook, there are notes of what needs to be done to what."

I nodded and sat next to him at the table, he began to show me how to fix a speaker. After an hour or so, I began to understand, some of the things that weren't working were easy to fix, changing cables or just replacing old parts, Junior was very organised and had everything in place, even if the room didn't look organised at all.

Junior didn't talk much, which I was okay with. He didn't seem to mind me much either, he didn't treat me like I had expected to be treated, he just… answered my questions and with a lot of patience explained things to me.

It was weird, never in a million years did I imagine myself working with broken devices. I was meant to do great things, I was supposed to lead (even though I was really bad at it), not fix old things that nobody seemed to take proper care of. The realisation felt heavy on my chest. I did all this because of Sam and to think that I wasn't even allowed to see to her.

I was never the type of person who acted out irrationally, I always thought about the outcome of my actions before I made a decision. And for once in my life I did something irrational and look where it led me, look at where I am now, chained and trying to tolerate the very same people I told myself I was supposed to hate.

Hour after hour went by, my wrists were hurting because of the chains, I could've easily taken them off but I didn't want to bring myself more trouble than I needed. Junior seemed nice enough and after a few hours, he got up, said he needed a break and left. I got up to look out the window, people were walking by, their voices were carried by the wind, some of it I understood, some wasn't English. I was looking at everybody, admiring them, this was nothing like I thought it would be, *they* were not like I thought they would be.

I was focused, looking at people when a certain boy caught my attention. Isaac was walking towards this house. I felt the sudden urge to run out of the house and make him regret his lies. unconsciously, my nails dug into the palm of my hands, I welcomed the pain.

Pain was better than anger; I could control pain, anger controlled me.

I looked away, sighing I got back to my work. I didn't want Junior to think I was incompetent or lazy. I had to fix an old music box. Junior told me what it was, I knew of music, my brother played the piano quite well, I just didn't know about the music box. The music box to me worked perfectly fine, but apparently, there was a little doll, a ballerina that was supposed to spin as the music played.

It was quite a cute invention, if I do say so myself.

I could hear Isaac's steps as he walked in the room, I could even feel his eyes on me, room and somehow it just made the air thick, I never wanted to punch someone so bad. He cleared his throat a couple of times because I was trying to ignore him.

"Are you going to stand there all day?" I asked after a while, not being able to stay quiet. I kept my eyes focused on my work.

"Do you even know what you're doing with that thing?" There was mockery in his tone. "I don't expect a girl—"

"So I can't fix a music box, but I can make two 6-foot-tall boys fall on their knees?" I interrupted with a defiant tone.

"I'm not 6-foot-tall," He commented, "Also, you're a girl from the Government; you're not supposed to know how to fix old useless garbage."

"I already fixed the music box," I rolled my eyes, opening the box as I twisted the little handle from underneath it. The sad melody began to fill the room, reminding me of the times Nate played when he was bored.

I raised my head to look at him, and then I rolled my eyes at the sight of him. I *really*wanted to punch him.

"I thought we already discussed the 'you know nothing about the Government' conversation. If you have something to fix, leave it on the table; I'll get to it when I finish with the music box."

"I don't have anything to fix. And you just said you finished with the box. You're just staring at it," He answered. I raised an eyebrow, waiting for him to carry on. "I came to talk to you, to remind you that you have to keep your part of the deal we made."

I decided to focus on the pain the chains were causing me instead of how annoying his voice actually was, I rubbed my right wrist, where the chains were leaving marks. They were way too tight.

"Chains bothering you?"

"I owe you nothing. You said you'd help me find her—"

"And you found her."

"First of all, it was plain coincidence." I carried on, still looking down at the music box, twisting the little handle ever so often so the melody wouldn't stop. "But anyways, I'll give you that: you 'helped' me find her. That wasn't the whole deal. Don't forget the other part. It has now been weeks, I'm guessing she's still here, I'm not even allowed to talk to her, so your part of the deal hasn't been completed."

He laughed mockingly, making it harder for me to keep calm.

"Sam ain't gonna leave," He said, shaking his head at me. "Even if I help you do that, which I won't, she don't wanna leave."

"Either way, you didn't keep your part of the deal. Yes, I did find her, but you didn't get her out of here, why should I keep my part?"

"You were never gonna keep your part, were you?"

"I guess now we'll never know," I sighed, trying to reach for a tool at the end of the table but because I forgot about the chains, I ended up hurting myself.

"José can be a little animal sometimes," He tried to carry on the conversation, reverting to the subject of the chains.

"And an idiotic one for that matter," I reached for the tool and grabbed the music box. The ballerina had stopped moving, but the music kept playing. I took the music box in my hands and removed the ballerina in order to fix the mechanism. "Doesn't he know I'm working with enough tools to break these rusty chains?"

"Oh really?" I could imagine his mocking smile. "You know, you talk and talk, but you do nothing. You think you're so smart, yet here you are with rusty chains on your wrists."

"I don't think I'm smart," I snapped but quickly resuming to my calm demeanour. "You're the one with a big mouth."

He smirked, folding his arms across his chest. "All day calling us animals, savages, idiots, and whatnot, but you don't do anything, not even try to escape. What a shame. I expected more, to be honest."

"I don't need to prove anything to you," I sighed, giving him a cold look. It was obvious what he was trying to get on my nerves. "I know what I know, which is, or so it seems to me, way more than you people know."

I bit my lip, I told myself not to do anything, to remain calm. However, the way he looked at me, like he really believed that I couldn't do it, it bothered me.

I spent my whole life trying to prove that I was capable, I wasn't just going to let a rebel, a *savage* look at me like I was "all talk". I took the tools I needed, slowly hid my hands under the table and began to take the chains off.

"Go on then, show me," He dared me, mocking me and trying to provoke me. "Take the chains off. Show me you can."

"I don't need your validation," I wasn't angry or annoyed but he definitely bothered me and it didn't help that I already wanted to punch him. He had this smug look on his face that really bothered me. One of my hands was free, what I found most difficult was trying to keep quiet.

"Ah, I knew it," He continued, giving me a satisfied smile. "Too much talk."

When he turned around, walking to the door, I slowly got up, the chains off my hands, quickly I made my way around the table and I stood behind him. Right when he was about to reach for the door's handle, I chained his right hand. When he turned around with a confused frown, I smirked and chained his other hand.

"Come on, your turn, *smartass*." It was my turn to mock him.

"How did you do it?" He asked with a confused frown. "You already had them off, didn't you? I was looking at you. How did you do it?"

"You get distracted really easily," I explained. "When you started to 'provoke me,' you weren't looking at my hands. You were focused on my eyes. And that's what strong eye contact does – it distracts you.

Do you really think I'm that dumb not to see what you were doing? I'm good at what I was trained to do, and most importantly, I do not get distracted. You might have fooled me once, but at that time I was already distracted by my personal issues. It wasn't really you."

"Is that what they teach you?" He quickly asked, he seemed very curious. "To be a soldier and that?"

"Take the chain off and I might tell you,"

"Easy-peasy," He had a cocky smile as he took a seat and made himself comfortable. I sat in front of him.

Isaac had been trying for five minutes to take the chains off with the same tool I had used, but he couldn't do it. After a while, I was so bored of waiting that I just sighed and took the chains off his wrists.

However, he told me to put them back on, but not as tight. I looked at him, debating whether if I should waste my time or not, but I was bored, so I did.

This time he watched me while I took the chains off so that he could see how to take them off later on. When he tried the second time, it took him seven minutes exactly, with my help. When he finished, I told him that he had done it as quickly as a 12-year-old cadet would do it. But at least he tried. I took the chains and put them back on my wrists, but looser.

"You know, if you try to escape, they'll catch you. And it won't be nice once they get you back." He shouldn't have been concerned about me, after all it was him who got me here.

"That's the last thing I have on my mind right now," I answered, going back to my seat. "Like I said, I haven't been able to talk to Samirah and so far, the time I have spent here, I haven't really been awake."

"I'm – It was your fault. I told you to drop the attitude."

I didn't say anything, I shrugged and tried to carry on with my work. He didn't say much either.

"Why don't you want her to be here? Sam's happy here," He broke the silence, I looked up at him with boredom.

"I don't know, I guess I thought about everything: finding her, taking her back home, arguing with the higher-ups from the

Government so they would allow us back in, living again. But never for a second did it cross my mind that perhaps Samirah wouldn't want to come back with me. It is illogical to me, to be honest, but we all have different ways of thinking."

"But you—"

"I don't think you came to talk about me or my family," I interrupted him, feeling a little irritated by his questions. "You came to ask for something, so go ahead and ask."

"I want you to teach us,"

"You're going to have to be a little more specific than that," I raised my eyes to look at him, teach him what?

"To do what you do," He explained, wiggling his finger around, pointing at me. "What they taught you there. I asked Sam yesterday. She said you were the second best to graduate as a soldier or whatever. That means you're good. So why not make use of it and teach us?"

I snorted without meaning to, then I looked at him from head to toe, it seemed to made him feel uncomfortable. He was muscular, and he was quick, agile. But I wasn't going to waste my time teaching rebels anything. When I was done, I went back to repairing the music box.

"Let's say that I like the idea, which I don't," I told him. "What would I get from it?"

"Nothing," He quickly replied, frowning. "This isn't one of those quid pro quo situations. You're here and over here, we earn our living."

"I'm already earning my living." I pointed at the table with all the things I had to repair.

"You can do more than that."

"If I get nothing from it, then I'm not interested." I showed no interest whatsoever, which he didn't seem to like. "Besides, I'm not from here. I don't have to help you."

"You know that even if you don't want to help us, we can make you, right?" He narrowed his eyes at me, looking like he wanted to shout but was trying not to. "You're here thanks to Miguel's pity."

"Well, I'm sorry to disappoint you." I sighed, giving him a cold stare. "But you can't make me do anything I don't want to do. You want a favour. You think I am obligated to fulfil all your commands—"

"You need to stop—"

"*You* need to listen and not interrupt." I shot him a look, for a moment I felt like I was back in the Government, giving orders. "I am not going to help you, not even if you ask me nicely, and not even if you lock me in a room and beat me for days. I am not going to help you or anyone here."

The frustration was clear on his face. He most definitely didn't like me and I quite liked that.

He was turning around to leave, but when he was halfway through the door, he turned around and stared at me coldly, his jaw clenching.

"Do you really think you're better than us?" He asked me. I was going to reply, but he stopped me. "You're not leaving. And with your attitude, you ain't gonna last long. No one will stand up for you when something happens, not even Samirah. Look around you. You not better than us, and you ain't in a place to be thinking you are."

*   *   *

"I'm not going to repeat myself, walk faster." José pulled hard from the chain, hurting my wrists as he did so. I bit my lower lip, keeping myself from saying anything at all. We were walking towards Junior's workshop.

I had not seen Sam once and it had been days since Miguel allowed me to leave the cell. *Where was she?*

José slowed down his pace once I started to walk faster. I wanted to snap at him, ask him what was the point of all the pulling and telling me to walk faster if he was going to slow down? However, it wasn't until I looked up that I began to understand what was happening.

We weren't at Junior's, we weren't on our regular route, we were in some kind of town centre. There was a lot of people and they were all looking at me, the air grew thicker with whispers, I felt their eyes on me, I couldn't understand what most were saying but I knew it was about me.

"I thought I'd show you around since your sister wants nothing to do with you, might as well do it myself." José smiled at me widely, his words created a void in my chest, I could feel the last bit of hope fading. I had left everything for Sam and she didn't even want to see me.

"Come on," José yanked the chain, it caught me off guard and I was thrown to the ground. At first, all I heard was the snickering, then José's voice came. When he spoke, I didn't understand what he was saying, it wasn't English.

José pulled me up, hurting my wrists once again. With his huge and rough hand, he grabbed my face and made me face him. The words that left his mouth felt like a weight on my chest, "Be careful with the savage, darling." He winked at me before pushing me off him, I fell once again. All he wanted was to humiliate me, to make me suffer because of my words. And he was accomplishing it.

A short man made his way to me, he didn't look like a threat, if I had been standing, I would have probably been taller than him, he was a scrawny little guy with anger written all over his face. He looked down at me with disgust, "We don't want people like you here." He said, I thought he was done but before turning around and leaving, he spat on me.

I took a moment to process what had happened, I didn't feel anger or pain or anything at all, I just wanted to get it over with.

I wiped his saliva from the side of my face as I stood up, I took a deep breath in and slowly released it. I straighten my back and put on a poker face while I waited for José to move on.

It was fair to say that I wasn't used to that, to any of that. I was prepared to be one of the best soldiers in the Government, I was prepared and I thought I was ready to face many challenges but I was not ready for this kind of humiliation.

They wanted to humiliate me, to hurt me, and they had but I'd be damned if I let them see it.

# Chapter 9

Location: La Cruz
Narrator: Aliana

"YOU'RE ACTING LIKE a child," Miguel looked down at me with boredom, resting his body against the wall of my cell. "I thought we had agreed you wouldn't give me trouble."

I decided today I was going on a strike.

"I want to see my sister."

It had been days since Miguel finally allowed me out of my prison cell, I thought maybe I would get to see my sister at some point, but right after I finished work, José took me straight back to the prison cell. And every day I was walked around their city through different routes like I was some sort of freak he wanted to show around. On the good side, I was beginning to know my way around the city.

"Have you thought about the possibility that maybe your sister doesn't want to see you," Miguel spoke slowly, making eye contact with me. His words felt like a stab to the heart. His facial expression gave nothing up, I couldn't tell if he was lying or not.

José told me several times that Sam didn't want to see me but from José's mouth, I believed nothing. He wanted to hurt me, he wanted to break me. I held a little hope that maybe Sam just couldn't see me. Maybe she lived far away, maybe she was busy, maybe she wasn't allowed to… something other than her not *wanting* to see me.

Sam was independent, she could go about her day completely fine without me but I couldn't do the same. My sister to me was some sort of lifesaver, she kept me afloat when everything else was pulling down from my feet. Did I need Sam? Yes, that was something that didn't need to be questioned. But did Sam need *me*? Did Sam want to see me, did Sam *care* about me? That was something I had no answer to.

I stayed quiet, there was nothing I could say. Sam said that I shouldn't have come, that I should have stayed where I belong. Her words hurt me beyond explanation. I've always known I was a burden to Samirah, we were two completely different people, two opposites with similar faces. While Samirah was always the centre of attention, I was her shadow, I was no one. And although before she decided to leave the Government we were close, it wasn't always like that. There was a time when Samirah wouldn't glance my way twice, a time when she truly believed Aurora's words. There was a time when Samirah wouldn't even speak to me unless she had to.

"You want me to leave, is that it? Fine, let me see Samirah once and I'll leave," I muttered through gritted teeth.

"I can't allow you to freely walk around my city."

"I am no threat to you or your people," I wish I was, though. "You can just let me go, I'll never be allowed back home, so you have nothing to worry about. I'm not going to cause you any trouble."

"Trouble? A small little thing like you?" He laughed sarcastically, I looked up to meet his eyes.

"I might not understand much about your people but I understand enough to know they do not want me here," I looked down at my wrists as I spoke, they were bruised because of the chains. Time after time, José would drag me by the chains around the street. He'd do it just to show off as if I was nothing but a tamed animal, he was humiliating me and he wanted to take pride in it and how the people laughed… they all proved me right, they were savages who got off watching others suffer.

"Like I said, you're my guest and you will stay here for as long as I want you here."

"I haven't precisely been treated like a guest, though, Miguel, have I?" His name rolled off my tongue, leaving a bittersweet taste in my mouth. I didn't like all these familiarities.

"If you have any complains, I'm all ears." I could hear the mockery in his voice, it was like nails on a chalkboard. "Be grateful, if I treated you like you people treat us... you wouldn't last a day."

"I'm not a threat to you. Look at me, I have *nothing*," I couldn't keep my voice from breaking, I was tired. I thought I was stronger than this but I was *so* tired and Natalí's medicine didn't help much. "All I wanted was to save my sister."

"You and I both know the moment you stepped foot out of the Government, you wouldn't be allowed back in." I frowned at his words. How did he know that? "There's nowhere for you to go, you're staying here whether you like it or not."

"And you're going to keep me locked in here?"

"You'd certainly give me less trouble that way," He joked, standing away from the wall, "But no, I'm not keeping you here. Samirah lives in a house ten minutes away from Junior's place, she's waiting outside to take you with her."

"Does she— does she want me to live with her?"

"She has been coming every single day trying to see you, I didn't let her," He informed me, I could feel my eyes filling up with tears, did this mean Samirah *did* want to see me? I stood up so quickly I got a head-rush.

"Wait," Miguel lifted up his index finger, standing before me. "I know my people don't want you here but I also know you don't make it easy for them to tolerate you. José might not be the greatest, but if you get him to stop, people will follow. I don't want problems in my city."

"And how exactly do you expect me to do that? Perhaps you should control your—"

"I think I have done enough for you," He interrupted me, raising his voice. He didn't seem to like being interrupted. "You will be watched, but you'll be able to go home with your sister. Imagine house arrest, you go home and then work, work then home. Keep things simple until I figure out what to do with you."

"What does that mean?"

"I don't know yet," Miguel sighed, the conversation was over, even if I asked, he wouldn't answer me. He turned around and walked out my prison cell. "Well, come on then, or you wanna stay here?"

He didn't have to ask me twice. I followed after him, my heartbeat racing with each step I took. Sam was waiting for me; she *did* want to see me. I was fidgeting with my hands the whole way. Once we made it out of the hallway and into the big room with the big windows, I saw Natalí, she was talking to some lady, the other healer.

"Lynn-Lynn," I heard Sam's voice before I got the chance to see her. She was practically running to me, and once she got to me, she did something she had rarely ever done. She threw herself at me and wrapped her arms around me tightly.

Sam was hugging me.

It was the warmest hug I had ever received. It took me a second to hug her back; I didn't get many hugs, I could count the number of times I had ever been hugged with my hands. I never liked being touched, anyway, I thought of it as unnecessary. And yet, knowing that Sam still cared about me, it made me feel whole again.

Sam cupped my face with her hands, carefully not to hurt my bruises and swollen face. "Does it hurt?" She asked, her voice breaking a little, her eyes watering. She looked at my eye, moving my head around just to get a good view.

I shook my head, not trusting my voice. I knew if I opened my mouth, I would've cried. Sam was crying and it was so odd seeing her cry, I don't think I've ever seen her cry.

"Can you walk?" she asked me, wiping her nose with the back of her hand, her hair was in a messy bun, some locks of her hair falling. I had never seen Sam being so carefree about how she looked. "Oh, look at your hands, I'm so sorry, Lynn, I tried but Miguel said—"

"It's okay, Sam," I interrupted her, "I'm okay."

"Can I take her home, Miguel?"

Miguel looked away as soon as we turned to him, he cleared his throat before answering, "Sure, I'll walk you."

* * *

When we got to Sam's place, I didn't get to look around because Sam walked me to the kitchen. Miguel left right away, said he had to do something important. He was different with Samirah, he was a little more talkative and he even made jokes, it was something that made me feel uneasy. Miguel made me feel uneasy.

Sam stood in front of me, she was dressed in different colours. She had bags under her eyes, her cheeks chubbier than the last time I saw her… she looked so different. But there was something more, something that had been on my mind ever since I was told she left.

She could feel.

"Why'd you leave?" I finally managed to ask her, we had been sitting in silence for a while, not knowing what to say to the other, I guess.

Sam took a deep breath in, "It was too much," She began, swallowing hard as she did so, "You wouldn't understand, Aliana, even if I explained it to you, you wouldn't really understand what it was like."

"Try?" She looked away from me, biting her lower lip. "I think I deserve to know why you left because Johan said that … Sam, if it was because of me—"

"The things I had to do, Lynn, the things I had to see… it was too much. I needed to leave. Marrying Roc didn't mean a thing to me. Yes, it isn't a secret I dislike him but I didn't care," She looked at me with her eyes filled with pain, making my heart sink. "There are things you don't know, what the Government does is inhumane. I couldn't stay there knowing that I was going to be used to hurt the very same people I was supposed to protect."

"Is it because of your training?" My throat suddenly felt dry, something changed in her facial expression, guilt. "Johan told me, they were training you to be a member of the board."

She nodded, "I didn't tell you because I didn't want you to feel like Aurora had—"

"Aurora picked you as her successor, so what? She never liked me, that isn't a secret," I tried to smile, looking down at my hands. "I just… I didn't know that you had, you know, *feelings*."

She smiled at me sweetly, one of those charming Keenan smiles. The thing about my siblings and my parents, it was that they had a charm, they had this vibe, I don't know, something that just dragged you to them, that made you want to have their attention, their approval. It was insane how alike they all were and how different to them I was.

"You were always so busy trying to hide your own feelings that you didn't see what was in plain sight," She smiled while she took my hand. "And it isn't just me, Lynn," I frowned at her, confused, wanting to ask but scared to do so. A part of me already knew or more like already suspected of some people but I was never sure.

"Aurora?" I asked, Sam nodded. That was an easy guess. Her dislike or more like her hatred towards me was something that didn't just go unnoticed. "Could've fooled me, huh?" Sam didn't find my joke funny, in fact she looked at me with pity. "Who else?"

"The members of the board, all of them. Every single one of them," She shook her head with shame. "They were all trained since they were kids. It's wrong, Lynn, everything they do it's wrong. And it was not just one thing, it was more like one thing on top of the other, they made us all do things that were slowly stripping us of our humanity. The worst part is it isn't really their fault because that's exactly the same they had to do when they were trained. I'm not surprised they all turned out the way they did. Father included."

I was confused to say the least, I did know some of the stuff the Government did but I knew enough to know that I didn't want to know more.

"I don't know how much you know and I don't know how to explain it to you either, Lynn, but what I do know is that the Board is not what you think. Have you ever wondered why there's so much secrecy, underground facilitates, so many restricted accesses?"

Sam looked away from me, letting go of my hand as she did so, "And you think these people are any better?" I looked at her straight in the eyes, I didn't want to argue with Sam but I was still slightly angry at her.

"You left your home, you left us for this?" I looked around the small kitchen, "I understand that maybe it got too overwhelming for you but if you felt that way, there were other options, Samirah, do you think you're the only person who had to do horrible things?"

"You don't understand, Aliana." She raised her voice, it was almost as if she was losing her calm but quickly calmed herself down. "I don't expect you to understand but what's done is done, I can't and I won't go back, I know the deal you made with Isaac, I won't go back."

"So you'd rather stay here?" I asked her, trying to remain calm. "With these people?"

"You don't know them, Aliana, you think they're savages and cruel because that's what we were told. You fear them because we were told to fear them, but you don't know them enough to judge them."

"I don't know them? I think the time I've spent here was enough." I muttered angrily, my nails were digging into the palms of my hands, how could she defend them? "You don't know what these people are capable of. You're blinded by this excitement of this new-found life you have here, and just like always, you think of no one but yourself."

"I never asked you to follow me, Aliana." She snapped at me, a fire in her eyes that I had never seen before. "I have a life here, I can do what I want and I can be whomever I want; there's nobody telling me how to live my life and I am not going to apologise for wanting to be free."

"It was your home, Samirah." I raised my voice, not really wanting to but losing some control. "You had as much freewill as you have now."

"Really?" She laughed at me, making me a little angrier but before I could say anything, she continued, "You have no idea what it was like for me. You have no idea. You can't just cross the bridge and come looking for me because you think I need saving? You don't get to judge my decisions and tell me that I'm wrong, this is my life, I will do with it what I please. I suggest you look at things differently from now, I'm not leaving and you don't have a choice but to stay."

* * *

97

After my ... *chat* with Sam, José came looking for me. I was in a mood and José was making things worse.

"Junior hurt his knee, gotta be at work earlier," José informed me, I ignored him, standing straight.

He didn't say much afterward, he handcuffed my wrists, and we made our way to Junior's. When we got to Junior's, Natalí was there, she was arguing with Junior quite loudly, it was their language so I didn't give much attention to what they were saying. The image was quite comical, actually, Junior sat with his bad leg resting on a coffee table, his right hand massaging his temple as if he had a headache, his eyes closed and his posture calm. And then there was Natalí, standing in front of her father, practically yelling at him, a vain visible on the side of her neck, she looked worried and annoyed. It was almost as if Junior was the child and Natalí the concerned mother.

Without saying a word, I made my way to the workshop, I didn't want to interrupt what looked like a family discussion. Also, I wasn't in the mood to talk to anybody.

And I worked. I did my job the best I could and I tried to keep myself busy, keep myself from thinking about what Sam had said.

Sam and I were completely different, I bore a resemblance to Samirah; we were sisters but that didn't mean that we thought and acted the same. I hated when people compared me to Sam because they never had anything good to say, at least not about me. People often made sure I was aware of what they thought when it came to Sam and I. It wasn't really her fault, it was just her... her methods, her ways, *her*– everything about her was better.

At first, I hated it. I hated the fact that we looked alike and because of that, everyone expected me to be like her. Sam was my sister; I loved her, but I also envied her.

When we were younger, Sam grew to be elegant and beautiful. She developed a delicate figure and a fine bone structure, and to top it off, she had always been so smart.

And then there was a time when I wanted to be a little more like her and a lot less like me. I couldn't shake away the thought that if I was like her, if I dressed or talked like she did, maybe people would've liked me a little more. Truth was, no matter what no one ever looked at me like they looked at her.

It wasn't any different with me, all I saw was Sam. And all I wanted was for Sam to see me, to noticed me but she never did, not at first anyway. It wasn't until we were older when Sam started to really see me.

And I couldn't really blame her, how could I? She was so used to being the centre of attention, it wasn't her fault. Trying to blame Sam for being loved by those around her was like blaming the sun for shining. I couldn't blame her for being who she was. I couldn't blame her for liking the attention or holding onto it. I really couldn't.

My siblings were the most important thing to me, I would do anything for them without hesitation. That's why all that envy, that jealousy I felt towards Sam made me ashamed of myself. It showed me once again the kind of person I was.

I was not a good person; I was not an innocent girl with a clean conscience. I had done wrongs, I had done things and I don't know if those things can be forgiven. I was a mistake that shouldn't have happened. I was my father's mistake, Sam didn't know this and yet, somehow, she knew that I wasn't right, that there was something wrong with me.

When the day came to an end, I waited for José for thirty minutes, I waited and I waited but he never came. The anger I felt right at that moment made my eyes fill with tears and my body tremble with anger as I walked towards Sam's house. It took me about 20 minutes to get to Sam's, I barely remembered the way.

I was willing to bet José didn't show up because he was trying to prove something, he had to show up and remove the chains, he had to because Miguel said so but he didn't show. And that was the last of it.

José knew what he was doing, he wanted to humiliate me, to make me regret my words. I called him names, I degraded him. I got his message loud and clear: I might have called him an animal, but I was the one practically sleeping in a cage, I was the one in chains, wounded and humiliated. I could practically hear him laughing at me.

Oh, I was going to break those chains and wait for José to come the next day and try to chain me again. Please, let him try to chain me again. He had humiliated me enough.

I was not an animal.

When I reached the house, the lights were on and, from the front window, I could see people in the kitchen. Sam sat facing the window and playing with a tissue. Sebastián was behind her, resting his hands on the back of her chair. His hair was gone, as he shaved his head. He looked very weird; his head seemed bigger. With their backs to the window were two other people. One was a boy with dark brown hair and light brown skin, his back wide and strong. I couldn't see him, but I knew it was Isaac. Sitting next to him was a girl. Her long brown hair was in a ponytail. She had her long, toned legs all over Isaac's lap, wearing nothing but really short shorts covering her.

I sighed and went inside the house.

"She'll come around. I know her." I heard Sam's voice and I knew she was talking about me, "I know she will come to understand."

When I walked into the kitchen, they all looked at me, I couldn't form any words and even if I tried to speak, the lump in my throat wouldn't have allowed me to. I had to focus on keeping my head high. The chains made a sound, reminding me of José's smirk. Anger flowed through me.

"Sam." I saluted my sister as I walked to get a knife I needed, ignoring their eyes as I walked past them.

"Why do you have those chains on?" Sam asked. I wished she hadn't. I had never felt so humiliated in my life.

I shook my head and smiled at her, swallowing the ball that had formed in my throat. I placed my hand on her shoulder and smiled at her again. I needed to make up with Sam, I never liked arguing with her. I missed her a lot. I shouldn't have been so thoughtless.

"Do you want me to help you take them off?" There was something in Sam's voice that made the ball in my throat bigger. She felt sorry for me.

"Don't worry, Sam. I got it," I told her, walking out of the kitchen and ignoring everyone's eyes full of pity as they looked at me.

100

"Lynn, I—" Sam was saying, but I was already gone.

Once I got to the room Sam had said to be mine, I sat on the bed and stared at the chains and the knife. I was a prisoner in my own "home". I almost burst out laughing at how funny this situation was. What was funny? Nothing, but I'd rather laugh than cry.

About an hour passed before Sam's company left. I had been trying to get the chains off, but the kitchen knife bent, which bruised my wrists even worse than they already were. I was starting to loathe José.

After a long while, I gave up and went to sleep with the chains on, like a chained animal who wasn't even trusted in my own cage. I couldn't help the tears that fell down my face. I hated the power José had over me, a power that not even Aurora had and the worst part was that it was me who gave it to him.

I thought back to Sam's eyes, the way she looked at me, the way they all looked at me. The look in their eyes wasn't one of curiosity; it was one of pity.

José had done it: he humiliated me. And had enough. I was going to make him wish he had never laid a hand on me.

# Chapter 10

Location: La Cruz
Narrator: Aliana

"SLEEP ALL RIGHT, sunshine?" José's grin got wider when he saw me coming out of Sam's house.

I hadn't slept all right. I actually had just left the house because I needed him to take the chains off so I could have a shower.

"I need you to take the chains off so I can have a shower and go to work," I said with a cold tone, barely looking at him. I couldn't believe I was asking him for something but I needed to remain calm, Junior needed help, his knee wouldn't let him work properly and Miguel said I needed to work on gaining his people's trust.

But José was making it so hard.

He laughed at me. I told myself to calm down and relax. I was at the edge of losing it. I hadn't taken my pills since yesterday and I was noticing the rough edges. The lightness of my mood was changing, and the anger was returning.

He had what he wanted, he had humiliated me enough. What else could he possibly want? It seemed this wasn't enough for José. He took a few sips of water, gargled with it, and then spat it at me.

"You clean. Now let's go." He laughed and I lost it.

Everything happened very fast. I dried my face, then looked at him. He was laughing and I joined him, which surprised him.

"You would have saved yourself all this if you just kept your mouth shut, you stupid bitch," he said. I was laughing hysterically.

And when my laugh died, I punched him right in his nose and then kicked him in the stomach. I punched him again. And he was punching me too, but I didn't feel a thing. The rage I felt, the sweet and overwhelming rage, took control of me. José was to blame. I wanted to make him regret every single bit of humiliation he'd made me feel. And I was ready to make that happen.

Everything was red and I was not in control.

He got up from the ground. I smiled at him. I didn't care what got in my way; I had enough of him. He lunged for me, and I fell on my back to the pavement. He punched me once. The second time, I moved away, which made him hit the pavement. He let out a groan of pain. With my nails, I scratched his face, his eyes. He lost focus. I somehow managed to kick him off me, he was really heavy.

I was done with games.

I hit him in the face with the heavy chains. He was on the ground with blood dripping from his mouth, from his eyebrow and his cheekbone. I could feel my own blood sliding down my face, mixing with the water and my sweat, my head was pounding and it was hard for me to stay balanced but it didn't matter, all that mattered was José and all the things he said and did to me since I first got here.

He was trying to get up, the chains had hurt him, made him lose balance. With my right foot, I kicked the left side of his head. I walked around him, put my chains around his neck, and pulled.

Somehow, he managed to keep hitting me, even when I was choking him. But then he stopped. He was now only worried about getting air into his lungs. Air. It amazed me how everything came down to air. Now he wasn't worried about humiliating me. I bet he didn't care who I was right at that moment. All he cared about was air. Air. Air. Air. Air he could not get because of me.

I was killing a man.

Again.

And that's when it hit me: I was killing a man, a man who probably had a family. A rush of guilt hit me. What on earth was I doing? It seemed as if it wasn't me acting this way. José had opened the door

I'd been trying hard to keep locked. I'd lost all control. I was about to kill a man.

Quickly I removed the chains from around his neck. I stared at him as he coughed blood and breathed harder. I had almost killed him. The void in my chest got bigger, it was big enough to swallow me whole.

Realising what I had just done, I did what I do best: I ran.

I ran and I ran until I was in the town centre, but I didn't stop there, not even when Natalí and Junior shouted my name. I ran and kept running. I ran into the woods. I didn't know where I was going – somewhere far enough where the memory would go away, where I didn't have to remember the joy I felt when I tightened the hold on José's neck. Tears were running down my face as I kept running into the woods, making my vision blurry and making me trip. I quickly got back up and carried on running, ignoring the pain on my side.

I ran until I had an option: I could go back home, where I could be free of all of this.

Anxiety was taking over me until I couldn't breathe any longer. I fell to the cold, wet ground. How ironic that I had strangled José until he was out of breath but now I was the one who couldn't breathe. And when I thought I was going to pass out, I saw him.

Isaac was running towards me. Isaac threw himself on the ground next to me, at first, he just watched me with worry, with his hands inches away from me as if he didn't know if he should touch me or not. But then he took my face in his warm hands and made me look at him. His eyes were gazing right into mine.

His eyes were the colour of his skin, a caramel colour with a certain glow to them. It was all I could focus on. Then he smiled at me, a sad smile. My lungs were hurting, my whole body hurt, José had hurt me more than I had realised.

He was saying something, but I couldn't hear him, his voice was background noise, all I could hear were José's gasps. I kept feeling the pressure of the chains around José's neck. It was all too easy. All I did was pull. It seemed so easy. What kind of person was I? I should have never crossed the bridge. I was supposed to come and save Sam, but all I was doing was endangering her.

"Breathe, just breathe," Isaac was saying. As if I wasn't already trying. "It's okay. Whatever happened, don't worry, it's okay. We'll figure a way out. You can trust me, okay? I'm not going to hurt you, but you gotta breathe with me."

I instantly had the instinct to get away from him. I tried to move, but he grabbed hold of me. He was holding me to him and I couldn't get away.

"Calm down. Let me help you!" he shouted as I kept trying to get away from him. "I just want to help you!"

"Why! Why would anyone want to help me? I almost killed him." I shouted back, finally finding my voice. "I lost it and almost killed him. I couldn't stop. Tell Sam that I didn't mean to. You have to tell her. Tell her I'm sorry." I was trying to get Isaac off me. I needed to get to the bridge and end all this.

"Let me go. I need to get home," I cried out. I was now sobbing… I was pathetic.

"This is your home now. I won't let José get near you," he said. I wanted to ask why, but tears kept coming and all that came out of my mouth were sobs. It felt as if my tears were poison coming out of my system. "For Sam, you have to stay for Sam."

Isaac let go of me and turned my head to face him once I stopped crying. I felt embarrassed and weak. I didn't want to look at him. He looked at me with his serious eyes and then wiped the tears off my face. I almost told him to stop, wanting to say that it wasn't appropriate, but I didn't have the strength to move away from him.

"What happened?" he asked me.

I took a deep breath before beginning to talk. So I told him, I told him what José had been doing ever since I was allowed out of my prison cell. I told him what José had been saying, how he had humiliated me time after time.

"I lost it but I swear I didn't mean to. I really didn't mean to. I just couldn't stop. You have to believe me. Believe me, Isaac, I didn't mean to. I really didn't mean to. I – I lost it. I'm not bad. I swear. I didn't mean it."

"I believe you, okay?" he said. And for some reason unknown to me, I felt relief. "But we have to go back home. Miguel will understand."

I shook my head, wanting to cry again. "No. I can't go back. Being there makes me like this. Don't you see?" I must have sounded crazy to him because he looked at me as if I were. Then I remembered: he was one of them, why was I telling him all this?

"I can't let you go back to the Government. It would give the wrong impression. And Sam would have to explain why you left. They will hurt Sam if you leave."

I didn't answer him, they wouldn't hurt her, she was one of them now. She fitted here with them, she could fit anywhere she went.

"We can stay here for as long as you want. And when you're better, we'll go back home, okay?" he carried on, I didn't say anything in reply. I didn't nod or anything. I just stared straight into the woods. He sighed.

What was home? I wasn't even sure. Was home with Sam? Or was home with the rest of my family? *Home is where your family is. Home is where your heart is,* Johan often said. I didn't know where home was, because there wasn't a single place that had ever felt like home to me.

After a while, without saying anything at all, I stood up and started to walk towards the city. Isaac didn't say anything either, but he walked by my side in silence. I was nervous. I didn't know what they'd do to me once I got back there, but whatever it was, I deserve it and I wasn't going to let Sam get hurt because of me.

Once Isaac and I got to the city, Miguel came out of the blue, took me by my arm, and dragged me to the interrogation building. I didn't fight him.

"Miguel, it wasn't her fault," Isaac shouted, following us. He got in front of Miguel and tried to stop him, but Miguel pushed him aside. Isaac stood his ground. I wanted to tell him to stop and move away, but before I could say anything, Miguel slapped him hard, that moved him away. Isaac shouldn't have gotten in the middle.

Miguel was hurting me. His hold was so tight around my arm that it felt as if my blood wasn't circulating and the chains were making my wrists feel numb. I knew where he was taking me, back to the prison cell. Isaac was still following us, telling Miguel not to do anything to me. His lip was broken, his lower lip was bloody.

We went into the large hall, there were people there, quite a few people. I didn't mind their curious eyes but my heart stopped when I saw her.

Luna.

Not Sam, but *her*. She was here. Our eyes met and I wanted to run away, now more than ever I had more reasons to run away. I tried to get away, turn away or something but Miguel's hold tightened then.

She looked different, I had never seen her face to face but I knew it was her. And everything made sense. *Miguel*. That's why his name was so familiar, that's why he looked at me the way he did, that's why he allowed us to stay. Miguel was Luna's brother.

"Miguel, don't!" Luna begged, there was concern in her eyes. "Miguel, *please!*"

She looked desperate, but Miguel was ignoring her as he kept walking towards the cells. It was really her. I couldn't help but laugh at this situation. Out of all the places, we ended up in the same place as Luna. What were the fucking odds?

"You wanna laugh!?" Miguel snapped at me, throwing me into a room and closing the door in Luna's face. She started banging on the door and shouting his name.

"After what you did, you laugh!?" he shouted, his face so close to me, I could see the anger in his eyes. "Tell me what's so funny."

"She's your sister, right? That's why you allowed us to stay. That's why you left right after Sam said I was her sister that day," I laughed without humour. Miguel's face expression changed for a second, but right away his anger returned. "That's why you asked me if I knew who you were. Listen to her, she sounds so concerned, but you know what she did, don't you? If you know about me, then surely you must know what she did."

"You're not making this easy for me."

"Take these chains off me and let me go," I tried to persuade him. Miguel clenched his jaw but didn't say no, so I continued. I had to get out of here, I *had* to. Luna being here just confirmed it; my sanity wouldn't last much longer knowing she was somewhere near me. "Think about it. I'm nothing but a problem for you. Let me go, Miguel. I don't belong here. *You* don't want me here, I can tell. The only reason you've allowed it was because of her, wasn't it?

"She's going to ruin you. She doesn't see the problems that I'm causing you. And if she does, she looks the other way. What would your people say? What kind of leader would allow an outsider, a *threat* to stay after making fun of his right hand and after almost killing said person? What kind of message would you be giving your people? I do you no good staying here. Let me go."

Miguel stayed still, I could tell he was thinking about it.

"This is where you belong, you have a place here," he said after a long pause as if trying to convince himself and not me.

"This place means nothing to me!" I snapped, losing my calm. I took a deep breath before I continued, *"Let me go."*

"Family," he calmly spoke as he walked towards the door. "Family is all that matters. Without it you are nothing."

"I am *not* your family!" I shouted at him, pushing him away from me. I didn't say it, but I agreed with him: Family was important, but this wasn't my family.

"Maybe you think that way but I happen to think differently. You stay here until I know for sure you ain't gonna hurt anyone," he turned to look at me before he opened the door. "I'm doing this for your own good. I'm trying to make things easier for you."

Miguel closed the door, leaving me alone in another cell room, away from everyone.

Day after day passed. I think it was a few weeks before Miguel came looking for me. I felt alone, alarmed, nervous, and *bored*. I wasn't angry anymore; I was numb. At some point during my imprisonment, Sam came to see me once. Miguel wouldn't permit anyone in to see me, though. Only he was allowed. He'd bring me food and things, but he wouldn't take the chains off. Luna came over once, which was awkward. Through the door, she tried to talk to me, but I told her to leave me alone, to go away and never to talk to me again. To my surprise, Isaac came once too. He asked me how I was, but I didn't answer him. When he said he was leaving, I thanked him for what he had done that day at the woods. He didn't say anything after that but he never came back either.

While I was locked up, I had no problem when it came to my pills. I told Miguel I needed the pills and without asking questions, he got them to me. I don't know how many days I spent in that room but I was gone for most of it. I was supposed to ease up on taking the pills, but it was very hard for me to do that. Every time I wanted to stop, something new happened and my emotions were getting the worst of me. I didn't want to feel, I didn't want to think, so I took the pills.

Isolation wasn't easy. It was a period of time for which I have almost no memories of. The lights were on and off for days; I didn't know if it was morning or night. It took me a while to realise Miguel wasn't bringing meals following a timetable, I don't think… at times it felt like not even three hours had passed when Miguel was back with another tray of food. Once I didn't eat my food to see how long it'd last until it went bad, I thought that was the only way I had to figure out whether Miguel was playing with me or not. But a rat ate my food. Even though Miguel kept denying the existence of said rat with the excuse that there is no way a rat could get into that room.

I thought I was going crazy when I started hearing steps and murmurs but that could've been another of Miguel's doing but I knew I was starting to lose it by the time I started seeing things in the corner of my eyes. I'd see a shadow, someone moving beside me and I'd turn around to find nothing.

Isolation was messing with my head.

One morning Miguel came in, I thought it was the middle of the night and I had trouble sleeping so I was awake when he came. He asked me what had happened with José, and I told him. He kept asking me the same question over and over again as if he didn't understand what I meant. I was very tired and numb, I wanted – and needed – a proper shower.

Miguel told me he hoped my month and two weeks in isolation was enough to calm me down and that Junior was waiting for me at work, he told me to stay out of José's way, that he'd take care of things but that he needed me to stop 'acting up'. After that, he took me out of my cell and I had never felt so disoriented. The sun was brighter than usual and it hurt my eyes.

"It messes with your head, doesn't it?" Miguel asked, looking down at me. "I don't want to lock you up until isolation drives you insane but you're not making it easier for me. Just… stop, okay? Just stop fighting everything, *Mijita*."

That was the last thing he said to me before he took me home where he finally took the chains off and left me alone.

I avoided looking at Sam when I got to her house. I went straight away to the bathroom. I took ages in the shower. I was late for work, but I didn't care. My wrists were wounded and they really hurt.

When I came out of the bathroom, Sam was waiting for me, sitting on my bed with two white bandages next to her. I sat next to her, waiting for her to say something. But she didn't say anything, she just took my hands in hers and began to clean my wounded wrists. And then she started crying. It began with a little sob, then one single tear fell down her cheek, but then tears were flowing down her face like rivers. She was trying not to make a sound. I tried to keep calm and not cry with her because I knew what she was thinking, I was thinking it too: there was something wrong with me…

Once she finished bandaging my wrist, I kissed her forehead, telling her I was really sorry and that I was going to control myself. My voice shook a little, making Sam cry even harder. After that, I left.

I didn't go to work. It was 1 p.m., and I was in no mood to go to work, I don't think I was ready either. Instead, I went to the woods near Sam's house and hid there for hours. I stared at the sky as I laid on the ground. When the sun went down, I made my way back to Sam's. Sam was worried, but I told her I was okay. Then I made my way to my room. She knocked on my door late at night, but I pretended I was sleeping. I knew she wanted to talk but I didn't know what to say to her, I didn't want to make her cry again.

Was I bad? Was this what I was? Was I an aggressive, violent person? I kept thinking back to what happened and the way I felt when I was choking José. I liked it. It almost seemed like what I did was fair. I didn't want to be that person. I didn't want to be ill, and I didn't want to be bad. I knew that was what Sam thought. I should've left when I had the chance; she'd be better off without me. I was just a burden that was getting heavier with each passing minute.

Date: 2 June 102 AW
Narrator: Aliana

I was back to the routine: work at 8.30 a.m. and back home at 7 p.m. The same thing over and over, day after day. People were giving me dirty looks and whispering, pulling their children away from me like I had some viral disease. If they hadn't liked me before, they certainly didn't like me now. I was used to it by now, I barely even noticed it anymore.

After fixing what seemed like hundreds of machines, including bicycles, lamps, radios, and whatnot, I was about to ask for my half-hour break when the front door opened.

And there she was.

Luna stood at the door and I didn't know exactly what to expect from her. I had always thought that she had no interest in me. But here she was, in front of me, standing with her sharp hazel eyes and her light brown – almost blond – hair, falling down like waves down to her shoulders. It was weird seeing her right in front of me. She was taller than I had thought. She was nothing like I had expected.

Behind her was a boy with short brown hair. He had the same haircut as Isaac had, short on the sides and long and messy at the top. His skin was tanned, and his eyes were the same as Luna's: hazel in colour and small. His nose was a little wide, and his lips were in a little grin as he approached the table where all the machines were. I had seen him before a couple of times before, at times he was with Isaac, other times he came with Junior.

"Hello," Luna said, breaking the silence and looking a bit uncomfortable.

In my time as a prisoner, I had a lot to think about. I didn't know that Luna was here, had I known, I would've taken Sam with me and left ages ago, dragged her if I had to... but now it was impossible to do anything. I didn't want to think about Luna, but it was inevitable. Sooner or later I would have to face her. I just wished it was later rather than sooner – way later than this.

I raised my eyes to meet hers, not knowing what to answer. I didn't have to talk to her. I wanted nothing from her.

"Eli, why don't you go find Junior?" Luna said to the boy.

"All right, Mum," Eli replied. He went back to the stairs.

Mum.

I swallowed hard, ignoring my pounding heart and I looked back down to my hands.

"You know," Luna began, walking towards my worktable, "I know so much about you, like the fact that you graduated a year ago with merits."

That's not true. Samirah was the one who graduated with honours *and* merits. Johan lied about that, probably because he was ashamed.

"I'm sorry, do I know you?" I frowned, narrowing my eyes at her. "Maybe you're mistaking me with Samirah."

"Miguel said it was better if we didn't see each other for the first few months... but you saw me that day," She smiled at me, I wanted to erase that smile off her face. "There's no point in hiding now."

I shook my head, looking down at the tools on the table. I tried to think back to Sam, her tears and the way she looked at me. I didn't want that again so I tried my best to control my impulses.

"Like I said, I don't know you."

"Well, we can talk and get to know each other like Sam and I have."

"I have no interest in knowing you."

Luna snorted. I frowned, lifting my eyebrows at her, waiting for her to say something more, but she just tensed and looked angry. She blinked a few times and I could tell she wanted to say something but she was holding back.

"Listen, lady, I don't know you, you don't know me and I'd like to keep it that way, so just stay away from me," People often told me that I had the ability to push all the wrong buttons and make the most patient person get mad. I just didn't think I could do it *this* fast.

Luna was pissed and she didn't even try to hide it. "You're very ungrateful, you know that?"

"And I should be grateful to you? You are *nothing* to me. Ever since I've known about your existence, my life has gone from shitty to shittier. Do you really think you can throw some words around and we'll just hit it off from there? *You don't know me.*"

"Perhaps you should see I'm trying to help you," Luna snapped back at me, taking a step forward. She looked taller then, she stood tall and a little intimidating. "I've already done enough for you. I've given you a job and a place to stay with Samirah. And yet you refuse to accept my help and you spit it back in my face. Fine, I won't help you anymore. But just in case you think about doing something stupid *again*, neither Miguel nor I will be able to do anything to help you and the consequences of your actions will affect Samirah. I won't let you hurt her too."

And just like that, Luna turned around and left. Who did she think she was? *She* would hurt Sam if she dared tell her the truth. She was the one hurting people, not me. I grabbed a pair of scissors and started to cut on a bicycle's tyre, not caring if the bike was for use or not. I was so angry that I just needed to destroy something. When I was feeling a little more relaxed, I looked at what I had done. The tyre was destroyed beyond repair. Junior would want an explanation.

I didn't realise that Luna's kid was at the door looking at me with a confused frown. "What are you looking at?" I muttered, angry.

"You look kinda crazy,"

"Do you think it's safe to call a crazy person crazy?" I gave him a wicked smile as I quickly opened and closed the scissors in a threatening manner.

"I ain't scared of you," he said, indifferent to me. He walked towards the table and grabbed a machine and a tool. "So, my mum, where is she?"

"I don't know, maybe she's hiding under the table, why don't you go and check?" I rolled my eyes. "If you don't see her here, then I guess she *isn't* here, right?"

"No shit, weirdo," he rolled his eyes as he spoke with the same sarcastic tone I used. "Junior said I have to help you. He said you've got a lot of work that I could help with."

"I don't need your help, nor do I want it," I said, although I didn't intend to sound so rude.

"Oh, that's cool. Happy to hear that. But as far as I know, this is Junior's shop, not yours," he showed me a *real* fake smile. "Junior says that I should help you, no matter if you need my help or want it."

He was holding a blender in his hands. He ripped the bottom bit and tried to take the motor out of it. "What did my mum want?"

"I don't know,"

Eli rolled his eyes at me and repeated what I said with a mocking tone. Then it was time for my break. Junior usually showed me how some things worked during my break, but since his knee was still hurting him, he wasn't working. So I spent my break eating Spanish limes and watching as Eli did whatever he wanted. It wasn't until an hour later that he decided to speak to me again.

"So, you good at fighting and that, right?"

"Depends," I said, trying not to tense up.

"I mean, you beat José up. Like, not everyone does that – and you're, what, 5'5"? You ain't very tall," he said, taking me in as if he wanted to catalogue every detail. "And you don't look like you got much muscle. How did you do it?"

"I'm 5'6" actually, and it's not like you're huge," I was a little offended by his comment. "And I don't know how I did it. Luck, I guess."

"So," he said, holding the word for a while before changing the subject. "You and Samirah, huh? Sisters ..."

"Yes."

"Sebas likes Samirah," he informed me, giggling.

"That's the one who used to have very long hair, right? Sebastián."

"Yes," He smirked, "And I think Samirah likes him. Don't you?"

"I don't know," I sighed. "What are you doing with the blender, anyway? You said you were going to help me; you're making a mess."

"You said you didn't want my help, remember? Besides, Junior knows I take what can't be fixed. The blender's sharp thingies are too bent. It wouldn't work."

"Basically, you're just making a mess that I'll have to clean up after?" I asked, pointing at all the old machines he had in front of him. In the little time he had been here, he managed to make a huge mess.

"Basically, yes," He nodded, not looking at me but concentrating on whatever he was doing and he even stuck a bit of his tongue out to the left side of his lips, as if it helped him concentrate better.

I let out a little laugh. We kept on working and talking from time to time. I had been locked in a room for quite a long time and I didn't realise just how much I missed talking.

Eli explained to me how things worked in his city. His uncle Miguel was the leader, which I already knew. He told me that people did what they could to help out. Some taught what they knew: medicine, numbers, reading, a bit of history, hunting, building, fixing stuff. They all had a place to live and food to eat, and Miguel kept the peace.

When my shift was over and night came, Eli showed me what he was doing. Junior and I just stared at what Eli had made.

It was very interesting, to say the least. I was amazed by how he took garbage and old machines that had no use and that nobody wanted and made something that looked good. It was very creative. At first, I didn't know what it was but the longer I stared at it, the more I recognised it.

Eli made a little building the size of my hand. It was a replica of the church at the centre of the city where I was held hostage. I could tell by the clock at the top of the building. The clock in La Cruz wasn't working, but Eli made the clock on his little rusty-metal building work and just like the church, it also had the cross. I couldn't hide my surprise. It was actually a very nice thing to look at.

"Isaac taught me how to work with my hands and how to make things, but he works with wood," Eli explained. "I like doing it with metal. It's better."

Not knowing exactly what to say, I just nodded. The building thing was very pretty.

"Aliana, I need to show you something before you go home," Junior interrupted, placing a hand on my shoulder.

Junior made his way to the other garage, the one that was always locked. Eli and I followed.

"I can't figure out how it works. See, I'm not very familiar with the Government's work. I was thinking that maybe you knew, maybe you could help me fix it."

I was going to ask what it was when we walked into the garage and Junior turned the lights on. There was something in the middle of the garage. It had a white sheet over it, but I knew what it was.

Junior removed the cover from it, it was a car. It was a very old model, but it was beautiful: A Luxair 5v. If you knew how to drive it, you could make it go a thousand miles per hour. And it could go even faster than that, way faster. It had a Turbo Max 10, which Roc was obsessed with. You could either have it on normal mode or levitating mode which made the wheels would go out to the sides. You could reach your destination within seconds. The exterior was white and with thin blue pinstripes. The vehicle didn't need petrol; it worked with solar energy, just like everything else in the Government.

"How long have you had this in here?" I asked walking around the vehicle. "It's old, but this is literally the best model ever made."

I walked around the car. It had dark windows. The body was in the shape of an arc. The doors didn't have handles.

I walked to the driver's-side door. Without touching the door, I moved my hand from right to left as one did when one wanted the door to open, but nothing happened. I tried again, but nothing.

"It has been here for ages now," Junior told me.

"It runs on solar power," I explained. "Also, the motor is down here. All you gotta do is lift the car and take off the metal plate."

"Well, we tried the sun thing. The doors opened and all, but we couldn't make it work," Junior said. I was very glad that he showed me the Luxair.

"Can I help you fix it? I mean, if I can – if you'll allow me," I said. Remembering that I had just come out of prison, I added, "If Miguel allows it."

"*Mija, I'm* asking you to help, Miguel got no say in here," Junior chuckled. "Please, help me because this thing has been mocking me ever since we got it."

My heart jumped in my chest. I couldn't believe that something so little made me so enthusiastic.

"I wanna help," Eli shrugged, walking over to the car. "I wanna ride it."

"Okay. All very interesting and nice," Junior began, placing both of his hands on Eli's shoulders, "but I gotta close now. Should I walk you back, Eli? I don't think Luna will like it if you walk home alone."

"Nope," Eli answered, the three of us walked over to the garage's door. "I'm going to Sam's. Isaac's there. He told my dad he'd take me home."

Junior said goodbye as we both walked away. After two minutes, I heard the sound of the door being closed.

"So, your friends are at my house,"

"Technically speaking, it ain't your house. In any case, it would be Samirah's," Eli pointed out, "But yes, they are. They always there nowadays. They used to come to my house because Isaac was always there, but now they always at Samirah's."

I had the little impression that he didn't like the current state of affairs. I waited for him to carry on.

117

"You see, it was the only way I could talk to Rebecca. She's *so* pretty!" Eli said. So that was the reason he didn't like it that the group now met at Samirah's.

"How would you know? You're just a kid." I laughed. "What are you, 10, 12?"

"I'm almost 15, for your information," he shot back, offended. It took him a whole minute to talk again. "Aliana, what is it like to live there? I just... I don't know, just wondering."

"Well, it's pretty simple, really," I shrugged. "You do your job, you get paid, you buy a house and stuff, and that's it. If you don't work, you have no money so you can't have food or anything. Simple."

"No, but I mean, what about the people, what are they like?" he asked, he looked so eager to know. "Because people here say you lot are different from us. But I never know it, 'cos you and the people who come look the same to me."

"The difference is that some people over there have no emotions," I told him, burying my hands deep in my jeans pockets.

"People can feel physical pain. It is just that emotionally, they are dead." I continued, "I don't know exactly how it works, but what I do know is that they put something inside us, something that blocks the emotions but at the same time, it also helps the people to have the ability to be aware of certain things. They can't get angry or feel ashamed, but we do have an idea of what it is to be ashamed or angry. People know of ambition and pride and they all want to achieve goals, goals that were set by the Government, but still goals. That's how we know of pride and shame. You achieve the goals, you're the pride and joy of your family, you fail... shame follows you around." *Like me*, I wanted to say but decided against it. "People are very opinionated about these things; you will be reminded of your failure for a lifetime. I guess human beings can be a little cruel, even those who have no emotions at all."

"Woah, that's so cool, I mean... it isn't, but still, it kinda is." He shook his head, frowning at his own comment, "What about the city, is it different to this one? I've *always* wanted to see."

"Well, the city is beautiful. I'm not just saying that because it's my home. It's very different from your city, it's like once you cross the bridge, you step out of a time machine. Government City is like the future compared to your city. Oh, and the cars, Eli... we have vehicles that work with solar panels like the one you saw back at Junior's. But the new models are astounding vehicles. Only people from the high and middle classes can afford to have cars, though.

"We got farms, where the animals are and where everything we eat comes from. We have a harbour, you can only go to the working island though, that's where everything is made. That's where the factories are. We have this huge building in the centre of the city, everything that's important is there. It also houses the board, they are our leaders, the ones who rule the lives in the Government. From the last floor of the building, you could see the whole Government, even a little bit of the farms."

"What about your parents, what do they do? Samirah does a lot of stuff here, Tío Miguel is always throwing flowers at Sam, saying how she's smart and that..." Eli commented.

"Sam studied different things all at once and so did my brother, so yeah, they're both smart. My mum studied medical science. She works in the labs with my father before he was appointed to the board, he's basically something like a politician." I told him, kicking a little rock as I walked. "Sam was going to be part of the Board. And when you're a member of the Board, you've gotta study many things at once, you've gotta be the very best."

"And you're like a soldier, right? But hear this, okay? If the only people that are left, are your people and my people, what's the point? It's not like we're gonna have a war with you lot." He moved his hands about a lot while he talked, he was very into this topic, he seemed to have a lot of unanswered questions. "Like, who do you fight? What do you do?"

"There's no wars anymore. There's no crime," I confessed. His smile vanished in an instant, his mouth becoming a straight line. "There's really nothing to do except train and maintain the peace, the latter of which we don't really need to do because no one breaks the rules."

I knew this was a total lie. There were crimes committed in the Government. I had seen the evidence with my own eyes. *I* had committed a crime, I had killed a man in cold blood. That man had committed several crimes, he raped and killed five other women. Of course nobody asked any questions about why the man killed those women because to ask was to say you didn't believe in the Government's words when we were told it was nothing to worry about. And to go against the Government's word was treason. If you were convicted of treason, you were taken to prison, from which there was no escape.

And prison was really just a cover-up. The Government ran tests on the prisoners, they used them as lab rats.

"Boring." Changing the subject again, Eli asked, "Do you miss your family?" He had so many questions I didn't know how to answer, but I found myself answering anyway.

"I – I think so," I replied honestly. "I don't know exactly what it feels like to miss someone. I've experienced the loss of a loved one, but I wasn't allowed to acknowledge that he had passed or even to think about it besides, I was... younger when it happened. But now that I'm here away from the Government, and now that I'm old enough to begin to understand my own feelings, I find myself wanting to go and look for my family all the time, even though I know it's pointless and dangerous. I want to see them, my brother and my mother, but then I know I can't, so it feels like a weight in my stomach and my chest – really weird because... I don't know how to tell if I'm sad or not, does that make sense? I don't think it makes sense."

"What about your dad?" Eli asked. I had to think about it before answering. Talking about Johan, or talking to Johan, felt like walking on thin glass.

"Um, I do, I guess. We didn't talk much, but I miss him too,"

"I see." He nodded. "My dad and I have our rough times too, mostly 'cos of my mum. But I'm sure if I leave one day, I'll miss my old man too."

I didn't say anything, I felt my muscles tense but I didn't say anything.

"He's good, you know? My dad." Eli chuckled, looking at me, he must've misinterpreted my silence. "It's just that you had him on a bad day. People are cool, you just made the wrong first impression, and on the wrong person. No one really cares what you did to José. Well, they do, but they will forget it... at some point."

"First impressions are important after all," I added. We were now at Samirah's place. The lights were on, and voices were coming from inside.

"When you see Rebecca, you'll understand what I mean. She's *so* pretty," Eli said with a shy smile. "Pity she's into ugly Isaac. She's alone too. She doesn't have a family."

"Ah, *ugly Isaac*, is he now?" I laughed, remembering how while we worked, Eli would talk about Isaac with such admiration and love.

"Yes, why? You like him too?" he asked, his tone changing to one of boredom as he entered the house.

"No, that's not what I said." I quickly said. "And that's gross, by the way." I laughed and pushed Eli's head as I tried to comb his messy hair with my fingers. He laughed as he moved away, walking towards the kitchen.

Eli said hi to his friends, the ones who were looking at me funny. Sebastián was, as always, sitting next to Samirah. The Rebecca girl was there; she was having a conversation with Eli, and she was, in fact, very pretty. Isaac was looking at me with a friendly smile. I felt a bit awkward standing there, so I started walking towards my room.

 **Chapter 11**

Location: La Cruz
Narrator: Samirah

"THANKS FOR HELPING me clean up," I told Sebastián as I cleaned the table. Feeling a little awkward.

"No problem," Sebastián replied from the sink, where he was washing the dishes. "Plus, it wouldn't be fair to you. We come to your house and mess about when you like your things organised. And I like to spend time with you."

I smiled at his comment. Sebas was very nice to me, Rebecca said it was because he liked me which at first, I kind of doubted. Sebas found me in the woods, he brought me here. He was a friend but I don't know how I felt about him liking me the way Rebecca thought he did.

"Interesting," Aliana's voice came from the kitchen's entry, she was watching me carefully with her eyebrows furrowed.

Aliana's brown hair was longer than usual. She never liked to cut her hair. She had black circles under her eyes. I knew she struggled to fall asleep because of her insomnia and her nightmares, and the pills she brought with her didn't always help; sometimes I worry the pills do more harm than good. And to top it off, she had been locked in a prison cell twice. The thought of Aliana locked in a dark room, isolated from everything… it broke my heart.

Everything was okay with us, I was still a little angry and I thought she was still angry at me too, but aside from that, we were okay. She still had nasty wounds on her wrists, but her face wasn't swollen anymore, she had a few bruises here and there but she wouldn't have any scars. I didn't think so, anyway.

When Aliana walked into the kitchen, I was suddenly very embarrassed. I wanted her to leave, but I also wanted her not to leave me alone with Sebas. Aliana took a sweet guava from the fruit bowl. She was standing near Sebas, who was pretending not to be there, trying not to make a single noise.

"I changed my bandages," Aliana said, taking a bite of the guava, I fought the urge to take the guava from her hand and wash it or at least peel it. "I need your help with something at Junior's. Can you help? If you have time, that is…"

"Yes," I happily answered. "Whenever you want. Just let me know."

"I guess your friend can help too," she said, looking at Sebas, who looked at her with a confused expression. "You fix vehicles, yes? Junior wants to fix a Luxair. Maybe you can help."

"Sure," he answered.

Aliana nodded and then looked down at her feet. "Night, Sam," she said, walking out of the kitchen with her sweet guava.

I listened to Aliana's footsteps as she walked up the stairs and into her room. I then turned my attention to Sebas, who was still cleaning the dishes. He looked less awkward now. Sebastián told me that he didn't know how to act when it came to family moments. It was awkward for him, he told me he had never been in that sort of situation. And when he told me about his family, I kind of understood why. His mother left him and his father was a drunk, it was his grandmother who raised him. It was strange to me because I didn't want to judge his mother, I do not know her reasons for leaving but I couldn't understand how a mother could leave her own child? How could a father simply not care about his son? I couldn't understand but I tried not to judge.

"I told you, she just needed time." I smiled, and he smiled back at me. "She even talked to *you!*"

"It was a bit awkward, to be honest, with all that business about the bandages and whatnot."

I punched his arm. His dark eyes got smaller and his face lightened as he laughed. He was something else. It was unexplainable how I felt when he smiled at me because I felt slightly awkward but at the same time, it was nice that I had a friend who I could laugh with.

I tried to not think much into it; it was supposed to be something normal, boys liking girls. Was that not one of the things I had dreamt about my whole life? For someone to like me, to look at me the way Sebastián was looking at me right then. I didn't understand much of what was happening, but I did wonder why I felt so strange and so uncomfortable when he leaned in and kissed me.

Sebastián was kissing me. I was kissing someone for the first time. I was *kissing*Sebastián.

To say I was in shock would have been an understatement. My whole body went rigid, and my eyes were getting wider with every second. Sebas moved away and said he was sorry. I couldn't say anything. I didn't know what to say or what to do. I stood in the same spot and blinked as Sebas moved away. I heard him say something but I couldn't concentrate on what he was saying. When he realised I wasn't going to say anything, he left the kitchen and then the house. After he was gone, I could still see him leaning in and kissing me, the same moment repeating again and again in my mind. When I finally could react again, I sat and tried to make sense of what I was feeling.

I didn't know what to make out of this situation. It was a puzzle I couldn't solve, not alone. So I went to the one person whom I knew would never lie to me: Aliana.

Narrator: Aliana

I was finally falling asleep, my eyelids felt heavy and it was getting harder to keep them open. I was hoping tonight I wouldn't wake up in the middle of the night, but then someone burst inside my room, making me jump.

"Bloody hell, Sam." I put my hand to my chest. "You can't just burst in like that. I—"

"I need your help," Sam spoke fast, interrupting. She walked from one side of the room to the other, her hands behind her back. "I need my sister right now, okay?"

"What is it?" I asked, rubbing my eyes. Sam stopped walking and looked at me with a worried expression. "Go on, then. You came to tell me something, right?"

"Okay, okay." Sam sat at the edge of my bed. "Where to begin? … Well, the thing is – I, well, I don't know. I mean, this is—"

"Stop mumbling, Sam. Just spit it out." I chuckled. One didn't often get to see Samirah mumble. When she did, it was funny.

"Okay, so, you see the boy who was here, Sebas?" she asked, I nodded but she wasn't looking at me. "The big one, with light brown hair and dark eyes and big muscles—"

"The ugly one that likes you?" I interrupted her. She blushed and tried to hide her face from me. I didn't know if I wanted to roll my eyes or laugh at her reaction. "Do *you* like him?"

She stayed quiet for a long second to then sigh dramatically, "Well, the point is, you see how he was helping me clean and such. Well, at one point, I don't know how or why, um – well – he was—"

"He was what, Sam?" Samirah was nervous and to be fair, I knew what she was going to say before she even said it but I needed her to say it.

"He kissed me."

Samirah waited a few seconds for me to say something but I had nothing to say. I was actually surprised that I didn't care as much as I had thought I would.

"So? Say something, Lynn."

"Was it gross?" I sat up and I rested my back against the wall. "Your first kiss, I mean, with the ugly boy."

My first kiss was gross. It was weird and awkward. Of course, I never told Samirah about it or about the ones after that. Maybe it was gross for Samirah too, maybe all kisses were gross.

"He isn't ugly. He's nice and kind and friendly, and I laugh a lot when I'm with him." She defended him, yet something in the way she spoke told me that there was a but coming, however she didn't say anything after that, she stayed quiet, thinking.

"Sam, I'm not the one who has to like him." I laughed, trying to get her to talk to me. "If I think he's ugly or annoying and not funny at all, it has nothing to do with your opinion of him. What I think of him shouldn't change the way you see him."

"I don't know, Lynn. I don't know what I like? I don't know how it should feel like when you like someone, how am I supposed to know if I like him like he seems to like me? We lived in a place where even something so dumb as this situation is prohibited. I feel like a child who is brought to the real world for the first time and I lack the right tools to fit in. I have what I've always wanted, I have freedom, I have someone that likes me for real… so why doesn't it feel remotely close to what I thought it would feel like?" She shrugged and smiled sadly, looking down at her hands.

"And well… when he kissed me, I didn't do anything."

"Ew." I chuckled trying to lighten the mood, Samirah gave me a look. "Okay, sorry. What do you mean you didn't do anything?"

"I stood there frozen with my eyes wide open. I did nothing," Sam was talking faster than usual as she stood up and started to pace. "What do I do now, Lynn? What am I supposed to do when I see him? Do I kiss him? Maybe if I kiss him again I'll feel different? Do I just say, 'Hi, hello, how are you doing'? I don't think I will be able to look at his eyes again. I'm such an idiot!"

Sam pressed her hand to her temple. She was squeezing so hard that her skin turned white where her fingers were pressed. She then started to pace again in my small room.

"Oh God, what must he be thinking? What if he doesn't want to be my friend anymore? Maybe he thinks I don't like him? Maybe my face told him I was disgusted by him! Oh, my dear God, what do I do, Lynn? Imagine if—"

"All right, enough" I held my hands in the air in an effort to make her stop pacing so fast. "Your pacing is making me dizzy, and you're talking really fast. I'm sure tomorrow you will see him. Tomorrow you can explain to him how you felt and I'm sure he will understand."

"Do you think?" Sam sat back down, looking at me like I had all the answers. "What if he doesn't? Or if he's angry?"

"Sam, I'm sure he will understand."

"I'm sorry for waking you up," Sam apologised when I yawned. "Do you have to work tomorrow?"

I shook my head. "My free day is tomorrow."

"I have to work tomorrow," She told me as she laid next to me in my bed.

"If you even *think* about putting your leg over me, I'll push you off the bed."

I laid facing the wall and not even a minute later, Samirah hugged me, putting her leg over me, making me roll my eyes. It was good to know that Sam still wanted to tell me her things and come to me when she didn't know what to do.

Sam had her first kiss and her first thought was to come and tell me about it. I never told Sam about my kisses with Roc. And I didn't kiss him once but three times. I guess I was afraid of what Sam may think and how she would react, but also because I didn't like people knowing them type of things about me.

When Roc and I kissed the first time, I thought it was kind of gross. Neither of us knew what to do and we giggled the whole time. That was when I began to like Roc. I was very confused about my feelings. I didn't know if I liked him or if I felt something more for him. After that, Roc treated me differently and kept asking me if we could kiss again. I always said no. I might have liked Roc back then, but I still didn't like kissing. It was weird.

The second time was when we were 15. Roc's father had passed away. I had never seen him so upset. He wouldn't speak to me. He was my best friend, the only one who knew I could feel. He accepted me and protected me. I was there for him when he needed me but Roc misunderstood my actions and for some reason, he decided to kiss me. And I let him.

At that time, I was naive enough to think that Roc and I could end up marrying, so I told myself it didn't matter if I kissed him again or not. That time it wasn't as gross as the first time. It also lasted longer. We didn't laugh either.

It was a little selfish from me to do that, perhaps now thinking back to it, I guess I allowed it to happen because I wanted to keep Roc with me, I didn't want him to shut me out. At that point in my life, if Roc would have pushed me away, I have no doubts that I wouldn't have survived.

When I was 15 years old, things got difficult for me. I had a lot of low times. And Roc was the most important thing to me. I loved him to the point that I would have risked everything just to show him how much I cared for him. I would feel at my highest when I was with him. When he was gone, I'd be at my lowest. That's when it happened, when I gave him my life and the power to choose for me, to talk for me, to pick me up and drop me, and to do anything else he wanted, my life was his because I certainly didn't want it. At that point in my life, I had lost the will to live. Nothing was all right. And nothing made a difference, just Roc. He was there for me. He took care of me. I don't know what changed. I don't know what happened or what made me love him so much, but I did.

And then one day, I didn't.

I was shocked by my feelings for him. They had come out of the blue. But also, out of the blue, they were gone too. I loved him, I would risk my life for Roc's if needed but it was a different type of feeling, it was intense and overwhelming but it just wasn't the same as before.

Now, in the darkness of my room, I thought about Roc. I wanted to see him. The thought of knowing that I would never be able to be with him again seemed wrong. I didn't know if I was in love with him. I didn't know if I've ever been in love with anyone but I did know that I loved Roc and that what I felt for him, whether friendly feelings or more, was the closest I'd ever get to loving someone who wasn't part of my family.

Feelings were very hard to understand.

 **Chapter 12**

Location: La Cruz
Narrator: Aliana

"ALIANA!" A LOUD bang against the door to my room and a scream woke me. I jumped in my bed, banging my head against the wall. As I opened my eyes, I tried to find where the giggling was coming from. It was Eli, that much I knew.

"What the hell?" I didn't know where I was, what time it was, or who I was. That was no way of waking a person.

When I finally opened my eyes properly, I found Eli standing by the door, behind Eli, Isaac was leaning against the door with his arms crossed against his chest, tapping his right hand's fingers against his arm. I had noticed how he was never still, always drumming his fingers on something. I saw a little grin on his face amid the beard along his strong jaw. He was wearing a tight white T-shirt and baggy jeans. The way he dressed made his muscles stand out. It was as if his clothes fit perfectly onto his body as if they had been tailored especially for him. He stood like he owned the wall he was leaning against.

"What do you want, ugly little dwarf?"

"Isaac, she wants to know what you want," Eli joked, punching Isaac as he spoke.

"Yeah, well, I was asking you," I groaned at Eli, rubbing my eyes. "but I guess it works for him too."

I laid back on my bed again, using the bed sheets to cover myself. I felt uncomfortable having Isaac there. It was very weird for me to feel uncomfortable with a boy around given that I had been around boys in the changing rooms, although I'd never seen a boy fully naked. Thank God for that. It wasn't a big deal. But those boys had been around me for years; having Isaac around while I was in my pyjamas just made me feel nervous and uncomfortable.

And there was also the matter of clothes. I had never liked to show my body – my breasts, my butt, my thighs… I wore clothes that covered most of my body. I wore a sports bra on top of my bra. And I did prefer to wear jeans instead of skirts. I had big breasts (bigger than I would have liked, at least). I did love my strong thighs, but I simply didn't like the idea of someone looking at me as if I was nothing more than a body. And when I slept in my bed, well, that was my safe place where I didn't have to wear big T-shirts to cover my body or a bra for that matter. I wore comfy shorts as pyjamas.

"Come on," Eli said, I felt him poking my feet. "Get up. I wanna show you something."

"Why does it have to be so early in the morning?" I whined. I wanted to sleep, it's been ages since I had a good night of sleep. "Don't you have something to do? A school to go to? Work? Other people to annoy? I'm tired, Eli."

"Aliana, it's two in the afternoon. It ain't morning anymore." Eli laughed. I opened my eyes, but I didn't remove the sheet from my face.

"Told you she wasn't going to wake up easily." I heard Samirah laugh.

"It's my free day. Junior said I didn't have to go work."

"Yeah but you're gonna stay all day in your house, you gotta go out, sun's good for you." Eli argued back.

"I'll open the windows and let the sun hit me while I'm in bed."

"Don't be lazy, Lynn. It's one forty in the afternoon," Sam sighed.

"Aha, don't be lazy. Come on, I promise you'll have fun." Eli whined, pulling the sheets. "*Please.*"

"Okay. But stop pulling the sheets!" I groaned as I sat up, glaring at Sam and Eli.

"What's this monkey doing here, anyway?" I asked, pointing at Isaac, incapable of looking at him.

"Be nice, Aliana," Sam said. Her tone was a warning that she was getting bored of my jokes.

"What is this *boy* doing here?" I corrected myself. Isaac smiled a crooked smile.

I couldn't forget his threat, the fact that he said that I was going to be humiliated. Indeed, I had been humiliated. They humiliated me and treated me like trash. Maybe I did deserve it, but only up to a certain point, not to the extent to which José had taken it. And because of that, now I couldn't let my guard down.

"He's coming too," Eli explained. My heart banged in my chest, I didn't feel completely comfortable with that. "At first, it was him and me, but then I remembered Junior gave you the day off, so I thought we'd keep you company, it's not nice being all alone. You have ten minutes to get ready."

Sam laughed as she followed Eli. I was left behind with my mouth hanging open, who did that little boy think he was? I moved my eyes to meet Isaac's. He was still there, I was going to tell him to leave, but he spoke before I got the words out.

"I ain't ugly," he said with that dumb smile of his.

"And I ain't ugly," I repeated once he was gone, imitating him as I stuck my tongue out at him. Then I got up to go to the toilet.

Narrator: Isaac

I was going down the stairs when I heard Aliana imitate me. I laughed, fighting the urge to turn back and mock her. When I got downstairs to the kitchen, Samirah was at the table doing her hair and Eli was looking at her as he ate an orange. I took a guava out of one of my many pockets and bit into it as I sat down next to Eli. The sweetness burst into my mouth. I just loved it. I loved eating guavas.

"You two back to normal now?" I asked Samirah, referring at her and Aliana.

"Yes. I told you she only needed time." Samirah said, looking around for something. "Well, kind of normal."

"What you looking for?" Eli asked.

"My bag with my books. I'll be right back," Samirah answered as she got up. She then went to another room to look for her bag.

"Dude, I need your help," I whispered, flicking Eli's ear.

"My help?" Eli asked, lifting his little eyebrow. He looked so small that I wondered when he was going to hit puberty. When I was his age, my voice was doing the most. "With what? And what do I get?"

"Whatever you want. When we're with Aliana and you start talking to her, can you, like, include me in the conversation?" I asked him. I didn't want to ask Eli for this, mostly because I felt stupid doing so, but Miguel told me to get close to her, the problem was that I always got awkward around her so I couldn't really do that. "If I ask her, she won't answer me."

"You like Aliana, don't you!?" Eli laughed, pointing at me with a cheeky smile. "Uh, well, you best unlike her, 'cos she don't like you."

"Shut up, man." I put my finger on Eli's mouth. "I don't like her. I need to know stuff about her, *Miguel* wants to know about her but he says she won't let her guard down around him. And José wants Miguel to kick her out because of what happened, Miguel needs to know she's calm and *I've* gotta make sure she's calm."

"Nah, she ain't bad like that, Isaac. Trust," Eli shook his empty hand, looking at me with his hazel eyes, so sure of what he was saying.

"Yeah, but José talks too much and people believe him. If you like her so much, then I don't think you want her to leave, do you? We need to keep her in line but she won't talk to me. So help me out, yeah?"

"What will you give me?" Eli asked, looking away.

"My God, I thought you wanted her to stay. Besides, we're like family, are you really going to blackmail me?"

"So? Family ain't got nothin' to do with business, boy." Eli smirked, pointing at me with the same hand he was holding his fruit.

"It's a high price you gotta pay. I like the girl," Eli whispered when Samirah came inside the kitchen.

I wanted to pull his ears. Cheeky little bastard.

"I'm ready to go," Sam sighed, putting her backpack in her back, "Should I wait for you, or should I leave?"

"Aliana has about four minutes left. If you want to wait with me and Isaac, we're going to the plaza," Eli said to Samirah.

"Back home she was always the last one to get up. My brother and I had a hard time getting her up or trying to get her to leave her room"

"Nate, she said his name is," Eli commented, eating his orange.

"Yes, Nathaniel." Sam smiled. "So you guys talked, huh?"

I looked at Samirah very carefully. I still couldn't see how they looked alike. Samirah's hair was lighter, and her eyes were different. Their smile, the way they stood, the way they talked – all different. Sam had all these beauty marks on her neck while Aliana had none. Aliana had freckles that Sam didn't have. I don't know, I just couldn't see it.

"She told me everything, really," Eli bragged with an air of superiority.

"Really?" Samirah mocked, not believing him. "Even our father? And her lousy friends? Roc?"

"Your father, Johan, yeah," he answered. "Not about this Roc person. And what do you mean, 'lousy friends'? Ain't you two twins? You're supposed to, like, have the same friends and shit."

"No. We never really hung around with the same people. Her friends and my friends were completely different. Roc was in her little group." Sam took a seat by the table and looked through her bag.

"Natalí had a dog called Rocco," I joked. Eli nodded with a smile, remembering the dog, probably.

"He was, well is, Aliana's best friend."

"Mm, kinda like a boyfriend, you'd say?" Eli asked, cleaning his hands in the sink.

Samirah was about to answer Eli's question when Aliana walked into the kitchen. Her hair was wet. She was wearing a black top and ripped jeans that I had seen Sam wearing before.

133

Aliana took about ten *mamoncillos* and then we all walked out of the house. Eli and Aliana started to talk about something related to a car. They both seemed to be very enthusiastic about it. Samirah appeared to be lost in her thoughts. I just wanted to get to the plaza.

"So, changing the subject a bit, Aliana, who is this Roc guy I keep hearing about?" Eli asked loudly.

My eyes went right away to Aliana's face. I was expecting to see a reaction. She blushed a little and looked over at Samirah, but Samirah, lost in her own little world, wasn't even paying attention.

"He was my partner," Aliana answered.

I wanted to pay attention to what she was saying, but out of the corner of my eye, I saw a silhouette that caught my attention.

"Flaco!" I whistled to get Sebas's attention. He looked in our direction and began walking towards us with a smile on his face.

"Well, this is going to be awkward." Aliana sighed. I frowned when the two sisters began whispering to each other.

"What are you two talking about?" I asked. Eli shrugged, as lost as I was.

Sebas and Eli bumped fists. Sebas then nodded as a salute to me. He looked at Samirah and gave her a little awkward smile. *OH.*

"Where you lot going?" Sebastián asked. Eli was about to answer, but Samirah cut him off.

"I gotta go, bye!" Samirah shouted. I frowned. Aliana closed her eyes and bit her lip slightly, shaking her head.

"What happened?" Eli asked no one in particular. I shrugged. Aliana gave Eli a know-it-all smile, a devious smile, a full-on grin. We all looked at Samirah as she practically ran away.

"Nothing," Sebas sighed. I gave him a look and he shook his head at me, "I gotta go, I'm gonna be late too."

We watched as Sebas walked away. After a minute, Aliana, Eli, and I carried on making our way to the plaza. I wanted to say something, but I simply didn't know what to say. I lost my chance when Aliana started to talk to Eli again about some building thing.

Eli asked Aliana questions about the Roc guy, but Aliana managed to answer him in a way that didn't really answer anything. I wanted to say something, but I kept thinking that if I spoke, she would just ignore me.

When we got to the plaza, Eli ran to his mother and the rest of the training group. I waved my hand, saying hello to Luna. Eli left Aliana and me alone for about a minute, which felt longer than that because, oh my god, was it awkward. I was suddenly very aware that she was right next to me. I wanted to move away, give her space but I realised that if I did that, it would most likely make things even more awkward. I was being an idiot. I was also standing like an idiot, balancing on my heels. I almost tripped. I had never before felt this ridiculous in front of anyone. When Eli came running back, I felt the awkwardness leave.

"My mum said she ain't got a problem with you staying and watching today," Eli told Aliana. Aliana shook her head but before she could say anything, Eli carried on. "You'd only be with me and Isaac. You ain't gotta worry about no one else. Come on, please, Aliana?"

Aliana sighed and took her hand to the bridge of her little nose, nodding.

Eli grabbed hold of Aliana's hand, dragging her as he walked. I followed behind, wondering again why I was there.

"Isaac said you like knives, so begin with the knives then. I'm very good with those,"

We got to the far end of the plaza, where there were a lot of different knives displayed near cartons with bullseyes on them. Aliana looked uncomfortable, but she held her head high. It was easy to see by their look on their faces that nobody in this place liked her, they didn't trust her because of what happened with José. They were all acting like it was the first time there was a fight.

I kept thinking back to that day when she tried to run away. She looked so vulnerable, practically begging me to let her go home. I couldn't let her go. As stupid as it sounds, I wanted to protect her. I kept trying to convince myself that she didn't mean to hurt José. It was José's fault. He pressured her to the point that she could no longer control her anger. Yes, she hurt José, but José hurt her too. It surprised me how easy it was for me to defend her, but I saw her, I saw the guilt in her eyes. I saw how much hurting José affected her. She didn't mean to do it.

Eli was telling Aliana how Cairo, his father, had him train with knives since he was just 9 and how he really liked to use them. The whole time, she seemed truly interested in what Eli was telling her. And even though she was surrounded people who didn't want her around, she looked strong and untouchable. I was completely sure that if the roles switched and I was the one inside Government walls, I would surely watch my back 24/7.

Aliana nodded at Eli, she was trying to hide a smile, paying attention as he happily explained to her how each knife worked. If he only knew the arsenal she had back in her bag. Aliana raised her eyes to find my eyes on her. I felt like an idiot. I wanted to look away, but if I did that it would be worse, so I simply gave her another very awkward smile. She frowned, but a hint of a smile crossed her lips.

"So, you know your knives," Aliana said to Eli, looking away from me. "Now show me how you throw them."

Eli's smile reminded of Cairo because of his dimples. Eli took his aim and threw a knife at the whiteboards at the far end of the plaza. His knife hit the red-painted X in the centre. Once he was done, he turned to Aliana with a satisfied smile.

"Nice." She smiled back at him. There was something familiar in her smile, but I couldn't quite place it, it wasn't like Samirah's. "How about a moving target?"

"Moving target?" Eli repeated with a snort. "Easy."

Aliana dared him with a smile as she took four white pieces of carton board, each with an X in the middle. She counted to two and then let the pieces of carton board fly. Eli was good with knives. He had done a lot of training with knives and seemed to like it, so it was no surprise when he hit the first three carton boards. Although, he missed the fourth one.

"Three out of four, my friend."

"That ain't fair. It was too quick …" Eli complained. It was almost as if Aliana just insulted him. He was very competitive. "Let me do it again."

"You are not going to hit the four of them." Aliana laughed, but Eli was very serious.

"All right, then, if you know so much, try to hit all four," Eli dared her.

"Okay, *but* when I hit the four, I get to go back home." Aliana proposed with a great deal of confidence. She no longer looked uneasy or uncomfortable. She was back to being the girl I had seen that first time in the woods, minus the whole aggressiveness.

"*When* she says." Eli laughed as he nudged me with his elbow. "*If. If* you hit the four of them, I'll let you go home and I won't wake you up whenever you have a day off. But if you don't hit the four pieces, which you won't, you will have to answer every single question that we ask you."

I almost snort at Eli's part of the deal, but I knew I had to stay quiet and if I didn't want to make a fool of myself. I tried to disguise my laugh with a cough. Aliana moved her eyes to me.

"No way."

"Well, well, well… where's all the confidence gone?" Eli went back to his knives, disinterested, trying to make her fall for his ploy, which she did.

"You know what, you midget, throw the cartons," She was trying not to smile as she grabbed Eli's knives.

"Isaac, throw the boards," Eli ordered, crossing his arms across his chest and looking at Aliana. I looked down at him and lifted my eyebrows. "Please?" he quickly added with a smile.

I took the four pieces of carton board and looked at Aliana, waiting for a petition or something, but she just nodded. When I thought she was ready, I threw the boards into the air the same way she had done for Eli.

Aliana began with the last piece of carton board, hitting it right in the centre of the *X* just as I let it fly from my hand. She went for the next one, and she hit that one in the centre too. I turned to look at her. She was very focused as if nothing was there but her and the pieces of carton board. At that point, I knew she would hit all four. Then she hit the third one.

Well, shit then.

She was ready to let the fourth knife fly when a smaller knife got in the way, hitting her hand and making her drop the knife she was holding. Within seconds, her hand was covered in blood.

"Sorry, wrong turn," Claudia shouted, smiling as she apologised. Claudia was José's daughter. She was 15 or 16 years old, and she was very, *very* annoying.

"It wasn't a wrong turn. You did that on purpose, you little rat!" Eli shouted, walking towards Claudia. Aliana followed him. So did I.

Eli didn't like Claudia either, mostly because, apparently, Eli had a crush on Claudia but she laughed at him when he told her and then she told everyone.

"I'm not as good as you. Sorry." Claudia shrugged, her tone was as fake as her apology.

All I could think was what Aliana would do if she lost her temper again. I was not afraid of her, but I didn't want her to make another mistake. If she did, then Miguel would really have to kick her out. Or worse... and since Miguel told me to make sure to keep her out of trouble while he tried to control José, he'd be pissed off at me if Aliana does something crazy.

"Oh well, what can you expect from a—"

"What's going on?" Luna interrupted before Aliana had the opportunity to insult Claudia. Insulting José's daughter wasn't something she needed right now.

"Claudia threw a knife at Aliana," Eli said, glaring at Claudia.

Luna took a look at Claudia and then at Aliana. When her eyes dropped to Aliana's hand, her face completely changed to concern. I followed Luna's eyes and saw Aliana's bloody hand closed in a fist. She was putting pressure on her wound, making the blood come out faster. The blood was dripping on the sand. It probably looked worse than it really was.

Luna tried to hold Aliana's hand, but Aliana was faster and pushed herself back from Luna. Luna dropped her hands and looked away. "I'm going to find a piece of cloth, some water, and some alcohol for your hand. Claudia, you wait here."

"It's just a little cut." Claudia rolled her eyes.

"Ah, you're just a little—"

"All right, come on," I cleared my throat, interrupting Aliana before she insulted Claudia for real this time. I took Aliana by her arm, careful not to put too much pressure on it, and tried to walk away, but Eli … Eli, God, Eli always had to have the last word.

"I don't even know why you here anyway. Yesterday you said you weren't coming back," Eli spat.

"Shut your mouth." Claudia raised her hand to hit Eli. I was going to pull Eli towards me, but Aliana was faster.

She grabbed Claudia's hand before it could reach Eli. Her bloody hand was on Claudia's wrist. Claudia and Aliana were of equal height, but Claudia was bigger overall. Plus, Claudia had four of her friends behind her waiting for Aliana to make a move, at which point they would jump in. Despite all this, Aliana looked bigger than all of them. She stood her ground without hesitating. The way she stood – God, it was like she feared nothing. Her body tensed and her face was a wall. It showed no emotion, no expression.

"Don't *ever* raise your hand at him again," Aliana said in her deadly voice, raspy, slow and low.

"How dare you!" Claudia shouted as she shook Aliana's bloody hand off her. "God, that's gross."

"And there it is, what I didn't want." I sighed, grabbing Aliana and Eli by their hands. "Come on, both of you with your big mouths."

I took them to the stairs and then up to the sitting banks. I told Eli to go get the bandages and alcohol from Luna, without complaining, he ran back down. I sat in the middle of the bank, facing Aliana. We were right in front of each other.

"She's José's daughter," I explained. Aliana's face changed. A little smile on her face told me she understood. "José told everyone not to trust you. He's been saying that you think you're better than us, that you're probably a spy, and that you and your people are going to attack us all."

She didn't look at all shocked.

"If that was true," she began with a wicked smile, "then José and his daughter would be the first ones to go."

I frowned, not knowing what to say. She had to be joking.

"I'm joking," she clarified. "I've been here for months now. If I was going to do something, I would have done it already. Besides, I had my chance with José, I didn't do anything."

As if to save me, Eli appeared from behind Aliana with two bottles and two large rolls of white bandages. He gave the items to me, and I put them between me and Aliana.

"She's an idiot," Eli told Aliana, "but let's look at this from the positive side. You lost…"

"No, not really. I would have hit them all if that girl hadn't gotten involved."

"Yes, sure. Still, a deal is a deal. You lost, so you gotta pay." Eli looked back at the plaza, where his mother was calling him to return. "I'll talk to you later."

Eli left us, running and jumping through the banks. I turned my attention back to Aliana's hand. I held my hand out for her. She hesitated for a moment, but then she carefully placed her hand in mine. The wound was close to her wrist, too close. The cut wasn't deep, but the fact that Aliana held her hand tight in a fist made blood come out and made the wound appear worse than it was. I very delicately tried to clean her hand with the water. She remained silent, and so did I, being as careful as I could be. It was a long cut but it wouldn't leave a scar.

I wanted to say something but I didn't know if I should talk to her. Perhaps if I did try to talk to her, she'd ignore me and that would be very awkward. Besides, I didn't know what to say.I was panicking. She was just a girl, and it was just a conversation, but I couldn't forget the fact that I had told her that everything would be okay and yet she was locked in a prison cell for weeks.

I figured that I may as well just stay quiet and clean her hand, wait for her to say something. But what if she didn't say anything? I could feel her eyes looking at me as I cleaned her wound. I was drawing a blank. Every time I wanted to say something, my mouth would open. But nothing seemed right, nothing seemed like conversation material, so I closed my mouth, regretting even thinking about saying something.

"Are you going to say what you've been trying to say since we sat down, or are you going to think about it a bit longer?" she asked and I had never felt so stupid in my entire life. I wanted to hide under a rock somewhere far away. No one had ever made me feel so embarrassed. I didn't even know where to look.

"Who says I wanted to talk to you? I was just working out my jaw," I joked, opening and closing my mouth to pretend. To my surprise, she smiled, not a proper smile but a little grin. At least she hadn't ignored me, so that was something.

She turned her attention to the Plaza, it was probably the first time she ever came. I was used to coming to the plaza, so it was nothing special to me, but I could see why she would be amazed by it. It was a huge rounded place. In the middle was the ring of sand where the shows and fights happened, and all around the sand were the banks where people sat. The banks were close to the arena but higher up.

"When I was a kid, my dad would bring me here when no one was around. He liked it a lot," I began, not being able to stop the words from coming out of my mouth. I didn't know if she'd be interested but I continued, saying, "He used to say that this was the most calming place. When there's no one here, it is." Aliana was now looking at me. I expected a silly comment from her, but she said nothing, so I continued.

"My dad liked history. He would spend hours and hours reading about the old times, the good stuff. We don't have any record of what actually happened during the rebirth or why it happened but we do have records of some of the things that happened before."

"The rebirth happened because of wars, everything was destroyed, we were all that was left. And those who remained said it was a new start, so we started from zero, rebirth." She told me, I smiled nodding.

"Yeah, I know that much. Anyway, he told me this place used to be a bull thing, a bullring arena."

Aliana's face was serious, but her eyes were asking me to continue, to explain what I meant.

"He once told me he read a book that explained the previous use of this place. People used to pay to come here to see a man play with a bull. It was called bullfight. Apparently, the man played around with the bull until it died. I guess it was part of the culture. We don't do that here anymore, though, because we need the bulls to reproduce with cows and provide us with food. We now use the plaza as a fighting arena and activity centre. Sometimes we even celebrate stuff here."

"People have been cruel since the beginning of time," Her face, no longer serious, was full of curiosity. She was letting her guard down. I liked that. What I did not like was the way she was looking at me, as if I had all the answers. I had none. My spelling, for instance, was terrible. Numbers were easier than words were. It took me ages to finish reading a book. "See, that's exactly the kind of thing the Government tried to fix."

"There are things about those people – the people that were alive before the rebirth – that we can't understand. Yeah, people did a lot of bad things and I don't know what the Government does to its people but I know enough to know it ain't fixing anything." She frowned at me a little, probably analysing my words. "In my opinion, they had it coming, what happened to them – to the people before us. I mean, I don't know much, we don't know what exactly happened; we just know they were all fighting each other. And your people were smart, they left their country before things got bad and they came here and stole *our* land. The people who came before us, yours included, destroyed their world. They destroyed everything little by little and yeah, probably most of the people were bad and evil but I'm sure there were good people among them, people who didn't like cruel things, people who were against war and all the bad stuff that happened. There's good and there's bad. Some people are stupid, but what can you do? We all different. But over at your side, though, there's no good or bad, there's simply emotionless people, right? The Government tried to save humankind but they stripped humans of their own voice, over at that side there's humans but there's no humanity."

"And there's 'humanity' here?" she asked, her eyes lit up with a fire in them, I felt like I was being accused of something. "I don't see humanity here either, Isaac, I see a bunch of people who like to hurt others, I see people who laugh when they witness an act of violence and even *cheer*. I see people who hurt others simply because it makes them feel better, or just to humiliate others. Don't look at me like that, like I'm lying. *I* was at the centre of your people's laughter, I was humiliated and dragged about, I was José's punching bag and they all loved it, they cheered when they saw me flinch, they laughed and cheered when José spat at my face, and when they thought of me as weak, others followed José's actions and I saw their true colours.

"See, your people, your neighbours, the woman who waves at you when you walk by, all of those who look so innocent, they have the capacity of being even crueler than José ever was, your people have shown me time after time that what was done in the Government was the right thing, and that this," She pointed around the room, making me look around, "Everything that's around you is what's truly wrong. Say what you want but there's no humanity here, there's no love and peace either, there's just survival. If you want to see peace, *real* peace, then look at the Government."

I didn't know Aliana well but now I knew just how much she believed in what the Government did and to be quite honest, it was a little frightening.

"Peace without love?" I asked and as soon as the words left my mouth, I wanted to punch myself. *Peace without love?* How stupid was I?

"Nothing comes free of price, Isaac."

"So you'd rather not have a say in your life?" I asked her, it was impossible for me not to frown, was she okay in the head? "You'd rather basically be a living robot? You have no say in your life, no right to choose, you'd have a life and you wouldn't even be living it."

"And what's so great about having a say in your life, about choosing? I chose to come here, and now I can't go back home."

She looked away for the first time, breaking eye contact with me but before she did so, I saw anger in her eyes, annoyance in her face. I knew it wasn't because of me but her anger was most likely directed at herself instad, at the choices she made that led her here.

"But you're with Sam and you've met Eli. And even though we ain't what you prefer, we ain't – although I know it's hard to believe – bad people. Take Cairo for example. He looks like a beast, after what he did to you, you see him as a bad person, but to Luna he's her loving husband. To Miguel he's a brother, and according to a lot of people here, including me, he's a great person. But you only know one side of him." Aliana looked back at me. Her green eyes were all I could focus on. "You've only shown us one side of you but I know there's more to you than what you've shown so far. I see it when you're with Eli. When you came here, it was pretty clear that you had a wall up. You wouldn't let anyone get close to you, not until you talked to Eli. I was wrong to think that you had nothing to offer us. It isn't all black or white, Aliana." I was trying to hold her stare as I took the alcohol bottle and wet the piece of cloth. "I'm gonna put some alcohol on the cut now, okay?"

"Don't worry, it doesn't hurt," she said. I looked at her straightaway.

She had to be joking. She had claimed not to have emotions, but I knew that she cared for her family, so she did have emotions. Had her ability to feel physical pain been removed? I didn't know if they could remove that, but then again, I knew little about the Government. For all I knew, they could bring dead people back to life.

"I'm joking. I can joke too, you know. I know I'm not the funniest person but I'm – I'm trying to be nice," she cleared her throat, looking away from me, bouncing her leg up and down really fast. She was trying to be nice. "I do feel pain. In any case, this would cause me physical pain, which I, and everyone else who lives in the Government, do feel. And just so you know, we don't hate you. No one at the Government even cares for your existence, not unless they are told to care. Over there, we're told not to worry about your kind. We do know of rebels, but we don't see your kind as a threat at all."

She flinched as I put the wet cloth on her open wound. I had done it as carefully as I could.

"Then why do you seem to hate us so much?" I asked. "Samirah was a little scared when she first arrived, but she didn't *hate* us."

"I don't hate you. I can't hate you because I don't know you. It's just—" She frowned. Once more I wanted to press my thumb against her brows and softly get rid of that frown. "I don't know; I guess – I just have my reasons."

"So you're saying that you wouldn't hate it if per say, Flaco, I mean Sebastián had a little crush on your sister?" I asked without thinking about it. I lowered my gaze to her wounded hand and began bandaging it. I felt her eyes on me, so I looked back at her. Her facial expression now looked like it usually did: serious, impossible to read. Even her eyes were unreadable.

"I didn't say that, it's not that I oppose to it, I just think it's weird. Also, my opinion doesn't matter, it is Sam's life and she has made sure to let us all know she does with it as she pleases," she spoke, I've come to notice that whenever she spoke, she barely opened her mouth. "Sam and I are two completely different people. I was raised to think and act a certain way. I am not like Sam, who easily opens up to new ideas, I cannot do that. I don't like change but I can adapt, it just takes me awhile to get used to new things."

I nodded, narrowing my eyes. I had finished with the bandage and was now holding Aliana's hand for no reason at all. I should have probably let go, but I didn't want to. I couldn't. I looked back at her and saw that she was looking at me with her usual frown and narrowed eyes. She stared into my eyes just as I was staring into hers but then she lowered her gaze, looking everywhere but at me, her cheeks reddening a little.

"I'm starting to think that I make you nervous. I mean, I know I'm handsome, but—"

"*Please*. You need to stop flattering yourself so much. Self-love's okay up until a certain point, and you crossed that point a while ago." She chuckled.

"Do I, then?" I smirked.

"Make me nervous?" she asked tilting her head a little, I nodded. She took a moment to think about it. "A little bit; not because of the reasons you probably have in mind, to be quite honest with you, I don't know why, I'm still trying to figure it out."

That caught me by surprise, I thought she was going to lie. I thought she was going to avoid the question, but she answered. I didn't want to look away, it was her who looked away first, taking her hand with her, leaving me with the very strange sensation of vertigo.

"She's not okay, is she?" she asked, pointing down at Luna, who was standing still and looking at everyone with angry eyes. I could've sworn she was looking at us for a second. "She looks angry, aggressive even."

"Well, no one really likes to talk about that," I sighed, scratching my neck. "I don't know much about what happened to Luna. I was just a baby when she came back. My aunt told me she wasn't like that before. It was when people from the Government took her that she changed. I know you ain't gonna believe me but people from the Government do bad stuff. She's the only one who was taken that has ever come back and ever since she's been like that, she said they did something to her, made her sick, I don't know. She's better now, though. With time she gets even better. Or maybe I have just gotten used to her, I don't know."

Aliana bit her lower lip hard, making it go white. I waited for her to ask whatever that was going through her mind. If she only knew how much damage the Government did…

"You know, if you would have agreed to help out when I asked you, you would be down there teaching with her instead of working in the repair shop," I spoke up when I figured she wasn't going to, I wanted to keep the conversation going.

"I like the repair shop," she answered quickly. "Besides, if the people I'd be teaching were like you, I would most likely be wasting my time. Eli's quite good, though."

"You should give my offer a second thought. You'd be surprised to see what we can do," I assured her. "And about Eli, what did you expect? He's Cairo and Luna's kid, Miguel's nephew. He *has* to be good. There's a lot of pressure on that little guy. Although he's different from them, so that's good."

"People here are very strange – well, different." She shrugged, softening her frown a little. "It is almost as if being different is something good. Over there we are all the same. Kind of ..."

"You ain't like them, though. Most people who come from the other side of the bridge have feelings and emotions and all – like you, even though you try to hide it."

"I don't see why that's so good. Before, people could feel everything, all those feelings you rebels are so attached to, and they made mistakes. People did wrong to others. Countries destroyed each other all out of greed, desire for power, and even love – all because of the emotions everyone is so eager to feel," she explained. I wanted to say something, but she seemed so into what she was saying that I didn't dare interrupt her. "And once they found a way of fixing those mistakes, the mistakes within us, all the wrong disappeared. Corruption, hate, treason, murder, thievery ... all those things were gone. We had a chance to do things right again."

"I don't get it. When you do that to a person, you're literally taking their free will. People should have the right to choose, to make mistakes and learn from them. How can you take away something so important? I've always wondered. I just don't understand."

"Only a few people know the ways of the process, if that's what you mean by 'how'," she explained, calm and steady. "My father and mother know how to do it. I don't know anything about it, so I'm afraid I can't rid you of your confusion. I simply don't know."

But something told me that she did know more than she was letting on. "So there's more people like you and Samirah? People who can actually feel?"

"I didn't even know Sam was capable of feeling. I mean, she cried and seemed happy and upset at times but that's not odd. That's why seeing her with Sebas or just seeing her here was very shocking," she let out a shaky breath that sounded like a laugh mixed with a sigh. Then she looked away to the ground, lost in herself as if she hadn't really been talking to me but had just been getting something out of her system. I couldn't make a sound. I took each breath carefully. I didn't want to move in case it made her stopped talking, because for some reason it felt like a privilege to hear her honest thoughts.

"If it were up to me, I'd have no emotions. Back home it felt like emotionless people were right and I was wrong. I felt lonely at times. It was actually funny. I had all these emotions, but all I felt was loneliness, I felt hopeless. It was almost as if I was disappearing. I was alone. Nothing made sense. It felt like a punishment to have feelings. Somehow life had found a way to make me pay for something that I had no control over, as if life was saying: 'You have this thing others don't have, so you have to suffer for it. You have to pay for it.' It wasn't as if I wanted any of it. If I could, I would have gotten rid of all my emotions and become oblivious to all of their lies, to the pain, and to the truth. Maybe that way I wouldn't have felt so alone. I wouldn't have felt hopeless or miserable. I wouldn't be the person I am today.

"I have emotions. I should've felt good things. I had a family, money, a good education. … I had *everything*, yet I've never known happiness, love, or enthusiasm. All I've ever felt was this drowning sensation. I couldn't ask for help because the problem were my feelings, they were destroying me. If I asked for help, everyone would know the truth. They would have probably killed me. To be quite honest with you, Isaac, at some point, the idea was actually appealing. And more than once, I was about ready to give myself in, to give up, to end the torment. I was different and I hated it. I was broken. And I was ready, not to ask for help but to stand in the middle of the crowd and shout that I couldn't stand it anymore. That way, I'd get it over with."

"What happened?" I whispered. It felt like a secret like I had been blessed with a piece of her and I had to hold onto it and not let anyone see it. I wanted to reach for her hand. I wanted to tell her that she'd never been alone here but that was a lie and a stupid one at that, it was ridiculous for me to even think about saying that.

"Roc helped me. Roc saved me," she whispered back. It felt like we weren't in the plaza, that we weren't surrounded by people but were alone in a bubble where we could talk. A part of me thought that she was telling me this because she just needed to say it, because she *needed* to speak, to let it out, not because she wanted to tell *me* in particular.

"He didn't give me in, even when I spoke with hatred of the Government. If someone showed any real sign of emotion, then that person would be sent to prison until they were 'fixed'. Roc's father had emotions and he died because of that. He loved his wife, even I could tell.

"My mother, on the other hand, feels nothing. She has never looked at my father that way. She has no emotions, so she cannot love him or us. He is just another man to her. Maybe she looks at him with what she imagines is pride or admiration, but love? No. Marriage over there is nothing. It's just a way to keep the 'old culture'. Marriage is nothing but a paper."

"And you wanted that for yourself?" I asked. Because of the way she talked, and with her calm face, her steady voice, and just the way she was, she had all my attention. "Being with someone not caring whether you loved them or not?"

"Yes. Well, I don't know. I got used to the idea of one day being with someone. It doesn't matter if you love them or not," she answered, still looking at nothing. "I thought I was going to be with Roc. And I thought it would have been easier with him because he and I were really close and I – I owe him my life. Besides, when you know you have to do something, your only option is to accept it, you can't change it, you can't say no. I thought Roc and I would be a good match. We were equal in a lot of things, but then the certifications and results came. After our graduation, I was second and he was no longer my equal. I was no longer a match for him. I accepted it and I obligated myself to move on, but he didn't."

I didn't completely understand what she meant. I found myself trying to understand what it must have been like. I remember her in the woods, angry and fearless, beautiful and powerful. And then she wasn't so fearless. When she was vulnerable and hurt, when she was delicate and unstable. And from what she was saying now, it was clear that she just accepted what other people had planned for her. It seemed unreal to me. It seemed impossible that this girl just accepted that her future would be not what she wanted but what other people had already chosen and planned for her. I wanted to understand her, I wanted her to explain herself so I could know more of her. What I'd seen thus far was nothing, but I was already surprised, fascinated and confused.

"What results?" I decided to ask about that first.

"The results and the certifications you get when you finish your academic studies. We finished last year. When you finish your studies and you graduate, there is this big ceremony where everyone's business goes public and there are supposed to be the first students for every career, male and female category. I was supposed to be the first for the female category. Everyone had high hopes that I would be first. It was down to me and this girl called Iris. The last test was given on the same day the certifications and results were revealed. Once we completed the test, the results were put on display. What a surprise it was when I was classified as second. Roc was first in the male category, my other friend Mathias second. Iris was first and I was second. And, well, bottom line is that for someone like me, with my family name and all, being just second isn't enough or acceptable."

I felt the mood drop. It was obvious that she wasn't ready to talk about the whole test thing. There were some unresolved issues there. She seemed not to want to touch the subject, so I tried to lighten the mood.

"So he was just your 'best friend', huh?" I joked, wiggling my eyebrows. She half smiled, shaking her head.

"He is," she answered. I could have sworn she blushed, but I couldn't tell because she wasn't looking at me and her hair was covering her face. "Well, he was. Besides, he was assigned to marry Samirah. None of that matters anymore. I'm here now. What happens in the Government is no longer my concern."

I nodded. I did understand that part. Maybe that was why it was so easy for her to talk about it, because she no longer "cared" for who she had been in the Government. That didn't matter anymore to her because she accepted that she was never going back. I couldn't help but admire her for that. If I ever left my home or my people, it would take me a long time to get used to it. It must have been hard to know she couldn't go back home or see her loved ones. It must have been even harder when all that stood in the middle was an old bridge. She was strong.

"Can you dance?" I asked, changing the subject. She looked at me with narrowed eyes, a spark of curiosity in them.

"Pardon me?"

Of course she didn't know what I was talking about. Rebecca had to teach Samirah how to dance because Sebastián was too shy to ask her.

"Oh yeah, I forget you people are a bit boring," I joked. "We have fun, and one fun thing to do is dance to music."

Her face was no longer calm or serious. She had that interest and curiosity in her eyes.

"I can't explain it. Becca showed Sam, but I can show you, teach you how." A smile appeared before I could stop it.

"Teach me what?" she asked with alarm in her tone, once again frowning.

"To dance and all. Today is my aunt's birthday. There's gonna be a party around six o'clock. The sun goes down around that time, so it won't be as hot," I told her. "Some people are going. Miguel invited them all. My aunt ain't a party person, but she does it for Miguel. Eli wanted to invite you, but I might as well just ask you myself."

I thought Aliana was going to say yes, but despite her curiosity, she shook her head. "I don't think that's a good idea."

"Why not? You'll come with me. I won't leave your side," I assured her.

"I don't think I should go, not after what I've done, your people won't be happy with me there."

"No one blames you for anything, you know? People barely talk about the fight; José won't let anyone remember he was outmatched by someone half his size." I laughed and that got a smile out of her.

She shook her head, but she had curiosity written all over her face. She wanted to know what dancing was. When she finally gave in, I wanted to jump and scream "*Yes!*", but that would have been a *little* embarrassing.

"Okay, but if I don't like it, I can leave at any time?"

"Of course," I answered. "What do you think this is, a prison?"

"Yeah, right." She rolled her eyes. I laughed.

"Hey, at least you ain't got chains now."

 **Chapter 13**

Location: La Cruz
Narrator: Aliana

I SHOULD HAVE said no.

I was already regretting having said that I would attend the party. I was a bit nervous about it and even tried to say no several times once Eli finished his practice, but he wouldn't take no for an answer. I at least tried to make him have a shower when he finished his practice, but he said he didn't need one because he "smelled of roses", as he clearly put it.

Why was I even going? I wasn't one of these people. Going to their gathering could start trouble. I really didn't want to fight anyone.

"You can't turn back now, we here," Isaac told me as he opened the door.

I spent about three hours talking to Isaac, which made things less awkward. It wasn't his fault how everything turned out, and I shouldn't blame him when it was my own inability to keep my mouth shut that got me in trouble in the first place. We talked about the Government, about my job mostly, I had his undivided attention and it surprised me but I quite liked it. It was nice to talk to someone who was actually interested in what you had to say.

It was easy, though, talking to him was easy. He was curious, yes, but it wasn't just noisy curiosity, it was as if he wanted to learn from what I was telling him, he wanted knowledge. I wasn't stupid; I knew some information I couldn't give him but I did tell him enough so he'd know I wasn't a threat to him or his people.

I wanted to ask Isaac why he took the time to talk to me, to listen to me, and to explain things to me. I had done bad things to Isaac and I expected him to give me the same treatment, instead, he was being nice. Maybe that was one of the reasons I was now trying to be nice. I couldn't fool myself, though; I talked to him because I wanted to talk to someone, to have a conversation and not to be alone for a minute.

"What's that noise?" I asked, frowning at Isaac, expecting an explanation. Eli laughed. Isaac smiled at me again.

I hadn't realised at what point exactly, or how, I began to look at Isaac differently. I didn't even know what had made me do so. But he was no longer the dirty, ugly rebel. He hadn't been ugly, to begin with, but he *was* a rebel. That being said, now I was seeing something I didn't see before. To my disgust, I had to accept that the word *sexy* had popped into my mind a couple of times today. Perhaps it was his T-shirt. I was pretty sure it was because of his tight T-shirt. Or maybe it was his three-day beard, which was absurd because I had never liked beards. I had always thought they made men look unkempt and even sick, but on him, it looked different. It looked good.

"Music," Isaac told me, I felt the need to look away.

"I'm gonna find Andrea," Eli told us as he walked backwards. "I haven't said happy birthday yet."

And so he walked away, dodging some people and pushing others so he could get through the crowd. There were quite a lot of people. Thank God no one noticed us.

I looked around and tried my best not to look helpless or scared. The last thing I wanted was someone to know how afraid I really was. I was afraid of everything lately. If I wasn't taking my pills, I surely would've snapped days ago. I didn't want what happened with José to happen again. I had to face my fears and control myself, the thing was I wasn't ready to do that just yet, not when Luna was walking around wanting to have a conversation I was not ready to have. I had to keep taking the pills if I wanted to have some control over my emotions.

I had no reason to be at this party. I was out of place, if not outright unwanted. No matter how many times I told myself that I didn't care, deep down I did care. Just like everyone else, I wanted to be accepted. But if I hadn't been accepted by everyone at the Government, the people I lived with for years, what made me think that I was going to be accepted by the people here, especially since I already tried to kill one of their own?

"Come. Natalí's are over there," I followed after him when he began to walk towards a table where two young people sat very close together.

"Hello," Isaac said, smiling. "This is Aliana, Samirah's sister."

"We already met," Natalí said with a knowing smile. Actually, Natalí and Junior were the only people I actually liked from this place.

"And I'm Thiago," the boy next to her introduced himself as he stood to shake my hand. He was taller than I was but not by much. His hair was black, and he had it close-cropped. His smile was somewhat attractive, but something about him seem a little dangerous, he had a bad boy vibe. He had a drawing on his neck, it went from the side of his neck to his back. I couldn't see more of it because part of it was covered by his T-shirt. He was kind of attractive if you were into that sort of thing ...

"You do look like Samirah, except for the eyes and the hair," Thiago smirked, shaking my hand.

"So I've been told," I replied, feeling a bit weirded out by his smile.

"It is very nice to meet you, Aliana," he said, finally letting go of my hand.

"I'll be right back," Isaac informed me. "I'm going to see my aunt. I'll only be a minute."

I watched him walk away after he'd said he wouldn't leave me. I felt my anxiety growing as he took another step, I was starting to notice the difference between taking six or so pills every day and taking three each day.

"So, you came with Isaac?" Natalí asked.

"And Eli," I told her, taking a seat next to her.

"That little shit!" Natalí laughed. "The other day I found him in my garden throwing rocks at my sister's window!"

I laughed, not because I wanted to, but because it was what I was expected to do. I could see Thiago from the corner of my eye looking at me. I didn't like it. It made me feel uncomfortable.

"You look stiff," Thiago said, looking at me. "Here, have this."

"Don't," Natalí warned him, shaking her head disapprovingly. Thiago reached into his pocket and took out a little plastic bag. He extended his hand to me and then opened it, showing me a ... a mushroom? I stared at his hand, confused.

"It ain't bad. It will only make you see things different – lighter, prettier. ... It helps you people with the whole emotion stuff," he told me, "Pretty much everyone who comes from outside takes these at least once. There's others that make you have some crazy hallucinations, I don't like those."

"You don't have to take it if you don't want to," Natalí told me, lifting her eyebrows to make her point.

I had doubts. I didn't want to take the mushroom, but if it helped with my emotions, then it would be welcome.

"If I eat this, will something bad happen to me? Is it like being intoxicated?" I asked, looking at Thiago and then at Natalí.

I knew what being intoxicated was like. I hated it. It was horrible and disgusting. I couldn't understand why people did it.

"Drunk? No, this is nothing like that," Thiago answered, moving his hand forward. "This will only make things look ... better."

I reached for his hand, taking the brown mushroom and putting it in my mouth. Biting into it felt weird, it soft and easy to swallow. It had no taste at all and I felt nothing.

"And now what?" I asked.

"Now you don't drink or eat. If you do, you won't get the effects," he warned me. "And don't drink alcohol, you'll most likely throw up."

I nodded. Natalí and Thiago looked at me as if they were expecting something from me. I looked back at them, blinking, trying to detect the difference. After a few minutes, I didn't feel anything but I did notice the difference. It was as if I was looking at them for the first time. If before I had thought they were good-looking, now I was amused by their strong features and how respectively beautiful and handsome they were. I blinked a few times, looking around myself.

We were in a garden. There were light bulbs all around, hanging from the trees and from the ceiling inside the house. There was smoke coming from a barbecue. And the smell! I didn't like meat, but the smell was so tempting, it made my mouth water. Everything was shinier, and the grass was greener and prettier, I wanted to feel it. It was unbelievably amazing how beautiful everything was and I that hadn't realised it before. It was like before everything had been blurry and I was unable to see it all properly. Everything had been in black and white, but now it wasn't. Now everything was beautiful.

"Wow," I said, looking back at Natalí and Thiago. Thiago was smiling. Natalí looked a bit concerned.

"I think we're all gonna get along just fine." Thiago smiled as he got up and walked over to me.

He was going to tell me something, but at that moment Isaac walked over and reached out for my hand.

"Come, I told you I would teach you," Isaac said, taking my hand.

I looked up at him. I didn't know if it was the lighting or what, but there was a light all around him. His hand was warm and gentle, just like when he had bent my hand when we were at the plaza and he was being careful not to hurt me. I had never seen anyone so handsome in my entire life.

"Seriously?" Thiago laughed from somewhere close by, but I couldn't see him anymore. I couldn't see anyone, I could only focus on how his fingertips were softly touching the back of my hand.

"Ah, what can you do? She came with me." Isaac laughed.

I could hear Natalí laugh too, I turned to look at her. It was like seeing a goddess right before me. I had thought she was beautiful before but now it was like her beauty had been highlighted. I wanted to look away, but I couldn't take my eyes off her, she noticed me staring which caused her to blush and look away.

Isaac squeezed my hand a little and guided me to where people were walking and moving in pairs to the rhythm of the music. They turned in circles and held hands as one of each couple walked through the other's hand. Their feet were moving fast and perfectly. I knew there was no way I could do that. I looked at them moving, or dancing, and I was truly fascinated.

Isaac was saying something, but I couldn't hear him. I shook my head and frowned. He bent down close to my ear so I could hear him. His voice was deep and loud against my ear. I felt his jaw moving up and down as he spoke. The hair of his beard was tickling my cheeks. The hair on the back of my neck raised up as he spoke into my ear. I almost giggled.

"This is salsa. We dance it a lot," he explained. It was hard to focus when he was so close to me. "You have to do this. Look."

Gently he took my other hand. I felt a shot of electricity running from my hand to my whole body.

Calm down. Jesus, just calm down.

"One foot and then another. Let's start easy." He explained, moving his feet. I was trying to do what he told me but I got distracted by the realisation that we were holding hands, that we were so close together, and simply that I was "dancing" him with. Let's just say that when I got distracted, which was a *lot*, I stepped on his feet. He would just laugh it off and tell me what to do, "No, no. My feet, your feet. Let me take you. Don't rush." When I made a mistake, he would say, "Slow down."

He was very patient in teaching me. I was just embarrassed. My cheeks were probably blood red. My hands were sweating, and my heart was beating so fast I feared it would burst out of my chest, grow little legs and arms, and run to hide somewhere far from Isaac. He surely noticed my red face, because from time to time he would look at me and try to hide a smirk.

"If we don't rush and if we do the basics, it will be easy." He smiled.

"Basics? Easy?" I said. "What part of any of this is basic and easy? And as if that wasn't enough, you have to move with the rhythm of the so-called music. I mean, I'm good with my feet moving and all, but it's so hard to coordinate with the music." *And the distractions ...*

"I knew you couldn't be perfect at everything." He laughed, looking me straight in the eye.

Isaac thought I was perfect? He was probably just joking. It didn't mean anything. I was trying as hard as I could not to blush again. I didn't even know it was possible to blush so much. It felt like my face was on fire. I forgot how to move. My right foot stepped on my left one and I almost fell, but Isaac quickly caught me, saving me from—

His hand was on my lower back.

His pinkie was slightly touching my skin.

I didn't know if he noticed but *I* noticed that his finger was still touching my skin. It was nothing, but it felt so ... I didn't know how it felt, because I had all these mixed emotions ranging from feeling shy and to feeling uncomfortable.

"Ay, watch out." He laughed.

"So sorry," I replied, looking away.

"It's all right. You take a spin now." Isaac made me take a spin under his lifted arm. I tried to coordinate my feet and keep them moving. "It gets easier. You let go of my right hand and you spin under my left arm."

He was still holding my hand. He let go of the other one so I could spin again. I had to go under his lifted arm. It was very confusing to me, but he was guiding me, so the steps were actually quite easy to follow. He took a chance and took a spin too. When he lifted my hands and let go, I felt a sudden urge to reach for his hands again, to hold them again, but before I could do something stupid, he spun under my arms, my fingertips briefly touching his back as he was spinning.

He was right in front of me again, a bit too close this time, taking my hands in his. I knew that I shouldn't like this, that I shouldn't allow him this close to me, but I didn't say a word. I liked it and a part of me I wanted it.

"You see, easy ... when you get the hang of it." He laughed. I gave him a smile. This time I had to force myself to erase it from my face. I simply couldn't stop smiling, and that was strange.

I wanted to say something but I didn't know what, I had no words and when my mouth opened, a different song began to play and I lost the desire to dance. I felt a bit uncomfortable, so Isaac and I just went back to where Thiago and Natalí were still sitting. I sat down and watched people dance. I looked at their feet, seeing how they moved with no problem. They even made it look easy.

As Thiago had told me, everything was shinier, prettier, and better. However, I had thought that I would have greater control over my emotions, but the mushrooms did the opposite. I didn't like how careless I suddenly felt, but I couldn't control it. For once, though, I didn't really mind.

"Bored?" Isaac asked, moving his chair closer to mine.

"Not at all." I smiled, "I'm actually impressed. I see them moving – dancing. And they make it look so easy. Very nicely done."

I was smiling more than I wanted to. I was letting go. I realised that this was the first time I was actually having a good time without any worries. This was a glimpse of the Aliana my siblings wanted me to be. This was the person I would have been if I hadn't had all the hate and resentment I had inside. How sad it was to know what I could be if it weren't for my own stupidity.

"Are you okay?" Isaac asked, probably seeing the change in my face. "You're acting different. I mean, I ain't complaining, but, you know, you seem different."

"Yes, I'm fine," I answered, trying to smile at him. "I wonder if everyone sees things this way and if I'm the only one who doesn't."

"What?" he asked, confused. He was frowning at me. "What do you mean?"

I could have sworn I saw worry in his face again, but I couldn't care about that right now. I had enough to deal with given the crap inside me. It was like all I had hidden inside me was begging to be let out again.

"I am a hypocrite. Today I told you how I believed in the Government, but look at me, Isaac, I feel so many things that sometimes it literally drives me crazy. I supposedly hate my own father; what kind of daughter wants to hurt her own father? You know, my life was not "over" the day I followed after Sam, my life was over way before that; I singlehandedly destroyed my own life, I filled myself with hate and anger to the point where it controlled my life and I let it. I'm a murderer, I'm all that is wrong with the world.

"I spent years preparing to graduate with honours, to be first, but I failed. And I worked too hard, I did so many things. I had it all planned – well, kind of. And now I'm here and I have no future, I can basically do whatever the hell I want, but I have no idea what I want. I don't know what to do with all this free time. I don't know how to make choices on my own. I'm here while all my life is over *there*, across that bridge. Perhaps I should eat those little things more often. Everything looks better, even you!" I laughed as I looked back at Isaac. His face was serious and worried. He looked away from me to Natalí and Thiago. I looked at them too. Thiago was laughing. Natalí looked worried.

"What did you give her?"

"Don't look at me." Natalí put her hands in the air.

"Amplifier. I gave it to her," Thiago said, handing a couple of items to Isaac. "Here, give her chocolate and water. It ain't my fault, man. Everyone reacts to it differently. I didn't know she was gonna go full-on depressing on you."

"Here." Isaac gave me the chocolate and water. He was smiling down at me, but I still saw the worry in his eyes. "I like you better when you ain't saying sad stuff."

I frowned as I took the chocolate and water, but I didn't eat or drink. I was neither hungry nor thirsty. Natalí stood up and walked away, Thiago followed her and tried to talk to her. I followed them with my eyes to see how Thiago leaned down towards Natalí to kiss her and how she moved away. Ha, ha.

"I reckon this is all you people do, partying, dancing, musiciquing, laughing. Zero worries."

"*Musiciquing* isn't a word, love." He laughed, and I felt stupid. "Would you just eat the chocolate, please?"

"Don't call me love. I'm not called love, and I'm certainly not *your* love," I reminded him, rolling my eyes as I looked away.

But I had seen him smile. I'm pretty sure he calls me all those names to annoy me.

He reached for a little glass with an alcoholic beverage in it. I knew the glass contained alcohol because of the face Isaac made when he swallowed it and the smell of it in his mouth. It was about the fourth little shot he had had since we had arrived at the party.

"Okay, little soldier."

"I am no longer a soldier. Now I'm just a simple girl who repairs broken devices," I joked, but there was no mirth in my tone.

"Why are you like that?" He laughed. "You put yourself down. You don't give yourself the credit you deserve. Just because you ain't there, it don't mean that you're less of the person you are. You live here now and yeah, you repair broken devices, but your work or your profession doesn't define you as a person. That ain't what you are. Your actions and your ideals, what you say, the way you are, what you have here and here." He pointed at my heart and then at my head. "That's who you are, what really counts. Besides, I know I don't know you but I know enough to know there ain't nothing simple about you."

I looked at him for a while. What could I say to that? What he said actually amounted to a good speech, but I couldn't help but laugh.

"You *really* are a corny." I laughed. "I'm sorry for laughing. It was a good speech. I am no longer surprised that you have girls drooling all over you given all you say. That is so 20's, the typical rebel shouting with his fist in the air: 'Fight for your heart, fight for your freedom!'"

"Dude, have you seen this face? Who could resist?" he joked, touching his chin and giving me that cocky smile he had when we were in the woods.

"Yeah, sure,"

"No, but seriously, you shouldn't be so hard on yourself. I understand that you can't forget about what you've left there, but just because you aren't there doesn't mean your life is over or that you're going to be miserable for what's left of it. Now you're here. Maybe this ain't what you wanted, but this isn't so bad either. You got a roof, food, and work. With time, people will accept you. And if they don't, who cares? For what's worth, I think you're pretty amazing. With time, other people will see this too."

"Speak for yourself," I sighed as I laid back in my chair with my back straight. I saw José walking quickly towards us, pushing people around him, which only made them turn to look at him and then watch, as he would probably make a scene about me being here. I shouldn't have come.

"What's this one doing here?" José spat, raising his voice so people around heard. I guess it hadn't been enough that he literally pushed his way through.

So predictable.

"She's with me," Isaac answered, not caring about the whispers or about how people looked at him when he said that.

I wished I had taken the chocolate and the water when they offered it. It would be hard to keep my emotions calm when José was trying to humiliate me once again. One would think he'd leave me alone by now. What else did he want?

"Why would you bring her here?" José asked. "Respect the house of your leader. You can't bring all the whores you please."

"Be fucking respectful," Isaac snapped, standing up.

"Never mind, Isaac, I'll just leave," I muttered, grabbing him by the arm, which was a huge mistake. People around were looking, and the whispering got louder. I shouldn't have done that.

"No," Isaac said, looking at me, "you don't have to leave. You have as much right to be here as he does."

"According to who?" José laughed, folding his arms across his chest.

"Andrea said she could come." Isaac took a step forward, clenching his jaw when José smirked. I just wanted to leave.

"You *really* should leave." José pointed at me.

"What's going on? Who turned the music down?" a black woman approached the inner circle. Her curly black hair was braided up to her shoulders. Something about her reminded me of Isaac. Maybe it was her posture or that playful look in her eyes. She was tall, skinny,

163

and beautiful. Next to her stood Luna. "Oh, you came! I thought Eli was lying, but here you are!" the woman got carried away, smiling as she walked towards me. "Is there a problem with my guest?"

José growled out of anger and then walked away, saying something that sounded like "unbelievable". I couldn't care less what José said. I just wanted to leave. Everyone was looking at me now. I didn't know for how long I could keep up my "not bothered" attitude.

Luna stood back, I could tell by the way she looked at me that she remembered our conversation, if I messed up, Sam would have to pay for it and Luna would blame me. I couldn't stand the way she was looking at me, so I looked away.

"I'm sorry. José doesn't like people much," the woman said to me. She had a welcoming smile, I didn't know her and the fact that she was treating me like she knew me made me feel uncomfortable.

"Happy birthday again, Tía." Isaac hugged his aunt. "I'd like to get to 40 and look as young as you do."

"Very funny," Andrea said, pulling Isaac's ears. "I still got a few years until 40. I'm Andrea, by the way. I haven't had the chance to meet you yet."

"I'm Aliana. Nice to meet you," I said, introducing myself. Andrea probably already knew who I was, she looked at me the same way Miguel did, with recognition. "Happy birthday."

"Well, thank you, dear." Andrea smiled. "So, you're Samirah's sister, huh!? You two *do* look alike."

"No, they don't." Isaac laughed. I chuckled and tried not to look too uncomfortable. Why pretend when we both knew the truth? I knew Isaac didn't know, but still...

"Don't worry, people will get over it when there's a new thing to gossip about," Andrea said with a smile as she reached for my shoulder and squeezed it. I fought myself not to move away from her. "If you don't feel comfortable, you don't have to stay."

"Yeah, I think it'd be better if I left. I think I've caused enough trouble already."

"Nonsense!" Andrea laughed. "All these fools are here because Miguel thinks I like to celebrate things big. He gets very excited. I would much prefer a family dinner, which you and Samirah are more than welcome to attend!"

I politely smiled at Andrea, not knowing what to say. Sam and I weren't her family.

"I'll walk you," Isaac said. That was not quite what I was expecting, but oh well.

"No, don't worry, it's fine,"

"I wasn't asking," he said as he kissed his aunt goodbye.

"Isaac, come back here before you go home, I have some stuff for María," his aunt told him, her smile fading a little. She raised her long, thin finger to point at Isaac as she lifted an eyebrow. "And remember what I told you."

"Yes, Tía, I remember." Isaac rolled his eyes and sighed as we both walked away from the party.

We were walking towards Sam's place, the streets were empty, I could hear the noises from insects and sometimes, when we walked by a house people were sitting on plastic chairs out in their front yard, laughing and cheerfully talking.

Isaac and I didn't speak a word since we left Andrea's. I didn't know if I was meant to talk or if he was going to talk. At one point I just wanted to get home so the awkward silence would be gone and the horrible effect of the mushroom would leave my body.

"Can I ask you a question?" Isaac asked after a long, awkward silence. I nodded. "And you'll answer with honesty?"

"Well, I've tried to be honest with every single question you've asked so far because of that stupid bet I made with Eli. I don't see why I wouldn't answer your question now – I mean, as long as it isn't something inappropriate."

It was true. Well, it kind of was. I've been answering all his questions because I said I would. But I didn't really mind answering the questions he was asking. It was actually interesting to talk to him. He wasn't *just* asking; he seemed like he really wanted to know, to understand. However, there *were* some things about me that I didn't want to share, no matter how carefree I felt or how trustworthy he looked. Some things I couldn't say out loud.

"What you said before, about your dad and about yourself? Was that somehow related? You feeling that way because he hurt you." He began. I felt my muscles tense before I could even think about a reaction. I didn't want to talk about this.

With a frown I looked up at the night sky, there were so many stars. "Johan is my father and I love him. I *adore* him but he hurt me deeply. Some scars don't always heal and contrary to popular belief, time doesn't always help. More often than not, it tends to deepen our wounds."

"Your pride will ruin you," he said with a slight hint of annoyance in his voice. It didn't bother me. He was probably right. "So, you wouldn't talk to him, even if you could?"

"I don't know, Isaac." I didn't mean to, but I snapped at him. I was getting annoyed too.

"It bothers you to talk about it?"

"Yes, as a matter of fact, it does," I answered with a cold, harsh tone as I walked away from him, suddenly feeling angry.

 **Chapter 14**

Location: La Cruz
Narrator: Aliana

I NEVER THOUGHT I'd like to have days off work. We didn't have days off at the Government, and over here, it seemed I had way too many. Best part? Junior did not care at all, I'd make a comment about having a slight headache and Junior would tell me to go home. So, I was going to take today off too.

I hadn't been able to sleep at all last night, thinking about pretty much everything. Taking pills didn't have the same effect as it used to and I didn't want to take more pills than I should. Technically speaking, the pills could make my heart stop. But it wasn't the first time I took so many pills. My body was kind of used to it or so I liked to believe...

I should have really stopped taking them. I always told myself I'd start tomorrow. I'd begin to reduce the dose. And I tried. I tried but I couldn't do it. There were too many things I couldn't deal with if I didn't take the pills.

I didn't get up from bed until 2.30 p.m. Sam had tried to wake me several times, telling me that breakfast was ready, but I just ignored her. I was too tired and didn't want to talk. Once I did decide to get out of bed, I took a shower. I had no clean clothes, so I had to wear clothes like the rebels wore, jeans and a worn-out T-shirt.

I had a killer headache. The cold empanada Sam left me for breakfast didn't help much, but at least I wasn't hungry anymore. I sat in the living room on the large sofa by the window. Sam's house was comfy; it was small but it was cosy.

It was raining. I was trying to read one of Sam's books about the importance of quantum mechanics. I rolled my eyes at it; only Sam could read something so boring. I was almost asleep when I saw a figure running through the rain, shrugging as if that would keep him from getting wet. Before I realised who it was, my frown deepened remembering our last conversation.

Isaac came into Sam's house. He was whistling as he went to the kitchen.

"Samirah?" he shouted as he looked for her in the kitchen.

"She's not here," I said loudly so he could hear. I didn't look away from the window, but I heard him stepping into the living room.

I didn't know whether to look at him or not. He didn't say anything either. I could just imagine him standing with his tough pose, his hands folded across his chest, and his cocky smile. I was surprised when I decided to turn around and saw him biting his lip, his arms hanging at each side of his body. He was tapping on his leg with his fingers. He looked awkward and soaked in water.

"You're wet,"

"Oh, yeah, didn't notice," he said with a cold sarcastic tone. "I'm leaving, though."

"Suit yourself." I sighed, trying not to give it much importance.

Isaac walked away. I thought he was gone when I heard the door closed. I was looking out the window waiting to see him walk away and disappear into the rain, but I saw nothing. Then I heard his footsteps as he walked back to the living room. I turned my head to see him, following him with my eyes as he walked towards me. He sat right next to me without even looking at me. His curly hair was wet and messy. Drops of water were falling down his face. He had on a white T-shirt, which was also wet. Because of that, it looked transparent and was stuck to his body. I could see his chest through it. I quickly looked back at the rain before I blushed again.

"You okay?" he asked. I nodded.

"So, if I ask you questions, will you answer me honestly like you said you would?"

"What do you think? I've answered all your questions until now," I reminded him. "I don't forget what I say."

I didn't mean for my tone to sound rude. I actually kept a neutral tone. However, I was pretty sure I sounded rude to him.

"You want me to leave?" he asked, looking at me for the first time today.

I should have said, *Yes, I want you to leave*, but as hard as it was for me to admit, I felt *lonely* and I wanted company. Saying yes would have been the prudent thing to do, I didn't want to keep answering questions about myself, but I wanted company. I wanted to hear a voice that wasn't the one inside my head.

"I don't know," I answered. "I guess that depends on whether you want to leave or stay."

He sighed. For a moment I thought he was going to leave and I felt a weird feeling in my chest. I didn't want him to leave. I did not want to be alone.

"I want to stay, but I don't know how to talk to you. And you don't make it easy either. I want us to be friends." I stared at him, waiting for him to continue. It didn't seem like he was quite finished yet. But judging by his face, I was just making the situation awkward.

"See what I mean?" he finally said.

"No, I do not," I said defensively. I didn't see what he meant. I was waiting for him to continue, I was being polite.

"Okay," he said as he stood up.

I watched and felt the sudden urge to ask him to stay. I quickly reached out to grab him by the forearm. It was like my reason was telling me to let him go but I was so tired of being alone.

"What do you want to know?" I asked, still holding him by the forearm so he wouldn't leave. He sat back down and I let go of him.

"It's hard when you dodge all my questions."

"No, I don't." I *totally* did dodge all his questions. "All the questions you've asked, I've answered. I don't see why I wouldn't have answered your questions. I have no secrets … that you might be interested in."

He slowly nodded. A long moment of awkward silence passed.

"Ask me what you'd like to know," I offered in a neutral tone. I knew I shouldn't get close to him, but I very much wanted to do so. I was even nervous; I don't think I've ever had a *real* friend aside from Roc and Mathias. "And if I don't like where the conversation is going, I'll let you know."

He looked at me for a long minute, or what felt like a long minute, maintaining intense eye contact. I was starting to feel a bit awkward when he broke the silence.

"How old are you?"

"Seriously?" I chuckled. My shoulders dropped as I relaxed. "I turned 17 in December. You?"

"The first time I saw you, I thought you were my older. I'm 19 – 28 January."

"My brother's 19 too."

"Why does Samirah call you Lynn?" he asked.

"My mother didn't like Aliana but Johan did. So, my parents named me Aliana Lynn. Pretty ugly name, I know. I don't like to be called Lynn, Sam and Nate do it to annoy me. Mostly Nate."

"What's your brother like?" he asked.

"Nathaniel is… annoying." I smiled, remembering Nate.

"Do you miss them? Your family, I mean." I nodded, "What's your mum's name?"

"Cynthia. Yours?"

"María."

"What about your father?" I asked. He told me that his father taught him a lot of things. I knew his father was dead because he always talked about him in past tense, but I knew nothing more than that.

"Nicolás, he was murdered when I was younger," he answered, and then he quickly changed the subject. "Why did you choose to be a soldier and not the same as Samirah … or something else?"

I didn't have a straight answer. I had to think about it, because no one had ever asked me that. Besides, I never thought about it much, I simply liked the occupation. I didn't know all the things Samirah or Nathaniel knew, but I could make bombs, hunt, use hundreds of different types of knives, defend myself using different types of fighting styles, and determine my enemy's weak points just by seeing the way they stood. You could drop me in the middle of nowhere and be sure that I would find a way to survive. I just liked it because I was good at it. I didn't depend on anyone else to survive in combat situations.

"That's kind of hard to answer," I shrugged, looking down at my hands trying to find a way to express why I loved it so much. "It's the only thing I'm passionate about, and I'm good at it. I would've hated working behind a desk for the rest of my life."

And oh, the adrenaline was worth it.

"And you?" I shook the feeling. I had to focus. "I know people work here, so what's your job?"

"I hunt and I keep the peace in the *barrios*." He smiled again. "We have animals here but some animals we let them run wild. Like we let the cows walk freely wherever they want, so if you see a cow in your backyard, do not be frightened. Also, I'm Miguel's security guy or something like that. I go around to the *barrios*. The city's pretty big and has numerous neighbourhoods. I go around the whole city seeing if the residents need anything. If they all doing good and there aren't any complaints or whatever, then I come back and report it to Miguel. It's pretty boring.

"Also, there are two more cities in this island but we're not really on speaking terms with one of them. Sometimes there's issues with people from one of the cities getting too close to our borderline, so I tell Miguel since I'm not allowed to get involved or visit any of the other cities. To be honest I'd rather do the part where I take care of the hunting."

I made a face.

"What? You people over there don't eat animals or something?"

"They do. I don't."

"What you eat then?" He laughed again.

"It isn't that I don't like meat. I just prefer not to eat it. But I eat fruits, vegetables, rice, cereal, food made of flour, I do eat fish though... I sometimes do eat meat here. I have to. Otherwise, I'll starve. All you guys eat is meat."

"Why don't you like it?" he gasped. Given the way he responded, it was as if I just confessed I killed a puppy or something.

"I'll tell you if you promise you won't laugh." I pointed at him, he rolled his eyes at me.

"I can try?"

"Long story short, I had a bunny when I was younger but my brother was allergic to their fur. One day, I held it a little too tightly and I heard something snap. I got scared and I told my brother. He said I killed it. I ran and hid under my bed. Since then whenever I ate meat, I thought back to my bunny and I just lost appetite." I told him shrugging, feeling my cheeks warming up a little. "As it turns out, I didn't kill the bunny. Apparently, Nate thought it was a good idea to get rid of the bunny and my obsession with tiny animals. To be fair, he was very allergic to it."

"I'm not laughing." Isaac covered his mouth with one of his hands, his hair still wet from the rain was dropping little drops of water on his shoulders. I could see the way his cheekbones were lifting up, he was smiling but was trying to keep a straight face.

And then he burst out laughing. I rolled my eyes but I found myself chucking with him, I punched his arm hard which caused him to laugh harder.

"That's why you didn't kill the rabbit that day in the woods, ain't it?" He asked me once he was done laughing. I nodded.

"Lynn-Lynn?" Sam shouted as she came inside the house. When Sam walked in the living, her eyes fell on Isaac, probably confused to see him there. "Hello, Isaac …?"

"Hey, Sam. I was looking for you,"

"What's up?" Sam asked, confused. Her wet hair was stuck to her head the same way her wet clothes were stuck to her body.

"I forgot," Isaac said, stretching his jeans with his hands.

"I'll be right back. I'm getting the whole floor wet!" Sam shouted as she ran up the stairs.

"So, friends then?" he smiled at me, extending his hand out for me to shake it.

His eyebrows were curved in a way that made him look like an innocent child. He looked kind of adorable looking at me.

"What about your threat?" I joked, he rolled his eyes and stared at me for a long second.

"If I'm being completely honest with you, I don't even remember what I said that day." He laughed, putting his hand through his wet hair. "Tell you what, how about we forget about how we met and we actually try to be friends?"

I thought about it and nodded to myself. I extended my hand out to him, he took it right away, smiling at me widely. "Friends, then."

"Well, I didn't see that coming." Sam's voice startled me. "Lynn, you look ill."

Sam came into the room all smiles. She had changed her wet clothes and was now wearing a big old jumper and jean short. She had a towel and was trying to dry her hair with it. She always looked so good and elegant, even when she wasn't wearing fancy clothes and her hair wasn't brushed. I remember when I used to wish I looked like Sam. I still did from time to time, to be honest.

"Are you okay?" Sam asked me, marking her accent when she spoke to me. She spoke even fancier than I ever had. She frowned at me and placed her hand on my forehead. Her hand was freezing. "I believe you have a temperature, Lynn, do you want anything?"

"Nope." I sighed, moving away from her hand "I'm just tired. Couldn't sleep last night. I'm going to lie down for a while."

Sam nodded. I stood up and walked away leaving Sam and Isaac talking about some broken arm.

*   *   *

I awoke in the middle of the night.

As soon as I did so, I knew it was going to be one of *those* days. I could feel the void in my chest growing deeper. The emptiness I felt was consuming me, getting deeper and deeper, and somehow my body felt heavy, too heavy to carry. I felt so tired.

Who knew emptiness could be so damn heavy?

It was three o'clock in the morning. After a bit of tossing and turning in my bed, I realised that I would have no success at falling asleep, so I went downstairs. I dragged my feet to the garden and tried to exercise for about half an hour but I felt so tired. I could see the tears filling my eyes and my chest tightening, why was I crying?

Why? Why was I like this? All I had was emptiness. I felt nothing but anger and sadness. I loved my family. I loved my mother, my father, and my siblings … but did I *really* love them? I didn't know what love was, so who was to say that I didn't make myself believe that I felt love towards them, when perhaps, in reality, there was nothing, no love. What did love feel like?

My family was my family; I was supposed to love them. *Love your family. Know where your loyalty lies*, my mother used to tell me. Several times she said she loved me, but I knew she was incapable of feeling such a thing, perhaps I *was* like her, and I made myself believe that I could feel such things. She would pretend to get angry at me sometimes but she couldn't be angry since she did not feel anything at all. However, she kept saying it: "I love you so, so much, my angel." She kept saying it again and again. Cynthia saw me as her daughter. She knew a mother was supposed to love her daughters, but I knew she felt nothing for me.

Perhaps that was what was happening to me. Perhaps I knew I should feel love but truly felt nothing but anger and hate. Perhaps it was true that I was rotten inside. I was not able to love but could only feel emotions that would make the horrible emptiness grow each day. Perhaps I was ill like Sam thought.

I hated being like this. I hated the fact that I wanted to change while knowing that I couldn't be anything but what I was. I shouldn't have fooled myself into thinking that maybe if I tried hard enough I could change. I wanted to change. I wanted to love, to really love, to feel something that wasn't this emptiness.

I couldn't fool myself. The signs were there, and one should not ignore the signs. Perhaps that was me, nothing but a void, an empty human being incapable of feeling anything that wasn't anger or hate. It was pathetic of me to try to be anything but what I was.

Perhaps I was sick after all.

# Chapter 15

Location: La Cruz
Narrator: Aliana

IT HAD BEEN weeks and I was very proud of the progress I'd made. I was very proud to say that I had friends. Natalí, Eli, Sebastián, and Isaac were my friends. It was weirdly satisfying and at times it made me a little anxious, knowing that there were people who were not 'emotionless', people who could have rejected me actually liked me enough to be-friend me. They liked me enough to want to talk to me every day and trusted me enough to tell me about their lives. I never thought I'd have something like that with someone other than Roc.

I woke up late this morning. I was in a rush and was tired because last night, instead of sleeping, I spent hours with Sebastián trying to figure out how to repair the Luxair but Sebastián was a little bit of a brute sometimes and there were times when I had to take deep breaths in order to keep calm, and that was when Sebastián picked up a habit of teasing me whenever I got frustrated.

When I got to work this morning, I was surprised to see Isaac and Eli already there. Isaac was standing next to Eli, who was showing Isaac his little buildings.

"Hello, Aliana," Eli greeted, he was way too hyped in the mornings.

"Hello, Elías," I smiled back at him, trying to say his name the way he had taught me, the Latin way.

It turns out that I had been pronouncing people's name wrong the entire time. The people of La Cruz spoke Spanish and names were pronounced differently. I did have some difficulties pronouncing some of the names, but I didn't know this was the reason. It confused me, but it also interested me.

"What's up, buddy," Isaac tried to high five me but I just stared at his hand. Rolling his eyes, he took my hand and made me high five him. "Flaco said you two were working late last night."

I snorted as I walked to my working place, "More like *I* worked, Sebastián tried to mock me the whole time."

"It is kinda easy to mock you though," Eli laughed, "You get mad so easily."

"That's true." Isaac joined in. I rolled my eyes and read the list Junior had written for me telling me what devices I needed to repair by the end of the day, which ones were going to be picked up and who was coming to pick them up. It was not a long list but it was so hot that the last thing I wanted to do was work.

I wanted to ask Isaac and Eli to help me but any hope I had banished the second I laid eyes on them. They were both concentrated in some toy car they were building. All I knew was that the toy cars worked with batteries and that they wanted to have a race to see who built the better car. It was interesting to see them working together, although that kind of beat the point of having a race but whenever Eli had a question or didn't know how to work with something, Isaac was right beside him, showing him how to make it work.

It was nice to see.

Narrator: Samirah

"Thank you for helping me." Natalí smiled while she picked up her books. She looked up at the clock hanging from my kitchen wall, her eyes widen. "Shit, we've been here for two hours, time flies."

"I don't mind, I enjoyed helping you." I smiled back at her, trying to calm my nerves. Why was I so nervous? I remained in my seat, watching her pack her things.

"So, how's you and Sebas?" Natalí didn't look at me while we talked and to be quite honest, it made it easier for me to talk to her. "You guys don't seem as close as you used to be."

"Yes, well, things are a bit awkward," I laughed, trying to make myself sound as calm as I could manage.

"I'm sorry if I'm intruding, I just... I don't know," She shrugged it off as she put the last book inside her bag. "I know we're not friends like you and Rebecca are but I don't know, sorry for asking."

"We *are* friends." I quickly told her.

Natalí stopped what she was doing and finally looked up at me, "We are?" She chuckled as she tucked a lock of hair behind her ear. "I mean, I know we talk from time to time and stuff but I thought, I don't know, that maybe you didn't really want to talk to me or something."

"I do," I told her, "honestly, I do but I just... I want to talk to you but I don't know what to say half of the time." I laughed, hoping I didn't sound like an idiot.

Natalí's smile grew wider. Her smile made her look ten times prettier and I was finding it hard to look away. I wanted Natalí to like me, to think of me as her friend but I always got so nervous around her that it was really difficult for me to speak. It was confusing and annoying because I had never felt like this aside from when I spoke to Grace back at the Government but that's different... Grace was freaking brilliant, she intimidated me and whenever we talked, I became a stuttering mess.

"So, you and Sebas...?" She asked again.

"I don't know, I like Sebas, he has helped me a lot and he's very nice but ... I don't know if I like him like he likes me? I don't think I've ever liked someone, I don't know; how does it feel like to like someone?" I asked her, looking into her eyes, hoping she had the answer to all the questions that were going through my mind.

"Why you asking me?" she laughed nervously, maintaining eye contact.

"Well, you're with Thiago, are you not? Certainly, you must love him."

"Just because someone's in a relationship, it doesn't always mean they're in love." She sighed, looking away from me, she sat back down and placed her bag on my kitchen's floor. "I care a lot about Thiago, I care about him but I'm just not in love with Thiago."

"Is that … isn't that the same thing?" I frowned, confused at her words.

Natalí smiled then, "No, it isn't." She shook her head, "You can love lots of people but I guess being in love is kind of like… a deeper level of love."

"Then why are you with him?" I frowned. It seemed like a waste of time to be with someone when you felt nothing for them.

"I don't know, because I have to? Because we've been together for years? I don't know, Sam, there's many reasons why just not the right ones."

I tried to ignore the fact that my heart skipped a beat when she called me Sam or ignore the way I felt my skin ignite when she looked at me and half smiled every single time she said *I don't know.*

"You don't *have* to," I told her, trying to make eye contact but she avoided looking at me. "You don't have to do any of it. Being in a relationship with someone, forcing yourself to act like you feel something when you don't."

"Nobody is forcing me to do anything." She replied, frowning while she looked out the kitchen's window, the sun was going down, it was a pretty shade of yellow mixed with red. When the sun hit her face, my eyes couldn't look away. I don't think I've ever seen anything so breath-taking in my life.

I couldn't take it anymore, I wanted her to look at me so badly. I softly cupped her face with my hand, turning her towards me. As soon as my fingers brushed her skin, I felt a current of electricity rush through my body.

"You wouldn't understand and I don't know how to explain." She whispered, for a moment I thought I wasn't the only one who struggled to find their voice. I was paralysed; I knew I had to move my hand away at some point but I couldn't bring myself to do so.

It was her who moved away. It was Natalí who looked away first and I had to fight myself not to reach out for her again.

"I could try to understand," I whispered back when I finally found my voice. "After all, I practically lived my life pretending not to feel anything at all."

"To be honest, not even I understand, Sam." Natalí stood up, grabbing her bag as she did so. "If anything, you more than anyone should understand that sometimes you have to pretend, maybe because you're scared or because you're used to it... but you just have to. It's complicated."

I stood up too, I felt myself growing anxious, trying to find an excuse that could make her stay longer, but it seemed she didn't want to talk about that subject and I couldn't find anything else to talk about. She was shutting me out, building some sort of wall and I wanted to fight my way in. But I didn't know how.

I followed after her as she walked out of my kitchen and stood by the front door, one of her hands grabbing the door handle and the other one holding her backpack. She looked down at her shoes and then up at me. The corner of her lips turning upwards.

"Thanks for helping me, honestly, I was struggling a lot." She told me, "And you should talk to Sebas, he'll understand."

I nodded, I didn't want her to go. This was the longest I had managed to talk to her without making a fool out of myself, I was getting over my slight fear and I was actually having a conversation with her. It was too short, the time wasn't enough, almost three hours weren't close to enough.

"Don't worry," I smiled, I was smiling way too much. "I like helping you. If you need help again just ask me."

She nodded and did something I was not expecting. It happened so quick, I barely had time to register it. Natalí leaned in and kissed my cheek. Her lips barely brushed my skin but it was enough to set my skin on fire. Before I had time to react, she was out the door, walking really fast down the street.

I raised a hand to my face, my cheeks felt warm, and my body felt *alive*. There was so much going on with my body right at that moment, I couldn't understand any of it.

What the hell was that and why did I feel it with Natalí?

Narrator: Isaac

"We're almost there, stop complaining." I rolled my eyes; hearing Aliana complain about how hot it was for the hundredth time.

"We have been walking for hours, Isaac." She complained, "I just don't understand, why today? I am actually going to burn alive, this heat is making me light-headed, also, there are too many mosquitoes."

To be fair, it really was getting hot. The sun was burning my skin, and mosquitoes were everywhere but I had to get Aliana out of town. Miguel's orders. I asked Natalí to keep Sam busy since Sebas gave me a bunch of excuses.

"We're here," I told her, turning around to face her with a huge smile.

Aliana looked around and did not look very impressed. "We've been here, we're still in the middle of nowhere. I want to go home, Isaac."

"You're not looking." Rolling my eyes, I took her hand and dragged her to stand next to me.

We were on a cliff, but it had a beautiful view. There was a meadow with different types of flowers in different colours: green, purple, red, blue, white, yellow, orange – all the colours you could think of. There was a little path made out of rocks that led to the end of the cliff. The view was amazing. There was an old tree with its branches curved to cover us, like a roof protecting us from the sun. Aliana walked over to the edge and looked down the cliff. She quickly held my arm and moved back. Down the cliff were rocks, as expected, but farther from the rocks was a lake. If you jumped from this side and not from the waterfall that was ten metres away from us, you would probably break your neck on the rocks. There was a river not too far away and very far in the distance, it ended and the sea began.

"Afraid of heights?"

"You could say that."

"I thought maybe you'd like this place, to clear your mind and stuff. It's pretty great, don't you think?"

She nodded, not saying anything at all, just staring at what was before us. I didn't say anything either. We sat in the meadow, not talking or doing anything, and it wasn't awkward, I didn't feel that need to fill the silence with pointless words. I was comfortable and she seemed to be too.

"What do you think is out there?" She asked me, looking at the horizon with a thoughtful frown. She looked beautiful right at that moment, it was hard not to notice just how beautiful she really was.

"I don't know. Nothing, I guess?" I shook my head, shooing the thoughts away.

"Surely there must be something."

"Like?" I chuckled, I never thought about any of this, it was pointless, these questions would never be answered.

"I don't know, people?" She shrugged, "I can't really believe that we're all that's left."

"My dad used to have this book, he'd write notes on it," I began, "There was some sort of map, but it was so much bigger than this. When I asked about it and where it all was, he used to joke and say the ocean swallowed it all. Cities under the ocean."

"Cities under the ocean," She muttered with interest, amazed by the idea of it, "I would love to see that."

"You like swimming?"

"I— I love it," She smiled at nothing, a slight shade of red covered her cheeks, "I think when you're underwater everything is calmer and there's silence, *peace*. Cities under water, can you imagine that, Isaac?"

"Maybe there aren't cities under the ocean," I told her after seeing the spark of interest in her eyes; I didn't want to give her false hope of anything. "My dad used to tell me a lot of made-up stories, you know, he had a huge imagination."

"Or, friend Isaac, but maybe there *are*," She shrugged again, looking at me with a grin, it was the first time I saw her smile in a while. "So, why are we here?"

I shrugged, not knowing what exactly to say, I couldn't tell her that Miguel asked me to get her out of town. She'd ask why and to

181

be completely honest I had no idea why, I just followed orders. All I knew was that leaders from the other cities were coming and Miguel wanted both Samirah and Aliana to be gone for the day. I did know why they were coming, Alex and Kiko, the leaders of the other two cities, they were coming to discuss the wall. A wall that Alex built around Kiko's territory with the excuse that we did not know if one day the Government was going to attack us. Miguel's father refused, as did Miguel when they asked him. Maybe they wanted something else, but I was willing to bet that they would mention the wall at least once.

"This is a nice place, I thought you'd like it. Plus, you haven't been here before." I said with a faint smile. "I come here often, this place is honestly breath-taking, helps you forget some stuff. Figured it'll help you since you've been... not *you* lately."

She didn't say anything, Aliana usually didn't talk much, but lately, she had been quieter than usual, there was something about the way she moved around, the way she went about the day, she just looked tired, as if her own body was too much weight for her to carry. She went work and she hung around with us but she wasn't really there.

We talked or more like I talked and she listened, nodding from time to time. I don't think she wanted to talk, I don't think she wanted to do anything at all.

After an hour or so, she told me she wanted to go back home but it had barely been a few hours, Miguel said to take as long as I could but without making it seem like I was keeping her away from town. So, when she said she wanted to go home, I told her that as a tour guide, I had to show her at least something else. I took her to the beach, and once we got there, she sat and played with the sand, watching the waves longingly as if she wanted nothing more than to run towards the water.

"My mum and I used to go to the beach a lot, study sea life. Those mornings were, I think, the few times in my life where I felt at peace with the world." That was the only thing she said during the whole afternoon.

 Chapter 16

Location: La Cruz
Narrator: Aliana

I THOUGHT THAT during my time here, I was never going to be saying these words out loud but I am going to see Luna.

This morning when I woke up, I went about my day, as usual, the same routine. I was working with Sebastián on the car, we were actually getting somewhere when a little boy came and told Junior that Miguel had sent to look for me.

Once I got to where Miguel was, he told a young man to take me to Luna's. "If you act like a child, then I will treat you like one," Miguel told me before the young man grabbed my forearm and dragged me to Luna's.

Fair enough, perhaps if I had gone to Luna's when I was first told to do so, I would not be in the situation I was then, standing outside Luna's house, looking at the front door. It was ridiculous but I was expecting for someone to come out and drag me in and beat the hell out of me. The young man pushed me, groaning at me as he did so.

"Go in or else I'll make you." He muttered through his teeth. Frowning, I contemplated the idea, perhaps if I had some random fight I won't have to see Luna.

The idea was tempting, but I did not want to get in trouble with Miguel. Besides, I promised Samirah I would try.

When I knocked on the door, an agitated Luna answered the door.

"Finally. I thought you weren't gonna come,"

Looking at Luna was something that made you both angry and scared. I hated the fact that there was a part of me that was scared of her, I hated to admit it but I was. I could never trust her, no matter how insignificant she seemed at times, or how crazy she looked right at that moment. She walked inside her house and I followed until we were in her living room.

"What do you want?" I asked coldly and disinterestedly as I followed her. She walked out of the living room, walking really fast, waving her hands about as she moved stuff around her house.

"I have been calling for you for days!" She said desperately, not looking back at me. She stopped walking in the middle of her kitchen, with one hand she scratched her forehead, her hair was in a messy bun and lots of her hair were coming out of it, she looked like she was about to lose her mind.

"Oh, yes!" She turned to look at me with a bright smile and her eyes wide open, she began to walk away again, I followed. "Your father has something very important to tell you."

"Johan? You talk to him?" I asked, frowning as I tried to keep up with her. Her house was pretty, old, and cosy, a family home.

She came to a stop when we entered her living room again, she pushed the door and with hurry began to look through her drawers.

"I asked you a question, why do you talk to father?" I asked again, louder this time.

"I told you, I talk to him from time to time," She replied without looking at me, still searching for whatever. I frowned, confused.

"Whatever Johan has to tell me doesn't matter now." I turned around to leave, I could feel myself growing angrier, this woman was crazy, she didn't know what she was saying, she probably didn't even talk to Johan.

"I wouldn't leave if I were you." Luna stopped me, she walked towards me and tried to grab my hand, I moved away. "Do you care about Cynthia?"

"Of course I care about my mother."

"Then you should stay," She turned away once again. I should have left, Luna could not be trusted, and I knew that, but I still couldn't bring myself to move.

I stayed and waited until Luna found what she was looking for, an old communicator. It was vintage, white and blue, a little-rounded thing with a square dialling pad and a plain platform for setting it up on the floor. When Luna put the communicator on the floor, a blue light came out of it. It was so old that I could see the little pixels on the LED as Luna dialled a number. The communicator quickly changed, showing a 3D image of Johan's body. It looked exactly like Johan but with no colour, just a blue light. With the communicator's camera, Johan could probably see us as we saw him.

Johan looked as he always did, dressed in probably a black suit, a white-collar shirt, and a black tie. His hair was combed as he had always kept it. He was shaved, and as impeccable as any other citizen of the Government. I felt a wave of happiness through my body upon seeing him after so long. Even if I didn't want to talk to him, even if our relationship was the worst, Johan was my father, I missed him. But that feeling was quickly replaced by anger and disappointment.

As a father, Johan wasn't supposed to hurt his daughter. As a husband, he wasn't supposed to disrespect his wife. But he did and it was easier for me to be angry at him than to act like nothing ever happened. Sometimes I wondered what would have happened to my life if I hadn't allowed myself to drown in my anger. Perhaps my life would have been different if I allowed myself to feel pain instead of shoving pills down my throat every couple of hours. How different would my life have been at this moment? Maybe I would've been a better person.

Johan didn't say anything. He just stared at me from head to toe. I remembered how I was dressed, untidily. My hair was out. Back at the Government, girls weren't supposed to have their hair out, it didn't look "smart". Instead of the usual bun most the women wore, I had my hair in a high ponytail.

"Aliana," Johan greeted with a smile, his face lit up with obvious joy. I felt relieved to know that after all I said and done to him, he still felt joyous to see me. Maybe he was still waiting for the day I would go running into his arms like I used to do when I was a little girl.

Too bad I wasn't a little kid anymore and I knew perhaps a little too much to think so highly of Johan. Sometimes I found myself wanting to tell him that I was sorry, wanting to have a normal father/daughter relationship with him but no matter how hard I tried, I couldn't forget what I already knew. And I couldn't fix all that had been broken. All that *he* broke.

"You look different," He didn't look nervous at all, but I knew he was. He didn't know what to say to me. And to be honest, I didn't know what to say to him either but for different reasons.

"How's Mum? Nate?" I asked, clearing my throat. "Roc? Have you seen Roc?"

"Well, Roc is… At first, he was confused. He knows it is not true that you've been kidnapped. He came to me looking for answers. He looked pretty shaken, though,"

Oh, Roc, if only you had trusted me when I asked you to. But then again, if Roc would've come with me, many things would have been different now. If people here didn't like me, I was sure they would have loathed Roc. I have no doubt Roc would have been murdered by the first week among these people.

"Nathaniel is doing okay. He doesn't stop working," Johan said, looking down at his hands.

"And Mum?" I quickly asked, remembering what Luna had said. "How's Mum?"

"Cynthia is a whole different case," he began. My anxiety grew. "I need you to pay attention and listen to me very carefully because you have to understand something before I tell you about Cynthia."

"What is it?" I was getting worried now. I could pick up Johan's nervous tone of voice.

"To create a better tomorrow, we must remember the yesterday," Johan carried on, ignoring my question. "To understand how we came to be, you have to understand what we do, why we do it and how it started.

186

"Since the beginning of time, the human race has always been at war, it has always been a constant fight. The last war that was recorded in human history started about a century ago. Everybody was the enemy. Refugees had nowhere to go, they weren't welcomed in other countries, nobody wanted the "enemy" living right next door. And when help was needed, the only help people received were an influx of soldiers with tanks and bombs. Soldiers who did more harm than good. There was no way to prepare human race for the Red War, billions died for no reason at all. It is said blood ran through the streets like water, nothing washed out the blood of the innocent. The Red War was the most inhumane act in human history, it destroyed us; war brings the worst out of us, Aliana.

"We came from a very wealthy and advanced country. Our ancestors were enslaved by King Morin. We were one of four monarchies, and his kingdom was the wealthiest and the strongest, making it the most important one. Judging by the information we have, it was when his experiments came to light that war began. King Morin wanted to control the people, keep them in line and keep himself in power. They wanted to demolish the monarchy and Morin wanted to rule over all the monarchs. Many countries and leaders supported him. Not because they shared his ideas but because of what was promised to those who stood by the king.

"The king had his people carry out experiments with slaves. They were his property, he believed there would be no repercussions for his actions. In a year, more than 10 thousand were killed under his experiments. People got tired of seeing their loved ones die for a greedy man who had no consideration for his people or for human life. So, people rebelled against the system, they didn't stand a chance but their anger, their grief, and their impotence were their strength and the other monarchs offered their help to put an end to Morin. My great-grandfather, Alexander, and his brother Aiden Keenan led their people in time of darkness. We were opposed to these experiments, we fought to end it; we didn't create this idea of the Government, we were the first subjects of the experiments.

"They brought an end to the cruelty Morin and his allies had put the world through. But it was too late, the damage had already been done and half of the world was already in ruins. They were threatened by the other monarchs, they were supposed to step down and leave the kingdom to a fitted king. But Aiden... Aiden didn't want to step down, he fought for his people and he was not going to freely give the power to a foreign ruler. Aiden became obsessed with Morin's experiments and he succeeded where Morin failed. Aiden created the perfect army; 12 emotionless soldiers who were loyal to nobody but Aiden. That's how he got rid of whomever that was a threat."

"How do you even know all this?" I asked him, trying to make sense of it all. I didn't understand why he was telling me this, I didn't care about any of it; I just wanted to know how my mother was.

"Recordings, files, books, newspapers..." He sighed, "It is all kept in the CB, nothing was ever destroyed, we just took everything with us. Everything worth remembering is kept in the CB. That's how we know that it was very unlikely that anybody survived the Red War. The Last thing we know is that North America became a threat, the entire world heard about what Aiden had done, they knew Aiden and Alexander controlled most of the continent, they wanted them dead. It wasn't long until nuclear weapons were used. We destroyed what was left of the world and in his desperation to fix it, Aiden selected people who could improve the human race in his eyes, people who would help him build a new place, a *better* place, leaving millions of their own people to die. That's how we ended up here, that's how the Government was born. They travelled across the ocean to this island in the middle of nowhere. This land never belonged to us, we stole it. We came here and we took their land, we killed and tortured people until we made them our slaves. After all the pain and the suffering that had been inflicted on us, we were so quick to do the same to others..."

Johan took a moment to compose himself, it seemed the subject affected him. He was a man with principals, morals... knowing that he was part of something that hurt so many people probably kept him up at night, convincing himself he was to blame for all those who died ages ago, trying to find a way to redeem himself, to fix what his family broke.

And yet he couldn't do right by me.

"Within days, Aiden neutralised the people and claimed the island as his. At first, Aiden wanted to do the procedure on a few of his soldiers and the natives. He had big plans for these islands, he had the bridge built and he was ready to start the constructions over at this side. What Aiden didn't see was that the people sympathised with the natives. Not everybody agreed with Aiden and soon they began to speak up. That's when the people rebelled, that's when the strikes, the marches, and the violence began. That's when Aiden's idea of a perfect world began to shatter right under his nose because the person who led this movement was his own brother, Alexander Keenan."

"Wasn't he your grandfather?" I frowned, Johan nodded. "I thought he was the Board's leader, not some revolutionary…"

"He fell in love. He loved a native and that love made him stand up to his own brother, to all that was wrong." Johan almost smiled and anger shot through me, making my head spin. "Alexander was leading a movement that would rid people of the procedures, that would give them back their free will and their lives. However, not everything went the way that it was supposed to. In fear of losing power, Aiden ordered every civilian to go through the procedure. When Alexander found out about this he knew he had to do something. But it was too late, by the time Alexander was ready to do something, Aiden had already succeeded.

"This procedure was done and still done today is extremely dangerous and inhumane. We hid away every person's emotions, making the people easy to manipulate with an implant, a chip. People were no longer a problem. Everybody does as they are told. Nobody complains, nobody fights. Nobody has free will, and that was what Aiden wanted from the start: people who were easily controlled. It was then when the natives, in fear of going through the same as our people, rebelled against the system. Alexander helped them escape and when Aiden was gone, he took his rightful place as leader of the Board."

"It seems to me, you're leaving pieces of the story out," I reminded him, watching his every move. "They killed a third of our population, they blew up the bridge—and now you're telling me your grandfather helped them?" I couldn't help but laugh, "The apple doesn't fall far from the tree, I see."

"Be respectful—"

"The only reason I haven't walked away is because I'm waiting for you to tell me what any of this has to do with my mother," I interrupted him. Seeing him made my body tremble with anger. "So you either tell me about my mother or I'm walking away."

Johan sighed, looking away from me. He hid his hands in his pockets and his whole attitude changed, he was distant and cold. "One of the many purposes of these chips is to block a part of the brain, or that is the intention. Right now, there are few people who know how to do this process. Sometimes when we're doing the process, we make mistakes. Nothing is perfect. And this is a very dangerous procedure, consisting of inserting the chip in the right location and making sure it is well attached to the brain. You never know how an individual is going to react to this procedure. The problem is that the possible mistakes are not able to be spotted visually. And we, the few who know about this potential problem, can't keep an eye on everyone who undergoes the procedure. Sometimes the problem is that the chip is cracked.

"The chip, trying to do its job and not succeeding, sends electric shocks to the cracks through its microscopic tentacles, which are supposed to be joined with the whole brain. The cracks are created when a chip isn't well placed. When this happens, some of the person's brain's electrical signals that are supposed to bypass the emotions allow certain emotions to pass through the gaps. This can make the subject paranoid or confused. Some people in this position are capable of feeling one thing only, it usually is the strongest emotion... all this makes them unstable. This leads to sickness, a sickness that we're trying to cure. But once the chip's tentacles are inserted, there is no way to readjust them. As soon as they touch the brain, they burrow under the surface, which is why we can't readjust them without severely damaging the brain tissue. Cynthia and I were working on a cure, a way to fix that problem. Are you following?"

I must have been making a face. The truth was that I was struggling a little, even if he was giving me the less complicated explanation. I understood that this was about what made people emotionless. I also understood that I could feel, that I had emotions and I wasn't supposed to. This was what Sam kept writing about in her journals. This was what she meant when she said there was something wrong with me. I had a thing in my head that didn't work properly and that made me the way I was.

"If you say these people aren't stable, why don't you just do the process again?" I asked, looking away from Johan, almost turning around so he wouldn't see me. I had to swallow hard before asking the one question I've always been afraid of asking. "Is there a way to cure this?"

"I'm getting to that," Johan cleared his throat, "As I said, trying to adjust the chip so all the tentacles go through the brain tissue, can be very dangerous to the brain, perhaps even lethal… there have been experiments where we test people who we know have an issue with the chip, we're trying to understand how—"

"The pills," I interrupted him, not really caring about what he was saying, my brain was working too fast for me to even try to understand what he was saying. "The pills you give me? You—are you experimenting with me? What have you done to me?"

"Do you really think I'd do that to you?" Johan asked through gritted teeth, interrupting me. There was hurt written all over his face and for a second, I felt joy. "You are my daughter, I would never let anything hurt you."

I looked up at him then, how dare he say such thing? How could he stand there and let those words out of his mouth?

"The pills not only help you with your anger issues; they also help you to remain hidden when they start seeking, don't you understand by now, Aliana? The people you grew up with, the people you called friends, *they* are your enemy. To them you are broken, you are a threat to the peace, to the Government. I gave you those pills because

I hoped that they could help you, but we both know they did more wrong than right—"

"Save it, Johan. Just tell me what's going on with Mum," I shook my head, interrupting him. I didn't want to know anything more.

"Are you ever going to stop treating me like I am not your father?" he suddenly asked with hurt all over his voice, it was enough to make me look up at him. He seemed tired as he waited for an answer I didn't have.

Johan sighed as he slightly shook his head before continuing.

"As I said before," he continued, "a few people know about this procedure. Cynthia and I were looking for a cure, as we had been told to find a way to cure the unstable. However, in addition to doing that, Cynthia and I started to do research into something else. We wanted to… *unblock* what had been blocked by the process. We wanted to remove the chip. At first, I wanted it for only Cynthia, but she said she would never hide from her own people. It was everybody or no one.

"When Samirah left, something snapped inside of your mother. She knew she had no emotions at all. She wanted to feel something, to feel pain for the loss, to be angry or frustrated. Because of this, she focused on her work. You saw her yourself. She's barely at home. And her hard work paid off. She found a way to remove the chip. We didn't know if it was safe, the first tests ended up with subjects not waking up at all. But she didn't give up, she wanted to do it to herself. She promised me she wouldn't do it, it was too dangerous. And then you left. Cynthia was the closest she could be to be devastated, and it… it could have driven her mad if she could feel anything at all. I tried to talk to her, but she pushed me away. Weeks later she asked me again to do the process. I thought she had forgotten the idea, but clearly, I was wrong. No matter how many times I told her you two were okay, she wouldn't believe me. She—"

"Where is my mother?" I took a step closer to the hologram.

"She's fine now," he answered me, looking down at me. "She had one of her students do the procedure on her, to reverse the process. It had to be more than one person in that room but only one was captured, Cynthia refuses to give up the other person. Apparently, she was awake during the whole thing. The young man who was there, the boy who assisted her is no longer with us; the student who got away could be dangerous to the government. They know too much. Your mother had a lot of students, it could be anyone. As for the procedure, I don't know how, but it worked. Cynthia did it. The first week, her emotions were all joy and happiness. She wanted to look for you and Samirah, but she couldn't, and that's when her emotions began to unbalance. All the sadness and pain she couldn't feel before overwhelmed her like waves. She started talking to people. Her voice was being heard. People started to ask questions. You know that every time a person disappears, we blame the rebels for it. So, if rebels had taken our daughters, what was stopping them from taking others? And that's when the board had to step in."

"I don't *care* about the board. My mother. How is my mother? Where is she?" I desperately asked.

"Cynthia is in prison. They want to do the process on her to prevent this from happening again, but she will not bear it. I'm trying to find a way. I'm running tests to see if I can change something to make the process less dangerous. The board can't risk anything happening to Cynthia. If something went wrong, it could deliver the wrong message to the people."

"Why don't you do something?" I asked him, "Do something like what you did with me. Give her the pills and control her. Don't let them hurt her, Johan."

"My hands are tied," he muttered, clenching his jaw. "If I show even the slightest hint of disapproval again, they won't allow me to take part in further decisions about this matter. I can't let that happen, I already changed their mind when they wanted to get rid of her."

I couldn't believe what I was hearing. Cynthia had been his wife for twenty years, but he wouldn't even take any risks for her.

"How can you be so calm? She's your wife. She has always been by your side, even if we all know you don't deserve it. Twenty years, Johan. Doesn't that mean anything to you? You owe her." I was disappointed and hurt, and Johan didn't seem to care. Because of this, I snapped at him like I always did. "You can help her; you just don't want to. When Luna was in my mother's place, you helped her. And when you helped this savage, you didn't care what she did or who she hurt. To help her get out you allowed her brother to slaughter and burn innocent people; you didn't care who died as long as Luna was safe but you can't do the same for my mother?"

I tried to blink the tears away, I couldn't look at Johan so I turned to look over at Luna, she had her arms crossed and didn't look very happy to be there. I was almost sure that if it was up to her, she would already have slapped me a few times for talking to Johan like this. I knew I shouldn't talk like that to my father. I owed him respect, but what respect could I have for him when he had no respect for others?

Johan had nothing else to say to me, at least he had no comment on what I said. I tried to walk away, tired of Johan's words. However, when I walked by Luna, she grabbed my arm, dragging me back into the room. She was quick and strong, I give her that.

"Listen to what he has to say," Luna told me, I shoved her hand away, glaring as she just stared back with an unbothered expression.

"Don't ever touch me again." I snapped. I was so angry that I felt the need to hurt them both. I felt the need to hurt the three of us. "I don't understand," I turned to Johan, it took all I had in me to keep my voice from shaking. "I really don't understand. I know you don't love Mum, but you must feel *something* for her. She's been with you for twenty years. She has been your partner, your friend, for *twenty* years. And here you are, calling and having weekly conversations with this... woman. Why aren't you doing something, Johan? You owe it to her! Don't let them hurt her. You said yourself that the process can be lethal. Do it for us – for Nate and Sam. Help her."

"I'm *trying*. If you'd let me finish, then you'd understand why I'm here." Johan was coldly distant and his tone was sharp as ice. My words hurt him. He was stepping back. I knew it was a matter of time until one day Johan would get tired of trying with me. "We need your help."

"But I know nothing about this, Johan. You know I know *nothing*. I'm not like you guys. Sam knows, why didn't you tell her instead? I can't help you!" I felt desperately helpless. I could do nothing for the person I would give my life for.

"I need your skills; you are the best at what you do. I need you for this, if everything else fails, I need you to step up." Johan took his hands out of his pockets and began to play with his wedding ring. It was something he did when he was nervous.

That was the first time Johan ever said that I was good at what I did. He had been so angry at me when I finished in second place, so disappointed. He wouldn't even talk to me after that. He told me a bunch of things I'd rather forget, and then he just went to his office and stayed there the whole day.

"Do what?"

"If I don't find a way to help Cynthia, she will need to leave this place, this place is not safe for her."

"You're joking?" I raised an eyebrow at him, laughing humourlessly. "You have got to be joking. What makes you think she wants to be here? She's not going to leave all her life for *this*."

"There's no other way, Aliana," Johan said. I was going to argue, but he carried on, saying, "There's a lot of things you don't know, things that you will find out in your own time. For now, all you need to know is if I don't find a way to fix this, you will have to get her out, no matter what. You have to understand that what Cynthia did was the highest form of treason. If I don't find a way to fix this, they will kill her and eventually kill me too."

"She can't be here!" I snapped again. My mother was not made for this place, not with Luna here.

"Would you rather her be there or dead, Aliana? I would rather have her miles away. At least she'd be alive. Either way, she will not be your concern. She will go to another place, another city. I just need you to trust me."

I swallowed hard, my mother couldn't die. If that happened I would never forgive him.

"Luna will let you know if something changes. And speak not a word of this to Samirah until I say so. Aliana, whether you like it or not, this is happening and you will have to be prepared." Johan left no room for argument and without saying goodbye, his figure disappeared, leaving behind only the pixelated blue light. I was staring right into the light, thinking about everything and nothing. My eyes were quickly filled with tears. I needed to sit down.

"Johan will do everything he can to protect her. He cares about her," Luna told me as if her opinion mattered to me. Her voice was like nails on a chalkboard. "And even if he didn't care for her, he wouldn't let anything happen to her."

"If he cares so much for her, why does he still talk to you?" I snapped, looking straight into her eyes, I hated her. "And what would you know? You are no one, you know nothing."

Luna had a half smirk on her face, a smirk that made my blood boil. She raised her hands up as if saying 'whatever you say.' I never wanted to fight someone so much.

"If this plan Johan has doesn't work and we have to bring my mother here, where will she be staying?" I asked in a demanding tone. I needed answers.

"That is not for me to tell you," Luna answered calmly. "When Johan thinks you should know, he will be the one to tell you."

"It's my mother we're talking about! How do you two just tell me this and expect me to let her go with whoever and do nothing? Johan said you would tell me."

"Johan said that *when* he makes a decision, I will tell you, nothing more."

"You're loving this, aren't you?" I asked her, she snorted and shook her head at me with a smug expression. "I have never in my life hated someone as much as I hate you." I turned around to leave and return to where I had come from, far away from Luna.

But before I could leave, she grabbed me by my forearm again, this time actually hurting me. I didn't like that she thought she could touch me whenever she wanted. It was the second time she had done it today. There would not be a third. I turned around, so we stood face to face, I was surprised to find Luna no longer smug but irritated and angry. She looked somewhat violent.

Finally.

"You should really drop the whole spoiled-little-angry-girl act; how far do you think this attitude will take you? Your dad isn't here to make up excuses for you, and you can't hide behind mummy's skirt anymore. Give it a rest or someone will get tired of it, and they will put you in your place."

Luna was finally showing her true colours. She was finally showing me the Luna I had many nightmares about, the cold woman who was willing to kill, the woman who hurt people with no remorse.

"Oh, you want to give it a try?" I smirked, daring her with my eyes. "I can defend myself this time."

Luna understood and my words must have felled on her like stones because her face dropped and she stared at me with empty eyes.

She didn't say a thing. I wanted to pressure her for answers, I wanted to get her to say it, to say what she did to me but she didn't move a muscle, like a person who was lost in their own mind. This was pointless. I was never going to get answers from Luna, no matter if I wanted them, I would never know why she did what she did.

"You stay the hell away from me or I swear to God, not even Miguel will be able to get me off you," I told her before I walked out of her living room and I ran all the way to the woods behind Sam's house.

Tears were running down my face. Anger flooded in my veins.

I tripped and fell on a tree, and I felt it all way too vividly, the anger, the pain, the memories. It was like a mist in my mind, it clouded it and I was *so* tired of always holding it in. It made me physically sick.

I lifted my fist and I threw punch after punch. I felt my blood dripping from my knuckles, I heard the wood cracking. It was her face I saw; it was her face I wanted to hit.

I hated her.

I hated the fact that a small part of me was actually terrified of her. I hated that I wanted her to explain herself and tell me why she did it. I hated Luna with an intensity that wasn't healthy. I hated everything that was ever touched by her.

I hated myself.

 **Chapter 17**

Location: La Cruz
Narrator: Isaac

SEBAS WAS SWEATING. His face was red from running, and his breathing was harsh. I laughed at my friend's red face as I stood up to greet him, placing my hand on his right shoulder. I was with Miguel, he wanted to let me know what we were going to do from now on, Miguel didn't trust Alex or Kiko, he wanted to double security just in case.

"What's up?" I asked, giving Sebastián time to catch his breath. "Need a little water?"

"Shush. I need you to come with me now," Sebas managed to say between breaths. "Into the woods, about two hours away from here. If we run, we can make it in an hour and a half."

"If we take the bikes, we might make it in one," I said as I rushed to the bikes, walking fast as we made our way far from Miguel's house. If it was a problem, I would try to fix it before telling Miguel.

Sebas got on his bike and was leading the way. I followed. I had never doubted Sebastián. If he said it was important, then it was important. We had gotten to the halfway point, but the bikes wouldn't go any deeper into the woods. We had to ditch them and run.

"What's going on?" I asked while we were running.

"I didn't know who else to tell. I'm sorry." Sebas was starting to sound a little worrisome to me. I frowned. Sebas continued. "You can't tell Miguel, okay? I don't know if people have already seen them, no one has complained yet. And I couldn't let that happen, 'cos, after all, she is Sam's sister, you know."

"What happened, Sebas?" I grabbed hold of my friend's jumper, maybe something had happened to Aliana. Maybe she did something again.

Sebas narrowed his eyes as he looked from my face to my hand's grip on the sleeve of his jumper. I let go of the hold on Sebas's sleeve. He kept walking without making a comment about my reaction, he just kept walking quickly but quietly.

"Do you think what José says is true?" Sebas asked, not looking back at me.

"José talks too much shit – so much shit that his ass must be jealous of his mouth." I felt a bit of anger at the question. Of course I didn't ever believe what José said, Miguel said it was all a lie. "She came to look for her sister. You know that."

"But Samirah always said how her sister was too given to the Government. Remember she said how them soldiers were trained to manipulate and lie in order to adapt to situations. She basically said they were the bad guys. And catch this. Samirah doesn't trust her. Like, yeah, sure, Sam loves her sister, she cares about her but whenever we talked about her sister, she said she was damaged, that her brain needs fixing. And she tried to kill José, for no reason at all. Samirah always said her sister was *special*. She always said she needed help, implying that her sister wasn't good."

"And what's your definition of *good*? José's the good guy now, huh, Flaco?" I was being defensive. Sebas raised his eyebrows at me. I heard Samirah talk about her family a few times. Whenever she did say something about her sister, she looked guilty about the way she talked about her. But I knew Aliana. There was nothing bad about her, maybe her anger controlled her a little bit, but that could happen to anyone. "Get to the point, Sebas."

I waited for an answer, impatient. My mood had changed; the air grew thick with each passing second. It bothered me, the way he spoke about her bothered me. The things Samirah thought of Aliana bothered me. Aliana wasn't the most talkative, she wasn't always nice, but she wasn't what Samirah made her out to be. I spent days with her, hours talking to her, studying her. Fair enough, at first, I spent time with her because Miguel asked me to, I didn't understand why Miguel cared so much but I followed orders and I did as he asked. At first, I thought she was arrogant, stupid, spoiled, and many other things but as she opened up, as she began to talk to Eli and me, my opinion changed. I knew her loyalty to the Government ran deep, but she wasn't damaged.

"You know damn well she a soldier!" Sebastián whispered. I didn't answer, I had nothing to say. I didn't want to argue with Sebas so when he turned around and began to walk, I followed.

"What if José is right?" Sebastián asked after a while. Hesitation in his voice. "What if people from the Government actually did send her to investigate us and then attack us from the inside? Like that old movie you like so much, the one with the queen you were obsessed with, the blonde girl? That freaking movie, you remember? The one about the horse?"

"You're saying that Samirah and Aliana are two Trojan horses? Are you okay?"

"Not Samirah. Let's be honest: I like the girl, but she sucks at lying. And when she has to do something that involves physical work, she's useless. But her sister? We know she was in the armed forces and is good at defence and whatnot. What if she still playing for the Government? I mean, she's actually cool, but what if she's just *playing* it cool?"

I stopped moving for a moment. "Oh, because Samirah couldn't be pretending too?"

"Do you really think Miguel would've allowed Samirah to get so close to Luna if he didn't trust her?" Sebas asked with a knowing look in his eyes. I looked away from him. "Don't let the fact that she's a pretty girl cloud your judgment, Isaac, Miguel doesn't trust Aliana, why else would he have you watching over her all day? Think with your head for once."

"It's not like that, man," I pushed his finger away from me when he tried to point at my head to make a point. "Yeah, she's beautiful and all but she's my friend. Like… Natalí kind of friend."

"Whatever you say, just… think for a second, yeah?"

"You got proof of what you saying? Or you just saying it because of what José said?"

"That's why I brought you here because you'll know what to do. If they find out, they probably will make Sam pay too."

"Show me then." That was all I said as we carried on walking.

If Aliana was really still working for the Government, that meant she was a traitor, which meant that Miguel would probably have her killed. We weren't very fond of traitors, not after the war with Príncipe City, Kiko's city.

After what happened with José, people would believe anything. If what Sebas was saying was true, then Aliana had to leave or else she'll be killed. Sebas chose the worst person to come to. I didn't know what to do. I had to go to Miguel, I had to tell him but I couldn't, I didn't want to, I didn't think I was going to be able to watch her die.

Sebastián stopped for a second and ducked. I followed as we crawled through the bushes, barely making a noise. It felt like we were going in slow motion. I wanted to hurry things up. I just wanted to know. Sebastián hid behind a bush. I quietly did the same. He pointed at something with his finger. I looked in that direction and saw nothing but trees. But then two men dressed in dark green uniforms started to move around, coming closer to us.

There was a tall one, around my height. The other one was a bit shorter but judging by the way he carried himself, his height was not a problem for him. They both were carrying rifles, and they both looked exactly the same as Aliana looked when I first saw her – except these two were dressed in a different colour. But it was the same air of confidence in the way they walked, the way they stood.

They were soldiers.

The two guys were about ten steps away from us. I could see them perfectly now. The tall one was white. His chestnut hair was all over his face. He had a very innocent face, but what stood out the most about him were his eyes, which were light blue, like the clear water at the beach. It made him look like one of those winter wolves I'd seen in movies.

The short one had a sly smile on his face. He looked badass with his weapons and the way he stood. His skin was light caramel, darker than mine, and his head was shaved. The bridge of his nose was thin and delicate, but his nostrils were a bit wider. His eyes were grey.

The short one turned around, his back turned to us. They looked very delicate, but at the same time, they looked badass. Just like Aliana did.

"I think we should go back, Roma," the white boy said. His accent the same as Aliana's, very elegant compared to the way I spoke.

"I think so too," the man called Roma replied. He looked at something on his wrist. A blue light came out of the device. I always did like the technology they had at the Government. "sundown's in about three hours. We've got four to make it to the bridge walking at a normal pace, avoiding the villages of course."

"Do you really think we'll find her, Mathias?" Roma asked before drinking from a water bottle. "It's been a while now."

"I don't know. I still have hope we will," the one called Mathias replied. "Nathaniel said she left a note, but she hasn't communicated. She hasn't let us know if she's okay or where she is. She surely must know we all worry. She must know *I* worry."

"Don't say things like that. Someone could hear you," Roma snapped quietly at his fellow soldier.

"But it's true. And I do hope we find her," Mathias replied calmly. The other guy just sighed.

"What do you think Roc will do if he finds her? He was the first one to volunteer. And then you," Roma said. It seemed like he wanted an explanation, but not quite. Roma's tone had a note of jealousy in it.

"We all want to find her. She has a lot of explaining to do, she shouldn't have left." Mathias replied, "I know at some point she will help us. She can make all this right if she wanted to."

"I think you think too much of her." Roma said in a bitter tone, "Nobody held a gun to her head, she did this because she wanted to."

"I still don't understand why you don't trust her." Mathias snapped, shaking his head in annoyance. "She's family, Roma, you trust me?"

"Of course I do—"

"Then trust me when I tell you to trust her." Mathias interrupted, his voice was strong and his posture firm, leaving no room for any more discussion. "We have to keep looking."

"Well, of course we do. It's Aliana. Everybody wants to find her." Roma sighed with annoyance, as he followed Mathias into the woods.

They were looking for Aliana.

* * *

I kept going over and over the conversation, trying to find something new, something that would make sense. I couldn't move. The soldiers were long gone, but I still couldn't bring myself to move away from the bushes.

Mathias, Roma, and Roc. Those were the names of the soldiers looking for Aliana. Perhaps there were more, but those were the ones I knew of for now. It could be true; Aliana could be working with the Government still. She was a lie. Maybe she had manipulated me. And Miguel would be so disappointed.

I stood up and sprinted back to the city. My head was spinning. Sebastián was running after me, asking me questions about Samirah, but I couldn't think straight. Aliana lied.

We were halfway back to the motorbikes when Sebas finally caught up with me and violently turned me around.

"Isaac, you can't say anything," he shouted. "At least give me time to get her to somewhere safe, okay? I'll get Sam out, and then you'll tell Miguel. Just wait, please."

Sebas was ready to leave with Samirah if he had to. He cared for her. He was so sure of it, he was risking getting hurt, risking dying over this girl, a girl that didn't feel the same way about him.

"I'm an idiot," I blurted out, looking away from Sebas to the ground. I was losing my composure. "If what you said turns out to be true, she was lying right to my face. Miguel will never forgive me for allowing Eli to get so close to her."

"It ain't your fault. You didn't know what she was doing."

203

"You go talk to Samirah, see what you get from her. They didn't mention her name but we have to be sure." We started to walk to the bikes. "I'll talk to Aliana."

"If Samirah finds out, she'll flip. She can say whatever about Aliana but Sam is very overprotective over her."

"Just try to get whatever you can out of her," I told him as we both got on the bikes and drove as fast as we could.

Location: La Cruz

When I finally arrived at Samirah's house, I still felt sick to my stomach. I ran inside the house, looking everywhere, but Aliana was nowhere to be seen. I ran up the stairs to her room. I burst inside, expecting to find her dressed up as a soldier with her badass attitude and aiming her gun at me, ready to shoot right through my heart.

How pathetic.

But she wasn't in her room. I looked around. The bag she had brought with her was on the floor next to the nightstand. There were three medicine bottles on the nightstand and a bunch of little figures made out of paper, but the pills? When I went through her bag before, I saw that she had a little pharmacy in there, but back then I didn't think much of it. Was Aliana sick?

I looked out the window to the balcony, where she was standing. Her hair was blowing to the side and she was looking up the orange sky. With two steps, I went out to the balcony. There wasn't a door to knock on, only a simple piece of cloth separating the room from the balcony.

Before she realised I was there, I grabbed her by her neck and pushed her up against the balcony, half of her body hanging, all that was holding her was my hand around her neck.

"What are you doing?" she asked, looking at me with unimpressed eyes. Her voice sounded a bit off but she wasn't bothered by the fact that she could easily fall and break her neck.

I never wanted to hurt anybody but if what I thought was true, she wanted to hurt my people, and I wasn't about to let that happen.

"What is your problem?" she asked again, louder this time, her voice raw with anger. Her eyes were red.

"My problem?" I said through gritted teeth. "You've lied to all of us. You manipulated me."

"What the hell are you talking about? Manipulating you?" She asked with a frown as if she didn't know what I was talking about. I pushed her further away so more than half of her body was over the edge, but she quickly wrapped her legs around me tightly, if she fell, I fell with her.

"Don't try to fool me." I tighten my grip around her throat, she then grabbed both of my hands. Her knuckles were bruised. "Your people are going to attack us, aren't they? Is this some sort of deal you made with Alex?"

"I don't know who Alex is!" She shouted, her voice raspy. People who were passing by stopped and gasped at the image. "I have no idea what you're talking about."

"You've been communicating with the Government,"

"Oh, really? And with exactly what device have I been communicating? Please, tell me because I'm actually curious now." She looked like she was ready to rip the world in two. "You went through my stuff when I got here. Did you find a communication device? A tracking device? I've been watched from the moment I stepped foot in this city. When I'm not here, I'm at that stupid store. And even though he thinks I don't see him, José is almost always around. When he isn't, *you* are there. So please, do tell me, you idiot, during what moment of the day and with what device have I been communicating? If I had been able to leave this place, don't you think I would have left ages ago?"

"Let go of me, Isaac." She said, looking directly at me, she was trying to stay calm.

"Isaac!" Samirah's voice brought me back to reality. She was standing at the front of her house, with Sebas behind her. Samirah ran inside the house and it wasn't long before she stood behind me. Fear clear in her voice. "Isaac, please let her go."

I ignored Samirah, instead, I focused on Aliana and she stared back at me. "Why are they looking for you?"

She let out a laugh, a tired, annoyed laugh. "How would I know?" She shrugged, holding my forearm tighter, her legs wrapped around me.

"There's people out there looking for you." I muttered, squeezing her throat tighter, "The Government had never before crossed the bridge, but they have now, for *you*."

"I'm sure there's an explanation for that, but please, Isaac, do *not* hurt her." Samirah's voice shook while she spoke, she was scared and it was easy to see but Aliana… if she showed anything, it was anger and boredom, as if she didn't care at all if I let go or not. Actually, I was willing to bet that the only reason she held onto me so tightly was so she brought me down with her if I did let go.

"Do you really think I would have gotten myself so close with any of you if I had a say in it? If I was with the Government, I wouldn't have looked at any of you twice. If I had come here to do attack your people? I would've killed all of you long ago."

"She doesn't mean that, Isaac," Samirah said, her voice tense as she took small steps closer to me.

"Actually, I do," Aliana smirked at me, nodding with a devilish look in her eyes, looking directly at me. "Why don't you go and tell Miguel. Go tell everybody. Or better yet, do it. Let go, Isaac, push me over the edge, go on, do it."

"*Lynn,*" Samirah muttered.

"Do it, Isaac, do it for your people. I would do it for mine." She smirked, looking at me with superiority. "You can't do it, can you?"

I couldn't do it, she knew it and I knew it too. Slowly, I brought her to solid ground and as soon as her feet touched the ground, she pushed me away from her and glared at me.

"I have no idea why they came." She muttered in anger. "You want to know? Go ask Miguel, I'm sure he knows."

I didn't have time to process what she said because right after she was done talking, she walked by me, pushing me out of the way. Samirah ran after her shouting her name. From the balcony, I saw her as she walked out of the house and ran to the woods, people stared as she ran. Samirah was following behind within seconds.

 **Chapter 18**

Location: La Cruz
Narrator: Isaac

"I THINK I deserve to know, Miguel." I tried to keep my voice calm, I tried not to let my annoyance show. "You tell me to follow this girl, to get her to trust me, to basically spy on her but you don't even tell me why!"

"The less you know, the better, Isaac," Miguel repeated, not even looking up at me, just going through some papers Alex had given him the last time they met.

I hated it when Miguel treated me like a child, every single time I asked something, he repeated the same: the less I know, the better. I was so tired of it.

"Then maybe you should know that whatever progress I made, I messed it up today," I told him, clenching my jaw.

"What?" Miguel looked up at me, finally, I had all his attention.

"There's soldiers out there in the woods, they're looking for her," I informed him. It didn't seem to affect him, which meant that he already knew and that only made my irritation grow. "You knew."

"Of course I knew, and so do Alex and Kiko." Miguel said, his eyebrows curled up, showing an annoyed expression, "What do you mean you messed up?"

"Why didn't you tell me?" I couldn't hold it in, I raised my voice at him. "I do everything you ask me to do, and just when I think I'm in, that I'm equal to the others, it turns out you're just using me when it is convenient."

"Isaac, what do you mean you messed up?" He asked again, standing up and walking towards me.

"I mean I messed up!" I shouted, throwing a chair against the wall. I was so irritated. I had been waiting for Miguel for hours before he finally had time for me and when I asked for an explanation all he said was: *the less you know, the better.* "I was angry and I—"

"What did you do?" Miguel sighed, looking at me with a disappointed look.

"I messed up," I told him, daring to look at him straight in the eye. "The less you know, the better."

Within seconds, Miguel had me against the wall. His massive hands held my face in place. For a moment, I thought he was going to hit me, I deserved it for my comment. But Miguel sighed and let go of me. He massaged the bridge of his nose as he avoided looking at me.

"Can you fix it?"

"I don't know," I answered, swallowing hard. "I can try."

"Thank you, Isaac, for trying." Miguel looked at me, he licked his lips and tried to calm himself. He then put a hand on my shoulder. "Aliana isn't a threat, she's just… she's unpredictable, which I don't like. I just need to keep an eye on her and I didn't tell you about the soldiers because it would only cause fear and there's nothing to fear. Trust me."

* * *

It was very awkward.

Aliana and I sat in the same room, fixing old devices and when I tried to talk to her, she would either ignore me or answer coldly. The day was almost over and she still didn't talk to me, not even once and it made the situation even more awkward.

Sighing, I stood up and went over to her table. I stood there for about two seconds, she didn't even look up.

"Hey, what are you doing?"

"Working."

"I see." I nodded, taking a deep breath in. "Aliana, I'm sorry."

"Okay." She sighed.

"I mean it."

"Okay," She repeated, looking up at me. "And?"

"I shouldn't have reacted like that, and I'm really sorry." I apologised, I really meant it. "I'm sorry and I understand if I've upset you and hurt your feelings, you—"

"Oh, why, Isaac, must you think so highly of yourself?" she interrupted, laughing at me, she pointed at me with a screwdriver. "You think I'm hurt because of what you said, because of what you think of me?"

"Then why—"

"What's irrelevant to you cannot hurt you," she said, interrupting me again. Her words fell like heavy stones in my stomach. "You don't trust me, and I shouldn't trust you either."

"I do trust you," I told her. What a dumb thing to say, when two days ago I was calling her a traitor. She shook her head. "Yes, I do trust you. But at that moment, I just… I lost it."

"If you did trust me, you would have come to me calmly and asked me, instead of bursting in like a beast and jumping to conclusions."

"I know, I know!" I felt desperate, I wanted her to understand but I didn't know how to explain. "Aliana, ever since I was a kid I was told that one day when I was old enough, I was going to defend this place, my people, with my own life like my father did. I saw a threat, my actions, no matter how wrong I was, were based on what I thought I had to do and I'm sorry because I didn't think shit through."

"You know, the funny thing is I can actually understand why you did that, why you reacted like you did. You saw a threat and your first instinct was to take care of it." She sighed as she laid back on her chair, playing with her screwdriver instead of looking at me. "I would've done the same, I was trained to do so."

"So, you're not mad?"

"No," she said, shaking her head after shrugging, "I'm not bothered."

"So, we cool?" I asked her, lifting my hand up for a high five. She nodded but didn't high five me, so I took her hand and I high-fived myself. And that made her smile at me a little.

That was better than being ignored.

Narrator: Aliana

I woke up with a *horrible* headache from overthinking and lack of sleep.

I did not know exactly what was happening to me, but I knew that something was changing. I mean, my surroundings were changing, the way I saw things were changing, and I even dared to say that perhaps, something in me was also changing. It wasn't like a huge change or anything, it was more like little things that made a difference.

The other day, I found myself *helping*Miguel. I don't remember exactly what was going through my mind, but I do remember I was with Eli at Plaza and Miguel asked me to help him show the girls how to defend themselves. I didn't even think about it twice, I stood up and did what he asked. It was a little something but it was… it wasn't something the me who arrived here months ago would have done. And I could tell Miguel thought the same because, since that afternoon, he treated me differently. He wasn't distant and serious, he was more like the way he acted around Sam. He didn't treat me like an outsider.

I still didn't know how I felt about that.

Everything was a little different but there were still bad habits that I needed to work on, like the fact that I was still shoving pills down my throat as if they were sweets. I still didn't like being here and I still wanted to fight half of the people that walked by and gave me dirty looks and whispered insults when I was close enough to hear them. And most importantly, the nightmares were still present.

They actually were getting way worse and I knew it was because of Luna. I was supposed to be over the nightmares and insomnia. I was supposed to stop taking the pills. I hadn't had a nightmare in over a year, but somehow the nightmares had recently returned, bringing old monsters to the surface and making it hard for me to sleep. I kept dreaming about her.

It was embarrassing, to say the least. Sam usually woke me up most of the times because I'd be whimpering or talking in my sleep. She'd wake up every morning with dark circles under her eyes from her lack of sleep because of me. I felt guilty and embarrassed. 17 years old and I still hadn't managed to get over my fears.

I couldn't stop thinking about what Johan said either, his words kept coming back every few minutes and it made me feel even more guilty when I spoke to Sam and I kept my mouth shut.

I should've told Sam, it concerned her as well but there were so many reasons why I couldn't bring myself to tell her. No matter how much it pained me to admit, Samirah truly believed that there was something wrong with me, something she could find a cure for, I was someone she could fix. She had never spoken a word of it to me, but I knew she thought so. Telling her what Johan told me would just be confirming it and even though we both knew it, saying it out loud was extremely hard.

I was incapable of loving, incapable of feeling anything other than anger and hate; it was who I was. I was a bitter and hateful person and the only way to fix it meant probable death. Fair enough, my mother was still alive but there was nothing wrong with whatever was inside her head.

I wasn't scared of death, I have never been. I was scared of living my life the way I had been living it so far.

I didn't want to think about all the events that had been happening, but that was literally all I could think about as I got out of bed and had a shower. No matter how hard I tried to push all it away, it just wouldn't go. I wanted to run away, and I was actually I was pretty good at that. I wanted to go somewhere where no one, not even my own thoughts, would ever reach me.

Everything was just spinning around in my head. I just wanted it all to go away.

I left Sam's house later than ever before. I was supposed to meet Junior by the church. We had finally gotten the car to start. The turbo wasn't quite working, so Junior had to use the wheels. I was walking and not paying attention to anything until someone bumped into me and brought me back from my thoughts. I was ready to apologise for being in the middle of the path, but the person who had bumped into me was long gone. I followed the person with my eyes. It was a little boy running. Everyone else was running in the same direction. They were all exchanging information in their harshly accented voices. I understood only a little of what they said.

I went to the fruit lady; she was always in the same spot with her fruit stand. She was nice and didn't treat me like scum. Or maybe that was just because she sometimes confused me with Samirah. And since the old lady thought something was going on between Samirah and her grandchild, Sebastián, she was actually nice.

"Do you know what happened?" I asked, pointing to the place where everyone was gathering.

"They found two of your people," the woman answered with no interest whatsoever, her accent thick and harsh. She was pealing a mango. "They brought one, and the other one died."

The other one died.

One died.

Roc.

The face of all my friends and the people who had trained with me popped up in my mind. One after one, I kept seeing their faces and bodies filled with blood. It knocked the air out of me. I couldn't stand the idea of one of them being hurt.

I started to walk towards the crowd. My heart in my throat. I feared what I would find once I stopped walking. The whole world seemed to be fading. I felt sick …

Out of the corner of my eye, I caught sight of Isaac walking through the crowd, trying to get to the middle of all this craziness. Sebastián was with him. Behind him followed Samirah. Her face was full of worry and annoyance. She never liked being in crowded places. Behind her was a familiar face, a girl with long brown hair tied in a braid. Her skin was tanned. She had one tattoo on her right upper thigh and another on her side near her stomach. People's eyes stayed on her longer. They all made space for her to walk by, a river of people opened up just for her. Rebecca was in fact very attractive.

I started to push through the people. I was getting close to the centre, where space was getting tighter. Once I got to the middle, I looked around. Luna was there frowning at Miguel, who was bleeding. He had blood on his arm from a gunshot wound, I guessed. He also had blood dripping from his forehead into his face. Cairo had his back turned, but I could recognise him from his arms full of ink. He had blood running down his neck. His grey shirt was dirty with blood. He was favouring his right leg where his dark blue jeans had a dark stain, just above the knee – probably another wound. José was standing next to him.

Cairo hit the person that was in front of him, it was impossible for me to see who because Cairo was so big that I couldn't see past him or José. Cairo gave another two blows, his body was so weak and tired that he lost a little balance, almost falling. People around were shouting and cheering, telling him to hit harder, while they laughed at and mocked his opponent. This could be one of my friends. At the realisation, I couldn't move. I looked around, trying to find help but my eyes froze when I found Sam. She had one hand on her mouth, tightening her hold on Sebastián's forearm with her other hand, recognition clear in her face and that only made my heart skip a beat.

I tried to move a little. I heard a cry of pain and saw the dark green uniform covered in blood. Everything slowed down. All the noise was gone. There was nothing but the sound of my own heartbeat slowing down. I saw a lock of blond hair dirty with blood. I saw his face covered in blood. Cairo hit him again.

Roc was trying to get up, but Cairo hit him again. People were cheering with their fists in the air. José was saying, "I told you so," to no one in particular. Sam was hiding behind Sebastián, who was the only person with a serious face. Next to him, Isaac was laughing out loud at something Rebecca had whispered to his ear.

I felt my world shatter in my hands. I was frozen, I couldn't move or even try to blink the tears away.

Cairo lifted his fist again and I snapped out of my trance. Before I knew it, I grabbed Cairo's hand and pushed it back, tripping him with my own body. He fell to the ground. José looked at me, ready to fight me. Everyone was silent. The cheering and the laughing stopped. José turned to me, ready to blow a punch but]I slapped his forearm and dodged it. Someone broke the silence by saying, *"Go on, José."* I looked at the person. It was the same guy who had spat at my feet when I arrived. I thought his name was Freddy. I couldn't believe he was eating slices of mango as he watched the fight. Unbelievable.

José looked at me angrily. He had a wound on his face. He was bleeding too. I knew what to do without humiliating him too much. He came at me again. This time I kicked the back of his knee, making him fall. I kicked his right arm, aiming to damage his muscle. I failed to do that, but at least I hurt him. I looked back to where Roc had been before, but he was no longer there. My heartbeat stopped, he was there a minute ago. It wasn't until I saw Luna that I found him. Luna had her arms around his waist, quickly walking away with Roc.

I was ordering my body to stay calm as I ran through the people. I saw Cairo getting up. I was not about to fight everyone when I needed to get Roc out of here. This wasn't a training game. This was real. Roc was here and he was in danger.

I shook my head as I ran towards Luna and Roc. The problem was that people were all around me and they weren't letting me get through.

Luna understood. Of all people, *Luna* was the one to understand. A few minutes ago, Luna was nothing but a memory to me, the person who I swore to hate. She was the reason behind my nightmares, a monster who killed every single person I loved but right at that moment, Luna understood why I acted out and she went against her own people and helped me by saving Roc.

# Chapter 19

Location: La Cruz
Narrator: Isaac

WHEN ALIANA HELD back Cairo's hand. My smile disappeared.

"Oh no," Samirah said. She was hiding behind Sebastián like a little kid.

"Luna took the guy. I saw her," Rebecca said, her tone full of mockery.

Luna walked away with the soldier while Aliana fought Cairo and then José.

I looked over to Miguel. Andrea was cleaning his wound. He was as tense as a rock. Andrea was talking to him, but Cairo was already walking away, walking towards Aliana. Miguel was angry. I could see the vein on his neck swollen and about to explode.

"Aliana!" Samirah shouted. I just stayed still. Had I really seen her do that? My mind was telling me to move, but my body was frozen. Samirah shouted her sister's name again walking towards Aliana, making me snap out of it.

Cairo was behind her. I was supposed to walk the other way, to walk away from Aliana, but my body didn't ask for permission. It just followed her towards trouble. I couldn't see them, but I knew Sebastián and Rebecca were following me and Samirah.

Luna and the soldier were already inside the church. Aliana was close but Cairo ran behind her to try to catch her, and he did. Cairo grabbed hold of Aliana's shoulder and pushed her back so fast and with so much force that she was shot down to the ground. The sound of her body hitting the ground echoed in my ears.

I saw her falling backward in slow motion. A wave of anger rushed through me. Before I knew it, I was fast walking towards Cairo, imagining all the things I wanted to do to him. Samirah covered her mouth and let out a cry. Before she could run to her sister, Sebastián held her in his arms, as if he knew how she was going to act before she did.

In an instant, Aliana got up with a jump. Her face was free of emotion. She didn't look angry or hurt. She was focused on Cairo, ready to fight him. Only Aliana was stubborn enough not to back down from a fight with Cairo. Cairo was about two heads taller than her and twice her size. Either she truly had a lot of trust in herself and a *lot* of training, or she hit her head pretty hard. Even though I did see her bring him down earlier, I couldn't help but feel afraid that he might hurt her.

Cairo tried to punch Aliana but she deflected his attack with her wrist and took advantage of his unprotected right side, kicking his right leg twice. Her kick was firm, fast, and strong, so strong that I thought she might have hurt herself. She unbalanced Cairo enough to hit him again. Cairo tried to hit her but he lost balance, Aliana took his hand and, making it look as easy as breathing, took him down again. She didn't look back as she ran to the church, although she was limping. Cairo stood up with a growl and followed her, limping too and zigzagging as he walked. When I passed by Cairo, I didn't look at him or acknowledge the fact that he was hurt.

I felt that familiar warmth in my chest. Aliana was definitely perfect. I was the dumb idiot who thought I was going to save her from Cairo. She didn't need to be saved. People who messed with her were the ones who needed saving.

When Aliana reached the church, I was close behind, close enough to say something to her that she would hear. I told her to wait, but she didn't stop. She went to the room where the interrogations took place. Looking back at me, she closed the door in my face. She hadn't even looked at me; she looked *through* me.

Cairo and Samirah walked in. Samirah was telling Cairo something about touching her sister but Cairo ignored her, looking straight ahead, finding support on the wall as he walked. There was a lot more blood running down his neck and his leg.

"Luna!" Cairo shouted out of breath. The church made it echo. His voice threatening.

Miguel and Andrea came in next. Behind them were Sebastián and Rebecca. José had probably stayed with the people, keeping them from coming in and filling their heads with whatever stupid ideas he made up. Miguel looked calmer now. Andrea had probably calmed him down. Whenever Luna did something that didn't make sense, Andrea went to Luna's rescue. She always did. Luna and Andrea had been best friends since they were kids.

"Where are they?" Miguel asked, anger clear in his voice.

"When I came in, Aliana locked the door. Luna's inside with the boy." I pointed at the door.

"Aliana and Luna are in there?" Miguel asked, his eyebrows shot up in surprise. At least it wasn't only he who was surprised by that fact. "Are you sure?"

"Yes."

"That little thing kicked me down twice." Cairo laughed, supporting himself on the wall. My aunt Andrea quickly went to check on him but Cairo shook his head at her.

Miguel, ignoring Cairo's comment, walked into the room next to the one Aliana had gone into. Andrea went behind him. Everyone else followed. Miguel had this room made because sometimes he didn't want to take part in the interrogation or just wanted to see how the prisoner behaved. The room was connected to the interrogation room. It wasn't painted yet so the walls were of cement colour. It had a one-way mirror on the wall, so I could see the other room.

Luna was saying something to Aliana. Aliana wasn't even looking at Luna. Her face was emotionless. I didn't like the way she looked. It was like she was empty inside. She was sitting on a mattress with the boy's head on her lap. She was cleaning his face and combing his hair with her fingers.

217

I didn't understand jealousy, mostly because I had never felt it before. I never cared enough to be jealous when the girls I had been with told me stuff about other boys or were around other boys. But the way Aliana was holding him, the way she so carefully cleaned his face and looked at him, made me slightly jealous and that not only caught me completely by surprise but it also confused me.

I didn't understand anything that was happening. Cairo was as confused as the rest of us and then without any warning, Cairo burst through the door that connected the two rooms. Luna stood up quickly, putting herself in front of Aliana and the boy, protecting them.

"What are you doing?" Cairo asked Luna. He didn't sound angry but rather worried. His tone completely changed, as it always did when he spoke to Luna. "Are you all right?"

"Stop treating me like I'm crazy, Cairo," Luna snapped at him. It suddenly felt very wrong to be in the middle of this. The two started to argue in hushed tones.

Aliana wouldn't release her hold on the boy. In fact, she was now holding him tighter as if she thought someone was going to take him away from her and she couldn't allow that.

"Who is he?" Rebecca asked with a sly smile. "He's kinda cute, considering …"

I found myself silently begging that no one would answer the question. I didn't want to hear that name. I didn't want it to be him. Because if it was him, everything was going to change and it surprised me how much the thought bothered me.

"Roc," Samirah answered, her voice shaking with nervousness. "The boy's name is Roc."

# Chapter 20

Location: La Cruz
Narrator: Samirah

IT WAS UNBELIEVABLE. I wanted to laugh at the situation. Sebastián, Rebecca, Isaac, and I were in a little circle, all talking at once except for Isaac, who had a confused frown and looked lost in thought.

"Is he going to stay too?" Rebecca asked with a worried expression.

"I don't understand," I said, ignoring Rebecca's comment. "I'm confused. Why would Luna defend Aliana? Do they even know each other?"

Rebecca was going to say something, but before she had a chance, Miguel approached us. He and Isaac walked away from our hearing range to have a conversation. Rebecca was saying something about how the situation was going to get 'real heavy' if Roc stayed. Sebas and Becca began talking about what they thought it was going to happen when Miguel walked back to us.

"I need you lot to leave," Miguel told us all, once he was done talking to Isaac. He seemed a bit irritated. "Samirah, you stay."

I nodded. Sebastián's eyes found mine, his were filled with worry while I was curious to know what was happening. When Sebastián didn't get anything from me, he sighed and walked out of the room, I honestly didn't know what he was expecting from me but I had more important things to think about. Rebecca followed Sebastián out, nodding goodbye to us. Isaac stayed behind Miguel, like a shadow following him around whenever Miguel moved. It kind of reminded me of my brother and my father.

"How are you doing, little one?" Andrea's voice startled me, I turned to look up at her brown eyes as she squeezed my shoulder.

"I'm okay. I just don't understand what's going on."

"Your sister and Luna want to talk to you and Cairo," Andrea told me as we walked to the centre of the room. "You can't really keep secrets here, so Luna thought it would be better if the family knew about it first."

I frowned but didn't ask her to elaborate. Soon enough I'd know.

I sat next to Aliana. She was still in the same place, doing the same thing: holding onto Roc. She was always so protective of her things... And I guess Roc could be considered as something that was *hers*.

"Are you okay?" I asked Aliana. She nodded stiffly, like a robot, the image scared me a little but I reminded myself that this was my sister, I should not be scared of her. "Do you know why he's here?" I asked, motioning towards Roc.

"He's asleep. Luna gave him something so he would sleep. She said we can keep him asleep until we figure out what to do with him," Aliana answered, her voice shaking a little. She was looking at nothing in particular. I don't think she heard me properly or if she did, she just didn't want to answer my question.

It was scary to see Aliana that way, so *empty*. I always clang onto hope that at least she was in her right mind, there was a problem with her, a problem that I promised myself to fix but right then she scared me a little. Her eyes lacked emotion, and the way she held onto Roc seemed a little obsessive. I was beginning to get anxious. I had questions for which I needed answers but I wasn't sure how to ask. If something, Aliana was unpredictable when she felt attacked or under pressure, and I didn't want her to lose it here, not in front of people.

"I'm sorry, Sam. I just – I thought that it would be better if you didn't know the truth." Aliana finally looked at me. As soon as her eyes met mine, they filled with so much emotion that it almost shook me to my feet. Her eyes were full of sorrow, real sadness, the kind I had never seen in her before, mostly because she always pretended not to feel anything. She was always neutral with her emotions, always had to be in control. Aliana, the *perfect* sister. There was a time when I envied her and I wanted to be like her. There was a time when I wanted to be as pretty as my sister, to have her confidence and skills. I wanted to be so much like her until I saw *her*, I saw what she had become. She was so consumed by the idea of being in control that she didn't realise she never really was in control.

"Whatever you've done, we'll find a way to figure it out, okay?" I assured my sister. What else could I say? "Together."

I took Aliana's free hand. It was cold as ice. Her body was shaking and her face was drained of all colour.

I was never as temperamental as Aliana. Well, I was, but my anger was different from hers. She stayed calm and took it all in, never snapping. Me? I got angry and said what was on my mind. Later I'd forget what I was angry about and end up talking normally, only to get angry again once I remembered. It was a vicious circle. I did say a lot of things I didn't always mean, I just wanted to hurt the person who made me angry, make them regret upsetting me. But I got over it eventually. I snapped and it was done. Aliana? She let every little thing affect her and she held onto her anger, swallowing it like a poison that only made her bitter and angry.

I didn't want to be another person from whom Aliana had to hide, another pain she had to endure – I didn't want to be that *anymore*. I wanted to be the person who held her hand and told her we'd find a way around whatever because that's what siblings did. It was Nate, Lynn and I. She was a part of me, and I was her better half. I completed her, and we both knew it. I loved her and I would not rest until the day I find a way to make her better.

Cairo raised his voice, bringing me back from my thoughts, he said, "I don't understand why we have to talk in front of everyone."

"Calm down," Luna muttered, placing a hand on his chest.

"At least take that one away." Cairo pointed at Roc. I felt Aliana's hold tighten. She tensed her body and held my hand tighter. She was hurting me but didn't mind.

No one but my family knew that Aliana had some… *issues.* She rarely had moments, but I recognised when she was going to snap. I knew it would be better if no one in this room – or in the city or anywhere else – saw Aliana snap.

"Lynn, it's okay. Look at me. Nothing's going to happen to him." I tried to calm my sister. I could see that she was nervous and scared, if she felt threatened, she would snap and I did know how to control her then. She looked at me, her eyes big and filled with pain, it broke my heart to see her like this. She blinked a couple of times making a tear fall from her eye. She was scared and I didn't understand why.

My relationship with Aliana wasn't always the best. There was a time when I barely acknowledged her and I kept my distance simply because I allowed my grandmother's words to have an effect on me. I believed every single word Aurora said. Aurora manipulated everything and I allowed her to manipulate the way I saw my sister. Aliana was spiteful, she was angry and bitter, cruel to our father.

It never made sense, one day she just wasn't the same, and it *scared* me. The person Aliana had become frightened me. At times I believed she held onto people to maintain her sanity. As if we were some sort of life jacket that she needed to cling onto in order to not drown but she had an anchor tied to her feet, dragging her down and she didn't know how to let go. At times I got scared by the thought that she might ruin me if I didn't let go first.

That's what she was doing right now. She was trying to hold onto Roc because she felt alone and scared.

"I'm here, Lynn." I took hold of Aliana again, whispering so no one would hear. *She's our sister. She's good. She's Aliana,* I reminded myself of Nate's words, shaking off all those thoughts I wanted to keep hidden. "Let go of him. I'm staying here."

Aliana relaxed after a long minute. Once she let go of Roc, Isaac, and Miguel took him out of the room. The air in the room felt heavy. Although it was only six people in the room, it felt like there were hundreds surrounding us. I had Aliana's hands in mine. It was obvious that she was nervous, which made me curious. What did we all have to talk about that made her so nervous? And Luna … Luna didn't know where to look. She kept moving her hands, not knowing where to place them.

"So," I spoke up, breaking the ice, "Who's going first?"

No one said a word. Everyone looked at Luna and then at Aliana. Aliana looked over at Luna. As if being asked for permission, Luna nodded. Aliana took a deep shaky breath. Since when Luna and Aliana had secrets?

"I talked to Johan last week," Aliana began. I thought about what had happened last week, how Isaac and Sebastián had told me that Aliana was a traitor. "Johan said Mum is in trouble and that they are going to practise the process on her again. You probably know what that means more than I do. He said it was dangerous and that he's trying to find a way to make the process less risky if it comes to doing the surgery, but he might not have enough time to find a way. I think—I think the board wants to get rid of Mum because she's a threat to them and Government."

"I don't know why there are soldiers out, I honestly have no idea. If I had to guess, I'd say they're trying to show people they're looking for those who left, trying to calm them down. I don't think It'll work anyways, Mum is the one who put ideas in people's heads, they have to see her to fully believe everything is fine but the board doesn't want her to be in the public eye. And as to why Roc's here? I guess it is because he's looking for me."

I waited for more information, as that was simply not enough, not even close. And for a second, I even allowed myself to feed the idea that maybe, just *maybe*, Aliana and Luna had lost their minds.

"Who's this Johan and the board?" Cairo asked with a serious voice.

"The board consists of the main families who make the decisions, like the governors. Johan is our father, the board's leader," I explained, looking at Aliana with a frown. "Carry on, Aliana."

"How do you communicate with your father?" Cairo asked with authority, demanding an answer that I also wanted to hear. "Ain't he supposed to be in the Government?"

Aliana didn't say anything. I could feel her pulse racing in her wrist. I narrowed my eyes at my sister. If this was true, *how* did she communicate with Johan?

"Johan communicates with me," I turned to look at Luna so fast that I hurt my neck. As soon as my brain acknowledged what she said, it started running wild with different scenarios. I did not know if I believed any of this.

"You know my father?"

I could see the colour vanish from Luna's face. Cairo looked down at her, expecting answers. Aliana squeezed my hand, making me look at her instead. Her eyes were watery. She wasn't a person to cry about anything, so if this was true, this was important.

"Yes," Luna slowly release a shaky breath before carrying on. "I was kidnapped by the Government for about two years. In those two years, they did *things* to me. Thanks to Johan and the medicine he sends me, I can control some part of what's happening to me."

Luna was talking slower than usual. She was sick, that much I knew, it was obvious. I looked away from her in shame, knowing fully well that I might not have treated Luna but I had treated people like Luna. I made them sick. I played with their brains. The difference was that out of the three people I treated, only one was still alive and to be quite honest, I would have rather she passed away like the others.

"The Government needed people who never had the process done to them. It worked better if the brain was "virgin" that's how they called it," Luna laughed to herself, resentment clear in her voice.

"So you have a chip?" I carried on as I could, Luna half nodded. "They made a mistake and you have one of the side effects. The side effects mainly manifest as what we could call mental issues: schizophrenia, multiple personality disorder, and bipolar disorder. Those are the main ones that we know of. With the difference that these were caused by the electroshocks from the chip, we know little to nothing of how this really works."

I wasn't talking to anyone in particular. I didn't need an answer, as I had one. It was obvious that Luna was sick. I just didn't know what caused it. Now I knew.

"Johan always said you were very smart," Luna spoke more to herself than to me or any other person in the room, but what she said made me feel uncomfortable and Aliana tensed. "I don't remember what Johan told me exactly, it was a lot of words. At first, I thought I was going to die, that I was never going to be *me* again."

"Bipolar psychosis or something like it." Cairo interrupted in a low but serious voice, looking down at the floor. It was obvious he wasn't comfortable talking about this.

"Why would my dad talk to you about me?"

"Johan was the first person I saw when I was captured. We were young back then. He was too curious for his own good, like you. After a while, Johan and I started to have a friendship. We would just talk about everything. He would bring me proper food and things for me so I wouldn't get bored. He was always nice to me."

"I don't know when or how, but Johan had gotten inside my head, and my heart. I couldn't help what I was feeling for him," Luna finished, lowering her head. Cairo tensed. His face dropped. Aliana's tears left her eyes quicker as a look of betrayal crossed her face.

I didn't know what to make of this. Why was Luna telling us this? If it happened a long time ago, it didn't matter now. My father loved my mother. He always had. He had a family with Cynthia. We were a family, a happy family. I wanted to tell Luna to stop talking, but I couldn't get my brain to think of words to say.

"As time went by, Johan and I were in some sort of relationship." Luna looked up. She took a deep breath as she shattered my picture of a happy family. "I was pregnant with Johan's child."

It was impossible. Johan loved my mother. And even if this happened when he was younger and not married, it would have been impossible, because Johan married Cynthia when he was like 15 and Luna was about the same age. It was impossible … *impossible*.

I looked at Cairo. His face was a wall, not showing any emotion. Miguel and Andrea were looking at Luna with sympathy in their eyes, but not with surprise, which meant they already knew. Isaac didn't even try to cover his surprise. It was written across his forehead in capital letters. And finally, I took a look at the only person who

I had thought would never lie to me. Aliana was still looking down at the floor, still shaking, but she was not surprised or angry. Tears ran down her face, over which pain was written. I tried to let go of her hand, but she wouldn't let go. And suddenly her hate for Johan made sense.

"Johan has another child?" I asked incredulously. "Is Eli …?"

But Eli can't be …I shook my head, trying very hard not to lose myself in this.

"I had two daughters. After a – an – incident, Johan decided that it would be best if he took care of the girls. With Miguel and another man's help, Johan found a way for me to escape. I wanted to bring you with me. I wanted you *both* to come with me, but you had no future with me. I was sick, and I … It was true that you two were better off without me. Johan said he would find a way to communicate with me and tell me how you two were. But he didn't. He didn't communicate for a year. I thought Aliana was dead for a *year*—"

"Do *not* try to make him look like the bad guy," Aliana snapped, a fire in her eyes that I hadn't seen before. That was the first time I ever heard Aliana defend Johan. "Tell the story however you want, but don't put all the blame on him. It was you too. You left because you *wanted* to leave. Don't act like the martyr here. Johan gave you a way out, you didn't even try to fight. You left without even saying a word. Johan has done bad things, but you have too. Own up to it."

Luna was hurt by Aliana's words, but her words made no sense to me. Aliana was Luna's daughter, which meant that I was too. Everyone was quiet, the only sound was Cairo's harsh, uneven breathing. He was looking at the floor, still as a statue.

"No, you are *not* my mother. I have a mother. Her name is Cynthia. *She's* my mother," I told her, shaking my head. What I had just heard was a lie.

"No, Samirah, I am …" Luna said, starting to walk towards me, but she stopped herself. She was sick. Maybe this was all a product of a sick person's imagination. This was her condition talking.

"I have a family. We have a family, and so do you," I said, louder than I meant to. "My father wouldn't do this to my mother. He loves my mum, okay? We're a happy family. My dad would never do this to us. I don't know why you're saying this, but it isn't funny. It isn't a nice thing to do, Luna. I don't—"

I stopped myself. I wanted to laugh. My brain kept trying to add up what Luna just said, but no matter how much I tried to make sense of it, I just couldn't make it add up.

"What was the incident?" I asked. Neither Luna nor Aliana answered. However, they both tensed up. Luna looked at Aliana. Aliana knew but wasn't going to say anything about it. I nodded to no one.

"Thirteen. You were 13 years old when you stopped talking to Johan," Drawing on all my strength, I got up, leaving Aliana's side. "You knew. You knew this and you never said anything! That's why you stopped talking to Dad. That's why you're – that's why you're like this because you knew we weren't—"

I took a big breath as I rubbed my hands on my face. I needed to calm down. I needed Aliana to say something but she remained still, not a single word came out of her mouth.

"Seriously, Aliana? All this time and you never said anything? Didn't I deserve to know any of this?" I felt betrayed, hurt, and lied to. Aliana wouldn't say a word. She wasn't even looking at me. "All my life I've been by your side. I've supported you, helped you, and never lied to you. And when everyone was pointing fingers at you, I held your hand, putting my reputation at risk for you! My future, my career, I risked them both for you! I never left you alone because you needed me. I respected your decisions, even when they made no sense to me. I never judged you because, of all people, you were honest, you were real. How could you not tell me?"

"I was 12 when I found out, I didn't know what to do. We thought it was better if you didn't know, Sam. I thought that—"

"We thought? *Who* thought?" I asked, interrupting her.

"Johan asked me not to tell you," Aliana said. I turned to look at Luna. Luna's eyes were full of doubt and sadness. "And I didn't want you to know. Cynthia *is* our mother. That's the truth, and there's nothing more to it. This means *nothing*. This changes *nothing*."

227

Aliana didn't look at me when she finished speaking. She looked at Luna and Luna turned to look at me with uncertainty. She had never looked at me like that. She always had a smile on her face, but of course, Luna probably thought that I was going to treat her the same way Aliana had. I couldn't help but feel pity for her. I didn't want her to think that this would change something between us and even if it did change something, it wasn't in a positive way. They all lied to me. They knew this for years and they all lied to me.

How was I ever going to trust Aliana again?

"You lied to me." I turned to look at Aliana. She looked down at her feet, unable to look at me. I shook my head, my chest felt heavy and breathing wasn't as easy as it should've been. I felt their eyes on me, they were all looking at me except for Aliana and their stares made something in me feel heavy. I didn't understand my own feelings but I did know that I needed to get out.

Without saying a word, I walked out of the room. Aliana called out for me, but I ignored her. Sebastián was waiting at the entrance to the church. He smiled at me but I didn't want to talk to Sebastián, I wanted to talk to one person and only her. So, when Sebastián tried to get to me, I dodged him and ran towards Natalí's house, ignoring Sebastián calling out for me.

 **Chapter 21**

Location: La Cruz
Narrator: Isaac

THE DAY PASSED in a blur. I don't really remember what was discussed after Samirah walked out, all I remember was that Luna had two daughters who were 17 years old. Aliana and Samirah were Luna's daughters and that was very odd.

Cairo walked out not long before Samirah did, almost falling on his way out. Miguel had the healer over to clean his wounds and he was sent home, Luna followed behind.

Miguel tried to talk to Aliana, but Aliana wouldn't respond. When Miguel was about to walk out, Aliana asked him to give her a day until waking Roc up. Miguel hesitated but gave her a day and then he walked out with Andrea and I following. That's when Miguel looked at me and with a serious expression told me to keep an eye on them.

And so I've been doing since yesterday. I didn't want to intrude, so I stayed in the hallway, facing the door where Aliana and Roc were in. She hadn't left the room, there wasn't even a single noise and when I went to the room to see what was happening, Aliana was lying next to a sleeping Roc. He was asleep on his back and she laid next to him, her eyes glued to the ceiling, her lips moving ever so slowly as she whispered things to him, moving her hands about as she spoke.

I did not want to go inside that room. Something about the way she acted around him, it made feel weird. I didn't understand what it was, but it was a slight annoyance towards them both. Feeling that way made me angry at myself. I was Aliana's friend, I had no right to feel like that but I couldn't help it.

I waited until the time Miguel had given her was up and even then, I waited another 20 minutes. She needed time alone before shit hit the fan and if I could give her 20 more minutes, then I would. When the 20 minutes passed, I knocked on the door and waited a few seconds before I walked in. I don't know what I was expecting, maybe the same imagine as before. But it was far from it. Aliana was sitting against a wall, far away from where Roc laid. Her eyes met mine and I couldn't look away. I was waiting for her to tell me to leave or to stay, if she needed more time, I would've figured out a way to keep Miguel distracted.

Friends, we were friends and if she needed me, I was going to be there for her. When she didn't ask for more time, I sat next to her, resting my back against the wall, our shoulders slightly touching.

"A lot of things make sense now." I whispered to her. She looked up at me, and when our eyes met, I felt chills going through my whole body. Her green eyes hypnotised me, I couldn't look away, even if I tried to.

Even though her face lacked of emotion, her eyes were so full of it, and she was looking at me in such a soft, sweet way that made the hair on the back of my neck raise up. I could get lost in her eyes and live there for the rest of my life.

"I guess so." Aliana sniffed. She smiled sadly at me before looking away.

I don't know why I did it, maybe it was because if I was in her situation, I would've liked someone to be there for me, but I held her hand. She frowned confused as she looked down at our intertwined hands. If I was in her position, I wouldn't want to be alone.

We sat in silence for a while. She was so stiff that it made me uncomfortable to watch her. I rubbed the back of her hand with my thumb, thinking that maybe it helped. Her hand was *very*soft.

"I know I'm going to have to wake him up at some point, but I just don't know how he's going to react or what I should do when he wakes up." She told me, whispering in a tired voice. "What do I tell him? I don't think I'm ready to face him. I mean, I was pretty disappointed when I saw Sam here. When I saw her dressed like she was, so much like *you* … don't get me wrong, Isaac, but I know the way he thinks and… I was disappointed by the man whom I trusted and loved the most. After that, disappointments just kind of came, like dominoes falling, one after the other. I don't want to do that to him.

"I know how it feels when someone you care about disappoints you. So I've tried my hardest not to disappoint anyone. And yeah, I've failed a couple of times and despite how hard I try to be the perfect 'Gobi' like you people call us, I am *not* perfect, I make mistakes. But Rocco – Roc has *never* let me down. He has suffered so much, Isaac and to see someone you care about hurt knowing that there's nothing you can do to make him hurt less is one of the worst feelings ever.

"He has lost pretty much everyone he cares about. He lost his brother when he was 8. And that fucked him up pretty bad. His brother was an ass him but Roc was *devoted* to Ronald. I think that was what pulled me to Roc, seeing the way his brother treated him. Somehow, I related to that. When I saw him, I kind of saw me.

"I remember the day his father told him that Ronald was gone. That was the word his father had used, *gone*. I remember him looking for his brother, shouting Ronald's name all over the house. We looked for Ronald for hours. He was so desperate. The last place we looked was in Ronald's room. I held his hand as we both went in. He called out for *Ronron*. I remember I cried that day when I got home. I couldn't get it out of my head, you know? The way Roc kept begging for Ronald to stop playing and just come out. I can't get it out of my head the sounds he made when he sobbed or when he fell to the floor and just sobbed uncontrollably. After that, I ran away. I left Roc alone in his brother's room. I ran all the way back home, where I hid under my bed, where my dad found me.

"We never again spoke of Ronald. I was confused at how Roc's parents simply never spoke of him again, like Ronald had never existed. And then his dad was gone too. Roc was very close to his father. He wanted to be strong, but he was devastated. I remember my arms hurt because of how hard I was holding him. I wanted to hold him together, to keep him from breaking down, but it was like pieces of him were falling and escaping my grip. He was breaking and slipping away and I felt so useless.

"The worst part? It was all his mother's doing. She turned Roc's father in. The same thing happened to his brother. It was his *mother*. How could I tell him that, Isaac? It would've broken his heart and he was alone with danger, because his mother meant danger to him, to who he was. The way we are, being able to feel these emotions, is dangerous.

"Roc has been hurt by those closest to him. I've done it many times. I've hurt him and I've put him back together. I gave him hope and I took it away. I thought that when I left, maybe he would be able to get over everything. He will always be in my heart, but I needed Sam. He didn't understand that, so I left him. I thought that finally I was going to be out of his life, one less let-down for Roc. And now he is here and I have to show him *this*." She turned to look at me with desperation clear in her eyes, she pointed at her clothes and her hair, shaking her head. "I have to let him down and show him what I've become. We were soldiers. We were the best, the captains, the leaders. We were partners, and I left him to be *this*. He will be disappointed, but what I fear the most is that he will pretend not to care, because that's Roc. He always pretends not to be hurt. He always has to be the strong one because he knows I can't be."

I had *no* idea what to say to her. This boy was her best friend, the person who had been with her since they were little kids. They had been together through things that I would never understand. I couldn't even tell her that things would be okay because I didn't know what would happen when Roc woke up.

"You know the reason why we call Sebas Flaco is because when we were kids, he was the skinniest boy in town. He didn't eat much while growing up, his dad wasn't the greatest dude and he pretty much spent his days drinking." I began, she turned to look at me with a frown, I knew I had her attention. I took a deep breath in and tried to find the words to carry on. "Sebas and I have always been very close but we don't always agree on everything and one of those things we don't agree on is the way—the way I am with my mother. One day, we had this *massive* argument, it was *so* fucked up that we ended up fighting each other. After that, I was so angry that I didn't want to talk him again.

"A few days later, though, Sebas's was taken to La Nueva because his dad had beaten him up so bad that the doctors here couldn't do a thing for him. The moment I found out what his dad had done to him, I felt my world was spinning. At that moment, I didn't care about the argument, the names he called me or the very hurtful things he said; all I could think about was that if something happened to Sebas, my fucking world would've shattered.

"Roc is to you what Sebas is to me, right?" I asked, she half nodded, her eyes were glassy and puffy. "He's here for you. He cares about you. And he won't be disappointed to see you like this because he will see you *alive* and that's the only thing that matter."

Aliana looked at me for a long second. She stayed quiet and then she smiled, turning to look at Roc again, leaning her head on my shoulder.

"Thank you," she whispered and then we both fell silent again.

# Chapter 22

Location: La Cruz
Narrator: Aliana

TALKING TO ISAAC was always oddly interesting. He always seemed to come up with deep, corny comments, but what he said always managed to stay in my mind. I often found myself thinking of something and wondering what Isaac would think of it.

I was scared, I didn't know what was going to happen when Miguel wanted to wake Roc up. And Sam… I still didn't know anything about Sam. She was mad, that much was obvious, but I didn't know what else was going through her head.

The secret was out, the one thing I had been trying to bury deep down and never let it see the light was out for everybody to know and I did not know how I felt about that. I didn't want Luna to think that now that Sam knew, she could get closer somehow. She needed to know and understand that she might have helped me, and I was very grateful for that, but I do not want a relationship with her.

A few minutes went by agonisingly slow. Isaac sat next to me the whole time, not saying a word. I let his hand go a couple of minutes ago when it was getting too hot and too sweaty for my liking. I appreciated him being there. It was nice to know that I wasn't as alone as I thought I was, it brought a fuzzy feeling to my chest. I wasn't alone. I had *friends*.

The door opened, startling us. I thought it was Miguel who had finally come to wake Roc up and make me *face the music*. However, I was surprised to see Eli's face at the door. He stared at me, his eyes empty of emotion, he just stood there. It was obvious that he knew and if it wasn't easy for me to accept the truth, I was guessing it wouldn't be easy for Eli either.

I didn't know what to say, so I just went with the simplest thing. "I know how it feels."

"So what now, then?" He didn't sound angry – maybe a bit sad, but not angry. "Are you gonna hate me too?"

"What? No." I shook my head rapidly, confused by his words.

"You hate my mother—"

"You are my brother." I interrupted him, looking directly into his eyes to make sure he knew I meant it. "how I feel about Luna, it has nothing to do with you." Eli shook his head, making me frown. "Eli, whatever relationship I had with Luna, it does not change what you and I have."

"But it does change things! It does matter and it has everything to do with me." He snapped, I could feel Isaac moving in his seat next to me, "She is my mother and you... she's my *mother* and just because you dislike your dad and you treat him like shit, it doesn't mean you can do the same with *my* mum."

I didn't even have time to think of something to say to him because as soon as he finished talking, he turned around and walked away. Leaving me with a strange feeling in my chest.

"Well, that was a little intense." Isaac joked, trying to lighten the mood. I rolled my eyes, turning around to look at him.

"Shut up." I shook my head. Isaac chuckled.

"He's really attached to her, you know?"

"To Luna?" I asked and Isaac nodded, biting his lower lip.

I was tempted to tell Isaac not to say anything at all because I just knew that if we carried on talking, at some point he was going to say something that would get stuck in my head for the rest of the day, because Isaac's words had that effect on me, they stayed with me for the rest of the day and somehow managed to make me see things from another perspective, and I did not want to see Luna any different because *I* knew what Luna was capable of.

"It's normal that he'd react like that." He said. I took my time to reply.

"But why now?"

"Okay, maybe it could have been my fault?" He said, smiling at me with guilt. I kept a straight face. "Sometimes, when stuff happens, Eli sneaks in the other room and he watches from there, says he wants to learn how to be intimidating from watching Miguel or his father in action."

"You knew this and you let him?" I turn around so my whole body was facing him.

"In my defence, I didn't know a bomb was going to be dropped, okay?" He put his hands up in the air, "So far, it hadn't done him any harm, I thought Miguel was just going to discuss how you fought José and Cairo and was going to interrogate Roc and when you guys began to spill the beans, I completely forgot about Eli. I'm sorry."

I sighed and turned around, resting my back against the wall again.

"I'm going to get Miguel, okay?" He spoke as he stood up from the floor. I nodded, feeling myself growing anxious. "I have to, he said a day, it has been a day."

I nodded and watched Roc while Isaac walked out the door. What was I going to say? When Roc woke up, what was I going to say? I didn't have much time to dwell on it because not long after Isaac was gone, Miguel opened the door. Behind him were Cairo, José, Luna and Isaac, who was the last to come in. Miguel looked tired and annoyed at something José was saying. José gave me a dirty look. I rolled my eyes. Cairo didn't look particularly angry or sad, or anything at all.

"Well, well." Miguel's voice broke the silence, his voice had a mocking tone in it. "We all know who's who. I want to be clear, Aliana. I should let you know that even though you are family, it doesn't mean you'll have a special treatment. You will be treated just as everybody else."

Miguel wasn't looking at me when he said it. He was looking over at José, who was clenching his jaw as Miguel smiled mockingly at him.

"I haven't asked any favours of you, and I'm not about to start. There's no need to remind me," I said with a defiant tone, looking at José as I talked. It was obvious Miguel was telling me that because of José.

"How about we leave our family issues for a family meeting, eh?" Miguel joked, with a mocking smile. He seemed to be in a good mood today.

"Why don't you wake Sleeping Beauty? Or should I do it?" José said with a sly smirk.

"I dare you to come near him," I snapped at him as he took a step closer. He stopped to look at me.

"You touch my niece and I will burn your hands." Miguel stepped in, wiggling his fingers. How dare he do that? As if I needed anyone to stand up for me.

Also… he called me his *niece*.

"I don't need you to stand up for me, Miguel. Need I remind you that you locked me in this exact same room for months?" I reminded him. I knew I should shut up because I was angry and hungry and tired, but I was also irritated, which was the reason for my diatribe.

"Well, if you had stopped being a little shit when I asked you to, I wouldn't have done that." He forced a smile my way, I fought the urge to roll my eyes.

"I—" I began but Miguel interrupted me, dramatically rolling his eyes. Isaac coughed but when I looked at him, he was really just trying not to laugh, with his hand covering his mouth.

"Can you just… wake him up," Miguel ordered, ignoring me. I could literally feel the tension in the room and the only one who was in a somewhat good was Miguel. He was mocking and being sarcastic, behaving like nothing had ever happened.

I rolled my eyes as I stood up and walked over to Roc. He did look like Sleeping Beauty. He was calm and steady. I sat next to him on the mattress and lightly touched his face, calling out his name so he would wake up. I was nervous and my mouth was very dry. How was Roc going to react once I woke him?

"We don't have all day," José groaned, pressuring me and making me angrier.

I took a deep breath and hit Roc a bit harder, maybe harder than I was supposed to. "Don't break his nose," Miguel said, I rolled my eyes and slapped Roc again.

"Roc?" I said when he opened his eyes a little.

Roc's dark blue eyes were looking right into mine. I had no idea how much I had actually missed him until I was right in front of him, with his eyes wide open taking me in. His face was clean of all blood, a little swollen but it wasn't bad. His lip was broken, and his cheekbone was between red and purple.

His eyes were open wide. He wouldn't look away from me. He wouldn't even blink, as if thinking that if he blinked, then I would disappear. He didn't look around and didn't seen anyone else. He took my hand in his, he pulled me into his arms and hugged me. I had to admit that hugging him didn't feel wrong at all.

"Tell me this is a dream," Roc muttered against my neck, holding me tight. "Better yet, tell me I'm dead and that you've come to take me with you. Reality is far too unbearable. They won't allow me to speak your name. I have missed you so much, Aliana. I've been looking for you everywhere non-stop. I am so sorry. I should have left with you when you asked. I should have listened to you. I should have never left you alone. Tell me you forgive me, and then I'll never leave your side. I will do as you ask. But please forgive me for not believing in you."

"Roc," I said, trying to push him away a little. Roc shouldn't have said those things, not in front of people. I could feel my cheeks heating up. I didn't know what to say, my brain wasn't functioning properly but it seemed as though Roc still had more to say.

"I have thought about you every single day." He was holding my face now. This situation was *very* embarrassing.

Roc's face changed. His smile faded as he took in my face and my clothes. I surely looked like one of *them*, a far cry from what Roc used to see. An uncomfortable silence fell over the room as a frown deepened in-between his eyebrows. I couldn't look at Roc any longer.

He wouldn't understand. I was getting ready for him to tell me how wrong this was. Instead, he just lifted my face with his hand to make me look at him. He had his charming smile on his face. Either he understood or he didn't care. And that was a huge relief.

"I'm touched." Miguel's voice brought Roc and me back to the room. His mocking tone was nothing compared to the mocking look on his face. What the hell was wrong with Miguel today?

Roc looked towards the voice. Everyone was looking at us, waiting for me to ask Roc why he was here, to get questions out of him but how could I do that when my cheeks were burning and I felt so embarrassed that I wanted to kick everybody out of the room and erase whatever it was that they heard.

"What are you doing here, Roc?" I asked, looking back at Roc and trying to ignore everybody's stare.

"I came for you, Ali," he answered as if it was the most obvious thing ever. He looked at everyone, taking them in. He appeared to be disgusted as if we were surrounded by scum. He asked, "What's this?"

"Roc, forget about them. Look at me," I said, remembering the day I went to Roc for help, the day he was ready to tell on me just because he didn't want me to leave. "You shouldn't have come, Roc."

He looked at me and frowned, giving me the *don't be a hypocrite* look. I knew exactly what he was going to say.

"But did you not do the same for Samirah?" he asked and continued whispering. "Well, I came for you. I don't know why you're with them or what is happening, but I don't care. We can deal with these lot. Ali, we can go back home. You can come back. I found a way for us to be together. We can—"

"Roc, no," I said, interrupting him before he could say something else. I had missed him, but I had not missed this subject.

"No, Aliana. Look, someone will help me. I found a way. Not even Aurora will be able to say no. I will not marry anyone who isn't you."

Oh, for God's sake.

"Roc, I *can't* go back," I said with a cold tone, suddenly becoming very aware of how close we were and how many people were in the room watching us.

"Yes, of course you can. We can go back, together. You don't belong here,"

"Even if I decide to go back with you, it will never be the same. Nothing will be the same again." My patience was running low. Roc was saying too many things in front of people. I wasn't feeling comfortable with them knowing any of this or hearing me talking my friend out of our non-existent love relationship.

A part of me wanted to leave with Roc. If I did go back with him, everything would be easier. I'd have no fears to face, no feelings to face. I'd be back to what I knew. If I went back, I'd end up living the life the board chose for me. And to be honest, at this point I had no problem with that. I'd marry, I'd have a kid, I'd have a job until I couldn't do it anymore, and I'd have a family. I'd be back home with my family. But I wouldn't really be going back to my family, would I? My mother was going crazy; my sister had a new life on this side of the bridge; my father had weekly conversations with a woman I kind of despised; and my brother ... God knew what my brother's doing. And as it turns out, I had another brother, one who was on this side of the bridge with me. So, what exactly would I be going back to?

"Your mother? You don't know how she is. She's been sick, and since you left she's gotten worst. If you don't come back for me, come back for your mother." Roc must have seen the doubt in my face. He must have known I was thinking about it and he used her to manipulate me.

I felt his words like a punch in my chest, knocking the air out of me. I was about to say, *Yes, take me with you. Take me back*, but if I did go back, it would change nothing. Cynthia wasn't sick. The board had said she was sick so they could practise the process on her again and, if something happened to her, blame it on the sickness. If I left with Roc, I would be giving my mother only one option, and that option was in Johan's hands. And I don't know if I trust him enough. If I returned and Johan failed, my mother would die.

"Roc, don't do that. I am *not* going back," I told him with a cold tone as I stood up, swallowing the lump in my throat. There went my last chance to go back home. "Now, either you tell me what it is that you're doing here or you will have to tell them."

"Seriously?" he asked, anger in his tone. "You'd rather stay here? With these animals?"

"Animals?" José stepped in. *Oh God.* "Step out of your bitch's shadow."

Roc stood up so fast, I almost didn't even see him. He stood his ground, waiting for José to make a move. José just smirked, provoking him. I could see Roc's anger increase.

"Roc, no," I said. To my surprise, he listened to me. "I will explain everything later, but please, you *have* to talk to me. Tell me why you're here. Tell me and I will answer all your questions."

"They sent us to look for you, for anyone we can find, but mainly you and Samirah. You were the last ones to leave. But they told us we can't leave the search radius. Day after day, we've been looking in the same place. It's like they don't even want us to find anything. We're like dumb dogs searching and searching the same place. I got tired of it, so Ben and I, we crossed the perimeter. Ben was just following me. And I just wanted to find you."

Roc sat on the mattress and placed his hands over his face.

"We walked around until we ran into them." Roc didn't look at them, but he pointed with his head at Miguel, Cairo, and José. There was anger in his tone. "Ben shot them and ran. I stayed because I thought maybe they had you or knew of you. But Ben ran until he fell into nothing. He shouted and shouted until his screaming stopped."

Roc squeezed his hands together until his knuckles were white. Ben and Roc were good friends. In the past, when Roc wasn't with me, he was with Ben. I sat back down next to Roc, placing my hand on his.

"This isn't something that you can take away, you know?" Roc whispered. It was like he could read my mind. It was amazing how well he knew me – almost a bit creepy, really.

"His friend killed one of ours. He deserved to die," José said.

Roc quickly stood up again, his muscles tense. He was ready to attack. As soon as he stood up, I could see the mistakes he made. He was angry, he didn't think things through. José was provoking him and was ready for his reaction. José smiled and waited for Roc to do something.

"That was my *friend*," Roc said, his voice tense. He didn't even move a muscle.

"A coward who ran away when facing danger." José laughed, shrugging.

"Shut your mouth," I snapped. I didn't mind José insulting me, but I did mind that he said this about a boy who had just died, a 17-year-old boy who had a little sister and parents waiting for him back home.

"Oh, this little skank—" José sighed, but he couldn't finish his sentence.

Roc lunged at José, putting him against the wall. Roc had his knife against José's neck and he was no longer laughing.

"How dare you, you filthy animal." Roc's voice was full of anger, his knife pressed hard against José's skin. I could see a drop of blood running down José's neck.

Miguel must have made a mistake. They hadn't searched Roc for weapons. They had just taken the visible ones, not even considering looking beneath his shirt, or around his ankles, where he always had two knives.

"How dare you insult her? You aren't even worthy of being in the same room as her. How dare you think you can even lay eyes on her? She could break your spine with one single blow. Who are you? You are *nothing*, nothing but a filthy little shit." Roc carried on. I must say that if the circumstances had been different, I would have been flattered at the comment, but right now wasn't the time to be giving me compliments. "One word from her and I'll cut your throat open."

Everyone looked at me, everyone but José and Roc. And I realised that not only Roc was really waiting for me to tell him to kill José but also that everyone else was waiting for me to tell Roc to back down. Incredible. When did they ask José to stop humiliating me? Where were they when José was beating me? Where were they when José had me chained and humiliated? I was tempted not to say anything, to let Roc do whatever he wanted, but I couldn't do that. I didn't particularly care what happened to José, but I didn't want Roc to have blood on his hands because of me.

I took a deep breath to calm down, and then I walked towards Roc. Yes, José was a pain in the back, but if we killed everyone who was a pain, then there would be no one left in the world.

"Roc, let go," I told him, grabbing his hand that held the knife. "He isn't worth it. Come on."

"It is worth it if it means he won't talk to you like that again," Roc said, not breaking eye contact with José. I looked over at José. I could have sworn I saw fear in his eyes. "Say it. Say the word and I'll do it."

"You do it and you will not walk out of this alive, bitch," José told me. Roc tightened the grip, his knife going a little deeper into José's neck.

"You know nothing of us. You don't know what we're capable of doing," Roc said, answering for me. "At least let me cut his tongue out. I'd be doing the savages a favour."

No denying that ...

"Aliana..." It was Miguel's voice, raspy and low, a warning in the way he spoke.

"Roc, give me the knife," It was not a question but a command. He looked at me. His hold loosened, but he didn't let go. I shouted, "Bloody hell, Roc, you will put me in danger. Give me the knife!"

Roc took his time, but he did listen. He let go of José, but he didn't give me the knife. He maintained eye contact with José for a long time before he handed me the weapon. As soon as Roc passed the knife to me, Miguel and Cairo jumped on him and held him down. Roc tried to get them off, but he couldn't. It was José who began to punch Roc. He was going to punch another time, but I held the knife against his back. As soon as José felt the sharp knife, he stopped.

"See, I've let you say and do whatever you wanted. I was humiliated. I was incarcerated, isolated because of you. I just saved your life and you're going to beat up one of the people whom I'd kill for? You really want to risk it?" I asked him, my voice sharp as my knife and cold as ice. "Your lungs are right here." I pressed the knife a little, trying to make a point, José let out a small groan. "Now, do you know how long you'll have until your lungs fill with blood? Let me tell you, it is not a nice way to go. I don't want to do it, but you're pushing it."

I looked over to Miguel. "Miguel, I've done all I could to not get into trouble. I've followed your rules, and I've done nothing but stay quiet to the insults and the humiliations your people have put me through. All I'm asking is that you let *me* deal with this. I will get your answers. I didn't start this; José did. I will keep us both calm, but you gotta help me. I give you my word. Neither of us will do anything, okay? We'll calm down but *let go of him*. Please, Miguel."

"No. Fuck no," José began, I pressed the knife deeper into him, enough to cut and that shut him up. Miguel nodded with a smirk on his face and let go of Roc.

"José, just let it go." To my surprise, it was Cairo who spoke. I let go of José. Cairo pushed him to a corner in the room.

Roc was going to say something, but I put my hands on his arms to stop him, holding him tight.

"Roc," I said, waiting for him look at me, which he didn't do. "Listen to me. You need to calm down and sit down, you're too tall, my neck's starting to hurt." I joked, trying to lighten up the mood, which I succeeded judging by his little smile. "Don't make this hard for me, please."

"They came out of nowhere, Ali. With their spears and knives. It was a logical reaction. Did they expect us to receive them with open arms? Of course he was going to shoot. We were told to shoot them on sight. That's what they trained us to do!" Roc seemed more angry than sad. I just took his face in my hand and turned it so his eyes were looking at me.

"His life shall be an example of bravery, and he shall be remembered as a loyal servant to the Government," I whispered as I tightened my hold on his hand. I used to be proud when saying that phrase. I used to think that when I finally passed away, my parents would say goodbye to me with pride because I had achieved my goals in my life. But what a stupid phrase with a stupid meaning. That phrase wouldn't make Roc hurt less. It wouldn't bring his friend back.

"And together we shall endure the emptiness," Roc replied to me. At least he still considered me worthy of a reply.

"I'm sorry, Roc," I didn't exactly know why I was sorry, but I *felt* sorry.

"You're supposed to make him talk, not comfort him," Miguel demanded. It appeared his mocking had come to an end and now he had no patience left.

"He already told you why he's here," I answered, copying Miguel's tone of voice. Perhaps I shouldn't have talked to him like that, but I couldn't stand feeling guilty and pressured at the same time. "What else do you want to know?"

"Uh, I don't know," He looked at me with his eyes wide open, sarcasm all over his voice, "perhaps start with how many they are? How many are willing to come closer? What are they planning on doing if no one is found? I want to know things I can use to be prepared."

"The search finishes in a week. The Face publicly said that if there were no positive results, the search would be suspended and the gone would remain gone," Roc answered dryly. He didn't like the way Miguel spoke to me. "There's fourteen of us, and no one's breaking any more rules. So you have nothing to worry about, rebel."

Miguel made very cold eye contact with Roc. Then he turned around to face Cairo and have a conversation with him.

"Have you seen Nate?" I asked Roc.

"Nathaniel is okay, I guess," Roc shrugged. "You know he doesn't talk to me unless he has to. I saw him talking to Mathias, though."

"He's still not interested in girls, I assume." I smiled. I was still waiting for Nate to say he'd found his life partner and that he was going to marry.

"No. No suitable girl for your brother."

"And Mathias? Roma, Iris, Mia, Liz, Arian, my team?" I smiled, wanting to know about my friends.

"They are all fine, all your team offered to come to find you. Honour, you know? You gave them a lot, and now they're trying to give something back to your memory, trying to show that they are willing to find you. They all think you're dead. They want to find your body and honour your memory by incinerating it and not letting it rot in these woods." Roc told me. His eyes were bluer than ever. What he said made me feel nostalgic. "Mathias and I were supposed to look for you ourselves – he and I instead of Ben and me – but Roma said it was dangerous and that if Mathias went, he would report us as soon as we got back."

"Roma's right. Do congratulate him for being responsible for once."

"It seems since you left, Roma has matured quite a bit, you wouldn't recognise your team—" Roc said.

Miguel interrupted him, asking, "What's this team willing to do? How well trained are they?" I was glad Roc didn't get to finish his sentence about Roma.

"My team's very well trained," I answered as if the question was an insult, "but they follow orders. If they are told not to leave the restriction area, they won't."

"What are we going to do with him?" José asked. "He can't stay here, Miguel. We can't trust them at all."

"No." Roc shook his head. "If Aliana is here, then I shall be here."

I tensed as I lowered my gaze to the floor. Feeling everyone's eyes on me, I couldn't help but blush. I hated my private business being out on display for everyone to see. I didn't want Roc to stay. If Roc stayed, it would only complicate things. I knew Roc better than I knew myself. He would never leave the Government if he had a say in it. He had left this time because he knew he would come back at the end of the day. If he decided to stay in the city for me, sooner or later reality would slap him in the face and he would regret having decided to stay. And when that happened, he'd blame me for making him stay and he would resent me and I couldn't even think about that possibility.

"Aliana," Miguel called to me as he pointed with his head to the door.

Miguel, Cairo, José, Luna, and I stepped out of the room. It didn't feel safe to leave Roc in the same room with Isaac, but I couldn't do anything else. I looked at Isaac when I walked by him. He stood with his arms crossed over his chest, staring at Roc as if he was a threat who needed to be watched.

"He can't stay, Miguel," José said once we were outside and the door was closed. "People don't trust her. If you allow another soldier to stay—"

"Oh, I wonder why people don't trust me," I snapped sarcastically. How dare he just pretend that people didn't trust me for no reason. People didn't trust me because *he* made up lies.

"People won't like it," José said, ignoring me, which was the worst thing to do at this point. "Just because he's this little skank's boyfriend, it doesn't mean we gotta give him a place."

I raised my eyebrows at him, daring him to say something else. I was close to losing it. I couldn't control myself, as I hadn't taken my pills today. José was very close to getting his teeth knocked out, but I decided to keep calm and ignore his insults. He was waiting for me to snap. Little did he know that I actually agreed with him. I was going to reply, but a very deep voice interrupted me.

"Watch your mouth. I'm so done with your shit, always letting your tongue get us in trouble," Cairo snapped at José, standing right in front of him. I was amazed by his face; he looked truly terrifying. It was impressive. "She's my wife's daughter, my son's sister, and your leader's niece. She got more right to speak than you do. If I can accept her, then so can you."

Wow. Just wow. My eyes flew wide open. Did that just really happen? I looked over at Luna, who was just as surprised as I was. Miguel, on the other hand, was trying to hide a smile. Cairo and José were right in front of each other, looking like they were about to rip each other apart. Cairo had stood up for me. Although I didn't really care for Cairo, I didn't like that he stood up for me, as if his knowing the truth about Luna, me, and Samirah changed anything. It didn't.

I didn't know Cairo, and I didn't want anything from him or from Luna's family, except of course Eli. Cairo had never spoken to me except on my first day in La Cruz when he had pulled a knife on me. I didn't particularly care for him, and I didn't want that to change just because he was married to the woman I was supposed to consider to be my mother.

"Shall we let the princess do what she wants then?" José said defiantly, looking right into Cairo's dark eyes. "Her friend almost killed me. *She* almost killed me."

"Keyword being almost," Miguel whispered.

"Are you being serious? If I had wanted to kill you, the first time *or* this time, you wouldn't be standing here." I stepped in. This was supposed to be my fight, not Cairo's or Miguel's. "I don't know what your problem is. So far, I have worked and have done all I have been asked to do, just like you. You've tried to humiliate me in every single way possible, and I've lost control *once*. I see why you might not like me. After all, I did try to kill you. But I think you're overreacting. People have tried to kill me many times. You don't see me complaining, do you? Get over it, just like I'm trying to get over all the stuff you pulled on me. I have not asked for any favours because I'm in some way connected to Miguel. And I never wanted the truth to be known. Besides, if you didn't rush to open your big mouth and jump to conclusions, perhaps you would have given me the chance to tell Roc he could not stay."

I was so done with José's insults and his intention to humiliate me. On top of that, I was sad and tired and angry. I wasn't in the mood. This man always had something to say about everything. I couldn't understand how Miguel had chosen José as one of his men. I would never trust a man with a big mouth. And José ... José had the biggest mouth ever.

"People have tried to kill you?" Miguel asked, his face all smushed in confusion.

"When they train us," I answered, fighting the urge to roll my eyes. "Sometimes the practices get a little too intense."

"But you didn't practice with real weapons, did you?" He asked, completely forgetting about the matter in hand, and a little too interested in my training.

"Yes, real weapons. Some people died when they trained to be soldiers." I told him, sighing as I looked down at my feet, what the hell was going on with Miguel? "Can we go back to the problem, please?"

"Oh, yes." Miguel's voice went back to the boring and dull tone. "You were going to ask him to leave, why? He's your *friend*, is he not?"

Miguel didn't trust me. It was obvious. No matter what Luna said, it was easy to see he didn't trust me or didn't like me. I wasn't too fond of him either. I mean, the guy locked me in a room for weeks. But that didn't matter, what did matter to me was the way he looked at me as if I was nothing but a little girl like I was some insignificant girl who was nothing but trouble.

"Believe it or not, we have careers. We do know of pride and honour, and ambition. And in our careers, we find exactly that," I explained. "Roc is one of the best soldiers. If he stays here because of me, because of what he *thinks* he feels for me … he will regret it eventually and he will resent me. I am not going to carry that burden."

"He wasn't going to stay anyway, even if you wanted him to. I brought you out here because I didn't want to cause a scene, and although romance is somewhat entertaining, I ain't in the mood for it anymore," Miguel told me, looking at nobody but me. "If you are going to tell him to leave, how you so sure he gonna listen to you and leave? We can kick him out, but what's stopping him from coming back with his soldiers and taking you?"

"I was planning on asking him not to," I simply said. I was getting a headache. I hadn't had a good night of sleep in days.

"I think it's pretty clear to all of us that the boy wants to be with you. I don't think he's just gonna leave, not just like that." Cairo snapped his fingers at the end of his sentence, trying to make a point.

"If we pressure him to leave, he won't leave," Luna spoke, shaking her head. "If he thinks Aliana's at risk, he won't leave without her."

"I'll find a way to convince him."

"Whatever you need to tell him, get him to leave," Miguel said. He turned around and put his hand on the door handle. But then he turned back and looked directly at José. His eyes were cold as ice, and his smile was lethal.

"José, if you ever act out like that again, I will forget that we were ever friends and I will cut your throat open and rip your tongue out," Miguel threatened José. His voice was as calm as ever, a small smile on his lips as if he didn't just threaten José. Miguel looked deep in thought, then he nodded to himself and walked inside the room.

Cairo snorted and followed Miguel into the room, Luna tensed as she walked in after her husband. I was going to walk inside the room, but then José took me by the arm, gripping me very tight. I turned around to see his angry face.

"Same as us?" José whispered as he held me tighter, tight enough to leave a mark. "No. You don't fool me. You think you're better than us. You will never fit in here. There's simply no place for you here. The fact that you're Luna's bastard doesn't mean shit. You don't belong, you never will. Remember that."

José spat at my face, I felt his saliva touching my skin, my cheeks, and my eyelids. The rage built up within seconds as I watch him walk into the room. It took me a minute for me to swallow my anger and clean my face, trying to control myself. I wasn't going to make Roc believe I was safe if I got myself into a fight with José. But I didn't want to just get into a fight with José. I wanted to kill him. And the thought scared me.

I had a straight face when I went into the room. I held my anger in, swallowing it like poison, which burned my throat and fed the monster in me.

I walked towards Roc, trying to think of how to tell him he had to leave. I needed Roc to leave. If they disliked me, they were going to *hate* Roc. His personality was a little bit too much. He knew he was officially the best soldier the Government had. He also bragged about it. The people over here wouldn't like that.

"What's wrong?" Roc asked. I gave him a fake smile and then sat in front of him.

"I need you to do something for me, Roc, and you can't say no."

"No, Ali, no," Roc began.

"You don't even know what I'm about to ask,"

"Yes, I do. I know you, Aliana," he said, still frowning at me. "You're going to ask me to leave." He let out a tired, knowing laugh. "Why?"

"Firstly, I need someone over there to look after my family," I said to him. I hated lying to him again, but I had to in order to keep him away from all this. "You know them, Roc. Mum needs someone to help her with her research. Keep an eye on Johan. And Nathaniel, well, I just need someone to check in on him. You know how much I care for them, so I know you will take care of them if I ask you to. You *can* go back, Roc. You don't have to stay here, but you think you do because you know that if the roles were switched, I'd do it for you. This time is different, okay? You think this is what you want, and you think you owe me but you don't. If you stay here, you will regret it. And all you feel for me will turn into resentment. You can't do that to me, Roc."

I was trying to be honest within the lie. It was surprising, the coldness in my tone, the way I said everything to him as if it meant nothing. I did care for Roc – he was my best friend – but I couldn't handle him being here. I was barely making things work as it was. If Roc was going to be here, it would be chaos.

Roc was looking at the floor. He was going over my words, probably analysing every single word.

"You know, if I leave, we won't see each other again," he said with a question in his voice. He didn't want to leave me, but deep down he knew I was right. I was glad he saw it that way.

"At least you won't have to work as hard, because no one will be fighting to get your job," I joked, pushing his shoulder with mine.

"That's going to make things very boring." He sighed dramatically.

"You can come back while they are doing the searching," I said, trying to change the subject.

"It's never going to be the same, Ali," Roc whispered. "You know everything will change if you stay. Come with me, please. Just come."

"Roc," I didn't want to tell him I didn't want to go back because I didn't want to say those words out loud, much less say them to my best friend. "We do what we must, right? You go back home; I stay here. We have rules, Roc. We follow the rules. Once someone is gone, they remain gone."

"What good are those rules when all I care about is gone?" he asked, his tone filled with both exhaustion and sadness. "Do you understand what you're asking me? Aliana, don't ask me to leave you here."

"You've always said how you're going to listen to me because I know better, but still, you never do and you always get into messy situations because of that. I'm asking you this time. I'm asking you to *please* listen to me, because I know better, okay?"

Roc sighed deeply, he didn't say anything but he nodded slowly and a sense of relief washed over me.

"I think you can come back for a while," Miguel said out of nowhere as he folded his arms across his chest. "As long as he agrees not to bring people with him and lets us take his weapons when he comes – security and trust issues."

"I will never do anything that could hurt Aliana," Roc said, looking at Miguel as if he had just insulted him.

 **Chapter 23**

Location: La Cruz
Narrator: Aliana

HALF AN HOUR had passed before everyone stopped arguing about who was going to take Roc back to the bridge. José was complaining that he didn't want me to take him alone, so he offered to do it. That's when Isaac said he would go instead of José. Miguel didn't like either of the options, so he said that Cairo would take Roc. Miguel allowed me to go with them.

Cairo, Roc, and I walked for a few hours, during which time I told Roc everything that had been happening. I told him about my mother not being sick and how I was hoping to do something to help her. I told him about the experiments that the Government ran on people and why Roc and I were so different from the others. I told him almost everything, leaving out the truth about Luna being my mother. Roc processed the information in the same way Samirah did, by focusing on it while looking at nothing and hearing nothing else.

I had to work up the courage to tell him something that I knew would crush him but I couldn't keep hiding. "Roc, do you remember when they told you your father was gone? And Ronald?"

Roc tensed but nodded. Talking about this was like walking on thin ice. If there was something I was uncertain of when it came to Roc, it was how he would react to a conversation involving his brother and father.

"Your father loved your mum, and they used that love against him." Roc was going to say something, but I carried on, not giving him time to argue. "They told you your father and Ronald were dead, but they weren't dead. Not when they told you anyway. They both died a while after the Government took them away, and they blamed their deaths on a sickness they apparently had not found a cure for. Your father was 'sick', but not because he was born sick. Your father was sick because *they* made him out to be sick. The same happened to your brother."

I knew I shouldn't tell him that his mother was the one who informed the Government, but I couldn't prevent him from knowing that information. I couldn't keep it to myself any longer.

"Someone told the board," I could literally hear the thin ice breaking. "Elizabeth Meylor. She told the board about your father and brother. She didn't know—"

"My mother would never do that," Roc said. The tension in his voice scared me a little. "Johan made a mistake, read something wrong or whatever. I don't know, something else happened."

"Roc, it wasn't Johan who told me. I saw it, I read the files. I didn't want to believe it, but it is true, Roc. It is true."

"If what you're saying is true, then how come no one has complained? How come people actually *volunteer* to be experimented on and never say anything about being tortured?" Roc said as he shook his head. He didn't believe me. "And you, how come you feel?"

"I don't know, Roc," I lied. I wasn't about to risk my father's job. "But my mother's in danger."

I hadn't seen Cairo standing by the tree. I almost ran into him.

"From here he can go on his own," Cairo said as he pointed to the sky. I followed his finger and saw the sun going down. "Follow the straight path, and you'll be at the bridge in ten minutes max."

Roc nodded as he took his gun back. I hugged him tightly as if I would never see him again. I felt a tight knot in my throat and a strange feeling in my chest and the pit of my stomach. I was going to miss him.

"It's not too late, you know. You know you can come back with me. They will accept you, Ali."

"If I come back, there's a huge chance they will do the same to me as they are doing to my mother," I told him. I had been holding my tears all day; my eyes were burning now. "Look at me in the eye and tell me that you'd be okay with them messing around with my brain. Would you still care for me if I was someone different? Because that's what they'll do. They will destroy the Aliana you know."

I never wanted to have emotions. I wanted to find a way to remove them, but now the idea of being emptied of any emotion seemed... cruel. This was me; I was messed up but I had a chance at being fixed and it wasn't going to be through the Government. They would just erase everything or kill me and I didn't want to give it all up, not just yet.

"Okay, now leave," I said, trying to ignore the pain in my throat while also trying to swallow my sudden urge to cry.

Roc looked down at me with his deep blue eyes. I wanted to remember him like this, calm and with a smile on his face, free in the woods. His blond hair was a mess, so I tried to comb it with my hand like I used to do when we were kids and he wasn't so tall. My best friend was about to leave me again. It felt as if I really was letting a part of my heart walk out on me.

Roc smiled at me and turned around without saying a word. He started to walk towards the bridge. I watched him until he disappeared into the woods and there was nothing left to look at.

The return trip was faster. I followed Cairo's pace. I didn't ask questions. I didn't ask him to walk or run slower, and he didn't say anything either. It was a bit awkward. I wanted to ask him why he had stepped in when José was being particularly nasty back at the church, but I really didn't want to know the answer, as that would mean having to get into a conversation with him. He alternated between walking and running. I kept up with him.

When we arrived at the city two hours later, I was dying of thirst. My mouth was dry as a desert, my face was burning, and I was sweating. I missed exercise, and I also missed the way my heart pounded in my chest. The streetlights were on and people were out. It wasn't hot when the sun went down, it was actually quite chilly.

I walked to a water fountain. Cairo didn't say a word to me as he walked towards a little house with people sitting at the entrance. I followed him with my eyes and saw how he leaned down to Luna and placed a kiss on her forehead. Eli was there too, as were Miguel, Andrea, Isaac, and a little girl sitting on Isaac's lap. They all seemed to be having a good time, like a big family, all laughing and talking about nothing at all. They were a family without lies and secrets, a happy family. I couldn't help but think about my family. Were we really happy? I missed them, but I was not going to lie to myself. We never looked as cheerful as their family did.

I drank water from the fountain. It was fresh and tasted very good. It felt like I hadn't had a drink in ages. When I finished drinking, I started to make my way home. I wanted to lie down in bed and sleep after the long day I just had. So many things had happened that it felt like the day was longer than twelve hours. I wanted to get home and hide from Samirah. Eventually, I wanted to talk to my sister, but not right now. I was too tired to acknowledge the big fat elephant in the room. I would ignore it until I had a good nine hours of sleep. Or more...

When I arrived at Sam's place, the lights were off, I walked in and tried to look for Sam but she was nowhere to be seen. And I waited. I stayed up until the sun came back out but Sam didn't show up. My eyes felt heavy, way too heavy, I couldn't keep them open so I allowed myself to give in to my sleep.

An empty house, an empty body, an empty soul.

If only Isaac could hear what went through my head, he'd be proud of my deep, corny thoughts.

Narrator: Aliana

When Samirah arrived home, things were pretty weird. She was angry and wouldn't look at me, so I gave her time and space.

A week had passed. I was still waiting for Johan to communicate. Eli still did not want to talk to me as we used to, but at least I got him to talk to me. Sam spent all her time with Natalí, Natalí often looked at me with an apologetic smile as she was carried away by Sam. Roc had visited me almost every day since he went back to the Government. I told him to come back on the days when I didn't have to work, but he, like always, didn't listen to me and visited me whenever he wished.

When he came, he was as punctual as always. Exactly at 9.00 a.m he was at the church. I asked him if he got in trouble for arriving a day late, he told me that he had his ways and wouldn't say more. They were now looking for a new partner for him given that Ben was gone. He tried to convince me to go back with him, I told him that it wasn't right and that a love relationship between us would never happen. I tried to be positive and told him he would soon find a suitable wife and fall in love with her, to which he replied in the same way he always did: "I shall never marry anyone who isn't you."

My fear of Roc causing fights with people was not something I needed to worry about. When he came, he was actually nice to everyone. Well, maybe he wasn't nice, but he was tolerant. He tried his best to behave and for that I was thankful. Roc helped me to stay in shape, and he even tried to help me when I was working at Junior's, which was a disaster but the effort is what counts.

Sometimes Sam, Natalí, Isaac, and Sebastián would show up in the woods where Roc and I were practising. Sam would refuse to make eye contact with me, she'd spend her time talking to Natalí, and Sebastián would try really hard to get her attention. Something changed between them two and I don't think Sam talked about it with him and I think it was hurting Sebastián, or at least bothering him.

Isaac was there most of the days, our friendship grew stronger and I could tell it bothered Roc. I couldn't understand why because all Isaac and I did was talk. We spent *entire nights* talking. I don't think I've ever talked to someone so much. There was so much he was curious about, I told him almost everything he wanted to know. He talked to me about his childhood, about his friends, and about what he liked. Most of all he liked music and movies. He'd spend days lying on his bed just watching old movies or listening to music. However, no matter how many times I asked, he never talked to me about his mother and I never met her, not even when I spent hours at his house watching movies with him and Natalí.

My relationship with Luna was non-existent. I knew she was mentally not well. A part of me didn't want to blame her or hate her, but I couldn't just forget. I couldn't just make what I felt vanish because she had an excuse for what she did.

Cairo had changed. He didn't speak to me at all, but sometimes I caught him looking at me weirdly like he wanted to talk to me but he didn't know how.

Cairo wasn't rude. From time to time he would show me an awkward smile. I sometimes thought he was angry. I'd be angry too if my wife had two 17-year-old girls I knew nothing about. I heard Eli talking to Isaac about it, he said how Luna and Cairo had indeed argued almost every night, but his father apologised to Luna afterward. Apparently, Cairo had told him that no matter what Luna did or said, he would forgive her because he loved her unconditionally, no matter what.

Apparently, Cairo was miserable when Luna had been taken. I guessed that was why he didn't seem to care about Luna's secret romance and the daughters. I could tell by Luna's face that she wasn't having the best time of her life. If what Eli had said was true, the arguments were taking a toll on Luna and I couldn't help but feel a little sympathy for her. Whereas I wanted her to hurt, I didn't want her family to fall apart, mostly because Luna's family was also Eli's family.

I thought about Cairo quite a lot. I was very curious to know how he felt when Luna came back when the love of his life came back to him and was a completely different person from what he remembered. Although Luna had changed, Cairo stayed by her side through sickness and hell. How deep his love must have been that he stayed with her even when she wasn't the same person anymore. His love was truly unconditional. How lucky Luna was to have someone who loved her like Cairo did.

I couldn't help but wonder if anyone would love me through sickness and hell, if anyone would stay with me when I wasn't quite myself anymore. When I was a demon surrounded by angels, would my loved one pick me up and stay with me? Would my loved one stay with me when he could leave me and be in heaven instead of hell?

*   *   *

"What does one even wear to these family things?" I asked Isaac as we made our way back from the woods.

Miguel had come up with the great idea of having a family dinner. He didn't really leave room for anyone to say no. I didn't want to go and I was tempted not to, but after all, they did help me with Roc. It was going to be very awkward though.

"No biggie, honestly," He shrugged as he dried his sweaty face with his t-shirt, "last year Eli didn't shower for like a week and when we had a family dinner, he stank the whole afternoon. It was horrible. They just want to spend an hour together, that's all. Miguel has been in a weird mood lately, he gets all "funny" when he's pissed off, so if you thinking about not going, I'd recommend you rethink that."

"I never thought Miguel could… make jokes." I chuckled, we were getting closer to the city, I could hear people's voices, they were so loud.

"José." Isaac sighed, "He brings it out in Miguel. I mean, José has been bugging Miguel about your people staying here, and it has gotten to the point where Miguel has had enough and he's so tired of it that I think he now just takes it as a joke to piss José off."

"That's the thing, though," I began, trying to understand. "Why would Miguel have José as one of his trusted men when he doesn't even seem to trust him that much in the first place? Miguel's smart, and I can tell he doesn't trust or like José."

"Yeah, but *people* like José. They like him way more than they like Miguel. Thing is, people didn't always agree with Miguel's decisions but José supported him so people were willing to do it too. This could surprise you but… José *is* a people person."

I gasped dramatically, "Shocking!"

Isaac chuckled and pushed me with his shoulder, "I don't know, José knows how to talk to people and Miguel doesn't. José knows how to convince people while Miguel uses intimidation to do so. Miguel didn't want to be the leader, but he had to be."

"What do you mean?"

"Before Luna was taken, she was the one who was supposed to take over, she was supposed to be our leader, not Miguel." He told me, "Miguel was never into any of this, Luna was. Apparently, she had been preparing to be the leader ever since they were kids. From what I've heard she was just like José... but nicer."

"Funny, she doesn't seem like a people person to me."

"Well, duh," Isaac laughed, rolling his eyes at me, "You don't talk to her, how would you know? And people think she's crazy so they don't listen to her anymore. Hey, now that we're talking about it, do you mind if I ask—"

"Yes, I do mind." I interrupted him, walking faster than him towards the city. I liked hanging out with Isaac but he was getting a little too curious about the Luna subjects.

"Fine! I'll see you tomorrow!" Isaac shouted as I kept walking, making my way to Sam's place.

I was a street away from Sam's place, the sun was burning the back of my neck. I was ready to have the longest, coldest shower ever when Natalí startled me, putting her arm around my shoulder.

"Well, hello, little one." She said with a cheery tone and a smile on her face.

"Why are you in such a good mood?"

"Why are you so sweaty?" She removed her arm, looking at me with a disgusted face. "Lemme guess, you went to the woods with Isaac?"

"How'd you know?"

"He goes for runs around this time, and since you look like you do stuff with your body, I'm guessing you went with him." She shrugged, walking next to me.

"You're right." I told her, "So, you're not with my sister today?"

260

"Your sister woke up with a bitchy attitude and we had a petty argument, so she went to the beach with Sebas." She rolled her eyes in annoyance, I almost laughed at her face.

"May I ask what the argument was about?"

"Like I said, petty stuff." She shrugged, looking down at her feet as we walked, she suddenly seemed a little uncomfortable with the subject and I didn't want to pressure her so I waited. "She just— I don't know, she wants me to change things that I can't change, you know?"

"Sounds like Sam." I shrugged, "But she'll come around, she just always tries to find solutions to problems and when you tell her no, she doesn't always listen. But she'll come around."

"Sure she will, just not sure I'm going to be in the mood when she does." Natalí snorted, "Besides, she's with Sebas, right? Let her have her fun."

"Okay...?" I frowned and tried not to laugh at how annoyed she sounded just then.

"So, how's your life?" She asked me as we both walked into Sam's place. Natalí walked really slow. "I feel like we haven't talked much. You're replacing me with Isaac."

"More like you're replacing me with my sister." I shot back, she raised her hands to her chest and looked at me with a hurtful expression.

"That hurt my feelings." She dramatically threw herself on the sofa and put her feet up the coffee table. I playfully rolled my eyes at her and made my way to the kitchen, getting two glasses and filling them with cold water. "So, how are you feeling about this family dinner thing, Samirah talked about it none stop."

"Um, I don't know?" I answered, walking back to the living room and handing her a glass of water. "Kind of don't want to go, kind of do. Kind of scared, kind of not bothered."

"Scared? Why?" She furrowed her eyebrows and looked at me with confusion.

"I guess I'd be lying if I said I didn't care about them not liking me."

"You scared they won't like you?" She asked and I nodded slowly. "Why?"

"I don't know," I shrugged, looking away from her, "I'm not very talkative, you know? And they already like Sam and we're so different, what if they—"

"Don't compare yourself to your sister." Natalí interrupted me, "I like you and I like Sam. You're different, not gonna lie, you're kind of a pain in the ass sometimes, but you're cool. Kinda nice to be around you when you're not being all serious and shit."

"Well, thank you. I would say the same but your cursing's a little too much for me."

"Oh, please, you love me."

"If you say so…"

"I *know* so." She rolled her eyes at me playfully, drinking what was left of her water.

Chapter 24

Location: La Cruz
Narrator: Aliana

WHEN I AWOKE, I was still home alone. I had a quick shower and got dressed. It wasn't a surprise when I saw only two pills left. A wave of anxiety shook me. What the hell was I going to do when I ran out? I was supposed to lay back on the pills, but I obviously didn't do it. I needed the pills if I wanted to function properly and there was a little too much going on for me to function without taking the pills.

I took the last two pills to get me through the day. I chewed them before making my way downstairs. I sat at the kitchen table, eating a cold empanada when Samirah and Sebastián walked through the front door. Samirah was laughing at something he said.

"Good morning." I startled them. Sebastián smiled awkwardly at me and Samirah just ignored me.

"Hello," Sebastián greeted me.

I took a few *mamoncillos* out of the fruit bowl and slowly ate them. I looked directly at Samirah as I did so, she wouldn't look at me. It was like I wasn't even there. I would laugh at Samirah's efforts to ignore me if she wasn't actually succeeding. She took some things out of the fridge and began to move around the kitchen.

"How are you doing, Sebastián?"

"I'm good, thanks."

I understood that it bothered Samirah that I lied and that I kept the information about Luna to myself, but what was I supposed to do, tell her that her biological mother had left us and not once tried to contact us? Yes, I had been wrong. Luna was mentally unstable, but I hadn't known that. Samirah was blaming me for everything and projecting her anger onto me. Although I deserved some part of it, I didn't deserve it all.

"I'm good too. Thanks for asking," I said.

"Aliana." was all Samirah said, breaking her silence.

Her tone was a threat, a warning that I was going in the wrong direction. What could I possibly be doing wrong? I hated when Samirah behaved like a spoiled and childish little girl. When she behaved like that, no one could say anything to her. When I stopped talking to Johan, everybody judged me, but when Samirah had her spoiled, childish- little-girl moments, she could say anything, do whatever she wanted, no matter how hurtful it was, and no one would say a thing about it.

"On second thought, lately my beloved sister has been acting like a little brat. She has decided not to talk to me, and it seems she will not do so for a while, so I was wondering if you know when exactly she's planning on talking to me?" I crossed the line judging by the look on Samirah's face. Still, I carried on, "Maybe you know what's going on in that little head of hers."

Sebastián looked down at his glass of juice. He seemed to be uncomfortable, peering again and again at the door. It was awkward, very awkward. It was wrong to provoke Sam, but I didn't know what else to do to get her to talk to me. In another situation, Sebastián's face would have been comical, but I was a little too annoyed with Sam. I had to keep a straight face, as I was in an eye contact duel with Samirah.

"Um, I'm gonna go. I'll let you two talk." Sebastián began to get up from his chair.

"No, Sebas," Samirah commanded. Sebastián sighed and sat back down. I tried really hard to keep my face straight.

"I have the right to be angry, and I want to be. You, on the other hand, have no right to—"

"Oh, give it a rest, Johan isn't here and Luna's sick, so you've decided to blame me. Do you even know who you're angry at? I stayed quiet. All right, you can punish me for that, but you can't punish me for Johan and Luna's mistake. You can't blame them so you take it out on me."

"Whatever you say!" Samirah snapped. She walked out of the house, slamming the door behind her.

Sebastián looked at me and I stared back at him. I was waiting to see if he said something or if my staring would make him feel so awkward that he'd get up and leave. I was almost sure it'd be the latter.

Sebas stopped our staring contests and looked away from me, he took a deep breath in and said, "She just wants to know why you didn't tell her anything,"

"Hasn't she considered that perhaps I didn't tell her because I was trying to protect her from something?"

"Protecting her from what? The truth?" Sebastián asked, laughing as if he was trying to make sense of what I said. "She knows there's something else you're not telling her, that makes her angry."

I looked down at my hands, I felt a sudden urge to bite my nails.

"She doesn't want any more secrets," He carried on as he stood up and shrugged, "I see you around, my dude, gotta work."

Sebastián walked out after that and I was left alone once again.

* * *

"Why don't you bring Mathias with you?" I asked Roc. I didn't particularly think it was a good idea, but I wanted to see him too and he meant no harm to anyone.

"Roma says they don't want to put themselves in danger just because I want to find you. They don't know I found you," Roc finished, looking away. I was going to ask him why, but he continued speaking. "If they come, they'll try to get you to come back and it'll be hard for you to say no. If you ever come back, it will be because you want to, not because you are being forced."

"Are you ready?" He asked me, looking around at the woods, we were alone today and I wanted to train.

Roc took his t-shirt off, folded it and dropped it near a tree. I rolled my eyes at the gesture. He was such a show-off. I wanted to make fun of him but without a warning, Roc attacked me. I dodged his punch by an inch. I was going to tell him not to hit me in the face because I had a dinner that afternoon to which I didn't want to show up with a swollen and bruised face, but if I did tell him that, then he would start to ask questions. And I didn't want to tell him about Luna.

I was a little rusty. It was hard to keep up with Roc. It had been months since I last trained this way with someone since I last proper fought someone. At first, I only dodged his attacks. The theory was still with me. I knew all of the martial arts forms in existence. I knew how to defend myself and attack, how to mix my kicks with my punches, and how to knock a person down with just one simple hold. It was just practice. It was the stamina that I no longer had. Even if I was going for runs with Isaac, *this* was different.

We trained for five hours non-stop. I didn't know that it was possible for me to miss being someone's punching bag. By the time we were done, I was gasping for air but I felt *alive*. At first, I couldn't get in any punches, but once my body woke up, I was punching and fly-kicking Roc. He got more than a few punches in. My cheekbone was on fire. Although it didn't feel swollen, I knew a few bruises would show up tomorrow and that my body was going to be very sore, but I liked the idea of being sore.

We were both sweating like pigs. Roc was laughing at me for being out of breath as we made our way back to Sam's.

When we finally entered the house, I headed straight for the kitchen and poured myself a glass of water and we sat at the kitchen table.

"I need you to do something for me," I began, looking down at my glass of water. I swallowed hard and tried to figure out a way to ask him without sounding too desperate. I knew Roc would help me but I just didn't know how to ask.

"You need more pills?" He asked when I didn't say anything. I could hear the concern in his voice but I tried to ignore it. "I thought the reason why you took them was because you were there—if you're here, you don't need them—"

"I still need them, though." I snapped, I didn't mean to but it always irritated me when people got involved in my business. "I promise I'm gonna stop but you know I can't just stop taking them, I'm doing it in a slow pace, but I'm doing it. It's not like last time, okay? I promise." I told him and when he was convinced, he nodded. I carried on, "You're going to help me or not?"

"I'll see what I can do," he sighed. He wasn't completely happy, but he hadn't said no. I relaxed, able to breathe again.

"How are things going here?"

"Well, aside from the pills, everything is okay. Sam's still angry at me."

"Keenan siblings, always arguing." He laughed, I wanted to share his laughter but the memory of Nate didn't let me. And as if he had read my mind, he added, "All you two are missing is Nathaniel."

I felt the air around us shifting, I didn't want to think about Nate because I knew I wouldn't be able to see him again. "Anyway, how are things over there?"

"All is the same." Roc's laugh was now a sad smile. "It's weird without you. I miss you. I find myself counting the hours until I can come back out to see you."

Roc moved a bit closer to me. My heart skipped a beat, not because I was nervous or because I liked it, but because I knew what he was going to do and I didn't want him to. I looked at the glass of water and nodded.

"I've been thinking." Roc swallowed loudly. "If we were both here then we could be together, right?"

I should have said something to stop him, but my brain was slow to process and couldn't find the words. I didn't want to hurt his feelings but I didn't want him to think that I would love him back one day, because that wasn't going to happen – not the kind of love he wanted, anyway.

"I've been looking at them. These people, they do not care who you decide to be with," Roc carried on, "I want you. You know you care for me too, right?" Roc was getting closer to me. I had to tell him. If I didn't, I would regret it later.

"I do care for you, Roc. … You're my best friend. Of course I care for you." I emphasised the word *friend* to make a point. Judging by Roc's face, I needed to try again.

"Then I don't see why not." He smiled. I hated to be the one to ruin his smile, but I had to tell him.

"Roc, it is not—" *Going to happen.* I would've said if Roc hadn't leaned in and kissed me. Before I noticed, he was already all over me and his wet lips were pressed against mine. My muscles tensed. Roc was my *friend*, I didn't want this. I pushed him away as I tried to process what had just happened.

I wanted to say something, tell him that it couldn't happen but before I could even form the words, someone walked into the kitchen.

"Hello," Eli said with a straight face and a serious tone.

"Eli …" I stood up from the chair as quickly as I could, suddenly wanting to be as far away as I could get from Roc. "What are you doing here?"

"Um," His eyes weren't leaving Roc. "Well, Isaac told me he was coming to get you, but I told him I'd do it 'cos I needed to talk to you."

"She's busy," Roc answered for me, his voice was sharp and full of annoyance.

"Nope, I don't think she is," Eli shot back at Roc with just as much annoyance.

"We were talking," Roc said, standing up. I frowned at him.

"Yes, Roc, we *were*, and we aren't anymore." I didn't like the way he looked at or talked to Eli. Besides, I was still in shock about the kiss that I did *not* want to happen. "And now I need to talk to Eli."

Roc tensed his jaw and took a deep breath before he spoke. "I'll come tomorrow. I'll get you your stuff, and we'll finish our discussion."

"Bye." Eli mocked him with a smirk. Once Roc left the room. I felt like I could breathe again.

"I don't like him." Eli's voice brought me back. He was now rummaging inside the fridge, probably looking for something to eat. He was always so hungry

"Nate doesn't like him. Neither does Sam. So, I guess my siblings just don't like my best friend," I said, trying to joke, but it didn't feel like the time to be making jokes. It was the first time that Eli had come to me to talk after we had an argument. I didn't want to ruin it.

"If you want a boyfriend, I can make a list of good men who will be willing to make you a lovely bride. You should find a strong man, an attractive, good guy, but not that one. He's weird." Eli pointed at the door, where there was no trace of Roc. Eli still had his head inside the fridge, but I could tell he was a bit annoyed or maybe upset still but he was at least trying to joke around with me.

"He isn't my boyfriend. Don't say that. And I don't want a boyfriend. Don't say that either."

"What do I say then? You want to reduce my vocabulary, sister? I can't deal with this, you need to get food, there's nothing eatable in this fridge." He turned around and closed the fridge door. He had a sausage in his hand and was biting into it.

"Any who …" he carried on, ignoring me as he poured a glass of juice and then sat down. "I came because I wanted you to do something for me."

"What?" I quickly answered.

"Promise me you'll behave around my mum." He spoke, looking directly at me as he chewed. It took me a while but I nodded. "Just one afternoon, you don't even have to talk to her, just… don't be an ass."

"I promise." I sighed. Eli looked at me with a small smile on his lips. "Did you go to Samirah too? Because she's been behaving *real* nice lately."

"I don't care about how badly you and Samirah want to hurt each other." He rolled his eyes, "That's your sister, siblings argue and fight, you'll probably get over it. My mum's different, what you say affects her differently."

"I'll try my best."

"No, don't try your best, *do* your best." He frowned at me with annoyance written all over his face. I sighed, nodding at him.

"Great, get ready because you don't want to be late. You kinda smell like sweat." He told me, "Also, Isaac will eat all the coconut rice and I gotta be there on time to not let that happen."

Without saying much more, Eli made his way to the living room and waited for me to get ready. I had a quick shower and put on the first thing I could find. Afterward, Eli and I made our way to Miguel's house.

* * *

"Everything okay?" Isaac asked once he saw me, he was coming out of the kitchen with a bunch of plates, I followed him.

"Yep, all great." I answered, "Actually, uh, I might be a little nervous. I think."

He laughed as we entered the dining room and Isaac began to set the table. "Well, I just heard my aunt and Luna talking about your dad. I cringed when my aunt asked if he's hot." Isaac visibly shook his whole body as he set the last place on the table.

"That's disgusting."

"I mean, they were together…" He half shrugged, looking at me from the other side of the table. I shrugged.

"I know it sounds stupid but I don't know… the thought of Luna actually knowing and talking about my dad is just— weird."

Luna was my biological mother and she had something with Johan, but I just hadn't thought about it in deep. I never thought that they actually had a *real* relationship. It was shocking and hurtful to come to terms with the fact that they did have a *real* relationship, they cared for each other and they knew things about each other.

"Well, she *did* say they were in a relationship." He pointed out the obvious, he then looked at me and instantly frowned, he pointed at my cheekbone. "What happened?"

"I was practising this morning." I didn't care about my face. I looked down at the table, there was so much food, I wondered how many people were actually coming. "That's a *lot* of chicken …"

"Okay, here's a plan." Isaac laughed. He knew that I didn't like to eat meat. If there was something else to eat, I wouldn't eat the meat. "Sit next to me. When my auntie gets distracted, you throw the chicken onto my plate and then eat the rice, potatoes, and salad."

I nodded, smiling at his efforts to lighten the mood.

"Sam's here. Did you talk to her?" he asked me, taking a small potato and biting into it.

"We had a little chat— yeah, you could say that." I watched him lick his fingers after he swallowed, I rolled my eyes and grabbed the napkins. "She's angry, which makes me angry."

He laughed and shook his head. "And you didn't by any chance try to provoke her, did you?"

"Uh…" I stood there, looking at the table.

"Sebas told me." He smirked, I rolled my eyes. Stupid boy with his stupid mouth.

"If I provoke her, she talks to me." I shrugged, trying to make him understand, "I don't even do it on purpose, she gets mad and I get mad and… I do it."

"No need to explain it to me." He shook his head, setting down the last plate. I nodded and finished setting the napkins. "By the way, don't tell my aunt you don't like meat. She gets annoying with the whole stuff about growing and needing vitamins and whatnot."

I was going to say something but was distracted by Andrea walking into the dining room with a big plate in her hands, as soon as she walked in the smell of food overwhelmed me. Isaac always said his aunt was a great cook. The smell confirmed it. My mouth started watering because of it. Miguel was bringing the juice and Luna was carrying two bowls. Andrea shouted for Samirah, Sebastián, and Catalina to come downstairs. Catalina was Miguel's daughter. She was the cutest little thing, she had her curly hair up in a bun. Her eyes were the same colour as Miguel's and she had a small little nose. Her skin was a mixture between dad's bronze and Andrea's brown. She kept staring at me when she thought I wasn't looking. Isaac said she was six.

Just in time, Cairo walked in through the main door with a huge smile on his face and a flower in his hand. He kissed Luna and placed the flower in her hair. I looked away. It felt wrong to watch.

Andrea was talking to everyone and I knew I should've paid attention to what she was saying but I couldn't concentrate. Sam sat across the table with Sebastián at her side. She wouldn't look at me.

We all started to eat in silence, the air around us felt thick. I could hear Eli trying not to laugh next to Isaac, who was whispering something to Eli. Samirah was avoiding making eye contact with me, and I was getting annoyed at the worst moment. Sam was being childish. I wanted her to snap out of it. It was wrong of me but at least that way we could finally have a proper fight and then she'll get over it.

Isaac was making small talk with Miguel and Andrea. Catalina was saying that she wanted more juice when Samirah finally spoke. I had to take my chance.

"Can I have the salt please, Isaac?" Sam asked. I laughed humourlessly.

The salt was *literally* right next to me. Did she really want to do this? It was ridiculous in a funny sort of way. Before Isaac could reach for the salt, I picked up the shaker.

"Here you go," I said as I stretched my hand out towards Samirah, offering her the shaker. She hesitated, but ultimately, she took it from me. "You're welcome. Rude much?"

"Aliana," Isaac whispered to me. There was a warning in his tone, but I wasn't going to back down. I had reached my goal, Sam looked like she was about to snap.

Congratulations to me! I was finally going to know what was really bothering Sam. Her cheeks turned red dangerously fast, her hand curled into a fist and she was visibly shaking. One thing about Sam was that when she got angry… she *got* angry.

"Why would I thank you?" Samirah's eyes were full of rage. I prepared myself for hearing mean comments and the truth about her anger. "You have done nothing but lie to me."

"Samirah, what in all—"

"What's going on?" Miguel's voice interrupted me.

"Nothing. Sorry," I answered. "I think Samirah and I should step outside for a moment if we're allowed."

"No, I am not stepping outside. And there *is* something wrong," Sam snapped. This was new. Samirah was never like this in front of strangers. She always liked to keep appearances.

Ha, but were they strangers, though? I felt more like a stranger to Sam than these people seemed to be. This family was more of a family to Sam than I was right now.

"What is it?" Miguel asked, for once looking clueless and interested. There was a piece of meat on his fork, it was halfway to his mouth when we rudely interrupted his dinner.

"What happened is that my sister lied to my face every day. She woke up every morning and looked at me in the eye for *years*, all the while knowing the truth. Day after day and year after year she *lied*, and now she simply wants me to forgive and forget."

Samirah's tone was angry and loud but there was a hint of disappointment in it. My plan had backfired. I never expected Samirah to snap in front of so many people.

"But is that not what we do with you, Sam?" I shot back, forcing myself to smirk at her. If something annoyed her was when people didn't seem to be affected by an argument. "Do we not forgive and forget when it comes to you? Did Nathaniel not forgive and forget? Did *I* not? Don't I do that every day?"

"Oh, for goodness sake, Aliana, we're talking about *you* lying to me, not about me," Samirah shouted. Of course she would say that, she knew that she had done more wrong than I had.

"Okay, so you're angry because no one told you, because you were the last one to know. Does it bother you that much to not know something?" I attempted to control my tone of voice and keep it neutral, but I failed. Samirah annoyed me a great deal sometimes, even now when it was my own fault that the argument was happening.

"You're asking me if it bothers me to not know that my mother isn't actually my mother? Jeez, Aliana, hard to say …" Seeing Sam angry was always funny, it would've been ten times funnier if I wasn't angry too.

"And I told you I had reasons not to tell you." I shot back trying not to shout, unlike Samirah, who apparently felt free to say whatever she wanted.

"Well, go ahead and share those reasons with me. Come on, Aliana, tell me. Tell me why."

I wanted to say it. I wanted to shout it to her, tell her that the woman she so freely talked to and easily accepted, tried to kill me. That it was Luna's face I saw every night in my nightmares, that even her name sent shivers down my spine, that I was *terrified* of Luna.

But I couldn't do it. I couldn't bring myself to do that to Eli. I wouldn't dare ruin Eli's view of his mother, I wouldn't forgive myself if I did.

"She doesn't have to tell us if she doesn't want to." Andrea's voice made me look away from Sam and at Luna, who was sitting next to Andrea.

Luna looked miserable as if she was about to run away from what she knew I could say. And at that moment I realised that I wouldn't tell the truth, not only because I didn't want to ruin Sam and Eli's relationship with Luna, but also because I couldn't ruin it for Luna too. The realisation shook me in place. Even if it was only with a small part of me, I cared enough not to want to ruin her relationship with her son and Sam.

Everyone else at the table looked as uncomfortable as I felt. They were looking at everyone and no one at the same time. Miguel just looked tired, as if he regretted asking anything in the first place.

"Ain't this a great family reunion?" Eli said seriously. Cairo gave him a little slap on the back of his head and told him to be quiet.

Samirah looked outraged. Sebastián leaned in and said something to her that made her look angrier. Even I was surprised by how angry she looked. I wanted to make her snap, but not like this. Sam wasn't like this. There was something more, something bigger, bothering her, making her upset and angry. I wondered how much longer I would have to push until she let it all out.

"You're blaming me for something that isn't my fault," I tried my best to keep myself calm, but it only made Sam get angrier. For a person who didn't like to be pressured, I sure did put a lot of pressure on other people.

"You *knew* and you didn't say anything. You are to blame too," Samirah shook her head. And then out of nowhere, she added something that would have been comical in another situation. She pointed at my plate as she carried on. "And you don't even eat chicken!"

Isaac snorted at the comment but quickly carried on eating. I had taken two bites of the chicken. It was actually delicious. I didn't mind eating it, but I would have preferred not to. I had tried to pass it to Isaac, but his aunt was *always* looking.

"And you think I wanted to know any of this? I didn't tell you because you were better off not knowing." I ignored the chicken comment and the horrified look on Andrea's face.

"Yeah, and who knows what other secrets you and Dad have and won't tell me, because 'We thought you were better off not knowing.'" Her face was turning a strange shade of red, as were her eyes. I had never seen her *this* mad. There was jealousy in her voice. She was Johan's little girl. Of course, she was jealous because I had a secret with him. *Unbelievable.*"I was here, I was fine, and then you came and changed everything. I wish you would have stayed on the other side of the bridge. You didn't think of anyone but yourself, and now Mum is hurt and about to die because of you. You ruin everything you touch, Aliana."

I stared at Samirah with a forced smile on my lips, trying to hide the hurt I felt. I wasn't hungry anymore and the few bites I had taken wanted to go back up my throat. I could see a slight regret cross her face but it was quickly gone. Often when Samirah said mean things to me, Nate came to the rescue and tried to convince me by telling me she didn't mean it, she was just angry and she *was* angry, she was saying whatever she could to hurt me, but she meant it. Otherwise, she wouldn't have thought of it. Maybe she wasn't thinking straight, but thanks to that, she was finally saying all the things she had kept inside her.

The room was so quiet that for a moment I thought everyone was gone, but then I heard Catalina making noises with her plate. I took a deep breath, trying to hold the last bit of control I had so I would not cry. I don't think Samirah knew how hurtful her words really were, I don't think she knew how unbelievably cruel she was when she wanted to be. I tried my best to keep all the emotions I felt from showing. I reassumed a cold, sharp smirk and a neutral tone of voice.

"My fault? That's really how you see it, huh?" I smirked at her. Her eyes burnt with anger and it was all directed at me. She wouldn't even blink. "Did you ever think of us while you were here, happy and enjoying yourself, playing love stories with him? In the meantime, we were over there, trying to endure the loss. I made a mistake coming here, I know that. I also know that you'd rather be here with these people than with your family." I swallowed hard, determining that I would not cry. This was *not* my fault. "And if I didn't tell you about Luna, it was because I did not want you to hate her or Johan like I did."

"Why would I hate my father? I am not like you, Aliana. I'm not sick and incapable of loving. I'm *nothing* like you." Samirah's anger was in each word she said, and all of her words felt like a punch to my stomach. I was not ready for that. I didn't even know what to say to that.

Everyone went silent, even Catalina. I was about to get up and leave, but then a voice broke the silence. I thought I heard the voice in my head because it was too familiar to be real. It was impossible for him to be here.

"That was just unnecessary."

I turned around as fast as I could. A young man was standing at the entrance of the living room. It was a projection, with blue pixelated dots and a glitch from time to time. I didn't need any colour to know who it was. Nate was wearing an elegant suit with a fancy tie. There was a handkerchief in his blazer's right pocket, he said his allergies forced him to always keep it close. Nathaniel was always elegant. Wherever he went, he had to make an impression.

"Nate?" I asked, not knowing if I was going crazy or if he *really* was there.

"Sister," Nathaniel smiled. He looked as flawless as always. He fixed his tie with his left hand and kept his right hand in his pocket, he never liked to show his burnt hand, so he always tried to keep it hidden. "Before you start pointing fingers and blaming whoever for whatever, I must say I do not like Samirah's new accessory. Who *is* that man?"

I turned to look at Samirah. She was standing, and so was Sebastián. They were holding hands. My eyes flew open. That was new.

"Better question: how are you here, Nate?" Samirah asked.

"Little one, I am truly offended that you have to ask. Is there anything I do not know or cannot do?" Nate chuckled, unbuttoning his suit. I stepped closer to the hologram. "I believe it is important that we all have a conversation. And if I might add, I don't think it's fair the way you're all angry at the poor man. We all make mistakes. Father's 'mistake' was feeling. You cannot blame a person for something he has no control over."

Nate walked away from me and towards Luna, who was standing. Cairo was next to her. They both looked equally uncomfortable.

"You must be Luna." Nathaniel's tone was neutral and calm. Luna smiled politely, and so did Nate. "Sam has your smile. Aliana has your cheeky eyes."

Anger burst through me. How could he say that?

"Am I the only one who thinks this is weird?" Eli asked.

Miguel was going to say something but Nate talked before Miguel got the chance.

"Actually, this is a bit weird and awkward for me too. I believe I haven't introduced myself. How rude of me. I am Nathaniel Keenan, Samirah and Aliana's older brother. What is your name?"

"Elías. You can call me Eli, though. I'm Luna's son."

"*Oh.*" Nate slowly nodded, taking both of his hands to his pockets, looking out of place. "Well, nice to meet you, Eli."

"*So*, what's new? Am I to blame for something horrible?" Nate chuckled. Then he sighed and quickly continued. "What have you done, LynnLynn?"

Nate was mocking us.

"Why ask a question when you don't seem to care about the answer, Nathaniel," I told him.

"I'm not angry at you," Samirah answered after me.

"Of course. How could she possibly be angry at you when I'm the one to blame for everything?" I smiled dryly at Nate. "She'll probably tell you that it's my fault she burnt your hand because it is also my fault that she's too stupid to understand what no means."

"He didn't lie to me. *You* did." Samirah furiously walked towards me, stepping like a heavy animal as she went. If I didn't know better, I would've been afraid of her. But then again, if Samirah was going to hit me, I was prepared.

"Is she serious?" I laughed and looked at Nate. "Can she not see you? Don't you see that *he's here*? He obviously knows, you idiot!"

"Of course, I know. The difference is that I didn't react like you did. I was angry at first, but I understood. I repeat: we cannot blame ourselves for something we have no control over."

"What?" Sam frowned, staring at him in disbelief, she definitely wasn't expecting that answer.

"Johan cheated on Mum and you're simply okay with it?" I laughed in disbelief. "Ah, of course you wouldn't be angry. The perfect son always accepting his beloved father's mistakes."

"Hey, that's not fair. I *was* angry. We're all adults here, so let's all be honest with one another. Aurora *forced* Father to marry Mother. They were 15 years old, for goodness sake. Of course, Father didn't want to marry. He was a kid. And if you think Mother wanted to marry Father, then you're really fooling yourself. Mother wanted one thing, to be successful – the prodigy – to graduate with honours to bring honour and pride to her middle-class family. She didn't want a family *or* kids for that matter because that would push her away from her life goals. I love Mother. I'm not judging her. We all have ambitions. Hell, I don't want kids or a wife, never have and probably never will.

"Mother didn't want to marry Father much more than Father wanted to marry her. Mother wanted to be known for her own intelligence and achievements, not for her marriage. If Mother had wanted to marry, she would have married anyone but a Keenan. It was Aurora's orders to get married. They had to accept it. It doesn't justify what Father did, I'm no one to judge him for something he did when he was just a boy. And neither should you two. And that's something I've been wanting to say to you, Aliana."

I didn't know what to say, I didn't want to think of that way, it was weird to think that my parents didn't want to be together, that they were forced into it. I knew it was true but it was not something I… liked.

"You idiots. Both of you!" Sam broke the silence as she pointed at me and Nate.

"*Why* are you angry?" Nathaniel laughed, this situation was just confusing.

"Because she's a fool, that's why," I commented before Samirah could reply to Nate.

"Oh, for Christ's sake, I can't stand you sometimes," Samirah snapped, frustrated and annoyed. Nate started to chuckle. I wanted to snap at him for being so annoying at a time like this, but Samirah carried on, saying, "You're such a hypocrite. You say you don't lie yet all you do is lie. Even when I ask you to be honest, completely honest with me, you still hide stuff from me." She pointed at Luna when she finished.

I turned to look at the rest of the people in the room with us, I had completely forgotten about them. Miguel was eating his food with no care for what was happening while his daughter was drinking from his cup. Cairo was playing with Catalina's hair, I think he was braiding it and that was quite honestly the oddest image ever. Eli, Isaac, and Sebas were watching the show with bored faces, Eli used his hand to support his face. Luna and Andrea watched us, standing and looking between confused and uncomfortable.

"I didn't even know if she was alive or dead. All I knew was what I saw on that stupid video," I whispered, looking away from Luna. I could feel her eyes on me, she probably knew what was on the video. "Johan told me not to tell you. I didn't want to tell you either, I thought it wouldn't hurt you not to know. What good would it do you to hate someone you didn't even know, to hate her but at the same time wonder who she was, and why she hurt us and left us behind? It was better if you didn't know. That way, you wouldn't ask yourself questions that no one could answer."

Samirah glared at me with such hate that it made my chest tighten.

"So, are we all forgiven?" Nathaniel spoke, interrupting us with his cheerful smile. "And let's be fair: Sillyana does have a valid point."

"Do *not* call me that." I gave Nathaniel a dirty look.

"Why do you always have to be on her side?" Samirah asked with jealousy. I couldn't understand how she could still be jealous. How could *she* be jealous of *me*? It was absurd and stupid, as she had everyone and everything. If she wanted to, she could have taken *everything* from me.

"Because he likes me better," I smirked at Samirah at the same time Nathaniel shook his head.

"That is not true. I don't like either of you. One day you two just appeared in my life and I was stuck with both of you, making you two girls my slaves was fun, though. Anyway, if it was me in her position, I wouldn't have told you either, Sam."

"Thank you!" I put my hands into the air. *Finally* someone understood.

"No one has explained to me who is that man looking very miserable over there. He looks so uncomfortable that I almost want to open the door for him to leave." Nate laughed. "I am yet to discover if I like him or not. I'm not entirely sure."

"He's my boyfriend, Sebastián," Samirah answered. Every single pair of eyes snapped to Samirah and Sebastián. I suddenly was very curious as to how all this would turn out.

"What? Since when do you need a *boyfriend*? How do you even know the meaning of that word?"

I would've laughed at Nate's face expression but I wasn't in the mood for that. Sam said I didn't think about anyone but myself, yet she was in a relationship with a guy when she didn't feel anything for him. She said so herself.

"You have a *what*?" Nathaniel sang, shaking his head. "No, no. No. You shouldn't even know the meaning of that word."

"Don't start, Nathaniel." Samirah rolled her eyes, but it was too late, Nate was already going on about how she was too young to date and I knew he wasn't going to let it go.

*　*　*

"Why didn't you say anything?" I asked him, playing with the ring on my middle finger. It was the only thing I ever kept on me (aside from my pills). It was my mum's ring, she gave it to me when I was 14. When Sam saw it, she was so mad she didn't talk to me for a week.

We all were in Miguel's living room. It seemed we lost our appetite, and apparently, Johan had asked Nathaniel to communicate to give us information. Since Johan couldn't because he was in a very important meeting.

"I wasn't supposed to." Nathaniel sighed, he was eating gummy bears, "I wanted to, I really wanted to but— knowing would've only put you in danger."

"Yes, but Sam knew…" I frowned, looking up at him to see him with his hand halfway to his mouth, I couldn't keep the hurt from my voice. "She knew all along and you just… you never said anything."

"Sam was supposed to be Aurora's successor, she *had* to know," Nate explained, his eyebrows curved in a way that told me he was sorry but it wasn't that what hurt me.

"Huh, favouritism since babies, I see." I joked, looking away from him back to my mum's ring.

"Actually, about that…" Nate spoke, I looked up at him to find a look of pity in his eyes. I didn't like it. "Aurora believes and I mean she has *convinced* herself that you're not Cynthia's daughter."

"But we aren't?" Samirah answered for me, hurt in her voice.

"Yes, but Aurora thinks you are." Nate looked directly at Samirah. It took me a second to understand, even if he was being vague, I understood. I laughed tiredly, shaking my head. Swallowing was suddenly very hard, it was like I had a knot in my throat, my eyes were burning.

do not cry, don't cry, don't you dare cry.

I pinched myself and tried to focus on their conversation. "That's stupid." Sam chuckled, trying to lighten the mood. I couldn't find it in me to say anything, I didn't know *what* to say. "We practically look the same."

"She believes what she wants to believe." Nathaniel shrugged. I swallowed harder this time, clearing my throat as if somehow that would help with the giant knot in my throat.

"So, what's happening with Mum?" Sam changed the subject.

"Revelations are coming up." Nathaniel sighed, "That's the only day where you could come in and get Mother out."

"What?" Samirah's spoke with confusion all over her voice. At this, I force myself to listen to their conversation.

"To be honest, I don't think Johan can find a way to make it safe for Mum. If he does it, it could kill her. Her brain's *sort of* damaged and she's— she won't be able to go through it twice." Nate told us, his eyes dropped to his hands, I could see how it affected him even if he tried to keep his face straight. "Even if he had found a way to not hurt her, the board will kill her. The same way they have done with every single person who has stood in their way. She needs to be secure and away from the Government. You have no idea how important this is."

"How are you going to get her out?" Sam asked.

"Revelation day is our best chance, everybody will be there, even the CB will be completely—"

"I'm sorry, Nathaniel, but why would we help you?" Miguel interrupted. I frowned, looking at him. "Why would I risk my people's lives for someone who has done nothing for us? No one would volunteer to help. Everybody here will see it like that; we don't help those who don't help us."

"You don't help those who don't help you?" Nathaniel stepped closer to Miguel. His tone was no longer formal but rather upset. The bag with his gummy bears still in his hand. I *really* wanted one of those gummy bears. "Do you think those pills Luna takes to stay sane fall from the sky? *My mother* made that possible. She makes sure that your sister gets the medicine she needs. And you want to tell me that she has done nothing for you? She's the reason Luna is still alive. Don't you forget that."

"And don't you forget who made her that way," Miguel spoke in a low, raspy voice as he locked eyes with Nate, pointing at him.

"Nobody's asking for you for help, though, Miguel." I stepped in, "You said you wouldn't risk your people, I'm not one of you. You can't tell me what to do and if it comes to it, I will do this."

"I told Johan I was going to help, and I will." Luna looked at Nathaniel, who nodded in gratitude at her. She then turned to Miguel. "I know what Cynthia did for me, I will never forget. It might not look like it, but we're *all* very grateful for what she did. No matter what it takes, if it comes to it, we will get her out. I promise you that."

 **Chapter 25**

Location: La Cruz
Narrator: Aliana

"MORNING!" ELI SCREAMED, making my heart almost jump out of my chest.

"What the hell?" I tried to not shout at him, I was walking to the kitchen when he just appeared out of nowhere… "Why are you here so early?"

"Delivering me," Nathaniel said as he walked out of the living room.

It took me a minute to understand what was happening. I had just woken up and the pills I took were making me feel a little dazed. I asked Natalí earlier if she could give me some of the painkillers she once made for me. It was nothing like my pills but they helped to keep myself in control.

Nate stood before me, he was wearing a white jumper with its sleeves rolled up to his elbows and dark jeans. He was holding a cup of coffee, I think. His hair was messy but wet, maybe he just came out of the shower. It was Saturday so he probably didn't have to work today. I watched him carefully, taking in every single detail of his face. The way his eyebrows were perfectly curved and how blue his eyes really were. There was a bit of colour on his cheeks and I could tell he hadn't shaved in a few days.

Seeing him there confused me. I felt joy and excitement rise up in me, he was *here*.

"Calm down," He told me, he was watching me carefully, "It's just a hologram."

"He had a communicator fixed. That's why you can see him in colour." Samirah added, walking right through Nate's projection.

"Yes, I did. It was so easy, even Sam could do it. I'm not blue anymore. You now can see my perfect face and my beautiful eyes in HD. What a great present, wouldn't you say?" Nathaniel said with an air of superiority. Wiggling his eyebrows as he took a sip of his coffee.

I stepped closer to him and passed my hand through his head. It was a projection, but it looked real. I had to look closer to see the little dots that made up his image.

"I said to myself, 'If they can't be here, why not go there?'" Nathaniel carried on smiling to himself, "I am *extremely* bored over here."

"Well, this is great and all but I gotta go back home." Eli sighed tiredly, walking towards the front door. "I see you lot later."

Sam was still mad at me, she didn't talk to me but we were both talking to Nate. It was a little childish of her. Nate asked many questions as Samirah cooked an arepa, he wasn't really interested, he was just trying to be annoying. Not 5 minutes after Eli left, he burst back inside Sam's house, out of breath and with a red face.

"Your... Aliana," he began, trying to breathe as he spoke, placing one of his hands over his chest.

"What? What is it, Eli?" I asked desperately, within seconds I was right next to him, watching him as he tried to get the words out.

"Isaac." He said, fear clear in his eyes. "Isaac and your friend, they're fighting. Roc punched Isaac. Come, you gotta stop him! He's going to kill him."

Eli burst out running out the door then. I didn't think about it, I just ran out the door following him. Sam was somewhere behind me, I could hear her asking Eli what was happening.

"It was him, Roc." Eli told us between gasps for air, "I saw Isaac walking with Roc, but then Roc stopped walking and next thing you know he's punching the shit out Isaac."

"Do you really have to swear?" Samirah said between breaths.

"*Look*!" Eli shouted as he pointed to the right.

There were people all around, yelling and whistling, shouting Isaac's name, cheering for him. And that's when I saw a body thrown to the road. And there he was, Isaac, being thrown to the ground like he was nothing more than a thin piece of paper. Roc, looking huge and angry, was in his uniform walking towards Isaac.

That was kind of Roc's thing. He was very strong and he liked being able to show it off. He loved being able to lift people up and throw them to the ground, just to show how strong he was. It all seemed very macho-like to me.

Isaac stood up. As soon as I took him in, my heart dropped to my feet. He had blood all over his face, and his t-shirt was all dirty. Roc rushed to him and, like a bull, tackled him. They both fell to the ground. Roc was on top of Isaac, throwing punches like crazy.

"He is going to kill him!" Samirah shouted. She sounded justifiably worried.

I didn't know how good Isaac was at fighting, how good he was at protecting himself, but it didn't look like he was too good at it.

I rushed to where the people were, in the centre of the fight. Isaac and Roc were still fighting. Roc was not on top any longer. He, too, had blood running down his face. Isaac threw a punch at Roc's face, but that was not where he should have been trying to land his punches, as Roc always protected his face first. Isaac should've been directing his punches to the body to get Roc to let his guard down.

Roc was never distracted during a fight. He always concentrated on his target and wouldn't give up until he accomplished his objective. I knew Roc's weak points, though. It seemed like Isaac had just learnt them too because he was now mixing his punches. Roc had made it very easy for me to win against him for exactly that reason, and also because he didn't fight me fairly, with my being the girl he claimed to love and all.

Isaac was punching Roc with firm, strong punches. I had never seen Isaac fight before. To my surprise, he wasn't *that* bad. Roc was dodging some of Isaac's punches. I wanted to step in, but how was I supposed to do that? From the way Isaac moved and the way he didn't flinch when Roc punched him, I could tell that he was angry. And in my opinion, being angry was no good during a fight.

Isaac managed to drop Roc to the ground and began to throw more punches at him. Roc was trying to protect himself, holding his arms over his body like a shield. Isaac wouldn't stop and Roc was just trying to get Isaac off him but Isaac would not back down. He kept throwing punches, one after another. He wasn't really hitting Roc; he was hitting the ground because Roc kept moving out of the way. Isaac was just hurting himself. It was like someone had replaced Isaac with a beast.

And it was a shocking image. One that practically made my body freeze.

I didn't see Sebastián until he was pulling Isaac by his t-shirt, screaming at him to stop but Isaac kept going back to Roc. I think his t-shirt ripped.

I had been worried about the possibility of Roc killing Isaac, but now it was the other way around.

Roc took his chance and stood up when he could, reaching for his ankle, where he kept a knife.

My heart dropped to my feet.

"Roc, *don't*," I shouted at him. Isaac heard me and turned to look back. He must have seen the knife, because he let out a groan and tried to lunge at Roc again, but this time I did something *really* stupid.

I stepped in the middle just in time that I could stop Isaac, placing my hands on his chest, pushing him back with all the strength in me. I looked up to his eyes, his once soft, warming and calming caramel eyes were now filled with rage, a frightening rage. Blood was dripping from his eyebrow and cheekbone; his lip was broken too and the bridge of his nose looked like it needed healing.

"Isaac, stop," I ordered him. I wasn't scared but I felt something at the pit of my stomach that I wasn't familiar with. I didn't like seeing Isaac like this, this was so different from what I was used to seeing.

"Get him the fuck out of here." Isaac pointed his finger at me in a threatening manner, I furrowed my eyebrows at him, he had never spoken to me like that, not even at the woods when we first met or when he accused me of treason. "*Now.*"

I was confused by the way he was acting, but I didn't stay there to question him. If Miguel or anybody else came, they would probably want to punish Roc and I very much rather that didn't happen. I grabbed Roc's hand and I dragged him towards the woods. Running with him as if I was running for my own life.

We ran for about an hour when Roc finally managed to grab me and make me stop. I was gasping for air; my thoughts were too loud and I didn't know what to focus on.

"Calm down." Roc held my hand tight, his dark blue eyes staring right into my green ones. I saw worry in his eyes. The way he looked at me, I wanted to look away, the way his eyes soften as he took me in, the way his eyebrows curled up in worry… I felt the urge to look away.

"Why did you do that?" I snapped at him, pushing him off me. "Are you out of your mind, Roc? Don't you understand that if you mess up, *I* have to face the consequences of your doings!"

"He started it." Roc spat, all the worry washed off his face, replaced by annoyance. "He said things that made me angry, things that he shouldn't have known and I can't help but wonder…" Roc searched for my eyes until we were looking directly at each other, "how did a nobody know all the things you and you only should know?"

"I—"

"Tell me something, Aliana," Roc interrupted me this time, "Do you— is this boy somebody to you?"

"What?"

"Do you like him?"

I cannot believe him.

"How can you even think about that right now?" I snapped, I was so, *so* tired of the same subject, over and over again, he was like a broken record and it was enough… "My mother is locked up in a prison cell. My family is being torn apart. I can't quiet the fucking voices." I shouted, hitting my head harder than I should have, I took another step towards him, "And you want to know if I like him? There are so much more important things than these childish romances. Do you want to know what I'd like? I would like for my mother to be safe. That is the only thing that I want."

"Are you really still on about that?" he shouted at me, I imagined the fire in his eyes matched mine. I didn't know which one of us was angrier, all I knew was this wasn't going to end well. "Aliana, the Government is *not* your enemy. You're making us out to be the bad guys just because of that stupid rebel. He's inside your head, and you let him in there!"

"You know, Roc, manipulating me when we were in school, I understood. You wanted to win and everything counted. But now, even now when there's nothing to win when this is not about you or me, you're still trying to manipulate me so I go back with you. When my mother's life is at risk."

"I love you." He snapped at me, finally letting his anger fade a little and showing some pain. The way he looked at me hurt. It was like I had betrayed him. "I told you I could find a way for us to be together, but you don't care."

"I don't love you the way you want me to." I lowered my voice. I didn't want to hurt him, no matter how mad I was at him. My intention was never to hurt him. "And it isn't because there's somebody else. It is because I can't feel love, I can't make myself feel something that isn't there.

"There's *nothing* in me, Roc," I couldn't control my emotions any longer and my voice broke when I spoke up. A look of pain crossed his face then. "There's nothing but anger and hate. All you do is talk about this love you feel for me; don't you see what it does to me? Can't you see that all you do is give me more reasons to despise the person I've become because I'm unable to feel anything close to what you say you feel." I sniffed and wiped away the tears that were filling my eyes, making my vision blurry. "I've come to terms with it, Roc, there's no love in me to give. So, if you want to find love, go look for it in somebody else."

"But what about what I want?" His voice broke when he spoke. I felt my throat closing in on me. I really didn't want to hurt him. "Don't I get to be happy?

"How would you be happy? You'd be happy if I lied to you? If I pretended to love you when we both know that I'm incapable of doing so? Would you want to live a lie, Roc?"

"If I get to be with you, then yes." He looked at me dead in the eye as he spoke his words. I shook my head at him, he wasn't going to understand no matter what I said. "With time it could work. If you just gave it a try but you refuse to allow yourself to try."

"No, Roc, it wouldn't work. It would just make us both miserable." I told him, losing the energy to even speak. I felt so drained all of a sudden. "All I have to offer you is my friendship without manipulation or selfish motives. You say you love me, but here you are manipulating me and making me feel guilty for something I have no control over. I don't know what love is, but I'm pretty sure this isn't it. This isn't love, this is an obsessive behaviour that you have developed over the years and it needs to stop, Roc."

"I do love you, and I *will* prove it to you," Roc told me, he reached into his pocket and threw a bottle of medicine at my feet. And then he ran away from me into the woods, towards the bridge.

 **Chapter 26**

Location: La Cruz
Narrator: Aliana

"SO," NATHANIEL LOOKED between Sam and I. Lately it was just the three of us; Eli, Natalí, and Isaac had been either busy or hiding. I hadn't even seen Isaac since the fight. "Any plans on how getting mum out?"

"I thought you and Johan had already figured that out?" I sighed, pretending to read one of Samirah's novels. She had so many books, most of them were quite boring, not really the type of thing I would read.

"I really want to see her." Samirah smiled. Nate nodded but a hint of guilt hid in his smile.

"Nate, do you happen to know why Mum isn't going to stay here?" Samirah asked and Nate gave a single shake of his head, it was enough for us to know he was lying. "The least you can do is tell us the truth, Nathaniel."

"You can't keep lying to us, Nate," I added, I could see Samirah rolling her eyes at what I said. Lately, she had been doing the same thing when I spoke.

"Because you can talk…" She whispered but loud enough for me to hear. I sighed, letting her comment go. To be honest, I couldn't care less what Samirah thought of me.

"All right, don't gang up on me." He rolled his eyes, taking a moment to think about what he was going to say next. "It's important to get her out of here because Mother knows how to reverse the process. She knows how to remove the chip without causing major damage to the brain. She's valuable because of that." Nathaniel told us, he was being vague, but it was something.

"How? The process is very complex. It's impossible. I've spent hours trying to figure out how it works. It is literally a labyrinth. The brain is so complex you never really know how anything will affect it." There was a fascination in Samirah's tone as she spoke. Her face lit up and her eyes were filled with curiosity.

"Which means she could have died," I reminded them, they both seemed so fascinated by the science bit of it, that they forgot that our mother could have died. Samirah's face dropped as if she hadn't come to that conclusion. Nathaniel gave a single nod. "Please, let's skip all the boring details of how she did it. Tell us, what does that have to do with Mum going to another place?"

"Actually, there are no details. I don't know how she did it." Nate shrugged. A hint of annoyance crossed his face. "I don't, nor does Father. And there's been no side effects yet, we studied her for days before they took her away... she was genuinely happy. But as expected there were also tears. She was sad, she didn't see the point of feeling if we were not together. Father and I helped her to control her emotions a little. She's, uh, very tender. She would spend the whole day hugging or kissing us, smiling while telling us she loved us. But then all hell broke loose and you guys know what happened after that."

Nate gave us time to process what he was saying before he carried on.

"There's a man on this side, he wants to help. This man, well him and some others, they want to give the people of the Government a choice. They want people to have free will, to have emotions. That's why Mum's so valuable. She's the only one who knows how to remove the chip without hurting the brain. They want to do more research, they want to study Mum closely and then take down the Government."

My eyes snapped to find Nate's but his eyes were lowered, glued to his hand.

They couldn't do that.

"That can't happen." I voiced my thoughts, breaking the silence. "They can't do that, Nathaniel. You can't force people into something they do not understand or know. What if later on, they don't like it? What happens if those people whom you 'cure' end up being sick again, truly sick? Free will means free will to kill, to betray, to rape, to steal … free will to regret being able to feel."

I was upset by the idea. Sam, of course, was not, I ignored her glares because I wasn't in the mood to fight her.

"So, you'd rather not have emotions? Not being able to choose *at all*?" Samirah asked with a serious tone.

"Yes. Well, I don't know, Samirah. It's not like I have any control over my emotions anyway." I told her but I knew my words fell on deaf ears, Samirah would *never* understand. "What about all those things they were trying to protect us from when they took our emotions away? Greed, envy, anger, pain, violence? They were trying to save us. Something had to be sacrificed; it was all given so we wouldn't make those mistakes again. So we have peace and live in a place where—"

"What are you even talking about? Do you know the number of people that are killed daily because of all the research we do?" Samirah snapped, sitting up and making eye contact with me. "No, of course you don't know because you chose to be a soldier, out of all the careers, you chose the most useless one."

"Samirah…" Nate's voice had a warning ring to it but Samirah carried on.

"Also, what mistakes, Aliana? You have feelings. You hate and you feel resentment. You hate the woman who gave birth to you for reasons you do not wish to share. You were selfish when you kept me from knowing the truth. I wanted so hard to cure you, to find a cure for you. Because I always thought there was something wrong with you. I told myself that maybe if I found a cure, if I studied hard enough, I would find a way to make *you* go back to being who you were before you became this, before all the rage and hate got into you. But to be honest, I don't think there's actually something wrong with you. It isn't an illness, it has been *you* all along. The decisions that you've made so far, the way you've decided to live your life have led you to be the person you are now.

"You know, there was a time when it angered me to feel sorry for you, I hated the fact that I couldn't look at you without feeling sorry for you. I hated that other people looked at you with pity, I hated that they didn't like you but how could they like you when you drown all that tries to help you? You are angry, you are selfish, you hate and despise the woman and man who brought you to life, and you treat them both with cruelty. You'd rather feel pain and anger instead of just talking to Johan. Even if you wanted to, you wouldn't speak to Dad, because your pride is bigger than—"

"Samirah, that's *enough*." Nate stood up and interrupted her with anger vibrating in his voice, but Samirah kept going. Oh, she wasn't going to stop, not until she got it all out. And I was completely frozen. My brain was frozen and all I could do was sit there and listen to what Samirah had to say.

"On top of all this, you refuse to let other people have the chance to feel good. You refuse to let them feel things like happiness or love. Just because you have never experienced them, it does not mean they don't exist. I don't think you realise that the mistake has already been made. *You* are the mistake."

Samirah had called me cruel, but that was exactly what she was being right now. I stood still as a rock and watched as Samirah took a deep breath in and slowly let it out, trying to calm herself, I suppose. And I wondered, did she know that her words were like small knives cutting deep into my skin? Did she know that her opinion mattered the most to me? Did she know she was practically breaking my heart in two? I stood there, unable to move or formulate words. My vision was blurry from the tears filling my eyes, I blinked a couple of times and I felt the hot tears rolling down my cheeks. I sniffed and turned to look at Samirah. When our eyes locked, I saw nothing but anger.

"All right then. Samirah," I sighed, wiping my face with the back of my hand. "I don't think right now is the time to bring old things out into the open. One day perhaps. Do you want to know why I hate your beloved mother so much? Go ahead and ask her what was on the videotape. Ask her what she did to me."

I got up and walked up the stairs at a normal pace. Feeling my heart grow heavy in my chest with each step I took. I heard Samirah and Nate bickering downstairs but as soon as I closed my room's door, their hushed voices were gone.

I reached for my nightstand and opened the drawer, taking three of the medicine Natalí had made for me and throwing them at the back of my mouth.

I wanted to hit something.

Why couldn't she understand? Wasn't she supposed to be smarter than me? She lived there, she knew how people were back at the Government. Couldn't she imagine how hard it would be for people to go from feeling nothing at all to feeling way too much? It was too drastic, too overwhelming.

Change like that would make them lose their minds.

They aren't thinking about all the ways this could go wrong. What will they do when people rebel against them because they *will*. Don't they understand that life at the Government was not all rainbows and sunshine for everybody like it was for them? Nate, Samirah and I had pretty much all that we wanted, but it wasn't like that for a *lot* of people.

What would happen to the poor sectors where people literally died of hunger. The poor, who were supposed to bow down to those who had money. They were treated like slaves. What would happen when these people have emotions and begin to feel oppressed? They will ask for a change, they'd want a fair treatment, which means they will ask for change, equality for all but despite what they want to believe, the Government has never known equality. The ones who have everything, people from the rich sectors? They will never give the poor a chance to grow. And no one will be able to blame the less privileged for no longer tolerating the way they are treated. Truth is, poor people aren't given a fair chance to escalate in society. And they *will* rebel. And where there's a rebellion, there's violence. And I do not want my people to die.

I understood that things had to change, I've always said it. It wasn't fair the way the Government treated its people. But their idea? That was too drastic, it was too much too sudden. It would only bring chaos and solve nothing. If they wanted to do something good, they should at least start off slowly. People have never reacted well to sudden change, I shouldn't be the only one who thinks that way.

I know Sam and Nate don't think the same way as I do. And I understood their reasons, I could see why they thought the way they did. But it was like they didn't even think past their ideas. They had good intentions, they wanted to do good but good choices had consequences too.

And they weren't always good.

* * *

"Where's your sister?" I asked Nate as I made my way down the stairs, surprised to see he was still here. It had been a few hours. He was reading a book. He was so into it that he was biting his thumb with a frown.

"She went out." He told me. I sat on a sofa in front of him. We stared at each other for a few minutes until he put his book down and it simply disappeared.

"You know she didn't mean it." He said, breaking our stare contest.

"Don't defend her," I muttered, fidgeting with my ring. "she meant it, and she had been wanting to get all that out for a while now."

"This situation is difficult for her too."

"Yes, Nate, and I'm sure this situation is difficult for Eli too but you don't see him making me feel like I'm a worthless piece of shit." I snapped, looking everywhere but at him. I bit my lip, taking my time before I continued, I didn't want to cry again. "Hell, this is difficult for me too but I would never say to her half of the things she said to me today."

"I'm sorry, sister, but you came out here following her." He reminded me, I rolled my eyes. "You came because you couldn't stand the thought of being without her, and now you're sort of stuck with her."

"You're not very good at making me feel better," I told him, the corner of his lips lifted upwards a little.

"Do you want me to make you feel better or do you want me to be honest?"

"Um, kind of tempted to ask you to make me feel better, see how you manage." I joked, Nate was horrible at comforting.

"You want to know what I think?" He asked me, I didn't answer because he was going to tell me regardless. "I think you should've never left. Don't get me wrong, I know you adore Sam, I do too. But perhaps what you needed was to be away from her to realise that you can be your own person too. You don't need someone else to make you feel better about yourself, Lynn, you know that, right? You're not ruined, you don't need fixing, you're not broken. You need to stop believing that you are."

"You don't know that." I struggled to find my voice. Lately, I've been crying more than usual and it was getting on my nerves.

I was getting on my nerves.

"Yes, I do." He slowly nodded, looking back down at something I cannot see. He then looked back at me. "You're not the horrible person you think you are, Lynn. Stop treating yourself like this."

"I don't know how."

"Actually, it is very simple, Lynn, but I think you just don't want to see it. You don't like the way you feel about yourself but you've gotten so comfortable with it, you feel safe with what you know. You don't think you can change, so you want to spare yourself the disappointment. Lynn, you will fail a lot of times, and there's *nothing* wrong with that. We all fail before we succeed. But you *have* to try. If being here is making things harder for you, if being in the middle of this madness and around Luna doesn't help you, then leave."

"Yeah, as if it was that easy."

"It is. All you have to do is go with mum." He shrugged his shoulders as if it was the simplest thing in life.

"I don't think I can just get up and leave."

"Of course you can. Miguel can't stop you. You said it yourself, he can't tell you what to do." I stared at Nate's eyes, something in me believed that maybe he was right. "Leave and be on your own, become your own person away from Samirah's shadow."

"But would she want me to go with her, though?" I asked, looking down at my feet, not daring to look at Nate when I asked that question.

"Who, Mum?" He asked to be sure, I slightly nodded my head. "Lynn, Mum loves you more than life itself."

 **Chapter 27**

Location: La Cruz
Narrator: Aliana

"WHAT'RE YOU DOING?" I heard Isaac's voice, coming from behind me. I took a deep breath in before I turned around to face him with a heavy box in my hands.

"Cleaning."

"What are you doing out so late?" He asked, following after me as I carried the last box inside of Junior's garage.

It was late, I had finished work hours ago but Junior had complained about how he couldn't clean his own garage because his leg was hurting again, so I decided to stay behind and clean up a bit. After all, I did help to create the mess he was complaining about.

"The garage was a mess," I told him as I carefully put the box next to the others in a corner of the garage. I scratched the back of my neck, turning around to face him. "So, you're talking to me again?"

"When was I not talking to you?" He frowned, burying his hands deep inside his jeans pockets.

"I figured since you have pretty much disappeared since your fight with Roc." I shrugged and decided to try to lighten the mood, I didn't want to argue with Isaac, I wanted my friend back. "I mean, it was a few days ago, I thought you would've calmed down by the next day."

"I'm sorry about shouting at you, by the way."

"Don't worry about it," I told him, walking out of the garage, Isaac followed. Once I made sure the garage was closed, we both started to walk with no direction.

"So, how's you and Sam?" He asked, trying to get rid of the awkwardness.

"Not better." I chuckled, there was no point lying. "I don't think it'll be better any time soon, actually."

"Eli said it was awkward."

"Awkwardness would be an understatement." I snorted, "You could choke someone with the tension."

Isaac laughed as he shook his head. "You know, the other day I was in bed, watching movies and having hot chocolate—"

"Hot chocolate?" I laughed, interrupting him. "Oh yes, because this weather's perfect for a hot chocolate. Throw in a blanket, why don't you?"

"Hold up, don't tell me you're one of them people who only drink hot chocolate when it's cold?" He asked me, both his eyebrows shot up in disbelief. "You know what, don't answer that. Anyway, like I was saying before I was rudely interrupted, I was watching movies and I realised, you've never watched a movie."

I waited for him to carry on, when he didn't, I looked up at him blinking a couple of times, waiting for him to make his point. "And?"

"And you *have* to watch a movie."

"I don't have to—"

"Dude, seriously, we cannot continue this friendship if you haven't watched Star Wars." Isaac's tone was dead serious and so was his face but his eyes were glowing with a hint of amusement.

"I have no idea what you're talking about." I shook my head, laughing at his serious expression.

"What are you doing now?"

"Walking," I stated the obvious.

"Well, no shit, Sherlock."

"Who?" I snickered, not understanding much of this conversation.

"Seriously, what're you doing now? Like when you get home? Do you have work tomorrow? Are you tired?" He spoke a little too fast, his eyes were wide open with enthusiasm, waiting for me to answer his questions.

"Well, I was thinking of going home and reading for a while." I lied, I wasn't tired but I wasn't going to go home. I was going to go for runs around the woods. Lately, I've found myself dreading the coming home part of my day. It was stupid but I didn't know if Samirah was going to be waiting for me to have another round at insulting me.

"Do you want to come watch movies with me?" He asked me, he was so excited that I found it hard to say no.

And that's how I found myself, dozing off in Isaac's sofa, while we watched a movie that was way longer than I had anticipated. He brought his mattress and dropped it on his living room's floor. He laid there a little too close to the TV. I don't think he remembered I was there with him, he was so concentrated, his eyes wide open never leaving the TV. At some point, I think I even heard him rephrasing what a character in the movie had said.

When the movie finally finished, Isaac rolled around in his bed until he laid on his back, looking at the ceiling like it held the answers we did not get from the movie.

"I always get frustrated whenever I watch this movie." He told me, looking slightly miserable like he didn't know what to do with himself.

"Well, is there a continuation of the movie? Surely it can't end like that?"

"Yes, actually, there is." He told me, sighing dramatically as he stared at the ceiling thoughtfully. "But I don't have it. I have all the movies, *except* for the continuation of that one."

"Isaac, did you really make me watch this movie knowing that you didn't own the next part?" I asked him, annoyance clear in my voice. When our eyes met, he stared at me for a second before nodding.

"I have to share my misery with someone." He shrugged. "Want to watch another one or want me to walk you home?"

"Actually, I think I should go home," I told him, looking at the clock hanging from the wall.

Isaac walked me back home, we talked about the movie and then he went on telling me about what he thought happened in the movie he didn't own. He glared at me when I told him that there was a huge possibility that the character he really liked died and that was the reason why the character didn't appear in any of the other movies.

When we made it to Sam's home, he stood awkwardly by the door, I thought maybe he wanted me to invite him in but it was 2 am and I wasn't feeling well. We said our goodbyes and I made my way inside the house. The lights were off. Sam was thankfully asleep so I just went to my room.

Since this afternoon, I've been feeling weird. It was as if my muscles were rigid all the time, and it wasn't like when I was sore from too much exercise because I hadn't done any exercise in two days. Actually, nothing in my routine had changed, the only thing I had been trying to change was the number of pills I was taking and the number of times I took them during the day. I was laying off and I shouldn't feel the way I felt right then.

Not taking the pills should've given me more control over my mind and my body but it seemed as if the pills were giving me control over my mind but not so much over my body.

When I laid in bed, I allowed my thoughts to flood my mind. I stared at the ceiling, playing with the little pill bottle that Roc got me. After my talk with Nate, I swore to myself that this time I was *really* going to try. It did help that I had been trying to reduce the number of pills I had been taking. I had been reducing the amount because I knew I was going to run out at some point and I wanted to have enough until I felt safe until I knew for sure that I could deal with being around Luna without feeling scared.

And there it was; the truth. I hated admitting it, but truth is, as much as I hated Luna, there was one feeling that surpassed the hatred and it was fear. I was *terrified* of Luna. I tried to make myself not think about it. I tried to convince myself that it wasn't fear, it was anything but fear. And yet, whenever she was close, I found myself looking for an escape. I found myself feeling threatened by her presence. And how could I not, when I saw her cutting into my skin with a pair of scissors, I saw her ripping me open and leaving me for dead. It was the most horrific thing I had ever seen and since the day I watched her scar me, I couldn't get the image out of my head. It was the reason why I woke up sweating and teary-eyed.

I remembered watching the video, thinking it was one of Johan's experiments. I watched the video of Luna's imprisonment. I watched as she met Johan for the first time and she punched him in the face. I watched her as she spoke to herself and screamed like an old lady. I watched her and I was fascinated by her, by all her rawness. But then I saw her getting close to Johan. I saw them falling for the other. I saw them.

And then I saw her giving birth. I saw Johan delivering the babies. I saw him as he walked away with Sam. And I watched, mortified and petrified as she grabbed me in her arms, she sang a lullaby and I saw her grabbing a pair of scissors. And she cut deep into my skin. The skin of a baby that had just taken its first breath. She cut into me like I was a piece of fabric. And she left me there to die. I couldn't watch after that.

So yes, I was terrified of the woman who did that to a baby. Her own baby.

I sat up in my bed when I felt my vision go blurry, the room was spinning and suddenly, everything went black. My heartbeat quickened as I raised my hands to my face, to my eyes. I had my eyes wide open but everything was pitch black. I couldn't see.

I stood up and tried to keep balance by resting a hand against the wall. I took deep breaths in and slowly let them out, something was happening to me.

"Sam." I tried to say but tongue felt swollen, heavy.

I tried walking out of my room, hands were shaking, my whole body was shaking, I couldn't control my nerves and was having a panic attack. I tried calling for Sam over and over again but I didn't know if I was making any sound or if my ears weren't working properly either. I couldn't hear.

My heart was beating so fast that I was convinced it was going to burst out of my chest. I couldn't control my breathing anymore. I was sweating and shaking and feeling that horrible hot-and-cold sensation, the shivers. I felt nauseous, and I couldn't find anything, I didn't know where the rooms were, where the bathroom was. I felt lost and disoriented. Everything was black.

My legs felt heavy, I couldn't lift my feet. I think I dropped to the floor shaking. Yes, I dropped to the floor shaking and I couldn't get up, couldn't move. I tried to raise my hand to cover my mouth but I really couldn't feel any part of my body. Before I knew it, vomit was coming out of my mouth.

My muscles tightened and I was made of rock. I didn't have the strength to ever move again. And then there was the pressure in my chest like my whole body was trying to kill me.

Johan, I said. I wanted help, I was scared and I wanted help. My tears felt hot against my skin. So *so* hot. My vomit reeked. I wanted to get up, but I couldn't.

 **Chapter 28**

Location: La Cruz
Narrator: Samirah

"YOU CAN'T GIVE her the freaking pills!" I snapped. But it was pointless. We've been arguing for two whole days, it seemed everybody was too shocked to discuss this with rational thinking. "She's in withdrawal, what part of that don't you understand? This is how withdrawal works."

Aliana had been at the medical centre for Five days. Five whole days until she was well enough to come back home. At first, I didn't want Luna or anyone to know what exactly had happened to Aliana, but since Luna wanted to give her the pills Johan kept saying she needed, I had to blurt out the reason why Aliana shouldn't get the pills. Johan tried to avoid the subject, he just kept telling Luna how Aliana needed the pills, how she *had* to give her one pill every six hours, how she had to be very careful and make sure Aliana took the right number of pills but he didn't tell her *why*. He kept answering her questions in a way where he gave her an answer but not the answer she wanted. It was hard for Johan to talk about this or about any family issue… he always said family issues were only for the family to know, nobody else needed to know.

"What do you mean?" Luna asked. I ignored her, unable to explain at the moment. I didn't think I should anyway, not to Luna. I hadn't even told Natalí about this. And even though she doesn't want to talk to me right now, I used to tell Natalí pretty much everything.

"The medicine Aliana takes, it acts a certain way," Johan began to explain. I rolled my eyes, tensing up. This was Aliana's business. I didn't think Luna or anyone in the room should know. "The pills don't block her emotions, but they do kind of suppress them for a bit, which makes it easier for her to control them. The pills make emotions harder to feel or act on. Aliana has been taking these pills since she was old enough to lose control over her emotions, especially her anger. Once she discovered the truth, I didn't see the point of lying to her about the medication. I gave her tablets to take daily, with precaution. She was doing fine until she was 15, which was when she had an overdose—"

"She had a what? You said this was normal." Luna cried. Miguel's eyes went wide open, as did Andrea's. Cairo's face was emotionless and Johan tried to remain calm. "How could you let this happen, Johan? Why didn't you tell me any of this? You said they would be fine with you, and you've—"

"This isn't my father's fault," I snapped at Luna. They were all looking at my dad like it was his fault, it wasn't. "If anyone is to blame, it is Aliana, for—"

"She needs *help*, not for us to blame her," Nathaniel muttered, jumping in to defend Aliana. I fought the urge to roll my eyes.

"This isn't Aliana's fault," Johan defended her in an effort to protect her from herself. None of these people were helping Aliana. Aliana needed to open her eyes and see all that was wrong with her. "She believed she was stronger. She didn't think the pills would take control of her. But they did. All the emotions she was trying so hard to repress and to control with the pills are still there, without the pills she just feels them all at once. When it first happened, she was… she wasn't herself. All she wanted were her pills. After the first week, she started to get better. I gave her one pill in the morning, one in the afternoon, and one at night. I don't know how this happened. I don't know how she got to this point. I really don't know who gave her so many pills. I just– I thought it was fine. I– I don't know."

My father's voice broke. He was nervous. He hated these sorts of thing. Whenever Aliana had an anxiety attack, he would freeze, his colour would drain from his face and he'd just watch with his eyes wide open as Nate or I tried to calm her down. I knew he would've liked to help, but he just didn't know *how*. I thought he felt helpless when it came to this. He couldn't do anything to help my sister.

"You should have told me," Luna shouted again with her hand on her forehead, massaging her temples, worried. I almost laughed. Why was she worried? But then I had to remind myself that apparently, she was my mother.

"Can we please stop with this?" I spoke up. "I don't know if you all remember, but we need a solution, we can't just isolate her or put her to sleep. She's upstairs with *Eli* watching over her. We need to think of what to do."

"But if she takes the pills, she's just going to be more dependent on them," Miguel said with a frown. He almost seemed worried. "I don't think giving pills to her is a good idea. Why don't we just wait for it to fade, and then she'll get better?"

"This isn't like a normal drug, is it?" Cairo asked, looking at my father for the first time today. "We know what the drugs do to you when you get addicted, but that's – she's different. I mean, she's just lying in bed and being depressed."

"Because this isn't like one of those drugs," Nate answered him. "These drugs are made for … These pills are for mental issues, but the mental issues they treat aren't normal either. They aren't normal because we created them. We played with the brain, making it react in ways it shouldn't. These pills were meant to help control that. She does *need* them. Her body needs them. It might be even bigger than a need. She might rip her own skin off if it meant getting one more pill. But right now, she can't focus on the need for the pill. The only thing she has in her mind is the pain she's probably feeling right now because, like my father said, all the emotions she was trying to block are probably so overwhelming that she can't get out of bed."

"I don't understand. I thought she was better. I really did," Johan said, as soon as he went to sit down, a chair appeared as part of the projection. "She was taking one every five hours. She shouldn't be like this. She shouldn't be withdrawing, not like this. Are you sure?"

307

"Look at the bottles!" I pointed at the coffee table where I had placed the bottles I found and wanted to show my father before I knew Luna, Andrea, Miguel, and Cairo were going to join our family discussion. Some of the bottles were empty, some were full.

"Mum!" Eli shouted as he ran downstairs. My heart skipped a beat when I saw his face. He was pale, fear in his puffy red eyes.

"What is it? Is she okay?" I asked him.

"She was throwing up again. She said she was okay, but there's blood. She looks—" But Eli didn't get to finish his sentence because Aliana was already making her way downstairs.

She looked *dead*. That was how she looked. She was wearing pyjama shorts and a muscle t-shirt, the type that had large armholes. Her scar was visible. She had black bags under her swollen red eyes. She had been crying. Her arms hung at each side of her body and her hair was a mess. She was shaking. Even from where I was standing, I could see the goosebumps. She looked like life had left her body. She was a dead girl walking. My heart broke seeing her like this, but it also broke my heart to know that this was *her own doing*.

"It was Aurora," she said, looking only at Johan. He stood up and looked at her. A tear fell from his eye. "When I ov— When I took too many pills and I was sick? It was Aurora who put me back on them."

She couldn't even say the word *overdose*. We couldn't say she was an addict. We didn't like to acknowledge it, much less talk about it. But she couldn't either. I've always known that Aurora and Aliana didn't really like each other but blaming Aurora for this ...? That was low. I didn't think my grandmother would dare.

"Aliana," I began, "I don't think you should—"

"Do you remember she came home that time, two days before I mysteriously got better?" Aliana carried on, not paying attention to me and looking only at Johan. "She came to my room and sat next to my bed. She stayed there for about an hour. I was stupid enough to think that maybe she was worried, that maybe she did care about me after all. When I dared to look back at her eyes, she said some pretty mean stuff but before leaving, she reached into her bag, took out a little bottle full of pills, and threw it at me. *If you wish to kill yourself, do it effectively and quickly. Do something right for once.* She said that to me. Those were her exact words."

Everyone was silent. Not a single sound. Johan looked away. With his hand, he wiped his tear.

"I know you're not going to believe me," Aliana continued, looking at Johan and only him. "I know how this looks but I swear to you, I *swear* I was stopping."

"Why would we believe you?" I scoffed rudely, shaking my head at her. I was so tired of this.

"Because this was different!" She shouted, catching us all by surprise. Luna even jumped. "Yes, I admit I'm still dependent on the pills but I swear I don't know what happened, I was reducing—"

"You *died*," I shouted at her, my voice shaking as I said that. My heart was in my throat. "Do you want to die, Aliana? Is that what you want?"

"I—"

"You had no pulse for a whole minute. Do you know what's like to wake up in the middle of the night to see your sister lying in her own vomit with no heartbeat?" I tried my best not to cry, I was mad at her but seeing her the way I saw her that night, it was terrifying. I didn't want to lose her. I loved her.

I remember Sebastián waking me up, shaking me awake because he heard something, I told him to let me sleep and go see for himself. I didn't want to get up, but when I heard him desperately shouting my name, I ran out of my room to see something that horrified me. I don't remember much, everything happened so fast. I do remember the way my eyes filled with tears and how my chest grew heavy when I couldn't find her pulse. That was a feeling I didn't think I'd ever been able to forget.

I sent Sebas to find the healer. I was relieved when I saw that it was Victor, the healer that lived two houses down from mine. With him, he brought actual medical supplies, unlike the other healer who thought that everything could be solved with herbs and creams. Victor brought her back to me, he said her pulse was faint but it was there and I swear I felt my soul coming back to my body.

"Sam, I know how it looks like and I know why you don't believe me," she spoke to me, her eyes were begging me to believe her, but I couldn't. I would not allow her to do this to herself again. "I had never gone blind from withdrawal. You know the effects, you know what it does, no one has ever gone blind because of that. Sam, I *couldn't* breathe. My muscles, I felt like my muscles were stone. Nate, please, you have to believe me."

"It can be explained. Yes, those aren't effects of withdrawal but your mind could've—"

"No!" She shouted again, Eli stepped away from her, fear clear in his face. She looked desperate. "I know what you're going to say and I didn't make myself believe I was blind! How could I even?"

"Anxiety can affect your vision, we all know that," I explained, shrugging carelessly at her attempts at making this not about her addiction.

"Yes, they can affect my vision, but they don't make me blind." She carried on defending her argument.

"You're looking at me," I said, she frowned, not understanding. "If it truly wasn't withdrawal and it was something else and it really blinded you. Why can you see me now?"

"When I woke up yesterday, I could see, I don't know how it happened but I swear, Sam." Her voice was raspy, I could hear the need in her voice, it was like she wanted nothing more than for me to believe her.

"So, do you want your pills?" I tested her, her eyes snapped to mine, a frown between her eyebrows.

"Of course I want my pills, I *need* my pills, but that's not the point." She seemed a little frustrated.

"I don't think that's a good idea," Miguel stepped in with caution.

"Seriously? You think I'm lying?" Aliana's eyes were filling themselves with tears, she sucked in her lower lip and bit it, tried to stop them quivering when I didn't answer. She then turned to Nate who was looking down at the floor, avoiding looking at her. "Nate? Dad?"

Aliana nodded to herself when they didn't even turn to look at her. Something seemed to change in her, she didn't look as vulnerable as she did before, she looked angry now. Her eyes lacked any emotion as she angrily wiped the tears from her face.

"I think we should give her the pills," Luna began, her voice shaking, I rolled my eyes at her comment. "They're going to make her better, right?"

"*Do not* give her any pills," I told Luna. Aliana turned to look at me, I maintained eye contact with her. "They aren't going to fix her. They're just going to make things worse for her."

"Because you know what's best for me, right? Do you really think *you* can fix me?" Aliana said with anger in her voice, she glared at me as she spoke. "All your life you've bragged about saving me, fixing me, helping me... I've always been so jealous of you. I've allowed you to do as you pleased with me. Always following you, always so devoted to you, I would have given up my life for you. Once upon a time, I would have died just to give you life but to you, I'm nothing more than an experiment, the messed-up sister you wish you never had. And deep down you know you can't help me. There is nothing to save, there's only anger. It is pointless to help someone that is already doomed, right, Sam?"

I swallowed hard as she recited a line from one of my journals, more precisely my journal about her. I uncomfortably shifted from one foot to the other, trying to think of something to say. But before I could, Aliana carried on with a sharp, cold tone. She wanted to hurt me with her words just like I had hurt her with mine.

And I deserved all of it.

"Don't look so surprised. Piece of advice? If you're going to write a journal about someone, don't write their name on the cover." Aliana laughed humourlessly, I could feel eyes burning holes in my back. I didn't dare to look back at my father or at Nate, I knew I would only see the disappointment in their eyes. "Did you know that was one of the reasons I went looking for you, to show you that my love for you was real, I felt love for you. Funny enough, that's the only thing I ever needed from you and it was the one thing you denied me of. It's fucking hilarious if you think about it: Mum can't feel for shit and yet, she was the only one who made me feel loved.

"You knew I felt, yet you stood aside without showing me a glint of love. Yes, at times you did your random act of kindness and you held me when I needed company. You did many good things, Sam, but what I needed was for all of you to tell me that I was good enough for you, to tell me that you loved me, to say that you didn't care what Aurora or anybody said because I was good enough for you guys.

"I needed your love, but I got nothing but empty smiles, and your shadow. You were like a long-lasting eclipse, you know? You covered the light, leaving me in the dark. I was never good when Samirah Keenan stood in front. You knew all this. You knew how I felt, but you did nothing. Why, Samirah? Why didn't you do anything? Were you jealous? You lived in that fascinating world where the word *no* was never heard. The world of a spoiled brat that couldn't stand the thought of anyone getting more attention that she did. You're just like Aurora, you always want everything to be yours. It always has to be you, Samirah. For God's sake, even Johan loves you more than he loves me. There's no denying it and you rejoice in that, don't you? You're a hypocrite and you're no better than me. You want to fix me, Sam? How about you fix yourself before you try to fix others?"

"That is not true Aliana," Johan said when he finally found his voice. He sounded offended. I was frozen where I stood. What could I say? Aliana rarely said anything, but when she did, well, let's just say that every word could kill.

"Yes, it is, Johan, and that's okay." Aliana carried on, saying, "I understand. I pushed you away. I mistreated you, whereas your perfect daughter here, she was everything you wanted a daughter to be. She did what you wanted her to, she followed you everywhere you went, and she did everything to please you. I was just a disappointment to you."

"Aliana, that's—"

"You always thought the worst of me, Johan. You think that everything I do is some sort of evil plan to hurt you. Tell me,

Father, did you ever stop to ask me what happened when I failed the test?" Aliana asked. This was an awkward subject. Aliana failed a *very* important test and in our family, no one ever failed. It was an embarrassment, more so because the results were shown in public. Dad was disappointed, *very* disappointed because Aliana failed on purpose to make a point, she could ruin herself if it meant she'd ruin him too. "I waited for you all night, Johan. I waited for you to let me explain, but you never even asked. I am a disappointment to you, but you are a disappointment to me too."

I was frozen to the spot where I was standing. I didn't know what to think of all the things Aliana was saying.

"Give me the pills, don't give me the pills," Aliana shrugged carelessly, her eyes weren't full of anger anymore, it was like she became stone cold. "Lock me up, isolate me, leave me in my room… honestly, I don't give a shit."

And with that, Aliana left with the same indifference she had when she first came downstairs. It was like she was running out of energy to care.

After we got over the shock from Aliana's words and attitude, we argued and argued. My father thought that we should try to keep a record of what she takes and when she takes it. It was the best option, it was dangerous to get her off the pill drastically. But I argued that giving her pills again was also dangerous. I told them that I couldn't trust myself to give her the pills, she could find a way to persuade me and I didn't trust her to have those pills at home. Nathaniel was angry. So angry that he left the discussion and disconnected. Miguel and Cairo thought everything was a bad idea. Everything seemed a bad idea to them. Getting Aliana back on her pills? Bad idea. Not giving Aliana her pills? Bad idea. I thought Miguel was just in shock and didn't know what to do. Cairo just seemed concerned and shocked too. I bet neither of them would have thought Aliana was an addict. I hadn't believed it either, not until I saw it with my own eyes.

Luna couldn't believe any of it. She was going through a lot of emotions. She was angry at some point, then she was shocked, then she went back to angry and then she was sad. At some point, she asked my dad why he never said anything. My father didn't have an answer for her which made her angry again. She wanted to give Aliana the pills.

It was Andrea who came up with a solution. She said she could come every morning and drop off the capsules, or else Aliana could go over to her place and get them. Andrea would be responsible, and not be affected by Aliana's words. Andrea would treat her fairly and with respect. After we argued about it and reached an agreement, Johan explained to Andrea how she had to give Aliana the medicine.

Aliana came downstairs. Eli was holding her hand. My sister looked out of her body like she wasn't even there. However, as soon as she saw the pills, her eyes lit up. The need, the want, was in her eyes. She had completely forgotten about her charade of being blind. I knew it wasn't true.

Johan explained to her how it was going to be and how she was going to be taking two pills at first and then slowly tapering off. Once he did and Aliana took her capsules from Andrea and she went back to her room holding Eli's hand. One by one, everyone but Johan left the room.

I sat on my sofa, facing him.

"She'll be okay,"

"I didn't know. How did I not know?" he shook his head, placing his hand on the bridge of his nose. "How did she keep all this inside her? I didn't know she felt this way."

"Even if we had known, she would've found a way around it. Aliana doesn't allow people to help her."

I couldn't get the anger out of my voice. I was angry at Aliana for not telling me, angry at her for doing this, and angry at myself for being so oblivious to what was happening, angry at myself for treating my sister the way I had.

I just... I loved Aliana so much that the thought of losing her broke my heart.

 **Chapter 29**

Location: La Cruz
Narrator: Isaac

I HAD BEEN lying on my bed almost all day, listening to sad music on cassette, CD, and vinyl. My hair was a mess this morning, I hadn't even combed it. I hadn't even showered yet, which was very depressing. But then my aunt walked in with a bunch of food and told me to have a shower or else she would bring the bucket. Knowing her, she would most definitely bring the bucket. She wouldn't care if I was in bed or had a broken cable in my hands; she would bring the bucket.

My mum left this morning to visit my grandparents again, they lived in another city. I stayed home all day long. It was very peaceful. I could have the music turned up to maximum volume with no mother to shout at me and tell me to turn it down. Better yet, I didn't have to watch out for what record I was going to play in case it reminded her of my father and she'd start drinking again.

It was Friday night. I was at home, alone and bored. There was a party somewhere near Natalí's house, and she practically forced me to say that I was going to be there. Needless to say, I was trying to find excuses as to why I wasn't going to show up. I needed a real good excuse; Natalí was good at catching my lies, I don't know how she did it but whenever I lied, she just knew it. It was kind of creepy.

I was ready to bounce when I opened the door to find Aliana biting the skin off her lips. I've come to notice she did that when she was nervous. She was wearing jean shorts and a white over-sized top. When she heard me chuckle, she looked up at me with those big green eyes of hers. She looked tired like she had overworking and not sleeping at all. She also looked nervous, she was on edge.

"Aliana." I greeted her. I was supposed to go out, but if she wanted to hang out … screw the party.

"Hey, um, are you on your way out?" she asked, looking at me from head to toe. My clothing was different than usual. Modesty aside, I looked good. "I can come back later. Tomorrow, I mean."

"No, don't worry about it." I smiled at her, being overly friendly. Natalí couldn't get mad at me now. "Actually, I was trying to make up excuses as I got ready so I didn't have to go to the party. Since you're here, I can tell Natalí you begged me to play a movie and I couldn't refuse."

She laughed then and shook her head at me, looking down at her feet. "I'll accept to take the blame as long as I get to pick the movie."

"But you don't know what they're about," I argued, frowning at her. I had lots of movies but there were some boring ones that I didn't really want to watch.

"That's the point." She rolled her eyes playfully at me as we both made our way towards my living room.

I brought my mattress downstairs again, but this time she laid on it and I stayed on the couch. She picked a rather boring movie like I had predicted, but she wouldn't admit it because she didn't want to agree with me. So instead of accepting that the movie was boring, she opted for making conversations with me during the whole movie.

When the movie *finally* ended, we stayed in silence for about three minutes. It wasn't awkward or uncomfortable, I didn't feel that urge to fill the silence with meaningless words. It was a comfortable silence. Aliana sat up and stared at her hands, she played with the sheets, like she was trying to distract herself. From time to time, she'd look at me and it seemed as though she was trying to find a way to say something, I waited for her to think through whatever she wanted to say, gave her time to be comfortable enough to say it.

"Everybody knows now." She whispered, just loud enough for me to hear her. "It has been like a month and all they talk about is me."

"They'll get over it at some point," I told her, not really knowing what else to say. "As soon as something exciting happens, they'll talk about that instead."

"I'm used to people talking about me." She shrugged, the careless expression was long gone, "It was so different back at the Government, though. Over here people talk about it because they want to entertain themselves, they make up lies and they're *so* mean."

"You just focus on getting better, what they say doesn't matter," I told her, she looked down at her hands and laid them on her bare thighs. "You're not the first one, you know? There's been others who have gone through it— addiction? They get better and so will you."

"It's weird, you know?" She frowned, she licked her lips before continuing. "It just… it doesn't feel like withdrawal. And that sounds very stupid, I know but… I don't know, I just—I don't know." She laughed humourlessly then, shaking her head at her own thoughts, probably. "But anyway, enough about me, how have you been?"

"Amazing; you saved me from the pit of hell," I told her, she lifted one of her perfectly curved eyebrows, rolling her eyes at my exaggeration. "Honestly, the only reason I was going was because Natalí said I had to, I've been locked in my room for too long."

"Oh, Isaac, you should socialise more."

"Funny *you'd* say that," I laughed, throwing one of my cushions at her. She grabbed it and kept it. "The only people you talk to is us and that's because we practically forced you."

"That's not true."

"Yes, it is. But aren't you glad, though? You got to meet me, what could possibly be better than that?"

"So confident." She rolled her eyes, trying to keep herself from laughing as she threw back the cushion at me. "Anyway, another movie?"

"Pick one," I told her, her eyes lit up and her whole face changed. I smiled to myself when she began to go through the all the titles and finally picked one.

We were watching our second movie of the night, a horror movie. I was trying very hard not to jump at some of the scary parts and Aliana kept criticising everything the characters did. Although at one point I saw her covering her eyes with my pillow.

I was concentrated, watching as the couple making out was about to get killed when an angry voice scared the living shit out of me.

"What the hell?" Natalí's snapped, we both turned to look at her with wide eyes. She turned the light on and oh boy, she looked beautiful. Natalí was very good looking, there was no denying that, but whenever we went to parties, she liked to extra beautiful.

"Jesus, Nat, don't you know how to knock?" I glared with my hand on my chest, my heart about to burst. "You scared the shit out of me."

"What're you doing? You said you'd come." She frowned at me, looking over at Aliana and smiling widely at her but as soon as her eyes were set on me, she glared.

"No, *you* said I'd come." I corrected her, she glared harder and pointed her finger at me, like a pissed off mother about to unleash hell on her kid.

"Actually," Aliana interrupted, sitting up with her legs crossed over. "that's kind of my fault. I didn't know he had somewhere to go until I was already at his door. I'm sorry."

Natalí squinted her eyes, trying to figure out if she was telling the truth or just covering for me. After a second, she seemed convinced enough.

"Party was a disaster anyway," Natalí sighed tiredly as she walked towards the mattress, she took her shoes off and sat comfortably next to Aliana. "Your sister's celebrating her month anniversary. *Yikes.* I had to witness so many unnecessary kisses. My poor, poor eyes."

Aliana snorted, I rolled my eyes. Natalí smiled at Aliana but her smile didn't reach her eyes.

There was something Natalí wasn't telling and I was pretty sure I already knew what it was.

There were times when I was convinced she was going to tell me, but before she could get the words out, she'd get frustrated with herself, she'd get scared and say, *Forget it. It's nothing.*

There were times where I wanted to tell her that I knew. Make it easier for her somehow but I figured it was something important to her, something she needed to come to accept herself before she felt comfortable enough to tell people. So, I wasn't going to pressure her.

I suspected for a few years now, it was her private business but she wasn't as discrete as she thought she was. She liked Samirah, that much I knew.

"What we watching?" She sighed, turning around to look at the TV. She rested her head on Aliana's lap and after a while, Aliana carefully brushed Natalí's curls.

And that's how we ended the night. Natalí, Aliana and I watched movie after movie. Not once did we talk about Aliana's problem, she didn't seem to want to talk about it either. I knew for a fact Natalí didn't care, what people said wouldn't change what she already knew of Aliana. I didn't care either. But Aliana did seem to care and it was understandable.

When everybody found out that Aliana and Samirah were Luna's daughters, people practically lost their shit. Some people were saying that their father *raped* Luna. Some *very* religious people at the church were saying, after what happened with José, that Aliana's basically the Devil's seed. They even went as far as to say that their own father didn't care for them and that they were used as experiments, that's why Aliana was nuts. They made up so many stories. Some people went as far as to talk about their mother, Cynthia. The rumours weren't really about Samirah, most of it was about Aliana, people didn't like her so it was easier for them to make up lies, I guess.

I knew I couldn't expect Aliana to open up about everything she was feeling, she lived her entire life hiding away her feelings. People like Samirah and Aliana, they have lived by rules all their lives. It was normal that she reacted to things the way she did. And it wasn't just Aliana that was going through a hard time. Samirah was too.

Even when she was open to everyone and she tried to fit in, at times she looked out of place, like she didn't quite belong.

It was weird because I hadn't noticed about how Samirah was also having difficulties fitting in until Natalí told me about it. But I had noticed Aliana's difficulties. I had noticed a lot about Aliana. I mean, how could I not when I couldn't help but stare at her whenever she was close.

 **Chapter 30**

Location: La Cruz
Narrator: Aliana

"WHAT'RE YOU DOING here?" Junior asked me, his eyebrows raised in surprise but the smile on his face let me know he was happy to see me.

"I was bored at home and I thought I could hang out with Nat." I smiled politely at him, I didn't have to force it, I liked Junior.

Then Junior did something that completely caught me by surprise. He wrapped his arms around me, in a warmly and fatherly way. It was the kind of hug that I never had but I've always wanted, the kind that made you feel as if everything was going to be okay. The same way Johan would hug Samirah and Nate. I was surprised by it but I found myself wrapping my arms around Junior and I just let myself relax.

"You are always welcome here," Junior told me when he let go, staring into my eyes. "But no working, I don't care what anybody says, you work when you feel okay. For once I agree with Miguel."

I wasn't supposed to work because Miguel didn't want me to, his excuse was that he didn't want me to get overwhelmed with stress. I couldn't stand the thought of all of them knowing, but what could I do? They didn't believe me, to them I hit bottom. And yes, I admit that at some point I was going to hit rock bottom but I knew that what happened that night wasn't withdrawal.

I am an addict, I know what withdrawal is like. Whatever happened that night, it wasn't it.

I was now getting new pills from Andrea. We've been cutting the doses slowly. Andrea was surprisingly good at this. There were times when I thought I was going to do something drastic, I told her and she helped me through it. I felt better. I felt the need and the aching and, God, the pain, but I needed to get myself off those pills. I've been wanting to do it for so long, and now I could finally do it. I needed to work, to keep myself busy but Miguel kept refusing. If I stayed home during the whole day, I'd go crazy. Andrea was trying to help me convince him.

Junior told me to go to Natalí's room and as I made my way there, I kept going over what I wanted to tell her. With a sigh, I knocked on her door and three seconds later, Natalí opened her door with a frown.

"I don't know whether to find it funny or adorable the way you always knock and actually wait." She chuckled, letting me in behind her. She laid on her bed with a book in her hands. "So, how may I be of service?"

"Nice room," I told her, looking around her room. It was a *mess*. But it wasn't a mess of clothes or dirty messy, it was a mess of books. There were books in every corner of her room. It looked more like a library than a room.

"Thank you, took me ages to get all these books." She told me, going back to reading whatever book she had in her hands.

"Have you read them all?" I asked, picking up a book from the closest pile of books. *Wuthering Heights.*

"Most of them." She answered with pride, I didn't have to look at her to know she had a smug smile on her face. "I've loved reading since I was a little girl."

"My dad has lots of books," I told her, placing the book back at the top of the pile. Natalí's eyes watched me with a glint of interest, before she asked, I continued. "And we have a *huge* public library."

"No *fucking* way." She quickly sat up and looked at me, "I have never been so jealous of you people in my entire life. Continue."

"There are lots of books?" I shrugged, laughing at how her face fell instantly.

"I often forget most people don't share my love for literature." She sighed, rolling her eyes at me, "Books are a form of escape to me. I don't know, fiction has always been more appealing than real life."

We stared at each other for a long second. It was like we were waiting for the other to speak first.

"I need a favour." I decided to speak first.

"I figured." She smirked at me knowingly, "What can I do for you?"

"You're like a doctor, right?" Natalí nodded but then shook her head, "You're training to be a healer, so basically some sort of doctor."

"Yeah, you could call it that, some *sort of doctor.*" She joked, laughing at me.

"I— well, basically, I was given these pills," I told her, taking the bottle of pills Roc had given me out of my pocket and throwing them at her. Sam had taken all the bottles, except for that one. Lucky for me. "And I— I think— well, I'm not sure what they are."

Natalí popped the little bottle open and took a pill out, "So this is the little drug, huh? Your poison."

I tensed at her comment but I tried not to let it get to me. This was Natalí, she basically said whatever went through her mind.

"Yes, but that's the thing, I don't think they are. Not really." I confessed. She frowned confusedly at me. "I— okay, I know how this is going to sound but I don't know if it was me going through withdrawal or if there was something in those pills that affected me in some sort of way."

"Poisoned. Like real, *real* poison?" She elaborated for me. I rolled my eyes at her, I didn't want to say that word.

"I don't know."

"Who gave you the pills?" She asked, putting the pill back in the bottle.

I hesitated, biting my lower lip. "Roc."

"Oh, dude, that's fucked up." Natalí couldn't help but laugh but when she saw my face, she contained herself. "I'm sorry. Why do you think he'd want to poison you?"

"I don't know if they are. I just— Nat, I know what going through withdrawal is, whatever happened to me that night, it wasn't it."

"Withdrawal is—"

"Yes, I know that." I interrupted her, walking so I was sitting next to her. "I know what you're going to say and I'm not trying to make it seem like I don't need to get clean because I know I need to get clean and I am, but I need to know for sure because nobody believes me and I *need* to know—"

"Yes, yes, I get it." She interrupted me, grabbing hold of my hand. "I can't do much for you here, we barely even have a hospital and I don't think you can even call it that… but I know a girl from another city where they have like amazing equipment that can be used to find out what these are made of. I can give her a call?"

"Please." I practically begged her. Nat took a deep breath in and reached for her nightstand's drawer, she took a sock with little banana patterns out.

"What?" She almost laughed, reaching inside the sock and taking out a communicator. "I needed to find a place to hide this shit, I didn't know where else."

I rolled my eyes playfully, watching as Nat pressed a few buttons, probably the other person's ID number. After three rings, the line went dead again. Natalí rolled her eyes, she called again. This time, after the fourth beep, they picked up.

"Yes, Natalí, what do you need?" A girl's mocking voice came out of the communicator. She sounded breathless like she had been running. "I thought you said you didn't want to talk to me again."

"Chill with the attitude." Natalí answered, "I have a friend here, she needs help."

"Of course, you need something." The girl snorted, I could tell by the tone of her voice that there were some unresolved issues between these two.

"I'm serious, it's important."

"Nat, even if I wanted to, I can't." The girl's voice changed a tone, she wasn't hostile anymore, she sounded sincere. "Alex's getting on my nerves and—"

"Wait, just before you continue, listen to me, yeah?" Natalí interrupted again, the girl sighed but didn't say anything, so Natalí carried on. "Somebody gave my friend Aliana some pills and she wants to test the pills for poisoning and I know you guys have like a huge lab, I mean—"

"Wait, what?" The girl interrupted, I rolled my eyes at the amount of interruption going on in the conversation. "Poisoning? Is she okay?"

"Yeah, dude, she's fine, she just went blind and stuff but she's good, apparently, she died for like a minute but she's good, still ugly but good." Natalí answered, winking at me. "She just wants to know for sure because—"

"Did you just say that she *died*?"

"Yes, for a minute. Her pulse was gone. Victor brought her back, though." Natalí shrugged, way to be sensitive.

I still wasn't sure how I felt about that little detail. The whole dying and all. At first, when Sam told me about it, I shrugged, not really caring about that and that really caught me by surprise. It wasn't that I wanted to die, but I felt nothing. It was as if there was a giant black hole in my chest sucking every single emotion that I could possibly feel. It was very frustrating because at times I felt too much and then I felt nothing. It was one or the other, there was no middle point and it was tiring. It was something horrible to be used to it but I've felt that way all of my life, I can't remember if there was a point in my life where things were different. It was too much or nothing.

"I'll be there to pick up the pills at night, same spot as always?" The girl answered. "I gotta go, okay? See you at night."

"Calli?" Natalí said a little too quickly, the other girl hummed. "Thank you."

"No worries, Nat." The girl, Calli, said before she ended the call.

Natalí stared at me, I stared back. There was a question in her eyes.

"Aliana," She began, I swallowed the knot in my throat, blinking a lot of times to get rid of the blurry vision. "Have you thought about what it'll mean if there is poison in those pills?"

325

I looked away from her honey-like eyes. Have I thought about it?

"There's not a single moment I don't think about it," I answered her. "I started feeling sick when I started taking those pills. I— I don't know what to think."

I don't know who to trust.

"Hey, I get it." Natalí grabbed my hand, smiling warmly at me. "I'll take the pills and we'll know for sure in a couple of days."

I nodded at her, trying to push away the sudden feeling taking over my body. I couldn't understand my emotions and I didn't know exactly what was happening with my body most of the time but at times, the feeling was so sudden and so strong that I found it impossible to breathe. Everything hurt. I couldn't understand how feelings could affect my body the way they did.

* * *

I was walking around the city, not a single thing on my mind. Lately, with Andrea's help, I've come to see that I worry about everything a little too much. Her exact words were: "You drown yourself in a glass of water." She was right. I knew she was right. So she was helping me to get rid of some stress. To do so, she took me on horse rides. At first, I thought it was a stupid idea, I didn't say it because she seemed excited but I thought it was a stupid idea.

Boy, was I wrong.

It was the most fun I've had since I kidnapped Isaac and Sebas.

Andrea was rather competitive, sometimes we'd race back to the city. We didn't talk most of the times but when she did get me to talk, we'd talk for hours and she'd make me talk about *everything*. She wasn't shy about certain subjects but she respected me and didn't pressure me to answer her when I didn't want to talk about it.

I sat on a bench at the city central and watched as people walked by. Some would stare and whisper my name followed by the rumours they made up about me. Some ignored me. Some glared at me. In other circumstances, I would've been too anxious to even sit there but, in all honesty, right at that moment, I didn't care.

326

The clouds behind the church looked grey and thick, it was windy today and the clouds just confirmed my thoughts: it was going to rain.

I watched as the clouds grew thicker and closer to me, yet I couldn't find it in me to move from the bench I was sitting on. I had been trying so hard to follow Andrea's advice, I was actually trying to control my emotions without the pills. It was so stupid of me to think there was a way out.

This afternoon, right after I got back from my horse ride with Andrea, Natalí found me.

"We need to talk." She had said, I could tell by the look on her face that I was not going to like what she was going to tell me. "Calli came by."

"What did she say?" I managed to ask her, walking by Natalí's side.

"You were right," She whispered. She looked around before handing me a paper.

I read what it said but I can't seem to remember the words in the paper. I don't think I even read much of it.

"Calli said each pill had a little amount of some sort of poison used in the Government. It would've slowly but effectively—"

I remember I shut her out. I don't remember the rest of the conversation, my brain shut down after I heard her say those words. I don't remember much of what happened after that but I do remember walking to the bench. My feet were hurting so I thought I'd sit for a while.

It is amazing how fragile our emotions really are. I was having fun this morning. For the first time in a long time, I felt free from all my worries, from all that was going on inside my head and then… and then it was all gone. I felt nothing but sore feet.

Roc tried to kill me.

I thought about that for a while as I felt the rain pouring down on me. There wasn't a single soul around but here I was, sitting in an old bench, letting the rain wash over me as if I was in one of those cliché movies that Isaac liked so much.

I was lost in thought when I felt someone's hands on me. With no real interest, I looked up to find a pair of brown eyes looking down at me. It was one of Miguel's men. The same one who took me to Luna's house when Johan wanted to talk.

"I've been looking for you everywhere." The guy told me, I forgot what his name was, to be honest, I don't think I ever got his name. "I need you to come with me."

"Where?" I asked, standing up to follow him. I didn't want to put up a fight or refuse to go. There was no point.

"Miguel's house." He walked fast, trying not to get too wet from the rain, I guessed. I followed his pace. "Two soldiers from the AFLN are here to talk to you and your sister."

"The what?" I frowned, I had no idea what he was talking about.

"Just follow." I could tell he was trying not to be rude. Some of Miguel's men treated me differently since the truth came out. A little nicer.

When we got to Miguel's house, the man showed me the way. I was soaking wet. As soon as I began walking, I knew I was making a mess in Andrea's house and I instantly felt bad about it. From our meetings I had come to notice that she was obsessed with cleaning. She liked to have her place spotless.

We stopped in front of a door, I could hear hushed voices but I couldn't make out what they were saying, I did hear Samirah's voice, though. The man opened the door before I could. I walked into Miguel's office, and the guy stayed by the door.

There were eight people in the room. Miguel, Luna, Cairo, and José, the other four people had their backs turned to me but I recognised one of them well enough: Samirah. Next to her was a boy who had a strong back. His sleeveless shirt showed his strong biceps. His hair was dark brown, and he was about a head taller than Samirah. Next to him was a girl with long brown hair that was braided only on one side of her head. And next to her stood another boy, he was skinny compared to the other boy but still muscly. His hair was of a very strange colour. It wasn't blond, it was a greyish colour. He was wearing a black t-shirt, I could see a tattoo on his forearm. The three of them wore uniforms.

"Here she is," Luna spoke, making everybody turn their heads to me. "Aliana."

I walked towards the circle of people, feeling awkward because they were all looking at me and all I could hear was the sound of my wet shoes against the floor. I looked at no one and everyone at the same time. The two boys and the girl were looking at me. They looked badass.

"This is Calliandra," Miguel said, pointing to the girl.

Calli had a long, straight nose. Her eyes were the colour of honey, a little lighter than Natalí's. Her eyebrows were in a sharp, finely curved line and towards the edge of her brow were two slits. Her lips were curved in a small smile. Her cheekbones were admirable and her hairstyle, although it was weird to me, went perfectly well with her face.

"Calli. Just call me Calli," the girl said with a smile. She was Natalí's friend. I recognised her voice.

"I'm Evan." the boy with brown hair spoke.

The dark-brown-haired boy had a charming smile on his face. His eyes, rounded, were the same colour as the moon, a pale grey. His nose was bigger than the girl's, and his tanned skin had the same tone as mine.

"Hi," The boy with greyish hair spoke, a sweet smile on his face, his voice wasn't what I expected from him, it was a soft voice, not very deep but raspy as if he had just woken up. His brown eyes were taking me in. "I'm Noelle."

"I'm Aliana."

"Noelle, Calli, and Evan are from La Nueva," Miguel told me, but I already knew this.

"We're here to help you get Mrs. Keenan out," Calli said.

"I don't think that's a good idea." I shook my head. "Too many people. We can't risk it."

"We're not here to ask you for opinion," Evan began, by the way he spoke I could tell he was in charge. "This is our mission now and I want to make one thing clear, the only reason you're going is because we need someone who knows their way around the Government."

"This is my mother we're talking about—"

"What Evan is trying to say," Calli intervened, glaring at Evan and turning to look at me, "Is that you will be part of our squad but you have to follow his orders. It'll be three of us, we have uniforms, we have guns and we have maps but it would be better if you came with us."

I looked over at Luna, I thought she was going too?

"About that… we agreed it would be safer if it was just us," Noelle stepped in, probably knowing what I was thinking.

"We have no mind in this business, so we leave," Miguel said, looking rather annoyed. "I hope all goes well."

"I stay," Cairo said. Miguel nodded.

"You gonna help them?" José laughed. "You gon' help the man who fucked your—"

Cairo was going to lunge at José, but Miguel beat him to it. He dragged José to the nearest wall, banged his head against it, and punched him. Evan was going to step in. To my surprise, Samirah took Evan by the arm and shook her head to say no. Miguel punched José again, and José looked about to pass out. Miguel slapped him in the face a few times to make sure he stayed awake.

"I'm not a great leader. We all know that. I'd rather solve my problems with my fists than with words," Miguel muttered through his teeth. "I have tried to do as you asked, to keep you happy and show that I have no favourites. I let you talk and get away with it. But there's a limit, José, and you're crossing it. I am your leader and you owe me respect, to me and my family. Respect and loyalty. Otherwise, you will end up at the bottom of the cliff. You know I don't make false threats."

Miguel dropped José to the floor and walked away with no regrets. Cairo walked over to José to help him up, but José rejected his help and walked away with blood running from his mouth, he looked like he could burn the whole city down with his anger.

"Well, that was intense," Noelle joked.

"To the point," Calli rolled her eyes, ignoring Noelle's comment. "What's the plan?"

Evan clapped his hands to get people's attention, he reached down to grab a bag from the floor and took out a map from it. He laid the map on the desk. It was a map of the Government.

"These are the underground pathways." Evan began, pointing at the blue lines on the map. "You know where the cells are, right?"

"Central Building," I told them at the same time as Samirah pointed the Central Building on the map.

"Underground facilities, right?" Calli asked and Sam, Luna and I nodded.

"This is a very simple mission, we go in, find her, and we get out, there can't be any mistakes or problems, we have exactly two hours to do this." Evan told us, "We spoke to Johan and it will be done next week during Revelation Day. We will provide weapons but please, do try not to use them. We've decided that it would be safer if Cynthia didn't know Aliana's there with us. Her emotions could get the best of her and she would worry not only for herself but for you too and it'll be a problem."

"We also brought computers, Nathaniel said you were good with that stuff, and we need someone to hack into their system, who better than someone who helped create it?" Noelle spoke, looking over at Samirah. Sam's face lit up as she quickly nodded.

"I can hack the system and give you a clear path so you don't have to use Nate's password to get in the underground facilities," Sam told them, her face expression showed just how excited she was. As if this was some sort of exciting game.

"Is that it?" I asked, they all looked at me, Evan nodded. "Seems a little too easy."

"It shouldn't be too hard, this is the Government we're talking about, aren't you people supposed to be all peaceful and whatnot?" Evan said with a half smirk on his lips.

"So that's it then," Calli clapped her hands together. "Now all we gotta do is train and wait."

"Is there a chance I could speak with this Alex?" I knew the leader of their city was called Alex, Isaac had told me so.

"Nope. Not any time soon, anyways," Noelle answered.

"Why?"

"Why do you want to talk to him?" Evan stepped in for Noelle.

"Because I want to talk to him."

"Whatever it is you need to tell him, you can tell us. We'll relay it to him. And whatever his response is, we'll let you know."

"I just want to know if my mother will be safe there," I lied. I wanted to know if I could leave with my mother.

There was nothing here for me. I needed to start again. And like Nate had said, if being here does me no good, then I should at least try to find another place for me to be. There was nothing for me here. Sam didn't want me here, she had made it clear many times.

"Your mother will be safe, you have my word," Evan reassured me.

"Well if that's all, I'll be on my way," I told them, turning around to leave. I ignored Sam's glares and I made my way out of Miguel's house.

The raining was lighter now. I took a deep breath as the drops of rain fell on my face and my body. I closed my eyes for a moment and I tried to forget everything that was going on.

"What's up with you?" Sam's voice startled me. I opened my eyes right away.

"Nothing. What's up with you?" I asked her as she looked at me. She knew I was lying but she didn't point it out.

"Nothing." She sighed, she stood there in front of me, waiting for me to say something but I didn't know what to say, there was nothing to say. "Are you okay?"

"I'm good. Are *you* okay?"

"Don't lie to me, Lynn." She sighed. "There's something going on with you, you look... empty."

"And you look like you haven't gotten any sleep," I smiled, trying to change the subject. "Trouble in paradise? Where's your boyfriend?"

Sam looked down at her feet, "I think I might've gotten in a relationship a bit too fast."

"Yes, you tend to rush into things," I nodded and by the look she gave me, I was not helping her at all. "Talk to him."

"It's not that easy," She rolled her eyes.

"It is, you're doing it with me right now and we both said some pretty mean stuff," I chuckled, she looked at me like she was about to apologise. I continued, not letting her, an apology wasn't going to change anything. "Maybe he will understand more than you think. Give him some credit."

"That's the thing, though, not even *I* understand what's going on with me," She shook her head, a genuine look of confusion in her eyes.

"Andrea said to me that everybody gets confused every once in a while," I told her, "She said you gotta give yourself time."

"Well, does it work? Giving yourself time, I mean."

"Who the hell knows, everything is just confusing as fuck," I shrugged. Samirah started laughing then, it began as a chuckle but then she began laughing louder, and her laugh was so contagious that I couldn't help but laugh with her.

It is amazing how fragile our emotions really are. I was numb an hour ago, I felt empty, I felt like I had nothing like I was nothing. I felt nothing but sore feet. But now, I felt a little bit of hope. Hope because soon I would be with my mother. Hope because even if Samirah did think horrible things about me, even if she didn't want me here, I knew we could improve our relationship, maybe what we needed was time and space. I was hopeful and I had sore feet.

Chapter 31

Location: La Cruz
Narrator: Samirah

I STILL COULDN'T believe my family was a complete falsehood.

I loved – adored – my father. I adored him to death. I looked – *look* – up to him, I trusted him, I relied on him, and then I discovered this. Discovering the truth felt like I'd been shot. However, instead of killing me and taking me into the darkness of death, it gave me light. It gave me eyes to see the truth, to see how little I knew the people around me, the people I loved and believed to be my family.

Now every time I looked at Luna or at Aliana, I felt like I was being shot over again. I felt like the lies were part of my body, that my life was full of lies and the truth was a bullet, a bullet aiming directly at the core, directly at the centre, of all these lies. And once the bullet hit me, it destroyed me. The truth destroyed the image I had of a happy family, of my family. Maybe it was not a very happy family, but it was still my family.

Nathaniel was hiding something. He hadn't been coming lately, and he avoided being around Aliana. He even avoided talking about her, when he did, a shade of darkness flooded his eyes. But before I could acknowledge his expression, he completely hid it and turned to another subject. If I didn't know him better, I'd think he was feeling guilty. But Nate had done nothing to Aliana. Since her *incident*, Nate simply didn't want to be around her much. I thought it was too much for him to see her like that. I remembered when she first overdosed. He wouldn't even go see her because he was hurt.

I was still angry at her. And even though I was very hurt, I missed her a lot. She almost died. Aliana almost died and that helped me realise a *lot* of things.

I said horrible things to her, horrible, horrible things. I wanted to hug her and beg her to please do something about her drug problem because I could not stand the thought of losing her, but I was too angry. I was enraged. It was Aliana. God, she had a way of pushing every single one of my buttons and make me lose my temper. I wanted to talk to her about everything, to ask her how she was doing, but she just kept doing things that displeased me, at times I believed we couldn't have a proper conversation without arguing.

We could talk, but apparently, we couldn't talk for longer than ten minutes because we'd start arguing.

And there was Luna… I thought she was nice, but now it all fell into place. She was nice because she knew I was her daughter. She had known since the day I arrived. I hated the fact that I liked her so much before, now it seemed different. She got in the middle of my mum and my dad. Or it was my father who put her in that place. Or it simply just happened. I didn't know and I didn't care. All I knew was that I had one mother, one and only one: Cynthia.

She was the one who raised me, the one who educated me, and the one who even tried to show she cared. She tried because she knew *I* cared. Cynthia at least tried to show emotions that she did not have. She did it for us, for her children, to show us that she loved us. I believed her. And I didn't know what to believe when it came to Luna. I don't know what she did to Aliana or what Aliana knew but it must've been pretty bad for her to hate Luna the way she did. And I hated to admit it, but the more I thought about it, the more I understood Aliana.

The thought, the knowledge, that Cynthia was not my biological mother … it broke my heart to pieces every night when I was trying to sleep. And I couldn't shake the thought out of my head. What would Cynthia do if she knew the truth? Would she act like she still cared? Would she drop the act and be indifferent to my love for her? My mother, my beloved mother, the woman who taught me everything I knew …

I just couldn't believe it, if anyone at the Government were to find out, this would be a scandal. Nothing like this had *ever* happened before. How could Johan do such thing? Johan was perfect. He was good, he was kind, he was the smartest man I knew, he was respectful, he was affectionate in his own way, he was caring, and he was my hero. How could he lie to and cheat on his family? How was I supposed to think of Cynthia differently when she was the only mother I've ever known. I didn't want Luna to be my mother. I didn't want to share her blood, I didn't want to look like her, I didn't want my hair to be the same colour as hers, I didn't want my lips to be like hers, I didn't want my nose to be like hers, and I didn't want my personality to be similar to hers.

I didn't want to be Luna's daughter.

I liked Luna, I really did, but I liked her before I knew she was supposedly my mother. That piece of information changed everything. I tried to be nice to Luna, really. Since I found out, I tried a lot of things. I tried to hide from her, to talk to her, to understand her… I tried all I could think of, but it just wasn't like it was before. I also had to accept the fact that I made an effort to do all those things simply because I didn't want to be like Aliana. I didn't want to hate Luna and didn't want to hate my father.

I didn't want to be Aliana.

It was actually funny to me now that I used to want to be like her. I wanted Aliana's looks because even though we were sisters, I'd always thought she was prettier than me. I'd always wanted to be able to do the things she did, to be able to communicate with people with just one look. I'd envied Aliana for so many things, like the way she carried herself with confidence, like Mother did. I envied her relationship with her friends, who understood her and worked with her as if they were one. I often had to tell myself that they *had* to do that, as it was the way the Government worked, the way people were supposed to be: follow your leader and never question.

And there was Roc. The way she was with Roc. The way he was with her. I envied her for having that, for having that bond with someone.

I disliked Roc a great deal. Part of it must have been because I always wanted someone like him. No, I always wanted to have someone to care about me like he cared for Aliana.

I didn't like him, that was for sure. I didn't like his personality or his looks. What I liked about Roc, probably the only thing I've ever liked about Roc, was the inexplicable love he had for Aliana. I never really understood what it was. Once, I even saw Aliana lose her straight and serious posture to laugh at something he had said – *really* laugh. I never liked Roc, but I had always wanted someone like him who would give his own life for the person he claimed to love. Aliana had that type of love, and I didn't.

Even though she was bitter and too honest (plain rude, if you ask me) sometimes, she still had known love before I did. The worst part? Aliana never cared for it. She didn't care if Roc loved her or not. She certainly didn't love him back. I was glad of that because Roc, while he may have loved her, was a manipulative person. I really did wish better for my sister.

However, all my envy vanished when Aliana and I started to grow up. All that jealousy turned into something else. I still envied her, but I didn't envy her for love or for her looks. I envied her for a completely different reason. I envied her because she did whatever she wanted. I envied my own sister for her freedom. How little did I know that my sister was a bird caged in her own body as a prison. How little did I know how much my sister suffered for her own bitterness. She was literally willing to kill herself with those pills in order to feel nothing. I didn't know her enough back then, but I did know her enough now to know that she was suffering because she didn't want to be like she was.

I might have been angry and disappointed in Aliana, but she was still my sister. She drove me mad and made me angry, but she was my sister. She was my blood. I would always forgive her, no matter how much time it took me to heal. My love for my sister was bigger than anything.

"You're thinking so much that I think your head is about to explode." Sebas's voice brought me back from my thoughts. I blinked a couple of times, looking up at him. "What's wrong?"

"I think we should talk." I blurted out. Sebas's face completely dropped as if he knew what I wanted to say to him.

To be fair, he had been trying his best to avoid this conversation and I couldn't wait anymore. I was too confused about everything in my life but there was one thing I knew for sure: I didn't want to be in a relationship with Sebas. It took me time to realise this, and it was Eli who helped me see it. Eli said something about how he'd rather be with Paola, Natalí's sister, than with anybody else. Apparently, Paola and Eli were getting a bit too close and Junior wasn't having it because they were just 14 years old.

So, if Eli, a 14-year-old boy, knew what he wanted, knew that he wanted to be with Paola, then why didn't I know? And I thought about it. I thought about it until I gave myself a headache. But I understood that it wasn't Sebas who I wanted to be with. Was it even a *boy* who I wanted to be with and the most confusing part of it all? It wasn't Natalí either, Natalí from whom I stole a kiss and made things completely awkward. I didn't want to be with Natalí even if she did make me feel certain things. I wanted to be with Grace.

Grace was one of my mother's students. She was the same age as Nate and she had the most beautiful brown eyes I had ever seen in my life. Her hair was always so shiny and it was an odd colour. At times I'd stare at her for minutes, trying to figure out how her hair managed to look brown but also red and even blonde. It was a mixture of the three and I spent hours wishing she'd let her hair down.

I often asked her to explain things to me, to come and help me out because I didn't know how to work my way around something. And because she the nicest person ever, she'd come every time with a smile on her lips and we would be so close to each other that I could count the freckles on her nose and her cheeks. They looked like little constellations in her face. To say the least, I was fascinated by Grace.

I always thought it was admiration because she was intelligent, nice and polite. And she always helped me. Nate said she had to be, it was her obligation but I refused to believe that.

It was Grace who I wanted to be with, I wanted to spend time with her again like I used to. And that's when everything was a little clearer. I understood why I was always so eager to go to work in the mornings and stay over hours whenever she was. Why I felt happy for no reason at all when she was around.

Liking Grace made sense but I was still confused. Liking a girl, it wasn't something that had happened before. And Natalí was too nervous or scared to talk about it with me. It was possible to like a girl, it was because *I* liked a girl. Of that I was sure.

I think it was the only thing I was sure of.

"You want to break up?" He asked, he held his head high, staring right into my eyes.

"It isn't fair to you," I told him, not knowing what better words to use. "I was confused and I went with what made sense instead of what I was feeling."

Sebas frowned at me, I could tell he was trying to contain himself. "And what were you feeling?"

"I— I don't like you the way you like me," I decided to be honest. I needed to be honest, he deserved that. "I think— well no, I don't think, I know I like someone else but I don't know what it means."

"What?" His eyebrows curled in confusion, he sat next to me and took a deep breath. "That's confusing, Samirah."

"Yes, very," I agreed with him, "I like a girl?"

Sebas's eyes widened at my words, he stared at me, trying to figure out if I was lying or not. He cleared his throat and tried to say something but nothing came out. His cheeks began to flush.

"You're… you're gay?" He whispered. I frowned.

"I'm a *what*?" I frowned, I had never heard that word in my life. "What is that?"

"People who like the same sex as theirs?" He answered but he was confused too, which only confused me more.

"Wait, there's others?" I asked, He shrugged slowly. "What are you then?"

"I'm straight."

"Oh." Was the only thing I said as I thought about what he said. "I'm a little confused."

And that's how Sebas ended up explaining to me what sexual orientation was. By the end of our talk, I was a little less confused. He told me that some people weren't very accepting but that it shouldn't matter to me and he reassured me that he would break someone's nose if they said anything to me about my sexual orientation. I didn't particularly care to tell people about it. Nobody else introduced themselves as 'straight' when they greeted someone new, why should I?

However, the more I thought about it, the more it made sense. It was like I had been trying to make sense of something, but I could never quite understand it. It was very confusing, it was like I had been trying to find a word that would explain what I was feeling and I had finally found it. Sebas gave it to me.

I am gay. I am a lesbian and I am *not* straight.

I could not explain how oddly liberating and satisfying it was to say those words.

And just like that… I wasn't as confused anymore.

# Chapter 32

Location: La Cruz
Narrator: Aliana

TODAY WAS THE day.

Today we were getting Mum out and I couldn't be any more nervous.

I had a shower and took longer than necessary just because I couldn't stop thinking about the events that would unfold today. I was walking downstairs, thinking about all the things I could say to her, trying to figure out how she'd react... It was too much.

Once I stepped foot in the kitchen, Samirah grabbed me by my hands and stared at me with her eyes wide open. A huge smile on her face as she uttered words that made no sense to me.

"I am gay. I am a lesbian. I am not straight." She told me. Squeezing my hands a little bit too hard.

"I... am nervous. I am confused. I am not comfortable with the creepy way you're smiling at me," I joked. It was nice that she was in such a good mood. I didn't want to ruin it but I didn't understand her.

"I like girls."

I blinked at her a couple of times. "You can do that?"

"Yes and I like girls."

I nodded while I stared at her. She looked so... relieved? "You like girls?"

"I like girls."

"You like girls."

"I love you." She told me, her eyes filling with tears. "I'm sorry for all that I said, I— I know I wasn't the best sister ever and I know that I failed you a lot of times and I am so sorry I left you alone. I love you, Lynn and I want to make this better and I can't wait until Mum's here so we can have at least a few hours together. I know you will get her out."

"I love you too, Sam." I smiled at her, "I'm sorry for what I said too. And I hope you can forgive me for all the things I've done that have somehow hurt you. I swear to you that in my mind, I was protecting you but now I see that it was wrong and I am sorry for that."

She hugged me then.

"I made you breakfast," She smiled and lead me to the table. She had made arepas with cheese on top.

"So, tell me about this liking girls thing," I asked her, her smile grew as she began to talk my ear off. She mentioned Grace's name quite a lot and all I could think about was my mum's telling us about Grace almost burnt her own eyebrows once because she forgot to put her safety goggles on.

When we finished eating and made our way out, it was 5.10 and we were supposed to meet Evan, Noelle, and Calli at 5.20 at the church.

I was nervous. My belly was spinning with every step I took. I had to calm down. The mission ahead entailed things that were what I did for a living. I had been trained to do this kind of stuff. The problem was that I never did it for real. None of my training had real consequences, this did. And it was my mother. It was time to save my mother. And I was nervous.

I walked to the back of the church, where the red gate was, the gate was open and we could see the inside of the back of the church. Everyone was already there. Samirah squeezed my hand before letting go and heading inside the church through the back door. There was a desk with two very old computers. Sam sat behind the desk and began to do her work, tapping a screen and concentrating on something she was saying through the little communicator clipped around her ear. Behind her with their arms crossed were Sebastián and Isaac, who were watching what she was doing. On Samirah's desk was a big communicator. Probably Johan and Nate would show up later on. Luna was there too. Cairo was talking to her, and she was just nodding. Eli was behind Cairo.

I headed to where Calli, Evan, and Noelle were. They were dressed in uniforms, with rifles and knives in their belts. They looked perfectly fine. Calli wasn't wearing her black make-up or her braids. All her earrings were gone too. With her hair in a long ponytail, she looked different, like a proper soldier. So did Evan and Noelle.

I saw Isaac look in my direction, he smiled warmly at me, making me smile back at him. Evan gave me my uniform and told me to get changed.

I felt like I was myself again. With my baggy dark green trousers and my shirt, I put on my holster. In my belt, I placed my well-loved knives, and to my back, I strapped the 6-mm calibre Nate had given me, just in case …

Dressed in my uniform made me melancholic. I remembered how overjoyed I felt the first time I wore it. I had been very happy, to say the least. I finally had something that could be my own career, not something that was the result of my following in another person's footsteps.

I put on the collared shirt and walked out of the bathroom putting my hair in a high, tight ponytail. There was not one single hair out of place, and my uniform was impeccable. I was Soldier Keenan again.

I could feel Isaac's eyes on me. In my peripheral vision, I could see him looking at me with a smirk, reminding me of his word when I told him that I wasn't a soldier anymore.

"Well, soldier Keenan," Evan said, taking a step closer to me and raising his hands to the collar of my shirt, fixing it. "I know you're used to giving orders but today you follow me and we shall get your mum safe and sound back here."

"Yes, sir." I nodded and Evan's lips turned upwards.

Evan was going to say something but he was interrupted by Johan's voice. Everyone turned to look for him. After a few seconds, his image appeared in a shade of blue.

"Good morning," Johan said. He had his hands tucked behind him. Nate, with his hands in his pockets and wearing the smile I was very accustomed to, looked like a copy of Johan as he stood behind him.

I hadn't seen Nate in a while. We barely even talked since that night. I felt my right pocket burn as I remember the letter Calli had given Natalí with the results from the testing of the pills. They didn't believe me when I told them there was something more and even though I understood their reasons for not believing me. It still hurt. However, today I was ready to get the answers that I needed.

"Good morning, Mr. Keenan," Evan greeted Johan as my father and my brother walked towards him. "It's nice seeing you again."

"I'm guessing you're all ready for this. You should leave soon if you want to make it in time," Nate said, looking at everybody but me.

"All of you know what you have to do, right?" Johan asked. For the first time in ages, he looked a bit desperate and even nervous.

"We're ready, sir," Evan confirmed. "We know what this means to you. We won't make mistakes."

"So, are we ready?" Noelle asked.

"I'm in," Samirah said, popping up from behind a screen. "Nate, come. I need your help with this. Too many cameras. I have to keep an eye on all of them."

Nate nodded as he walked towards Samirah, walking right through the desk, the show-off.

"Before you leave, I need to tell you two something," Johan began, speaking to me and Sam. My heart raced at his words. "You should probably know to avoid confusions later on."

"More secrets?" Samirah asked, taking the question out of my mouth. Sometimes I did think we were connected.

"I don't think that's a good thing to do right now, Father," Nathaniel said with tension in his voice.

"What is it?" I asked vaguely. I was irritated with all this, there were so many secrets, Johan was basically an endless pit of secrets...

"Cynthia. She knows the truth about Luna," Johan quickly said. "She knows she is not your biological mother."

My world shattered at those words – what was left of my world, anyway.

I quickly looked over at Samirah. On my sister's face, I could see my own fear and doubts reflected. Cynthia knew that Sam and I were not her daughters. What would happen now that she knew the truth? Dozens of questions popped into my head. Telling us now was *not* a good idea.

I didn't want to think about that now. I needed to have a clear mind so I could get Cynthia out of the Government. If once I got Cynthia out, she rejected me, then I would accept it. It would kill me, but I could not make her love me if she didn't.

Samirah looked over at Nate. He looked as guilty as ever. He already knew. Quickly Samirah looked at me, probably trying to find something to indicate that I knew too, but I had no idea. And I would have preferred not to know this, to be honest.

"She knows," Samirah repeated, her voice hollow.

"Yes, but—"

"Whatever it is you have to say about it, Johan, save it for later. I don't need to know this now." I said, coldly interrupting my father.

I was very tired of all the secrets, the ones I knew about and the ones I didn't know about. My family was basically was made out of secrets. It was like every time I blinked, another secret would come to light. I never liked lying. I hated it. Once you get caught in a lie, it isn't only the lie that hurts, but the trust you had placed in that person quickly fades. And that was what I had done to my sister. Sam was hurt because of the truth and because everyone she was supposed to trust had been lying to her. I understood that now. Cynthia wasn't our biological mother; Luna was. And Cynthia would reject us too.

"You ought to know that—"

"*Please*, Johan," I begged. He stopped. "We have to find her. We can't waste time. Once she's here, you can tell us whatever you want."

To my surprise, Sam nodded. Without looking at anyone or saying anything, I walked out through the red doors, heading to the horses. If Johan wanted to carry on, I didn't want to be there to hear whatever he had to say.

Once I was out, I heard someone's steps getting closer. For a moment, I wished for those steps to be Isaac's, I wanted to discuss this with him, I wanted to complain, I wanted to scream, I wanted to talk about it and for some reason, I always felt a little better after I talked to Isaac. I turned around hoping to see Isaac's face. What a surprise and disappointment it was when I found Evan's instead. I let out a long sigh and turned back around.

"I'm not *that* ugly." He laughed. I shrugged. "Come, let's get the horses ready."

Evan walked by me without looking back to make sure I was following. I didn't want to talk to anyone except maybe to Isaac, my good friend Isaac.

"In my opinion," Evan began, saddling Lucero, Andrea's horse. "You guys have quite a lot of family issues. And *you* have an attitude."

"In *my* opinion," I shot back at him, "You shouldn't get involved in other people's business. And you shouldn't make the saddle that tight. It'll hurt the horse."

"I know about horses, I know what hurts him and what doesn't."

He made a very ridiculous face as he smiled and kissed the horse. I couldn't help but laugh at him. When he wasn't being all official and commanding, he was actually kind of decent.

"I think, and this is my humble man's opinion, that maybe you should talk to your father instead of keeping whatever it is that makes you angry inside you. It will only make you angrier and grumpier, and you'll have wrinkles."

Evan was now putting the saddle on the other horse. I was glad he couldn't see my shocked face. He had just called me angry and grumpy.

"Who asked for your opinion anyway?"

"No one. I'm just simply saying you'd look prettier with a smile on your face," he told me. I rolled my eyes.

"First of all, I don't care about your opinion, secondly, who said I want to look prettier?" I snapped back and right when he was going to reply, Noelle stood by my side.

"Everyone's ready," Noelle said, looking down at me with a polite smile.

Noelle and Calli were having a conversation next to me, I was too nervous to try to participate and socialise. The bridge was a five-hour walk away if one were to walk at a slow pace, but with the horses, it would be about a three-hour ride. We would be arriving around 8 in the morning. I didn't know how big the tunnels were or how long it would take us to get to the CB, but I knew that we would have to run.

On the ride to the tunnel entrance, there was a lot of jumping. My back kind of hurt. Calli laughed at me when I almost fell, but it wasn't my fault. I was so nervous that I wasn't doing anything right. We figured that since we had three horses, Mum could ride with one of us. My heart was already shrinking at the thought of her. How will she react?

Once we reached the entrance, Evan informed me that the tunnel was underwater. And I was amazed by the way the water looked from the tunnel. I could see the fishes. I loved it so much that I wanted to go by it again. By then, I was starting to relax, I was calm, Calli's arguments with Noelle helped a little when it came to distraction.

The other tunnels were dark. We were underground and going around the city now. We took a few turns and then kept walking until Evan slowed his pace, telling us that we were there, right where we needed to be, ten minutes away from the CB but we were earlier than expected so we had to wait.

Breathe, just breathe.

Chapter 33

Location: La Cruz
Narrator: Samirah

I WAS STARING right at the screens. We had to focus on one thing at the time and I needed to focus so I wouldn't make mistake. But I kept thinking back to Johan's words. Cynthia did know that we aren't her biological daughters, but Cynthia had known this for a long time. That's what Johan said after Aliana left.

I've been staring right at the screens, at all the images, with all the cameras showing me the people I grew up with, the people I knew. My people. I hadn't realised how much I wanted to be there until I saw them. I had to wait for hours until the people started to leave their houses to go to the Revelations. There was a lot of people, and they were all sitting in their corresponding places.

"What's happening?" Cairo asked watching the screens as did the rest of us.

"Aliana, Calli, Noelle, and Evan are still in the tunnels. They're a little early,"

"Why is there so many people out?" Luna asked.

"Revelations," Nate and I answered at the same time.

"The Revelations are a kind of graduation," Nate explained. "Here they will reveal everything, who passed with what grade; who will work at the farm or go into service or be assigned a good job; who will not marry anyone; who will marry whom … Everyone goes; they have to. It's our way to know who is worth it and who isn't."

"How do they know where people go?" Sebastián asked.

"Intellectual coefficient, testing..." Nate answered again. "Although it is way more complex than that, way more complicated, it really all depends on who you are, who your family is."

"Oh, the requirements. If you don't meet the requirements, then you're not important." Sebas summed up.

"Yes," Nate quickly answered. "Well, no. More or less. ... The people who don't meet the requirements are important because they take care of other things. They do what no one else wants to."

"Without mincing words, they're your slaves," Isaac interrupted with a serious tone. "Basic, really. You rich people stay rich; the poor stay slaves."

"We all do what we have to do." Nate seemed uncomfortable. "For now."

"Sounds to me like a poor excuse to make yourself feel better about it. You were born in a nice family and other people weren't, so you look away when they don't even get a fair shot at whatever you people do – and all this just because some of them are born in low-class families. Seems pretty easy to understand. Actually, the Government says everyone has the same chance and that everyone is the same, but it's bullshit." Isaac laughed. He seemed like he wanted to argue with everyone, or maybe just with himself.

"It isn't fair and I agree with you," Aliana's voice came out of the speaker. "but you're acting like we had a say in any of this? We were born into this, Isaac, just like you were born and raised to cheer when there's a public act of violence."

"That's different," Isaac argued back.

"It really isn't." She carried on arguing, it was surprising to hear because she didn't seem to be angry or annoyed, she was just simply giving a piece of her mind. Calmly and respectfully. "You believe what you and your people do, either cheer at violence or many other things that I do not care to point out now, is normal because you were raised around it, you see it normal but I don't. It isn't the same thing, I know and I shouldn't compare one thing to the other, but I'm just making an example, I'm not making up an excuse for how things work.

"Unfortunately, things are the way they are. It isn't right and it should change but *we* can't do anything about it. Not Sam, not Nate, not me. Because if we did speak up about it, we would have gotten killed. Just like my mother is going to get killed if we don't do anything to get her out. She spoke up about one little thing and disturbed the peace the board had created, even if it's based on lies. Look at where it got her. She has done so much for the Government, but they didn't care, they saw her as a problem that needed solving. What do you think they would've done to *us*?"

It was sad but true, I always looked away when something that I didn't like happened. We all did. What else were we supposed to do? Stand up against a whole country when we knew perfectly well that no one would stand with us – and get killed in the process? It was cowardly and selfish, but at least now someone wanted to do something about it. And I wanted to be a part of it.

"Sometimes it's so annoying to argue with you because you actually make somewhat good points." Isaac laughed, shaking his head and letting the subject go.

"Can we get back to concentrating on the task at hand, please?" Nate cleared his throat.

"I am concentrating on the screens, Nathaniel," I answered with a sigh.

"If you call that concentration." Nate pointed at a little camera showing that Noelle was coming up from the tunnels. Evan was giving him a hand, and Calli was keeping an eye out.

"You're early. There's still people around and inside the CB," I told them, confused as to why they were coming out.

"There's no empty corridors?" Aliana asked.

"No clear way in?" Evan asked at the same time.

"Not yet," I answered vaguely. Aliana began to walk.

"Where are you going?" Nate demanded.

"There's houses five minutes away from the CB. We'll wait there," Aliana answered. Nathaniel nodded.

"All right. You have to wait for about twenty minutes more."

"Yes, we know, Nathaniel," Aliana answered with a cold tone.

"Stop taking unnecessary risks. I think you should go back to the tunnels and wait there," I told them.

"If you had been in the tunnels, you probably wouldn't want to wait there either," Aliana said, looking directly at the camera mounted inside the light bulb.

"She's afraid of cockroaches." Calli laughed. I would have laughed too. The word *afraid* didn't even begin to describe how Aliana would feel if she saw a cockroach.

"It's called a phobia," Aliana muttered. "You go back if you want. I'm going to hide over here, far away from that abomination. I mean, they survived a freaking nuclear war. Tigers are gone, elephants are gone, all of the beautiful animals are gone, and what do we have left? Roaches." Aliana walked into a house. The others followed. I couldn't see them any longer, as cameras weren't allowed inside houses. I could hear them though.

"Tell us when everyone is at the Revelations," Noelle asked, yawning.

"But we got monkeys." Calli jumped in, arguing with Aliana. "We got much more animals than just roaches. Like, have you seen a jaguar? We got snakes, we got bunnies, we got horses."

"Yes, Calli, but—"

"*Iguanas*, Aliana. We got iguanas." Calli interrupted her, she seemed very excited about animals. "I got a parrot in my house. It can count to ten. I saw a sloth the other day, by the way. Scared the shit out me."

"Monkeys are kind of cute," Aliana said, enthusiastic to share this topic with Calli. They spoke with such ease, when did they even start talking?

"Monkeys carry diseases," Noelle pointed out.

"You know who else carries diseases?" Calli shot back with a mocking in her voice. "Yo—"

"Not me. I'm clean of viruses, thank you very much," Noelle interrupted.

"Everybody is so nice." Aliana laughed.

"Can you three, like, shut up?" Evan snapped at them. *Rude much…* "I'm trying to do something over here."

Calli and Noelle would talk from time to time, whereas Evan and Aliana were in silence, Aliana sometimes would add something to the conversation. Twenty minutes went by. Aliana began to ask if they could leave yet. At the twenty-five-minute mark, they were clear to walk out.

"Tell us if someone comes," Calli called out to me. "Evan, go with Aliana just in case she needs you. I ain't good at faking accents."

"Keep up the pace, roach lover," Aliana mocked. She seemed to like Noelle and Calli. Why wouldn't she, they basically liked exactly the same things – guns, knives, running, fighting, shooting?

"As you wish, boss." Calli mocked, raising her hand to salute her like a formal soldier.

"Hello?" Evan shouted as they walked into the CB. There was nobody else there. I had already said so. Aliana jumped and turned to glare at him.

"Are you all right in the head?" Aliana whispered aggressively. Evan chuckled.

"Chill out, there's no one."

"I told you, everyone is at the Revelations," I reminded them.

"So, we go underground. Are you sure she's in the communal cells?" Aliana asked.

"How many cells are there?" Calli asked.

"That I know of? Three." Aliana answered.

They carried on walking in silence. I could see the tension in Aliana's shoulders. The fact that she was nervous made me nervous.

"There's a soldier coming to you, on your right, about five metres away," Nate told Aliana. "When you take the right turn, you'll see him."

Aliana began to talk with Evan about something of no importance. She relaxed and walked as comfortable as she could manage. The soldier didn't give them a second glance as he made his way out of the CB.

"Oh my God!" I shouted. I hadn't meant to, but the scream just left my mouth.

"What? What is it?" everyone asked. I gave a little nervous giggle.

"What is it, Samirah?" Luna asked.

"I'm sorry," I apologised, I got distracted by the first revelation. "Grace's at the Revelations, she cut her hair. She looks so pretty. Also, she got a promotion."

"*Grace*?" Aliana teased, looking over at the camera with a knowing smirk. I couldn't help but blush. "As much as I'm interested in what you just said, you don't have to look at the Revelations. Your job is to tell us if there's a problem, not to get distracted and scare the hell out of me."

I stared a Grace for a long minute, humming as a response to my sister, Grace was a big distraction.

"If you can, please stop with the Revelations talk and pay attention to the other cameras. Tell me if there's someone coming. I would really appreciate it." Evan spoke, I rolled my eyes at his tone.

"Anyway, I have no view of the inside of the cells. But there's no one outside, so just take the lift and go down." Something caught my eye. "Oh wow! Andy Volmus passed. He now has *my* job. What were they thinking? He is not capable. I'm making a complaint. Nathaniel, you better complain about this."

I wished I could be there at the Revelations. I had never missed one until now. I liked seeing the faces of the people trying to look surprised or amazed. It was rather entertaining.

"Why aren't you there? Won't they wonder where you are?" Sebas asked Nate.

"I don't like to be around people or waste time with dumb shows when I can be doing something else. I never go to those things. It isn't unusual that I'm not there."

I snorted. Nate never went because he didn't like too many people looking at him. And as the son of a member of the board, he had to be up front.

"By the way, we need the lift code," Calli interrupted, waving at the lift camera, "Once you guys stop talking about your cute little life back here."

"Way ahead of you, Calliandra," Nate said, reading the code from the main screen, the one I just got. "Code is 6-Y-5-1-B."

"'Calli' will do, *Nathaniel*."

"One level down," Nate reminded them.

"Lynn?" I began, swallowing hard as I saw the information on the screen. Aliana hummed, playing with one of her knives, fidgeting really... "There's a new sergeant. Soldiers are now under the commands of, uh, Sergeant Meylor. They just announced it."

"Congrats to him," Aliana spoke, her voice lacking any emotion. I frowned. "Is he there?"

"Can't see him," I told her, searching for his face.

"Sergeant Meylor as in Rocco Meylor?" Nate asked, looking down at the cameras showing the Revelations.

It was weird. Roc wasn't supposed to have that job. With his grades, which were just showed earlier, he was supposed to be in the CB, creating new intelligence, being where he was mostly needed thanks to his IQ, not misusing it. Roc was a lot of things, but he wasn't an idiot. He was actually very smart, too smart to be a sergeant. I mean, I knew little to nothing about the army but weren't they supposed to go through stages before getting to sergeant?

It surprised me the way Aliana reacted because if I knew something about her career goals, it was that she wanted to be a sergeant. She wanted to work towards that goal and for her to not say anything about Roc practically skipping a bunch of titles and getting to sergeant, was kind of weird.

"Open door number K304," Evan asked, bringing me back from my thoughts.

I started to look for the door he asked for. I had so many screens open that I could barely see the one with the door codes. I had hacked everything with Nate when Aliana and the rest of the group were on their way to the Government.

"Should I explain how?" Nate asked me when I couldn't find the code for the door. He was teasing.

"No, thanks, I got it." I rolled my eyes and found the door number. "Hack this, then that, then K302, K303, and – bomb – K304. *Open*."

"You're such a geek." Sebas laughed and tapped my shoulder with pride. After we had a very long conversation, Sebas was *very* supportive. He kept saying that he had noticed from the very first moment that I wasn't that much into him. He thought maybe it was because I had never experienced relationships. Turns out men just weren't my type.

Nate cleared his throat. Sebastián's hand instantly dropped from my shoulder as Aliana and her team walked into the cells. I didn't have sight of them given that the Government, not wanting records of their experiments to exist, a few years back stopped recording what happened inside the cells. But I had seen some records, just for my studies, so I knew what I could and couldn't do. The board didn't want those videos falling into the wrong hands and they couldn't explain any of that without saying more than they should.

All I had to do now was wait. The waiting was the worst part. My heart was beating hard against my chest. I wished someone would just say something. Johan had explained once Aliana left that Cynthia knew a long time ago that we weren't her real daughters. However, I was still afraid that she would reject us. Maybe she would see what I had become and be ashamed of me. Maybe she wouldn't see me as her daughter anymore and that would destroy me.

"What cell is she in, again?" Evan asked after a while.

"C25," Nate answered, his voice tense. "It's on the left side."

A second passed, and then another. Then five had passed, and so on. I kept counting the seconds until I reached 250. I was biting my lip, biting the skin from my lips, a bad habit Aliana and I shared.

"She isn't here." Aliana's voice broke the silence. It was a serious and straight answer, a punch in my stomach.

What did she mean, she wasn't there?

"What do you mean?" Nate said loudly, although apparently, it hadn't been his intention to do so. He took a deep breath. "She *has* to be there, Aliana. Cell C25, Cynthia Keenan. Look again."

"Nathaniel, she's my mother. I think that if she was here, I'd be able to recognise her. There's a bunch of people here that look dead but *she isn't here*," Aliana answered with a bitter tone.

"When was the last time she was moved?" Luna asked, moving closer to the monitors. "They moved me a few times but always brought me back to my cell after a couple of days. When did you see her here last?"

"I visited her two days ago. She isn't supposed to be moved around. Johan didn't allow it," Nathaniel answered.

"She isn't here, Nathaniel. We looked in all the cells."

"Sam, check all the cells, all of them, from the lower to the private," Aliana asked. "If she was moved, it should say so in the system."

I quickly began to search in all the registered prisons. Nathaniel was telling me how to do it, even though I already knew how. I didn't say anything or ask him to stop because I knew he was nervous and needed to do something to keep calm. It annoyed me, but it kept him calm. He was bossy when he was in a mood.

When I got access to the list of the people in prison, I typed my mother's name: Cynthia Keenan. The computer searched for her name everywhere but came up with no result. There were a lot of people imprisoned, but there was no Cynthia Keenan.

"Her name isn't in the history," I slowly said.

"Do it again, Sam," Nathaniel said to me.

"Nathaniel, when we tell you she isn't there, it is because she *isn't* there." I tried not to be rude, not when I knew how much this meant to the three of us but bossy Nate was an annoying Nate.

"What name did you type?" Aliana asked, walking out of the cell. Everyone followed her. I rolled my eyes.

"What kind of question is that? Mum's name, idiot,"

"Yes, Samirah, but which one!?" Aliana had lost her patience and seemed to be angry.

She gave Evan her large weapon and put the normal-size one on her belt. All those weapons looked the same to me, useless fighting things. Aliana took her helmet off and tied her hair in a bun. She didn't like buns. That's how I knew she was really getting irritated when everything bothered her, even her hair.

"Cynthia Keenan."

"Try her maiden name, Cynthia Brown," Aliana said, putting her helmet down.

I hadn't thought of that. I did as Aliana asked, and eventually, I found my mother's name.

"She's in the private cells. She was moved yesterday by" – I took a deep breath in and released a long, tired sigh. – "Sergeant R. Meylor. Why would he do that?"

"That doesn't matter. You have forty minutes left, Aliana." Nate hurried her. Aliana began walking back to the lift. "Don't waste time."

"Are there soldiers in the private cells?" Luna asked.

"I don't know," I admitted. "I didn't hack those ones. I thought we didn't need them."

I didn't have access to the doors in the private cells, only those in the communal ones. As fast as I could, I tried to hack the private ones with Nathaniel's help. It took me about ten minutes because I didn't know much about the private cells. I had been down there quite a lot but I didn't like it enough to inform myself about it.

Once they reached the private cells, how was I supposed to open the door? How was I supposed to hack into something that was supposed to be unhackable?

My fingers were tapping on the keyboard, sometimes missing letters. Nathaniel was trying to explain to me what to do but I don't think he knew much more than I did. My throat felt dry and for a second, I was contemplating the idea of getting up and getting a mango juice from Sebas's grandma's stand. We couldn't do it, there was no way to do it.

Nate was slowly coming to terms with it when he ran out of things to say.

But then... windows began to pop up in my screen, I wasn't touching anything, it wasn't me. I was afraid, my heart stopped when I thought about the possibility that we got caught. But within two seconds, a bunch of windows with camera feeds started to pop up on the screen. I saw empty white hallways and a bunch of doors.

"What did you do?" Nate asked, frowning as he watched.

"I wasn't—it wasn't me."

"Whatever it was, it opened up the private level." Isaac pointed out.

"Once you come out of the lift, it's the fourth door to your right," I told them, not giving it much importance to the fact that we got hacked. We, who were the supposed hackers, got hacked while hacking.

"We have about thirty-two minutes until the Revelations finish." Aliana began to talk really fast. "Let's say Samirah takes five minutes with the front door and another five with the cell door. We have to look for the cell where Cynthia is being held, which *has* to take another four minutes, max. Let's say she doesn't give us any trouble in getting out. From here back to the tunnels is about ten to fifteen minutes. Let's just hope we don't have any complications."

I knew Aliana was nervous. She always tried to plan everything ahead when she was nervous. She wouldn't make mistakes. She would succeed. I knew she would.

"In and out, guys," Evan said, trying to calm the nerves.

The four of them were in the lift and I allowed myself to watch them, it was amazing how the four of them were able to follow orders and act as if they were one as if they had known each other forever.

I was already trying to find the code, which I had to give them so they could enter it once they reached the private cells. Otherwise, the lift's doors wouldn't open. Somebody got me access inside the private level but that didn't mean I had the codes just yet, I could only see, not touch.

It took me exactly three minutes to hack it. After I opened the lift for them, they exited and walked to the cell where Mum was being kept.

Everyone was so quiet. Nate was standing with his hands at each side of him. I could see his burnt hand clearly through the hologram. I looked from it, the guilt made it hard for me to look at his hands. He often said he didn't care, but who wouldn't care about having a deformed hand? Everybody cared at the Government. It was obvious that Nate did care, he kept his hand in his pocket at all times trying to hide it. I gave him a permanent mark. I did something that left a mark on him and it would never leave his body, and that wasn't right.

I made a mistake and I hurt my brother so bad that I gave him an actual scar. It was the same with Aliana. I had nothing to do with her scar, but it hurt me to see it.

I shook my head, trying to get rid of the thoughts. When I finally found the code for the front door, Nate began to give out the information.

"Evan, there's a panel in the door where you have to enter a code. Once the panel changes colour, you can open the door, do not open it before or you'll set the alarm. The code is X8529F45Y."

"X, 8, 5, 2, 9, F, 4, 5, Y," Evan repeated, spelling out the code as he tapped the panel next to the door.

"No cameras inside, right?" Noelle asked. "Just in the corridor."

"Cameras aren't allowed inside the actual cells, but we can still hear you," I reminded them, just in case.

"Does it say which door Cynthia is in?" Evan asked, finally opening the door.

"No,"

With my heart in my throat, I watched as they walked inside the room. Then they were gone. I couldn't see anything, and neither could anyone behind me. I grabbed hold of Sebas's hand and it wasn't until it hurt me that I realised I was hurting him.

"What are you doing here?" Aliana asked. I couldn't see her, but whoever she was talking to brought out anger in her.

"I should ask you the same," another voice said. Although it sounded far away, I could make out what they said.

I turned the volume up.

"You knew I was coming," Aliana replied, her tone dead serious and cold.

"And I was waiting for you," the voice said, this time louder and clear as water: Roc's voice. "Although I have to say, I thought you would come on your own," he finished.

"Congrats about the whole sergeant thing. Sergeant... what a waste, huh?" She joked. She was talking carefully but casually. I could hear the tension in her voice, though, even if she tried to keep it casual. "You actually went and got my job. I don't know if I should laugh or be mad."

"Your job is there if you want it. You know what you have to do to get it."

A brief moment of silence ensued. Everyone was so tense.

"So, are you going to stop me?" Aliana finally asked what we all had been thinking. "She's my mother, Roc. I'm sure you'd do the same for yours."

"I don't think I would, actually." Roc answered, "Don't look so surprised, after all, it was you who told me what she did. I'm curious, did you see her when you went through the communal cells?"

"I don't have time for this, Roc," Aliana spoke with desperation in her voice.

"She's in cell number 12P, down the corridor to the left." Roc's voice was bored and disinterested. "Not you. You stay, I need to talk to you."

I heard the rest of the rescue group talking, trying to make a decision in whispers, but it was Nate who told them to run. And so, they did. Or at least it sounded like they were running.

"What do you want?" Aliana asked, annoyance clear in her voice. "Care to explain why you moved her?"

"It wasn't me. I was following orders. I wasn't even supposed to put it in the records. I did it because I knew you'd be smart enough to think of looking. And I used her unmarried name because I knew you'd think of it. You see, I left you breadcrumbs to follow, and here you are." Roc sounded impressed.

"Do you want me to thank you? After what you did?"

"After what I did?" Roc sounded confused. I was confused too.

"I found her." Noelle's voice popped up. I was able to breathe again.

Evan told her that they needed to give Cynthia a drug to calm her. Calli said he would do it.

"I was planning on finding you after my mother was safe, but here you are, making things easier for me," Aliana spoke, I was suddenly curious. What was going on? "Why did you do it?"

"Why did I do *what*?"

"You're not stupid, don't act stupid." She snapped. I heard a noise that sounded like scrunched paper. "The pills you gave me. Care to explain why they had Kodeum in them?"

My heart dropped to my feet.

"What?" Nathaniel's voice was suddenly very loud.

"*Kodeum*? What are you talking about?" I asked her, frowning at the screen. She ignored me, though.

"No, they didn't," Roc said.

"What even is Kodeum?" Luna asked. Nate and I ignored her. I couldn't think straight.

"I think I would know seeing how I almost died right after I started taking those." Aliana snorted, I could tell by the way she was speaking that she was having a hard time controlling her temper. "I had them tested, Roc. Read it, it says it right there."

"Listen to me, Ali. *Listen*," Roc's voice sounded louder as if he was getting closer to Aliana's earpiece. His voice sounded desperate.

"Uh-oh, the boy's getting closer. Should I shoot? Give a sign and I'll shoot," Calli said. The sound of a gun getting loaded made me straighten up.

"Aliana keep away from Roc," Nathaniel ordered her. I was going to tell her the same but Cynthia's voice stopped me, making me forget about Roc.

"What is going on?" Mum asked, her voice confused and tired. My heart skipped a beat. "Is my son coming with us? Johan? Where is my family?"

Mum's voice was as sweet as always, a beautiful, elegant sound that filled my heart with joy.

"We need to get out. Cynthia's asking questions," Noelle interrupted.

"Wait for the drug to kick in. She will freak out if she sees Aliana." Nathaniel told them.

"I swear to you, I didn't know. It was— they gave me those pills." Roc spoke desperately, his voice was clear for us to hear him.

"All right, enough. We gotta leave," Evan ordered. His steps were loud.

"We gotta go, Aliana. Cynthia is with us. She's drugged," Noelle said. From the way it sounded, he was near Aliana now.

"They leave, you stay," Roc said with authority.

"That's not gonna happen." Calli sang and then, I heard the clicking of a gun. I swallowed hard.

"Get out," Aliana ordered.

After a very long minute, the door opened. The first one to walk out was Noelle. Behind him came Evan, who was holding Cynthia in his arms. Calli walked out next. Cynthia had her dark blonde hair tied in a bun. She was wearing a dirty but elegant tight grey skirt and a white-collar shirt. Even in jail, she had her white heels on. That made me smile. I couldn't wait to hug my mother.

Aliana stepped out of the room with Roc following behind her, a gun pressed to her back, making my heart skip a beat.

"So, are you going to kill me now?" Aliana asked with a hint of mockery in her voice. Why must she act like that? That was provoking him!

"I would never hurt you." Roc frowned got deeper, he shook his head at her.

"But you have."

"Aliana, we have to go," Evan muttered through his teeth.

Aliana turned around to face Evan as if Roc didn't have a gun aiming at her. I knew my sister was smart, I knew she was trained and she was prepared for this kind of thing but why did she feel the need to act so stupid?

"Go first, I'll catch up." Aliana nodded at them. Evan was about to protest. "Evan, the mission here is to get my mother out, remember? So get her out."

"I'll stay behind," Calli spoke, Noelle shook his head, looking over at Calli.

"Is he talking to someone?" Cairo pointed at Roc, Aliana must've heard because she turned to face Roc and asked him who he was talking to.

Roc removed an earpiece from his ear.

"They can leave, you can't," Roc repeated, ignoring her question.

"Sam, look at the Revelations' cameras. Whoever he's talking to, they have to be there." Nate told me. I did as he asked.

"Aliana, *let's go*," Evan ordered forcefully.

Roc sighed, bored of the conversation and he raised his gun again, aiming it at Aliana's head. And just like that, everyone had their guns out. Aliana, Calli, Evan, and Noelle were aiming their big guns at Roc. My mother hanging from Evan's free arm. She was so drugged that I don't think she was paying attention to what was happening.

"Oh, my God." Luna sighed, worry and concern all over her tone.

"What are you doing?" Aliana didn't lower her gun.

"You're not leaving me again," Roc groaned. Aliana lowered her gun this time, making everyone else lower theirs, everyone except Roc.

"Leave. I will find my way out," Aliana ordered.

She did the right thing. If she hadn't, Roc would have followed them or, even worse, would have called for backup. That was why I admired Aliana. Even though I had called her selfish and whatnot, Aliana always chose her family. We always came first.

"Sam, look," Isaac pointed at the screen, his finger covering the person he was pointing at. When he removed his finger, I saw Frank Hayes moving his lips slightly, his face filled with frustration.

"Isn't that Frank?" Nate asked. Squinting his eyes to get a better look.

"Please, just get my mum out," Aliana said to the rest of the team. Her tone was serious, but I heard past it. She was nervous. "If I don't make it in the next six minutes, leave. I'll find my way back."

Evan hesitated, but he put his gun down and walked inside the lift, Noelle following behind. Calli nodded at Aliana and went back to the team.

"Lynn, ask him about Frank." Nate told her, "See how he reacts."

"So, was it Frank or you?" Aliana asked. Roc stayed as still as a rock, "The one who came up with the Kodeum idea, I mean."

"Drop it with the Kodeum, they're lying to you." Roc snapped.

"You're not doing a great job at proving it to be a lie," Aliana chuckled, "You have a gun pointed at me."

"Take your helmet off," Roc told her, she hesitated but did as he asked. She threw the helmet to the floor and then put her gun away.

The team was reaching the ground floor, walking at a hurried pace as they walked through the reception.

"Stay with me," Roc begged. I rolled my eyes at the screen.

"Are you asking me or ordering me?" she asked very calmly. I admired that. I wouldn't have been able to remain calm with a gun in my face. "At least put your gun down. It isn't a nice feeling to have it pointed at my face."

Roc hesitated but then he lowered his gun. He didn't put it away though.

"Your mother is safe. You can stay with me now. There's nothing there for you," Roc said coldly.

"And what do I have here? You?" Aliana smirked, she looked so indifferent. I had never seen her looking at him like that. "You tried to *kill* me."

"Frank gave me those pills, even if it is true, I didn't know what they had in them!" Roc snapped, taking a step closer to her, she took a step back.

On the other camera feeds, I saw the team carrying Cynthia. They were walking out the CB, back to the neighbourhoods. Everyone kept looking back. Maybe they were expecting Aliana to come running. But Aliana was still at the underground facilities.

"I told you to be careful when Frank called for you the first time, I told you to be careful." She told him, "Frank cannot be trusted and because of you, I almost died."

Roc shook his head and put his gun to his head, scratching his scalp with it. I would be out of my mind if I was near Roc. How was it that Aliana seemed so flipping calm?

"He wouldn't cross me—"

"Frank is a snake." Aliana interrupted him. "You betrayed me. Knowingly or not, you betrayed me and I don't know how to trust you, Roc."

"Aliana, you have no time. Just do one of your flying kicks and run away," Nathaniel said with desperation in his voice.

"I'm leaving, Roc," Aliana told him attempting to turn away but he quickly grabbed her by her arm.

"I will not let anyone hurt you," Roc said through his teeth.

"We're inside the tunnel," Calli reported. I looked for them. I saw Evan going into the tunnel through the ground hole.

"You are the one hurting me," Aliana said with a cold tone. I could tell that she was losing her cool.

"Give me another chance, Frank will pay for this," Roc told her. "Stay and we'll make sure he pays."

"I need to make sure my mother is safe." She told him, shaking her head at him. "And even then, Roc, you can't touch a board member. You can't do anything."

"Then make me a promise," Roc said desperately when Aliana was turning around to walk away. "Promise me that when I'm a member of the board, you'll come back. You'll come back to me and forgive me for the mistake I made. I know you will learn to love me again. I know you, Aliana. Remember, I know you better than you know yourself, just like you know me better than I know myself. We can rule the Government together. You'll come back when I have everything we ever wished for."

I couldn't help the nervous giggle that escaped my mouth. The boy was out of his mind.

"You don't know me anymore." She told him, "Just like I don't know you either."

"*Stop.*" Roc snapped. I jumped.

Aliana put one of her hands on her back. She slowly pulled up her T-shirt.

Roc said, "You don't know what you're saying. I'm the same, you're the same. We'll be like we used to be because we will not change. Promise me and I'll let you go. *Promise.*"

Aliana didn't say anything. I could only think about the four minutes Aliana had left and the fact that Roc had lost his mind.

"Promise it," Nathaniel ordered, breaking the silence. "Tell him, Lynn. Tell him and he'll let you go. Just say whatever he needs to hear."

"We all gotta do things we don't like, Aliana," Isaac said, encouraging her.

"Your family needs you on our side. You'll do us no good in the Government," Calli added.

"Lie to him or knock him out but do it now," Noelle added.

Aliana still didn't say anything. The clock was ticking.

She was already moving forward, closer to Roc. She had taken a knife from her back, she held it in her hand, hiding it from Roc.

"I promise," Aliana said, her voice low and different. She didn't like to lie, but in this case, she had to.

Roc stood there for what felt like a long minute. He looked at Aliana, the gun still in his hand. He studied her and then he smiled. When he took a step closer to her, she tensed, as did everyone else. He cupped her face harshly and forced her face up to meet his eyes. I held my breath.

"You've never been a good liar." Roc smiled wickedly, "And I know you enough to know that for your family you'd put your morals aside. I'm not letting you walk away again."

"Fair enough," Aliana sighed, holding her knife behind her back and playing with it. How could she play at this moment? "I can't promise you that, but I can promise you that if you don't let me go, I will never forgive you. And you know that much is true."

A moment of silence ensued.

"Baby girl, you're either too brave or too stupid." Calli laughed. How could she laugh now? How could they all be so calm now? "Whatever. But you got guts."

Roc leaned in, enough so we could all hear. It was like he knew we were listening.

"That's not good enough for me," he whispered with a smirk on his face.

And what happened next happened too fast for my eyes.

Aliana stabbed Roc's arm with her knife and then pushed him away. She kicked him, but he caught her leg and pulled it, making her fall on her back. If that fall didn't hurt Aliana, it hurt me by just hearing the sound she made when she hit the floor. However, she stood up quickly and punched Roc a couple of times. And then, making it look as easy as breathing, she kicked him in the face.

Aliana started to run towards the lift. I stopped breathing for a moment. It was the longest moment of my entire life. The air was knocked out of me as Roc raised his gun and shot at her just as the lift's doors closed. He kept shooting until there were no more bullets. What was left was Roc shouting and hitting the lift's door like a madman.

And then, when I thought nothing bad could happen, a man burst through the doors, agitated and with fear clear in his pale face. He was bleeding through his shirt, it was too much blood. Cairo was next to him in a matter of seconds.

"José…" The man spoke, trying to breathe. Between breaths he carried on, saying, "He has taken over."

# Chapter 34

Location: The woods
Narrator: Aliana

ROC SHOT ME.

I couldn't believe that Roc shot me.

Pain was radiating from my arm, making its way through my whole body. It hurt so much, so goddamn much.

At first, I hadn't noticed the wound until I saw all the blood coming out of my arm. The shock and the adrenaline didn't allow me to proper feel it until I was almost out of the lift. It started off with a burning sensation. Not at all what I thought getting shot would feel like. But after the first few seconds of shock, a wave of pain shook my body.

I put pressure on my wound, tightly squeezing it with my hand as I made my way out of the CB, I knew Roc was following behind so I tried to go as fast as I could. My arm was dripping blood on the floor and I was afraid I was going to trip.

"I'm heading to the tunnels," I spoke through my earpiece. "Where are you?"

"Calli and Noelle left. There's a problem. Cynthia and I are waiting for you." Evan answered I could sense the tension through his voice. "Did you get shot?"

"My arm." I told him, putting more pressure on it. God, it hurt. "I don't think the bullet went through."

"Aliana you *need* to hurry up," Evan told me.

"Almost there," I told him, trying to run faster. When I finally got to the tunnels, I tried to run as fast as I could. Something had happened, I needed to get there fast.

I couldn't stop the tears running down my face, mixing with sweat because it was *so* hot. I walked and ran at the same time. I ripped the sleeves off my shirt, tied them tight around my wound, and kept running. I could feel my head spinning, I felt like I was going to faint at any minute but I had to force myself to keep going.

When I went through the water tunnel, I told Evan to get me out. I saw the light before I got to the end of the tunnel. Evan was there, offering his hand to lift me up.

"Water, please," I told him, gasping for air. Evan headed straight to my wound. My mother was asleep next to a tree, she looked so peaceful. "I'm okay. I— I just need water."

"Take this off. I've got bandages," Evan told me. I did as he asked while he went to the saddlebag. "Water, alcohol, bandages, morphine, scissors, and a needle. And hey, look what I found: your brain. Seems to me like you were missing it back there."

"What are you talking about?" I asked him, letting myself drop to the ground. I suddenly felt very dizzy.

"You got shot because you're an idiot," Evan told me as he looked at the wound. "On three, I'll pour the alcohol."

"I did lie. Didn't you—"

"Three," Evan interrupted me, pouring the alcohol over my arm. I groaned and turned to glare at him. He took the bottle of water and handed it to me. I didn't take it, I just glared at him.

"Didn't you want water? Drink or I will."

I gave him a dirty look as I grabbed the bottle and drank the water. I wanted to punch him so bad but I was so lost in the taste of the water. Water had never tasted so good, I almost choked on it. I was so thirsty, my mouth felt like sand. He poured alcohol on the scissors and told me not to move. I didn't know which hurt more, getting shot or getting the bullet out. God, the pain. I had to bite a piece of wood Evan gave me in order not to shout.

"Here you go. I figure you'd like to have it. Put it on a necklace or something," he said with a serious face as he gave me the bullet. Then he poured alcohol over the needle and some thread, getting ready to stitch my wound.

"What's happening?" I managed to ask. "Sam's not responding."

"José took over."

"What?" I tried to stand up. "Take me there."

"Hey, calm down." He grabbed me by my shoulders and sat me down. "You're not thinking straight. There's so much more going on, you can't just jump into a situation like this."

"Go to hell," I shouted at him, standing up. "My siblings are there!"

"So what are you going to do? He will kill you and it isn't just your life at risk, okay?" Evan fought back. "Calli and Noelle are on their way, they can handle it."

I sat back down and took the water from him. As I drank, I let him do whatever he wanted to do with my arm. He sat next to me. Once he finished with the stitches, he put bandages around my arm.

"Help me wake her up," Evan told me, pointing at my mother. I swallowed hard.

"Shouldn't we get a little further from the bridge?" I proposed, he shook his head.

"We already are far from the bridge. They won't follow." He told me. "It'd be a waste."

Evan leaned down and kneeled before my mother, carefully trying to wake her. But before he could achieve anything. I raised my gun and hit him with it until he fell to the floor unconscious.

Ignoring the pain I felt in my left arm, I leaned down and placed a soft kiss on my mother's forehead and carefully got on the horse, making my way to José.

Location: La Cruz

The first thing I saw was a bunch of people with weapons. Not just guns but machetes and knives. A man stood in front of the horse,

370

not letting me get through. I was expecting it, I knew I wasn't going to be able to get to José without being stopped first, so I made sure to hide two of my daggers in my sleeve. All I needed was to reach in and grab them.

The man told me to get off the horse, and grabbed me by my arm, dragging me towards the church. There were a lot of people around. Some weren't saying anything, some looked at me with fear in their eyes. Some didn't care enough.

This was Miguel's people and they had rebelled against him. Whatever the outcome of today's events would be, nothing would ever be the same again.

I heard him before I saw him. His voice was loud and cheerful, sending shivers down my spine. José had Miguel kneeling down, his hands tied behind his back, blood running down his face. Miguel's face screamed anger. There was blood on his white shirt, a stab wound.

That wasn't what caught my eye though. What really shocked me and made my stomach twist was the bodies lying on the floor not too far from where José had Miguel kneeling. I did recognise some of them, they were people who had escaped the Government and were staying here, in Miguel's city. Their supposedly safe haven. There was blood around their bodies, and some had their eyes open as flies flew over them.

The image made me sick to my stomach.

"Well, if it isn't the princess!" José cheered, making me turn to look at him. José made his way to me. He put his arm around my shoulder, making me walk next to him. "*Mira*, your uncle and I were expecting you."

"Get your hands off me," I muttered through gritted teeth. It would've been so easy to just kill him right there.

"I've put up a show for the people," He told me, pointing at the dead bodies. A huge smile on his face, it made my blood boil.

I looked around until I found a face that made my heart stop. Sam was on her knees, her hands tied behind her back, tears rolling down her face. Eli was next to her, trying to look brave although I could see his eyes filling with tears. Those two faces were enough for me to know what to do.

"Wanna know what the final act will be?" José asked me, looking at me with excitement in his eyes.

"Enlighten me."

"Your death." His smile faded slowly until he was staring at me with nothing but hatred in his eyes.

I swallowed hard as José pointed his machete at me. "It's nothing personal, I just— your people shouldn't be here, your stay here only confirmed that. Your people are dangerous and Miguel wouldn't listen," José shouted, looking over at Miguel as if they had this conversation many times before. "I didn't want to do this but it had to be done. Your people don't belong here."

There was a lot of things I had no control over. I had no control over Miguel's people and how they saw me or what they thought of me or my people. I couldn't change the way they saw me because to them I was nothing but a violent girl who tried to kill Isaac, Sebastián and José. I couldn't change José's opinion of my people because he despised us for reasons I couldn't quite understand anymore. I couldn't control how I felt about myself, or about others. I couldn't control my anger, my hatred, my fear…

I almost lost my mind trying to control things that were impossible to control.

This situation I was in, it was out of my control. But one thing I did know…

I was *not* going to die today.

So as José launched at me with the determination of a man who did not believe he could die, I reached for my daggers inside my right sleeve, I raised my left hand, I took a deep breath in and I let them fly.

It hit José's shoulder, I was aiming for his jugular but my left hand wasn't my dominant hand. With fury, José grabbed my dagger and pulled it out of his shoulder, throwing it away. He had a fire in his eyes that I couldn't understand. What did I do to make him hate me so much? Ever since he laid eyes on me, José couldn't stand me.

The situation escalated and I snapped, but he had it against me even before I tried to kill him.

José took two swings of his machete, one closer to hitting me than the other. My arm hurt, I felt lightheaded but I wasn't going to give up.

I dodged a couple more of his swings, trying to find a way to get close to him, a way to attack him. He was fast, unlike Cairo, José was actually fast despite his weight. I didn't have a way to attack him, not without getting hit by his machete and for obvious reasons, I was trying really hard to avoid that.

I could tell José was having fun watching me as I tried to get away from him. He was a hunter and I was the prey; I had nowhere to go or a way to defend myself.

The only option I had was to throw my last dagger at him but if I did that and I missed, I'd have nothing to defend myself with. I was practically running away from José, running out of options and ideas. He was too fast and he didn't underestimate me anymore, he knew better than last time. But then, when I thought I had to risk it and just try to get a blow at José, someone threw a machete to the floor, close enough that I could reach for it.

The betrayal didn't go unnoticed. José didn't mind me then, he went straight to the guy who had thrown the machete and with one blow, he sliced his throat open, making people gasp at the sight. And just like that, I realised that José didn't have as much backup as it seemed.

I didn't waste time, I grabbed the machete. José's back was turned to me and I didn't hesitate to swing the machete, cutting through his shirt and his skin, creating a thin line through his back. Blood rushed out of the wound, it was deep but not deep enough.

José turned around, his face was filled with sweat and drops of blood, he was panting, smirking at me. I thought he was going to attack again, maybe with much more force than before but he just stood there, watching me carefully.

"So, what's the plan?" I asked, trying to win time. My arm was hurting a lot more than before and it was hard to fight with my left hand. "You kill me and then what? These people don't follow you, you don't have their loyalty. They're just scared of you."

"They fear you and your people more than they fear me." He told me, unbuttoning his shirt. "At least I'm willing to do something to defend our people, what has Miguel done?" He shouted, speaking more to his people than to me. "How many people have crossed the bridge in the last two years, huh? There's more and more of them in our city every day and I've had enough! They are dangerous, they are prepared to overtake us if they wanted to, we have to defend ourselves, not let the enemy sleep with us."

It took me a second to register his words, he had unbuttoned his shirt and removed it, he was sweating and had a lot of scars on his torso. I had to look away from him, it was horrifying to think that someone or something did all those scars to him.

"You're wrong." I shouted back, shaking my head, looking down at the machete in my hand, thinking back to all of the people in the Government. They were rude, they were snobs, they were whatever you wanted to call them but not what José made them out to be. "They aren't dangerous, they aren't violent and cruel. You are."

"I think you're not doing a good job at proving your point, sweetheart," He said, pointing at my machete, "You are all of those things, you and everyone else who is like you. You are the ones who we should be afraid of—"

"I think you're forgetting something, José," I said, loud enough for everybody to hear. "I am one of you."

I used his hesitation, the seconds it took him to understand what I meant and process it, to lunge at him, ready to take a swing and end it once and for all but José was ready. His machete hit against mine. José used the closeness to punch me in my arm, right where the wound was. I couldn't help but shout as pain shot through me.

The pain was enough to unbalance me. Against my will, I dropped the machete and I tripped with my own feet. I heard Sam shout my name, I heard Eli's voice. I wasn't sure. It was so hot, so hot that I felt light-headed. I needed water.

I tried to get up but before I could, José's foot was stepping on my wound. My own screams rumbled in my ears. I tried to punch his leg with my other hand but my energy was leaving my body. I was tired and thirsty. I felt nothing but pain shooting from my arm to my whole body as José stepped harder.

José removed his foot from my wound and tilted his head to the side as he watched me struggling to move. I felt the tears flooding my face, my body felt on fire. I heard José laughing as he walked over to me. He sat on top of me, making it hard for me to breathe. He stared down at me, watching me as I struggled to breathe. He was putting pressure on me with his body.

"It hurts, doesn't it?" He asked, I couldn't focus enough to think of an answer when his hands found their way to my throat. Big and rough hands wrapping themselves around my throat like tentacles, squeezing hard. I couldn't breathe. "Trying to breathe but not being able to?"

I wasn't completely sure but I think I heard Miguel shouting José's name. I couldn't hear him properly, there was nothing more important that José's hands around my throat and the need for air. I was trying. I was trying but there was no air, I gasped and gasped but nothing.

I don't know what took over me, maybe it was Sam's pleas, or Eli's. Something in me was burning with rage and pain and I hit him. I kept hitting him as hard as I could, kicking and hitting, scratching his face until I poke him right in the eye with my finger. I felt the wetness of his eye as I pushed my finger in. I heard the noise it made and I heard him scream as his hands unwrapped off me and he took his hands to his eye.

I tried to get him off me but he was screaming, calling me names, not getting off. So I grabbed my last dagger from my left hand and with my right hand, I stabbed and sliced his throat open.

Blood came out from his throat, dripping on me and covering me with it. And when he lost consciousness, José fell on top of me, his blood making a pool around us.

After that I don't remember much of what happened. Actually, I don't remember any of it except for the void I felt.

When I woke up, I didn't know what day it was but I knew I was back in one of Miguel's prison cells.

My hands and my uniform were bloody, my wound had been restitched and the bandages were clean. Little by little the memories of what had happened came back to me and José was all I could see. I kept trying to wipe the tears off my face.

What had I done?

I shouted and I cried for hours.

The problem was not that I had killed José. The problem was that I felt no remorse. I ended a human life and I had no consideration for it, I felt nothing.

What kind of person was I?

*   *   *

I didn't know how long had passed. I think it was weeks, I'm not sure.

My clothes reeked of blood, I couldn't stand the smell so I took them off and I threw them away until they were in a corner, far away from me.

They would only give me water from time to time so I used that to wash my hands but no matter how many times I tried to wash my clothes, the smell wouldn't leave. I think I scratched my body a little too hard because I had little scars on my forearms and hands.

I couldn't eat whenever I tried to, I ended up throwing up all over it.

I was sure I was never going to come out of the prison cell until I heard the metal door crack open and I found a pair of eyes that I didn't think I would see again.

Narrator: Isaac

Cairo wasn't doing too good.

Victor, the healer said that he had an internal bleeding and that he was trying his best. Samirah offered her help and somehow, they managed to have a surgery with the madness that was going on.

I could tell she was worried about Aliana, but she was trying to keep herself busy.

I would be lying if I said I wasn't doing the same. Miguel was trying to recover from his wound too, so people decided that what was best was to lock her up and wait until Miguel got better to judge her for murdering José.

It was ridiculous.

Aliana did what she had to do. It was her or José and José had betrayed his leader, his people. But Aliana wasn't one of us, people refused to accept her as one, so she was to be judged for murdering José. Even if she did what she did to protect herself.

*　　*　　*

"José wanted to talk to me," Miguel spoke through the communicator in his ear, explaining what had happened the day José took over. He was lying on his bed; his lips were dry and he had bandages around his stomach from where José had stabbed him. "I had my back turned to him when he stabbed me. He had turned some men against me already, all he needed was to kill me but Aliana showed up before he could."

Miguel sighed tiredly while he listened to the other man speaking through the communicator. When the man finished, Miguel shook his head as if they could see him.

"No, even if I try to get her out of this situation, I can't tell you that she'll be safe. José had people backing him up, a lot of people who didn't like Aliana." Miguel said, the man on the other line spoke, Miguel listened and then carried on. "They fear her, they won't accept it. She needs to leave, otherwise, she won't be safe. Take her in like you took her mother in."

My heart dropped to my feet. I stared at Miguel as he spoke. The rest of the conversation was a blur to me, but I understood that when they came to an agreement, Aliana was going to leave.

*　　*　　*

377

"Isaac?" Aliana spoke, her voice was raspy and low, she hadn't spoken a word in days and from what I heard, she spent hours screaming at nothing.

"How are you?" I asked her, trying to get close to her but she moved away when I did so, so I stayed where I was, focusing on her face when I saw that she was only wearing her underwear.

"You shouldn't be here." She said, looking away. Hiding her face behind her hair.

"Your mum is safe, she left days ago."

"Days?" She looked up, a glint of hope in her eyes.

"It has been two weeks." It was what isolation did to you, you couldn't tell how long it had been since you had been locked up, it could drive you crazy.

"Sam?"

"She's worried about you, they won't let her come so she keeps herself busy," I answered and she nodded. Her eyes were unfocused, she was staring into the distance at nothing.

"Aliana—"

"I killed him." She whispered it like if it was a secret, looking directly at me for the first time. "I don't even feel bad about it, I killed him."

"There wasn't another way."

"Yes, there was." She shook her head, tears filling her eyes. "I could've done something other than what I did."

"He was going to kill you."

"I didn't even stop to think about it." She cried, then her cries turned to sobs and I couldn't stand being so far from her.

I kneeled before her and I brought her to me, holding her close to me. My heart felt like it was shrinking in my chest, I couldn't stand seeing her like this.

Once she stopped crying, I cupped her face and made her face me.

"Nobody blames you for what you did." I reassured her, "Nobody that matters."

"But I killed him."

"He would've killed you, Miguel, me and many other people," I told her, making sure she saw it in my eyes. I didn't judge her, I didn't think anything less of her. "You saved us."

She was so close to me, I could see the little brown freckles in her green eyes. I wanted to hug her and make her feel better again. I wanted to squeeze it all out of her, the bad thoughts and the hate.

"We're going to get you out of here, okay?" I told her, her eyes met mine and I felt mine starting to burn. "Two days from now, you'll be free from all this."

"I will?" She asked, lost in thought.

"Yes, that's what you wanted, wasn't it?" I smiled at her face. She nodded slowly. "You'll leave this shithole and you'll be free from all the hate that's here. You'll start over again."

Narrator: Samirah

Today was Aliana's trial.

I had tried so hard to talk to Miguel, talk him out of it but I knew he had to do it.

Something was happening. I knew something was going on but nobody wanted to tell me anything.

Luna was a mess, she had been crying non-stop. Once Cairo was out of danger, she stayed at the hospital every day with him. And when she heard about the trial, she was a mess of tears again.

Eli was hidden from everybody. I couldn't find him even if I tried. I was worried but I had other things to worry about.

With swollen eyes from crying, I made my way to the city central where Aliana's trial would take place, in the same place José had died. Right in front of everybody.

My sister was not going to die today. Miguel wouldn't allow it. *I* wouldn't allow it.

I had arrived late. Lynn was standing by Miguel; her face was drained from all emotion. Her arms hanging at each side of her. She looked like she was done with life. I wanted to scream her name, make her look at me. I wanted her to fight. She couldn't give up now. She couldn't.

"I know many of you think Aliana isn't one of us," Miguel was saying, "And you want to judge her for what she did. But I want every single one of you to know that not only Aliana will be judged, every single person who stood with José will be judged for treason."

A lot of people began to talk all at once, a little chaos was formed. Judging by Miguel's expression, it was what he wanted.

"She killed my father!" A girl shouted, getting everybody's attention. She had tears in her eyes. "She should be judged for it."

"Your father killed my brother." A man stepped in, he had a burning anger in his eyes. "I don't think the girl should be judged. José betrayed our leader, he deserved to die. Be grateful the girl got to him before I could."

A lot of people cheered at the man. The girl glared with anger as tears rolled down her face.

I was about to say something, I wasn't sure exactly what when out of the blue, men and women dressed in black appeared, pointing guns at everybody. People tried to run but there were too many soldiers, too many guns. The soldiers told us all to get on our knees with our hands behind our head. Everybody did so, there was nothing they could do. A moment of silence went by when I felt all heads turning back. I turned around to see what was happening.

There was a man, he was wearing a black sleeveless shirt and baggy pants with combat boots. His hair was as dark as the night, his skin the colour of bronze. He walked with a look of indifference in his face as he made his way through the crowd towards my sister. Behind him, Evan walked with his head held high.

"Nobody will be judged today." the man began, his voice loud and clear. "As I'm sure you all know, Aliana Keenan is a citizen from the Government. And every citizen of the Government will be and shall always be protected by the armed forces of La Nueva. If you harm this girl today, you will be going against one of the agreements that were signed 13 years ago when peace was made between our cities.

The agreement was for peace, do not compromise your peace because you want vengeance."

Nobody said anything. I stared at the man in confusion, not understanding what was going on.

"This girl will be escorted and brought to our city." The man continued, he took a knife and threw it on the floor. "Now, with that being said, if anyone opposes to me taking this girl, you can do something about it now. But know that your actions will affect all of your people."

Nobody moved a muscle, and when I thought nobody could be stupid enough to do anything, I saw José's daughter trying to stand up but a woman next to her kept her in place.

"I thought so." The man smiled, he leaned down to grab his knife and walked towards my sister. He grabbed her by her arm and walked away with her.

There was nothing I could do, nothing I could say because the gun pointed to my head was enough to freeze every single muscle in my body.

And just like that, my sister was gone.

 **Chapter 35**

Date: 20 August 102 AW (Revelations Day)
Location: The Government.

HOURS AND HOURS have gone by since the last time I saw Aliana.
I couldn't seem to remember properly. The last thing I remember
was being in those prison cells. I remember aiming my gun at her.
I remember asking her to stay. I remember that she lied to me, and
I remember shooting at her. I shot her after she stabbed me. She
stabbed me and I shot her.

Once everyone realised what had happened, Frank sent me to the
hospital to have me patched up. I think he was worried.

I shot her. I really did shoot her. And now the guilt over what I
had done was consuming me. How could I have done such a thing? I
swore never to hurt her. I promised myself and her that I would never
do anything to hurt her no matter what Frank asked of me. How could
I have done such a thing? All I ever wanted was to be with her, to
marry her and have kids running around our home.

I wanted us to grow old together and then have our grandchildren
run around our house. That's all I ever wanted, and now that dream
seemed farther away than it did before.

I don't remember when I got home. I don't remember walking
home or how long it had been since I let her slip right through my
fingers. This time I would not be able to get her back. I could have
killed her. God, she would never forgive me.

I looked at my surroundings. I was in my room. I was trying to
remember how I had gotten there, but everything was a blank. I was

sitting on the edge of my bed. The blinds were drawn, but they still let a little light in, enough for me to see myself in the mirror. I knew it was me but I couldn't quite recognise the person staring back at me.

I was trying to think of a way out of this, a way to make things right when someone sat down next to me. I felt the weight pushing down my mattress.

"Everything would be so much easier for you if you just had the balls to finish her," Frank sighed, my room reeked of his cologne. I looked over to him. His eyes were the colour of crystalline water, the same colour as Mathias's. I looked away.

"But I love her. I can't do it," I answered, desperation in my voice. "You made me do that to her, Frank. Why would you make me do that to her? I told you I didn't want to do it!"

"You love her?" Frank laughed. "You love her. Yes, right, I forgot about that. But does she love you? If she loved you, she would be *here*. If she cared about you, she'd be *here*. Where is she? In someone else's bed, that's where. I gave you a solution. I've been giving you a solution for months. If only you would've pulled the trigger like you were supposed to, then all of our problems would be solved. But you're so soft—you're just—"

"Why don't you get your son to do it, then?" I snapped, standing from my bed to face him. "Get your useless son to do all the things I've been doing for you."

"Jealousy won't get you anywhere, son." He laughed at me, I looked away from him.

"I will never hurt her." I snapped, changing the subject. "I will never hurt her. I will not."

"But you will never have her!" he snapped back, standing up right in front of me. He was a little bit taller than I was.

I couldn't keep the eye contact. I had to look away. Frank had that crazy, rabid look in his eyes. The way he always looked at me was as if I was nothing and he was everything like he owned my life and if he wanted to, he could destroy it all. To make things worse, he lifted his hand and put it around my throat, choking me.

"You wanted to find the girl, Roc, I made it happen but don't forget what the main goal is," Frank whispered, his voice so low, so soft, that if it wasn't for his hand around my neck, I wouldn't have thought he was threatening me, that he cared about me like he cared about Mathias. That he could be a father to me too. "I am not going to lose the Government because of one of your tantrums. She doesn't love you and she never will. Move on."

We both fell into silence until a laugh rang out, a laugh full of mockery. I felt my insides burn with rage.

"It's like you're devoted to her like you live thanks to her as if thanks to her you have air in your lungs. You're pathetic. You went to 'rescue' her and she pushed you aside. She asked you to leave, and you, like the idiot you are, came back to me with your tail between your legs. She asked you to leave because she has someone else to keep her bed warm because you were never enough."

"You know nothing. She *loves* me."

"It's hard to accept things sometimes." Frank's voice softened as he got closer to me. "It's a hard life. You missed your chance and you will never ever see her again. And now, look, look at what you've done. All because Aliana refused to stay with you. Look at what she brings out in you."

Frank grabbed me by the back of my neck and made me stand in front of the mirror, he turned the lights on. I felt bile rising up my throat. The memory of what I had done yesterday came back to my mind.

I remember walking home. I remember watching my mother as she walked up to me, I asked her about dad and about Frank. Her answer made everything a blur. Without thinking about it twice, I took my knife out and I cut her throat open. I remember looking into her eyes as she bled to death. I remember the smile forming on my lips as she tried to say something but couldn't. I remember seeing the blood rushing out, spreading all over her neck, on her clothes, on the floor. A pool of her blood.

I stared back at my reflection in the mirror, a tear running down my face where I had drops of blood. My hands were filthy with dried blood, as were my uniform, my shoes…

God, what did she make me do?

I stared right at my reflection. I was covered with blood, dried red blood. I dropped to my knees and stared at the reflection.

It wasn't me. It was someone else looking back – a person with blue eyes looking back at me with a smile on his lips. A wicked grin much like Franks. And I saw him in me, in the shape of my face, in the roughness of my jaw.

I really was Frank Hayes's bastard son.

Aliana was right, I had changed. This wasn't me.

 **Chapter 36**

Location: The woods
Narrator: Aliana

"ARE YOU OKAY?" I heard Calli's voice speaking to me but I couldn't concentrate enough to answer her question.

Everything was happening a little too fast. One moment, Miguel was trying to argue that he would judge others for their betrayal, then José's daughter said something and suddenly a bunch of people were there and a man tried to play politics.

Everything was happening too fast for my eyes or my brain to catch. But when I came to realise, I was inside of a car, Calli sat right next to me, Noelle on my other side.

"We're in a car?"

"Yes, and we'll be there in 20 minutes," Calli answered, looking at me directly in my eyes. "We didn't have time for you to say goodbye, we just needed to get you out of there, those were the orders."

"Who gave that order?"

"Alex," Noelle answered. I felt a slight pinch in my arm, I turned to look at Noelle, he injected something in my arm. I wanted to ask but my body felt heavy.

"Rest, okay?" Calli told me, smiling at me. "Alex and Cynthia will explain everything."

"Tonight's going to be a long ass night." I heard Noelle sigh before everything went black.

* * *

When I woke up, I was in some sort of room. My clothes had been changed and I felt... *new*. My wound had been cleaned and patched up. But I couldn't shake the uneasy feeling.

Where the hell was I?

I didn't look around the room much because I heard an unknown voice and I made my way out of the room and down the stairs.

On my way to the voices, I found a kitchen, I searched in all the counters and found the biggest knife there was. Holding it tightly, I made my way to where the voices came from.

I walked down a hallway until I stood in front of a door, I could hear the voices perfectly clear now, and I thought it was my head playing games with me. I opened the door and stepped in, not sure of what I was going to find.

It was an office. There were lots of books – way more than there were in Johan's office back home. On the desk, there was an old computer. Two people were seated, one behind the desk and the other before the desk. The one who sat before the desk I could recognise before she even turned to me. Her blue eyes met mine and within seconds, her arms were wrapped around me, holding me close to her in a tight grip.

"My beautiful girl," My mum cried, I felt my throat closing in, the tears burning my eyes. I closed my eyes and hugged her back...

She loved me.

When she pulled away, she looked down at me with emotion in her eyes. There was excitement, there was happiness, there was *love*. Tears left my eyes and my mother tried to wipe them away. Telling me how worried she was. I couldn't say anything, I wanted to but I was too shocked to think of anything to say. The knot in my throat was too big to swallow.

She loved me.

"We were worried about you." I heard a man's voice say. His voice was coming from behind my mother.

For a moment, I thought it was Johan. He had the same posture even when he was sitting. But this man wasn't Johan. He had black hair, but there was white in it. The man was wearing cargo jeans and a tank top. He was muscular, very muscular.

I thought I was going crazy. I was going mad. Maybe isolation finally pushed me over the edge and I lost my mind or maybe I was killed during the trial and this was some sort of afterlife because there was no way that the man standing five steps away from me was alive.

He was bigger and taller than I remembered, older. His light brown eyes, which were small, got even smaller when he smiled. He had wrinkles around his eyes and along the sides of his mouth. He looked like Johan, only if Johan was about 50 something years old.

"Gustav," I said to no one. Was I seeing right?

I tried to close and open my eyes. Maybe I was dead for real, but I blinked and blinked and he was still there.

"I liked it better when you called me Grandpa."

"But you were gone. They said you were gone. We had — you were cremated. You were gone," I said to myself.

"Everything has an explanation," My mother said. Gustav was getting closer to me, taking each step carefully. I felt the sudden urge to run from him. "There's so much you don't know."

"What does that even mean?" I frowned, how can you explain why you faked your own death?

"It means," Gustav began, turning to me with a warm smile, "Something is happening and we all have a part to play in this. Your mother, your father, your brother, and your sister. And so do you."

"What are you talking about?"

"The Government is founded on lies and absurd rules. The Government must fall. I will see it happen." He said, speaking like he came out of some sort of book or one of the movies that Isaac made me watch.

The empire must fall.

"It's already happening, my dear," Gustav continued. "There's no way to turn back now."

"What do you mean?" I asked, alarmed by his reply.

"Things are falling into their respective places, Aliana," Mum said, I frowned, was anybody going to *actually* answer my question without the dramatic choice of words? "We have to free the people of the Government, but to do that we must destroy it first."

And that's when it all made sense. I remembered what Nate told us and all that they wanted to do. This wasn't a game. This wasn't something you could start over if you made a mistake or if you failed. This was real. It was unbelievable that they were talking about it like it was nothing!

Isaac said I could start again, away from all the problems. I thought I could have an actual chance to have a normal life, which was stupid of me. I should have known better. There was no such thing as a normal life.

Acknowledgments

THE FEELING YOU get when you finally finish writing something you put your efforts and your deepest thoughts in, it is inexplicable. I started writing Emotionless when I was 16 years old. It started off as a paragraph in my English class, and 6 years later I'm finally able to say that it is getting published and it wasn't all by myself.

I would like to thank so many people for the help they have given me. Firstly, I want to start off by thanking my family. I want to take a moment to thank them for all the support they've given me, for all the sacrifices they have made for me and my siblings to give us a future.

To Sara Badran who spent hours with teenager me, reading over and over again the first draft and helping me understand the emotional side of this rollercoaster better. To Eleni Stabolidou who spent countless of nights helping me edit this book to make it what it is now, thank you, thank you and thousands of times *thank you* for working with me on this. Amal, Shukri, Tiff, and Tati who have taught me the meaning of sisterhood, friendship, and unconditional love. Thank you, my girls, for believing in me and for always coming to the rescue, ready to make banter out of any situation. I appreciate you all.

And lastly, I want to thank me (even if that's a little odd…). I want to thank 16-year-old me for writing during bus rides, during maths lessons, for writing the whole night, for writing through dark times and simply for writing.

It hasn't always been easy but I'm here and I'm not broken.

Lightning Source UK Ltd.
Milton Keynes UK
UKHW040650021218
333309UK00001B/25/P